Also by (

Dead Reckoning
A Caribbean Thriller

"Just what the doctor ordered." *The Key West Citizen*

"If you want seagoing adventure, this is the book for you."
David Linzee, Author of the *Renata Radleigh*
Opera Mystery Series

"A gripping Island Adventure."

"Pennington creates a suspenseful plot with unexpected
twists that will keep readers' attention to the last page."

"A well-written novel with vivid character descriptions and
an unexpected storyline."

WEST OF THE ALLEGHENIES

A Story of Survival During
the Revolutionary War

by
Craig Pennington

Cover Art:
Muted by the Vista
by John Buxton

Interior Maps:
after Homann Heirs 1784

For Claudia,
who has always
been my guiding star

CONTENTS

The Travels of
Fergus Moorhead
1769 to 1778

Lake
Ontario

Fort Niagra

Lake Erie

Canawaugus

Kittanning

Fort Pitt

Indiana

Chinglacmouche

Penns

Beeson's
Mill

Chamber's Town

Ft. Cumberland

Maryla

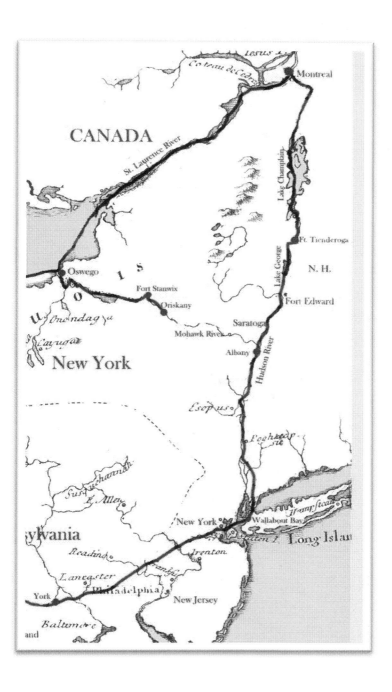

PREFACE

The story of Fergus Moorhead is a legend in Indiana County, Pennsylvania. Along with his great-great-great-grandson, actor James Stewart, Fergus is one of the County's best-known historical figures. What follows is a fictionalized account of the life of Fergus Moorhead. In reality, so little is known about his days as a pioneer, his capture by Native Americans and time as a Prisoner of War, and his escape and return to his family home that this tale could be true.

We do know that he and his family were among the first to settle west of the Allegheny Mountains. Additionally, the timeline of his life allows for Fergus to participate in the events described in the History of Indiana County and this narrative. Of his capture and trek to Montreal and journey home, all we know is that it happened.

The challenge in telling a narrative of a real person's life is to know where the truth stops and the legend begins. But, as the newspaper editor in Jimmy Stewart's classic film "*The Man Who Shot Liberty Valance*" says, "When the legend becomes fact, print the legend."

So here you have it.

WEST OF THE ALLEGHENIES

PROLOGUE

Monday, March 28th, 1816
Indiana, Pennsylvania

The warm spell a few days ago has left the snow with a hard crust that makes each step treacherous. You step forward, apply your weight cautiously, and then crash through the hard surface into a soft foot of wet snow beneath. It makes walking any distance a living hell, and I say so to Jane when she insists we go to town for the ceremony. She does not listen.

"There will be folks there wanting to see you," she says, gathering up my coat and turning me toward my boots warming near the hearth. "We're going. Jerimiah's already got Betsy hitched, so stop yer arguing."

So it was decided.

On this day, Indiana has officially become a borough, which is simply a fancy word for town. The ceremony should have been postponed, but Burgess Taylor said the senator had come all the way from Harrisburg, and he was not likely to delay simply because it was cold out. It has been a long winter, and it shows no intention of letting up. The wind is constant out of the north-west, and the snow, when it is not crusted over, piles up against the buildings and blocks the doors. I comment on this all the while I am pulling on boots and shrugging on the coat Jane holds out for me.

1

As I expected, outside, the wind cuts right through, and I am miserable in a matter of minutes. Old Jerimiah is a free man who has been with me for twenty years or more. And Betsy, our only remaining Belgian, nearly as long. She stands patiently in the shelter of the barn door, head hanging in resignation. The wagon and Jerimiah are ready to go.

"No point arguing," he says. "They's expectin' you."

"I am too old to be out in this weather," I try halfheartedly. Everyone is against me today.

Jerimiah, curly white hair blowing in the snow-laden wind, simply shrugs. "I'm older than you, an I'm goin'." He lays a blanket across my lap. "Not that either of us got a choice," he adds as Jane climbs on and nuzzles in beside me.

With a cluck of his tongue, Jerimiah shakes the reins, and Betsy ambles from the barn. We start the three-mile ride to the center of town.

Someone built a wood scaffold in front of the brick courthouse. From there, the dignitaries can stand upon it and look out over the crowd, such as it was. For such a miserable day, however, I am surprised at the turnout. Thirty folks, or so, stand opposite the wooden platform, huddling together to block the wind. Now and then, a strong gust raises the red, white, and blue bunting attached to the front of the platform and threatens to send it flying down the street.

Following a period just long enough to let us know that we're waiting for them, our newly appointed Burgess, John Taylor, and Senator John Reed come out of the courthouse door and climb onto the platform. Taylor's father came to Indiana sometime after Jane and me, and he never misses an opportunity to tell his family's story. He does go on. With introductory remarks and an overly technical explanation of what it means for us to live in a real borough, Taylor starts retelling the history of our new town and county.

Eventually, as I knew he would, Burgess Taylor points at me.

"There's a man can tell you a thing or two about history," he cries, a bony finger stuck out like Death himself. Everyone turns to look at me as if I had suddenly dropped down from the moon. "Fergus Moorhead," Taylor continues. "He needs no introduction. Why, if it wasn't for Fergus, we wouldn't be the town we are today. With a musket in one hand and a Bible in the other, he and his wife Jane cleared the very land upon which we stand!"

Even if it were possible to conjure up an image like that, it was not true. The land we own is three miles west. Still, everyone nods politely, and there is a smattering of applause. Whether it was acknowledging my accomplishments or their surprise that I am still amongst the living, I do not know. I smile brightly, give a quick wave, and having done my duty, turn away from the assembly. Jane and Jerimiah admit defeat and follow me.

Time to get somewhere warm and find a drink.

Charlie Bean bought the tavern from Sarah, the widow of my son, James. It always pleased me that he kept the Moorhead name above the door. There was family history in this building, and I would hate to see it not be recognized. My grandson, William, was born upstairs where James and Sarah once lived. James was always so proud to tell people that this was the first real tavern built in the county.

It is hard to believe three years have passed since we lost James. He had to do his duty, he said, so full of pride, marching off to join Perry's navy. Then came news of the great Battle of Lake Erie on September 10th, 1813, and the horrible loss of life on his ship, *USS Lawrence*.

Don't give up the ship, my arse.

Inside the tavern, a fire is roaring and reflects off the limed walls. The low ceiling beams keep the heat close, and I am at once content and sorrowful. There is no one at the tables, being as how most folks are still listening to the speeches. We shuck our coats and find chairs near the fire. Before I can become melancholy, Charlie is at our side with two rum toddies.

"Mr. Moorhead," he gushes. "It has been a while. So glad to see you. And you, Mrs. Moorhead!" Charlie is as round and balding as you might expect in a middle-aged publican. He is a bachelor and treats every patron like long-lost family.

Jane speaks for us, sensing that I am not in a talkative mood. " 'Tis nice to see you too, Charlie. Would ye mind sending one of those rums out back to Jerimiah? I'd so appreciate it."

Charlie crunches up his face a bit before agreeing. "On a day like this, who's to know." And off he goes.

I smile at Jane, and she returns it warmly. "Who's to know," I say. Someday soon, I am confident this deplorable situation will be corrected.

Knowing that I intend to sit for a while, Jane reaches for *The American* folded neatly on a nearby bench. It is a Federalist rag that I cannot abide. There is news of more fighting. She reads a bit describing how Madison has got us into war again off the coast of Morocco, a war Jefferson could have finished a year ago if Congress had let him. I shake my head. She smiles and keeps on reading.

I cannot help thinking of the wars I have seen, the death I have seen — the War of Independence, the Second War of Independence, or as they call it now, The War of 1812. Losing James. Then Joseph almost killed fighting with St. Clair in '91. We lost our Peggy last year to pneumonia. And the three other children that damn near killed Jane in their brief appearance on this earth. Maybe I *should* write down my story like Jane says, and then I would not have to tell it so often.

At seventy-four, the eyesight is fading even if the memory is not. I try not to let Jane know, but she notices I read less than I used to. Instead of mentioning it or nagging me to wear spectacles, she reads to me while there is light. Last, it was a book by Austin, do not know which, for I could not take it. Lot of poppycock if you ask me. If you want to marry somebody, ask them. It is what I did.

Taking another sip of the steaming rum, I begin to lose myself in thought. I have told this tale so many times, I am truly tired of it. Seems folks want to hear, at least they say they do. They shake their heads in disbelief and compare me to Boone, and that is ridiculous. I never wanted to be famous, and he wanted nothing else. However, the old fella did say one smart thing when he observed: 'All you need for happiness is a good gun, a good horse, and a good wife.'

I cannot argue with that.

Imagine, I first saw this land almost fifty years ago. They say a thousand people live in the county today. Back then, you could count your neighbors on one hand. There was my best friend Jim Kelly, whose son Meek married my little Janie. There was James Thompson, and of course my brothers, Samuel and Joseph. And, there were Indians, several of whom I got to know far too well. My story would have to include my 'friend' Cornplanter and that bastard Joseph Brant.

So, where to begin? I could start with my parents, who came to Chamber's Town from County Antrim in Ireland. Or, how I was born in Cumberland County, Pennsylvania, in 1742 and grew up farm-strong and rather well-schooled, always figuring I would be a farmer and a surveyor.

Then I met Jane and my life changed forever. You know, Boone was right. There is no story of this land, or war, or pioneering, or Indian attacks, or cruel winters, or breathtaking sunsets across an open prairie, without a good woman.

My story begins and ends with Jane.

PART ONE

The Claim
1766 to 1769

CHAPTER 1
Jane

Sunday, April 7th, 1766
Chamber's Town, Pennsylvania

Green eyes that captured the sun, a flash of perfect teeth, and a mass of dark red hair that refused to stay under her bonnet. That was my first impression of Jane White.

"I'm gonna marry that girl," I said to my younger brother Joe in a voice inappropriate for our surroundings. We sat on the hard benches in the Presbyterian church on a warm Sunday morning. From the constant shifting of positions throughout the church, I do not believe anyone was comfortably seated. Why being uncomfortable in his house was so important to our Lord, I never understood.

Joe elbowed me. "Quiet! We're in church. Have some respect. You can't talk about a girl that way when you're in church. It ain't proper."

I ignored him and continued to stare at the beauty before me. Jane's father, Joseph White, was our new minister and as severe a Scot as you could ever imagine. His constant ruddy complexion and ominous scowl told you from whence he came, even before you heard him speak. He and his family had arrived from Scotland two months before so he could assume the protestant flock of Chamber's

Town. Jane, John, and Hannah were the only children. Mrs. White sat in the first row beside Jane, hands folded in her lap, and a look on her face that rivaled the severity of her husband.

My family sat three rows back. Mother and father on either end, Joseph, William, my sister Jane, and me all clean and shining and ready to be saved, locked in between them. I had no ear for Pastor White's lecture. For the past two months, my soul had been in jeopardy and my mind on one subject — the beautiful young woman of twenty-one sitting not fifteen feet away from me. A woman I intended to marry. I only needed to explain that to her.

That day something made me bolder than I had been before. Jane knew who I was, she had often smiled pleasantly in passing, but she did not anticipate my intentions. Or, perhaps she did.

As we left the church, the Whites lined up near the door so we could thank them and compliment Pastor White on the brilliant service. Jane was at the end of the line. I stopped in front of her, and she smiled at me. I stood. She smiled.

"A pleasant day to you, Mr. Moorhead," she said in a soft, rich brogue, wondering why I did not move along. Behind me, heads leaned forward to observe the cause of the delay, knowing smiles on their faces.

"And you, miss," I stammered and did not move.

"Yes?" Her head tilted slightly.

So, I jumped in feet first. "I was wondering, Miss Jane, if I might call on you this afternoon? For a walk."

"A walk?" She smiled again. I loved that smile. "That would be nice, I think. Come round after dinner and speak to me faither."

Early in the afternoon, I rode to town and, with

trembling hands and a numbness I could not shake, I knocked on the parish house front door. Jane's brother showed me into a cool, comfortable study opposite the dining room with a knowing grin. In person, Pastor White was not as terrifying as I thought he would be. He welcomed me cordially, offered me a mug of cider, which I declined, and told me to stay on the main street and be back by four o'clock.

Unlike today, no one then was concerned that we walked without a chaperone. We were in public, in broad daylight, and I took her home in time for supper. What I failed to realize at first was that two months earlier, Jane White had decided to marry me. She just needed to explain it to me.

Saturday, August 9th, 1766
Chamber's Town, Pennsylvania

The drinking began early.

My house, the house of my father, was a mile or so from Jane's house. Our house was more a cabin than anything else, although it was two stories and sprawling, large enough for seven of us to be comfortable. It sat on the edge of my father's 300 acres of farmland with a long view of the East Branch of Conococheague Creek.

My older brothers, Tom and Alex, were married with homes of their own. Tom lived in Philadelphia, and Alex owned a farm five miles away. Today, they and their families were all here, the house stuffed to the eaves.

Jane's house was a mansion by comparison. It was also two stories, made of stone, and sat beside the church. The race was between the two homes.

The main contestants were my younger brothers, James and Joseph. Even James's brother John, although only fourteen, was allowed to try for the Black Betty prize. Two neighbor boys, both nineteen, also lined up. It was clear from the way they all jostled and pushed at the starting line that someone had already uncorked a bottle.

My father stood on the porch and smiled down at the obviously intoxicated boys. It was going to be a long day.

"Who's ready?" he shouted, and they all leaned forward. "Set! Go!"

Two strides in, brother Will stepped on the back of brother Joe's foot, and Joe went face-first into the dust. He cried foul, but nobody cared. The crowd on the porch shouted to get up and go, and he scrambled to his feet and tore after his brother, old Lucky barking at his side.

I sat on the porch steps and watched, remembering my race two years before as we celebrated Alex's wedding day. The race from one house to the other was a favorite tradition at weddings. The boys ran hard, shoving and tripping each other. The prize was a jug of Black Betty dark rum or whiskey, sitting on the parish house porch. The first one to grab the jug and run the mile back claimed the first drink and the first dance with the girl of his choice. Not that it would be their first drink of the day.

While the race carried on, cool hard cider was poured for those smart enough to stay out of the sun. My father sat down on the steps beside me.

"How do ye feel, son," he asked me once we both had a glass in our hands.

I thought for a moment before answering. "I don't know, Pa," I said truthfully. "I can't say I feel like it's real. I'm not scared. I feel kinda numb inside."

He threw his head back and laughed until he coughed.

"That's fine," he said, catching his breath. " 'Tis a perfect way to go through marriage."

Sitting beside my father on the porch steps, I realized I could not tell him how I really felt. I was proud. Proud to be his son yet pleased to feel like my own man. I was getting married and moving into my own home. At that moment, I stood beside my father as an equal, and it felt good.

We sat comfortably in the shade until a shout came from down the road, and we all stood to watch the racers make their return. Young John White was out in front of the pack, but his hands were empty. A stride or two behind, Joe and Will held the jug between them and fought for it as they ran. Both were covered in dust, and a trickle of blood showed at the corner of Will's mouth. It looked like Joe got his revenge for being tripped.

A hundred feet from where we stood, Joe gave a mighty heave, half turning in the air, and the jug came out of Will's hands. Will took a long stride, stumbled, and fell onto the road. Holding the jug over his head, Joe bounded up the porch steps. We all cheered mightily, and someone handed Joe a glass of cider. Grinning like a newly elected politician, he downed the glass in one long pull.

I gave him a pat on the back, avoiding most of the dust. "So, who do you intend to ask to dance?" I asked as if I did not know the answer.

He blushed and smiled at me sideways. In less than four years, he would watch the Black Betty race from this same porch while Mary Ann Riley waited at her father's house.

That's my last full memory of my wedding day until much later in the evening. The rest is spotty.

We all drank more cider and beer and waited for the

proper time to make the trek to the church. Joe consumed a hard-won glass of Black Betty rum, which, on top of the cider, quickly put him in the bushes.

Then the wagon came from the barn and we all admired the women's handy-work. A lattice arch, woven with summer flowers, framed the driver's seat. Sam ordered me to stand under it as Pa drove, and the women sat in the back. I climbed up and took my position, holding on with both hands, looking and feeling like a man on the way to his execution.

More wagons joined the parade, and we started down the road. I do not think Joe came with us.

I do remember standing at the front of the church with Samuel, my best man, and Pastor Bucher, who conducted the service since Jane's father had the task of walking her down the aisle. After an eternity of standing there, concentrating on preventing my knees from knocking together, Jane made her appearance. *That* I remember well. She was dressed in her mother's wedding gown, carried all the way from Scotland. There was a great deal of lace partially hiding her face, but when she reached my side and raised her head, nothing could keep those green eyes from shining through.

I have no idea what Pastor Bucher said to us. We stood, hand in hand, and looked at each other. Evidently, we both said, "I do," because the next thing I knew, the Pastor said, "Kiss your bride, son."

They say funerals and weddings bring people together. The Moorhead clan was large and getting bigger all the time. The Whites claimed fewer members, being brand new to this country, but my father and my mother absorbed them into our family like parched soil takes up water. From the moment I announced to the world that Jane and I intended to be married, regardless of whose idea it actually was, both families became one. The Scotch-Irish Moorheads from Ulster and the Scottish Whites from Angus, now two families joined as one.

The festivities that followed our wedding were a tribute to how much our families seemed to like and accept the other. Mother White presented a magnificent dinner with Jane, my parents, Samuel, and myself at the dining room table. On the brick courtyard between the main house and the kitchen, long wooden tables and benches held the rest of the rabble. Long vines of white flowers hung from poles above the tables created a festive atmosphere.

I believe we ate well, though I could not tell you what we had to save my life. At one point, Jane whispered to me that I should stop grinning, or her family may think she had married the local idiot.

As the afternoon wore on, my wits slowly returned. There was a period of rest following dinner, and then the dancing started. Weddings are one of the few times our community gathered, other than for the hard days of reaping, log rolling, barn raising, or attending a council meeting, and everyone intended to enjoy themselves. Men pulled the courtyard tables to the side and lit the torches. The fiddlers took up a spot on the rear porch. A layer of straw on the bricks eased the dancer's feet.

It was a grand time, and no one was permitted to sit for long. When any of the dancers claimed exhaustion, another cut them out without interrupting the dance. The dancing continued until the four fiddlers collapsed and begged a rest. Even old Mrs. Barclay was coaxed from her seat more than once. I tried to sit down for a spell, but Sam was there in a flash.

"No, you don't," he shouted over the clapping and the fiddles screeching out another jig. "No going above stairs until you're good and tired." Sweat dripped from his nose, and the hand I grasped to haul myself from the bench was slick.

"I need to save myself!" I protested.

He laughed. "You'll be plenty inspired, I believe. Now dance with your bride!" And so it went for many hours, our strength fortified with a light supper of cold chicken and cider, or Black Betty if it could be found. Now and then, we may have downed a glass of spring water.

Late in the evening, I stood on the side of the courtyard, entirely spent and realized with alarm that all of the young women were missing. I scanned the crowd for Jane, realizing she had disappeared. I looked at Sam, and he gave me a knowing smile.

Unbeknownst to me, the unmarried women had taken Jane inside the house. Two maids escorted her to the stair landing and helped her out of her stockings. With much squealing and clapping of hands, she rolled the stocking into a ball and, turning her back to the girls below, tossed the garment over her shoulder. I do not remember who caught the stocking, but they said the lucky girl was pleased with the result.

With a final wave to her well-wishers, her maids took Jane to her parents' bedroom above stairs. Mother and Father White had graciously given us their bed for the night, it being the most comfortable in the house.

Then it was my turn. When the bride's maids came back to the courtyard, a great cheer went up. Sam and Will took me by the arms and hauled me onto the porch. They turned me to the crowd, and I looked down on a sea of wet, smiling faces reflected in the torchlight. I was forced to make a short bow, and the mob cheered again.

Sam knocked once on the bedroom door and opened it without waiting for a response. He held the door back and gave me a solemn bow, sweeping his arm across the opening to indicate my direction. I stepped into the bedroom, and he silently closed the door behind me. I heard the fiddlers take up their music again, and it seemed far away.

Candlelight gave the room a soft golden glow. Vases of wildflowers sat upon the dresser and table beside the bed. More flowers were strewn like early snow on the floorboards.

I stood with my back against the door, staring at the canopy bed on the far side of the room. The most beautiful woman in the world lay in it, her red hair loose on the pillow.

"Kin ye not walk, husband?" she asked with the smile I loved so much playing on her lips.

My mind refocused. "I believe I can," I said.

"Then ye best try, or ye'll never make it this far."

I took a step, and then another, kicking off my shoes and pulling my shirt over my head as I went. At the edge of the bed, I looked down at the face of the woman of my dreams. She held up the edge of the blanket.

And that is all I will say about that.

CHAPTER 2
James Kelly

September 23rd, 1768
Chamber's Town, Pennsylvania

The following two years passed quickly in hard work and marital bliss. We moved to an old cabin on the corner of my father's farm. It was his gift to us, and I was eternally grateful. Jane came with a dowry that included a few pieces of ancient furniture, a chest full of quilts and blankets, and her grandmother's pewterware.

The cabin faced west on a slight rise with an excellent view of the valley below. It was solid, with a plank floor, but it required considerable improvements. The chimney had a wide crack, and the old windows leaked badly when the wind blew out of the north. As my livestock grew, we added a barn and split rail fences around the entire half acre. Each night after working sunup to sundown and beyond, Jane and I sat on our porch and watched the sky turn red and grow soft and held each other's hand. It's corny, I know, but we were in love. And soon, our love began to show.

William was born in June of '67 and Joseph the year after that.

I completed my surveyor apprenticeship with McFarland and his son. The work in those days was constant and hard. In my experience, a surveyor never works in an open field. Trees and rocks and swamps and thorn bushes were a requirement for any measurement job they assigned me. Hard as the work was, I spent my days outdoors, where I was most content.

Surveying was a respectable profession that every landowner needed, sooner or later. A good survey was like a good fence, making for good neighbors. Our town saw fewer conflicts than our Maryland neighbors to the south. There, for many years, the borderland was in dispute.

One time I met the famous astronomer Charles Mason. He came to Chamber's Town to discuss the line separating the land of the Penn's and the Calvert's. Stone markers now indicate where Pennsylvania and Maryland divide. One day, I feel, that line will be a source of significant irritation between our two states.

When we tell people of our happiness in those days, no one really believes us. The truth is, despite Jane's red hair and quick temper, we never once had cause to raise our voices to one another. We disagreed from time to time, though we never shouted, and we never went to bed angry.

That changed one fall evening when Jim Kelly returned from the Indian Territory west of the Allegheny Mountains. I had known Jim my whole life. He was tall and gangly, strong as steel, and just as dependable.

The three of us sat on the porch watching the sunset. Jane held Joseph on her lap, and William was asleep just inside the door. As the darkness grew and we listened to Jim talk of his amazing trek into the wild, I became more and more enthralled, while Jane became more and more agitated. She saw where this was heading long before I did.

"I tell you, Fergus," Jim said reflectively, stretching out his long legs, "you've never seen such land. Thick forests with cold rushing streams, valleys of open grassland. A man could own as much land as he wanted. All you've got to do is mark it off proper. Next year, the Penn family's opening a land office, and anyone will be able to apply for as much as they can afford. And it won't cost much, neither."

I smiled at Jane. "Doesn't that sound like some kind of country, honey?" I effused, oblivious to the head of steam building beside me. She did not answer my question.

"How long did it take you to get there, Jim?" I wanted to know.

Jim leaned forward on his knees. "Took but ten days, for I traveled light with four other men that knew how to walk. We followed Braddock's trail over the mountains and then turned north after we crossed the last ridge before the river valley. The spot we headed for is between two deep creeks, not far off the Kittanning trail. It is damn near as far west and north as you can go."

"Why is that?" I asked.

"See, at the end of the last war, in '63, there was the Royal Proclamation. Maybe you know."

I nodded. The Proclamation proved to be a major contention for years because it prevented settlers from moving any further west than the Appalachian and Allegheny Mountains. All of the land west of that line was Indian Territory.

"Now," Jim continued, "there's a new treaty made up at Fort Stanwix in New York. It moved the line all the way to the Ohio and Allegheny Rivers."

"And that's where you want to go? It's a long way."

He sat back and took another sip of cider. "And it won't be easy with women and children and livestock, cause you have to take everything you need. But it will be worth it."

"You're going, for sure?"

"Fergus," he said with a smile, "man is meant to keep moving. That's why we're here in Pennsylvania and not back in Ireland or Scotland. Aye, I intend to go. And I want you and your brother to go with me."

With that, Jane stood up and left the porch without a word. I watched her go. Jim hung his head, then looked up at me.

"I need you, Fergus. We need a surveyor. Someone who can mark off the homesteads and convince Penn's council that we did it right."

I looked back at the empty doorway and shook my head. "I don't know, Jim. That's a long way to go. And Jane just getting back on her feet with the baby and all..."

"Not more than a month, that's all it'll be. Once you see it for yourself, Fergus, you'll understand." He stood to leave and looked back at me from the steps. "We'll be the first in a new world."

I entered the cabin cautiously, painfully aware that any spark could ignite my redhead. Jane sat the shadows by the hearth, the fire banked low in the warm evening. She held Billy to a breast and did not look up as I came in.

Sitting across from her, I held my tongue and waited. I learned a long time ago that was the best approach in situations like this.

Finally, she spoke. "There's Indians."

"They call it Indian Territory, so I reckon you're right," I said, trying to keep things light. All I got for my effort was a flash of her green eyes before they dropped back to the baby.

"There's been Indians round here, you know," I continued. "It's only five years since the Conocacheague Valley was overrun. If it weren't for Colonel Jim Smith and his Black Boys making sure the Indians didn't get guns or rum, we'd still be fighting them. Right here."

"James Smith is a renegade. He was lucky not to be hung as a traitor," she countered. Sometimes I was convinced I had married a Tory.

"That's true," I conceded, "but he prevented the Indians from getting guns, and his attack on Fort Loudoun got Governor Penn's attention. Things are calm now — there's peace."

Jane gave a very un-lady-like snort. "Peace! Show me one *peace* that wasn't broken when it was no longer advantageous." Jane put the baby in his crib and faced me, hands on hips, in her fighting stance. "And tell me this, Mr. Moorhead, those Indians who no longer live here, where are they, then?"

That was a rhetorical question, so I tried a different tack. "We've said for some time that this land is getting too crowded and this house too small. Someday we'll want to give land to our boys like my father gave us. We don't have enough to give away. This is an opportunity to make a life for ourselves in a new world. The way our fathers did."

"We have a life here," she said, bending down to cover Billy with a blanket. "And ye have a profession."

"We do, and it is a fine life, no question." I hesitated, looking for the right words. "Have you never wondered what's out there? Wouldn't you like to see a land that no one has touched?"

"There's Indians," she said, and that was that. (1)

22

Five months later, the Penn family Land Office began to sell off Southwestern Pennsylvania land purchased from the Six Nations at the Council of Fort Stanwix. Immediately, applications were made close to Fort Pitt and down toward Virginia. The land northeast of Fort Pitt was now open for purchase at five-pound sterling per hundred acres, but no applications were filed. That area was considered hostile to settlers. It was, of course, the very land that Jim wanted to make his own.

To claim a piece of land, all you had to do was submit a letter with a detailed description, usually based on a tomahawk survey. After the settlements became more established, an actual survey could be completed.

A tomahawk survey was what we professional surveyors called a relative survey. It lays out a parcel of land relative to a specific point, though it is not tied to any world map. In other words, we know where we are, but we do not know where in the *world* we are.

Jim Kelly thought I could help make his claim stronger, being a professional surveyor and all. I tried to explain that we did not have the time or the equipment to do much more than walk off a plot of land.

"Least you can make it square," he said.

I shrugged. "That I can do."

"Well, then…"

We sat in Gibb's Tavern near the town square. It was busy, so we crammed ourselves into a table at the window. Now and then, a familiar face would come or go and raise a friendly hand. It was early spring in central Pennsylvania, and folk were happy to be out in the warm weather.

"I talked to Samuel the other day," Jim continued once the girl placed another round of beers on the table. "He seems open to the idea. I bet he can talk Joseph into going."

I snorted at that. "Joe could be talked into a trip to the moon. Boy's got no sense. And, he has no skill of any use in the wilderness. If it doesn't come from a book, he doesn't know it."

Samuel, however, was a different story. If he was even half considering this wilderness trek with Jim, then Jane might change her mind. At least, I could go see for myself. It does not mean I have to commit to buying the land.

"Let me talk it over with Jane," I finally said. We shook hands, and I headed home with a tentative step.

The discussion did not go well from the start. She accused me right off of being drunk, which I denied. Four or five beers with Jim did not get me drunk. I merely smelled like I was.

"Sam's going," I tendered.

"Sam has no family, nor more coming," she said, maneuvering her huge belly around the table. She carefully set the places for supper and used an overly harsh voice telling Jimmy to go wash up.

I had a thought. "What if we wait until the baby comes? You could stay with your mother. She'd be pleased to have you visit for a while. I'd be back in six weeks. Honest, I'm not saying I'm gonna become a pioneer. It's only to help Jim out and see what the country looks like."

Jane used her weathered argument. "There's Indians." And that was that.

Maybe I was a bit drunk. I did not have the energy or the head to argue. The sun was setting beyond the valley and I took up my chair on the porch. As the sky reddened, the glow enveloped our cabin, and long shadows stretched across the porch.

There was something in the way the sun set in the west, beckoning toward the unknown, the wilderness, the new world. I sighed in resignation, believing that it was a land I would never see.

Jane was standing behind me for a moment before I realized she was there. She stood quietly, holding her belly, watching me watch the sun sink below the far-off hills.

"After the baby comes," she said.

CHAPTER 3
The Long Rifle

April 29th, 1769
Chamber's Town, Pennsylvania

I did not have long to wait. A week after our talk, Euphemia came into the world. She was born early, according to Jane's calculations, but there were no complications. Looking at that tiny face smiling at me from the rocker made my heart leap in my chest. I questioned the sanity of any man wanting only sons.

I took exceptionally good care of Jane all through March and April. She recognized that my extra attention was purely an attempt to keep grease on the wheels of my advancing plans. She did not try to talk me out of it, nor did she mention Indians again. I know it worried her constantly, especially seeing as we had not been separated once since our wedding day.

As the date for our departure drew near, Sam and Jim came over for supper to finalize the details. We spent a considerable amount of time discussing the best route to our final destination.

There were three choices, three different roads west. We could take the longer, southern route on Braddock's Road that crosses the lower mountains out of Fort

Cumberland. Or, we could travel the more direct yet more challenging Forbes Road from Fort Bedford to Fort Ligonier. Both of those routes required us to turn north at some point and leaving the road for the uncharted wilderness. The third option was the far northern Frankstown Road that eventually joined the Kittanning Path. It was too close to Indian Territory for our liking. (2)

We argued back and forth, but in the end, Jim's experience won out. Braddock's Road it would be. He was confident we could join up with others in Fort Cumberland and be in a larger group, at least until the road turned toward Fort Pitt. After that, we would be on our own in uncharted territory, as Sam liked to call it.

Our departure was set for the last of April, and a week earlier, I discussed the upcoming adventure with my father. He did not voice an opinion one way or the other, only offering bits of advice on the gear we might need. My father was a stoic man of few words. He never let the family see his emotions, so it surprised me when he showed up at our cabin one evening. He carried his rifle over his shoulders.

I did not mention the gun as he leaned it against the doorframe and went in to play with his granddaughter.

"I swear," he said later, looking at Euphemia asleep in Jane's arms. "I truly do not know how ye produced such a beautiful creature. All the credit has to go to Janie."

Not certain how much I appreciated the compliment, I said, "Well, thank you, Pa, I'm sure."

He laughed self-consciously. "Just foolin', Fergus. You both should be mighty proud. Truth is, I don't know how ye kin leave her."

"We'll be back soon enough," I said, realizing the depth of his concern. "And we will be careful. You needn't worry.

We won't take any unnecessary risks."

Pa sniffed. "S'pose ye know there's Indians?"

Jane and I looked at each other and burst out laughing so hard we woke the baby, who immediately began to cry. Not understanding the joke he had made, my father smiled thinly, then stood to leave. Jane and I were still grinning as we walked him out to the porch. Pa picked up the rifle and held it out to me, all forty-eight inches perfectly balanced in one hand.

"I want ye to have this," he said, serious now. " 'Tis a far sight better than yer piece, and it shoots straight."

I knew it did. This was the long gun I learned to shoot with as a youngster. It was my father's most prized possession. The rifle was a Deckard, what we now call a Pennsylvania Long Rifle, made in Lancaster County around the time I was born. The stock was carved from curly maple with a fine brass buttplate and patch box.

A rifle has one great advantage and one great disadvantage. If you have the skill, the rifle, due to the grooved bore, was accurate up to 300 yards. On the other hand, it took much longer to load than a smoothbore musket like the flintlocks Sam and Jim carried. It may be quicker to load, but a musket isn't accurate for much more than a hundred yards — and only then if you're damn good.

"My musket will be fine," I protested, overwhelmed by his offer. "Besides, Sam's older, if you're lending it, he should have it."

My father shook his head and said, "If ye get in a fight, Samuel's the man you want in the front line. He kin load and shoot faster than most men. However, when it comes to hunting and feeding you fellas, this rifle and yer steady aim is what I would count on."

"Pa, it's too much. I couldn't take your rifle."

" 'Tis mine to give, and I'm giving it to you," he sniffed, leaned the gun against the doorframe again and held out his hand. He kissed Jane on the cheek and turned back down the hill without another word.

I stood and watched him leave, perhaps for the first time, realizing the enormity of our plan. That night I held Jane tight.

May 3rd, 1769
Fort Cumberland, Maryland

The first part of the journey was not too taxing. We tried to keep to our twenty miles a day. Each of us carried light packs with enough food to reach Fort Cumberland, seventy miles away. In addition, we each had a gun, powder and balls, a good knife, a hatchet, and an extra shirt. Because of the weight, I insisted on taking only the essential survey gear, and we spread that between us. We planned to buy the rest of our supplies and gear in Cumberland.

The extra food proved unnecessary. The first night we made it all the way to Mercersburg, where we knew of an inn. We celebrated a bit, excited and proud to be on our way.

Well-fortified with chops and cider for breakfast, we continued south as the sun rose. The sky was a deep blue, and the land was gently rolling with the Kittatinny Ridge on our right.

I commented on the height of the ridge and how glad I was that we did not have to cross them.

Jim spit a stream of tobacco juice onto the dusty path and snorted. "Those ain't mountains, Fergus. Just you wait!"

We made excellent time, walking hard all day. At an invisible point, we passed over Mr. Mason's line and entered Maryland without being aware of it. The end of the second day found us shy of Hancock, so we enjoyed our first night camping out. The hills rose steeply around us, and the air felt clean and fresh. We were in excellent spirits, congratulating ourselves on our progress.

The next morning we descended into Hancock and continued on without stopping. The Cumberland road was well marked, running through several deep valleys. We spent much of our time climbing up and down on the twisting road. Jim explained that this was merely the beginning of the Appalachian foothills, so we better toughen up.

Fort Cumberland sat prominently on a ridge above a sharp bend in the Potomac River. We passed the old abandoned structure on our left and entered the town. Caravans of wagons and carts filled the single dusty street, and the noise of bellowing oxen echoed across the water. Asking around, we discovered that they were all determined to go south into Virginia. We were the only people intending for the Ohio valley. It made me wonder if they knew something we did not.

We parked our gear on the porch of a general store brimming with barrels of axes and shovels and assorted tools. Inside, you would have thought it was the day before Christmas. Men and women congested the tight space, loaded down with purchases of tools, cloth, and flour.

Forcing our way to the back of the store, we located the shopkeeper taking a breather between customers and gave him our list of food and accessories.

He looked it over, nodding his head, and said, "Where you're going, you'll need an ax."

Jim shook his head. "We each got a tomahawk. An ax

will weigh us down."

The shopkeeper smiled at us and hefted a single edge ax from a barrel. "Got a have an ax. Why, a man could walk into the forest with nothing but his ax, yet fashion snares to catch game, fell trees, and build himself a cabin. Can't do that with a hatchet." He handed the ax to Sam and chuckled at our innocence. "Holding the sharp blade in the manner of a knife, you could even whittle with it when you have spare time. Ha!"

We laughed at that, adding the ax to our ever-growing list of supplies.

"Come back in the morning," he said, holding out his hand. "My name's O'Conner, says so on the door."

We all shook his hand and wandered out to find a place to sleep for the night. That proved to be more difficult than we anticipated. The town was full, and the lone tavern had nothing to offer. The publican warned us not to put our rolls on anyone's porch. So we located a pleasant grove of trees on the bank of the Potomac and made a campfire alongside a dozen other adventurers.

Two of our neighboring campers walked over to our fire and introduced themselves. To me, both men looked rough and none too trustworthy, but Jim and Sam seemed to accept them.

"Name's Bill Travers," said the older of the two. "This here's Alex Morgan." Travers was short and stocky, with strong arms evident through his shirt. I took an instant dislike to his companion. Morgan had a long angular face to match his frame, close-set eyes that refused to meet mine, and he did not offer to shake hands.

Jim waved at an empty space near our fire.

"Which way you headed?" Travers asked, making himself comfortable on his blanket. "Virginia or Ohio?"

"Neither," Sam said. "We're going up above Fort Pitt."

Travers and Morgan both gave us an appraising nod. "That's long way to go. Nothing there but Indians."

Sam smiled. "There will be, once we get there."

Both men laughed.

"So where you bound for?" Jim asked, peering more closely at the two strangers.

They glanced at each other again, then Travers said, "We've got work at Fort Pitt. There's need for hunters to feed the army there. So we're taking the Braddock trail all the way." He paused as if an idea had just occurred to him. "Say, we otta travel together, seeing as how we're on the same path."

"Maybe should," Jim said uncommittedly. "When will you be ready?"

"Ready now. We have all of our supplies. It's settled, then. See you in the morning." They both stood and went back to their fire.

"I don't like them," Sam said quietly, even though the men were out of earshot. That was an unusual statement from Sam, a man known to be as friendly and accepting as a man could be.

Jim nodded his head. "Maybe they ain't the most friendly, but it might be good to have a couple more guns."

And with that, we were five.

We arrived early at Mr. O'Conner's store to find our purchases stacked in the corner, a long handle ax included. We paid him fifteen shillings, an exorbitant sum, and most of the silver we carried. Then, dividing up the load among us, we met up with our new companions at the edge of town.

Ahead, an overgrown grassy path snaked up the deep valley between the sides of the Allegheny Hills.

We were on our way — five men walking quietly in single file. I glanced back at Travers and Morgan, bringing up the rear, and thought back to Jim's final words last night.

"We can always part company if things don't work out," he had said.

If only we had done so, then and there.

CHAPTER 4
Fort Necessity

May 5th, 1769
Braddock's Road, Pennsylvania

The trail we followed west from Cumberland rose quickly into a steep rocky pass. Boulders and debris that had fallen down the embankments littered our path, making it a difficult first few miles.

Despite what Jim had led us to believe, Braddock's Road was not much of a road at all. At most, it provided a general guide through the forest and high meadows. As we reentered Pennsylvania, the constant need to ford minor streams and clamber over fallen trees slowed our progress. Twice we came to old rotten bridges spanning fast-moving creeks. The main beams seemed solid, so, with a cursory inspection of the decking, we waded across the streams.

The light disappeared as the forest closed in around us. Trees taller and thicker than any I had ever seen back in Chamber's Town crowded the trail. Trunks so wide it would take four men to reach around the base towered overhead, their limbs forming a solid canopy of green a hundred feet in the air. And everywhere, the fallen and rotting behemoths lay in a jumble that clogged the forest floor. Thick layers of moss, half-round fungus and dark green bracken ferns occupied every open space. You could taste the air.

Sam kept clucking his tongue and commenting on the difficulties of bringing wagons with women and children and horses and cattle this direction. I, for one, failed to see how it could be accomplished at all. Jim, ever the optimist, was convinced we could do it.

By the end of the second day out of Cumberland, we had crossed the southern Alleghenies and the relatively easy rolling foothills and meadowlands beyond. The more foreboding Laurel and Chestnut Ridges still lay ahead. Thankfully, the weather held. It was not excessively hot during the day, and a fire at night kept the dew off.

All was not well, however. Travers and Morgan were proving to be unwelcome companions. In truth, Travers was all right. He drove me crazy with his constant chatter, though he was friendly enough. Maybe too familiar in that cloying way some people seem to have without noticing how much they irritate others.

Morgan was another thing. He would not lift a finger to help set up the evening camp unless someone spoke to him directly. At dinner, Morgan was always first to the skillet, managing to help himself to the best cuts or the deepest scoop of stew. Sometimes Travers snapped a harsh word at Morgan, who always barked back. Whatever friendship and plans they had of being hunting partners was slowly unraveling. We tried to be cordial, but it was clear a rift was developing between them.

In camp, each of us had a specific task. Jim was the cook and in charge of the food and the fire. Sam was our guard, and his job was to stay vigilant while we went about our tasks.

My job was gathering firewood and hunting. As my

father predicted, my skill and his rifle proved a deadly combination. I brought down a doe that crossed our path one evening as the ground fog began to rise. She stepped out of the woods into the clearing near our camp. It was a clean kill at 200 yards.

At the end of the third day, laboring over a rise in the trail, we came face to face with the red coat of an army sentry. The young man said he could hear us coming for two miles, so he was not spooked when we appeared. He escorted us to where a group of soldiers had made camp. Their captain's name was William Walsh, a handsome young man with a ready smile around twenty-one years of age. He welcomed us, and we spent the rest of the night at his fire.

Captain Walsh explained that they had come from Fort Pitt and were going east to Philadelphia, then back to England.

"They will be pleased to see you gentlemen at the fort," he said once Travers had explained his and Morgan's plan. "Things are heating up along the Ohio. There aren't enough men to hunt for all the people in the fort. You will make a fortune — if you don't get scalped."

He looked at the three of us and continued, "You should be extra careful, though, up north. We have had reports of marauding Shawnee and Seneca."

"I thought the Seneca are members of the Six Nations," I ventured. "Why are they on the warpath?"

"You know your natives," he replied appreciatively. "These Indians, we call Mingo, are Ohio Seneca. They're a different breed than the Iroquois. There are bands who do what they please. And the Shawnee are always up to no good."

Morgan broke from his usual silence. "Ask me," he

36

growled, "won't be long before they get back to payin' for scalps like was in the war. I made good money killin' Indians and hope to again."

It was well known that during the last war, both sides, French and British, paid for enemy scalps. There were men who made a living doing nothing else. Being from the east, we never saw it for ourselves, though there were stories.

Travers appraised Morgan with a look of disgust. "You might stop to think that we need to be friendly with them Indians you hope to kill if we're gonna be hunting on their land."

"Ain't their land, is it?" Morgan spat. "The treaty said white men now own this land. The more we kill, the better off we'll all be."

He stood and walked away from our fire.

Captain Walsh watched him go and sadly shook his head. "Much as it grieves me to say so, your friend may be correct."

"Not my friend," Travers said with force.

"Thing is," the Captain continued, "to stay alive in this country, you may need to consider one Indian as much a threat as another. It won't be long before there are no friendly Indians."

We digested that in silence for a while until Walsh spoke up again with a livelier tone. His voice was that of an educated Londoner and made me consider the difference between these soldiers and ourselves. We spoke the King's English, but we did not sound like these men. All of them were from Britain. The little I picked up as they chatted together sounded Welsh or West Anglican. None of them spoke like a Pennsylvanian. Although we were all subjects of King George, we were no longer the same people. I turned my attention back to the Captain's lecture.

"Why, I shall wager you gentlemen don't even know where you are!" He scanned our faces with a broad smile on his, waiting for an answer. Getting none, he continued. "You are sitting on hallowed ground, right here."

"Why is that?" I asked, looking around for ghosts.

Walsh pointed toward the gently sloping meadow where an earthen mound indicated a man-made structure had once stood. "Those are the ruins of Fort Necessity. You've all heard of it, I am sure. In July of seventeen hundred and fifty-four, young Major George Washington was forced to surrender to the French after his failed attempt to capture Fort Duquesne. Hard to believe it was only fifteen years ago. So much has happened."

"You speak as a student of history, Captain," I said. "What was so important about this fort?"

Walsh settled in, pleased to have a new audience. "Aye, I am proud to say I read history at the Old Royal. History and, of course, artillery. Not that I have much use for either in this godforsaken wilderness.

"As I was saying, the battle that took place here, and Washington's surrender, forced our county to declare war on France. The fighting on this continent soon created a global conflict. You might not believe it to look at this place now — the shots fired here between Washington and Louis Coulon de Villiers led directly to the last war."

Jim spoke up. "We call it the French and Indian War."

"Indeed. For you colonists, it was a war with the French and their Indian allies, but it went much further than that. My father fought with the Duke of Cumberland at Hanover in seventeen hundred fifty-seven, and now I am here. Funny how life works, eh?"

Walsh invited us to share their fare, and we offered them a fat steak from the previous day's kill. While supper was handed out, I considered the implications of this in-consequential piece of land. That war raged for seven years in most parts of Europe and America. And it all started here. Maybe ghosts were haunting the meadow. The thought that there were more likely Indians suddenly came to my mind.

I watched the soldiers move around their fires. They seemed relaxed and unconcerned with the possibility of hostile natives lurking nearby. However, the more I studied them, the more evident it became that they had not relaxed their guard. All of the men still wore their redcoats, with the crossed white belts, even though most had removed their cocked hats in the warm evening. I noticed they stacked their Brown Bess muskets with fixed bayonets, four each, within easy reach. Of the twenty men in the pla-toon, five were standing guard on the perimeter of the meadow.

"Tell us of General Braddock, Captain," I said as we ate. "We're on his road, yet all I know of his campaign is that it also ended badly."

Walsh smiled. "Ah, another disaster. It is a wonder that we won that war. It did not go well for us in the first few years. This road," he pointed with his spoon, "was an in-credible feat of manpower and engineering. It exists now as a path through the wilderness. Fifteen years ago, there was nothing at all.

"A year after Washington's defeat, he was back here again, this time part of a major force under the command of Edward Braddock. Braddock brought two regiments with him to attack Fort Duquesne. More than 1200 men, and heavy artillery, if you can believe that!"

I shook my head in disbelief. "I find it hard to imagine, especially when we spend all of our time climbing over trees, fording streams, and avoiding rattlers."

"Exactly. It was incredibly demanding work. Like Hannibal crossing the Alps! They made slow progress, I will tell you. Then, a mile or so south of Fort Duquesne, Colonel Gage's grenadiers ran into a party of French and their Indians. The battle was one-sided because those French bastards wouldn't stand their ground. Gage lined up his men in the proper formation and moved forward while the Indians shot at them from behind the trees. It was disgraceful."

Walsh sat for a moment, lost in the injustices of war before he continued. By this time, most of his men were listening attentively to their commander. I doubted any of them had heard the history of this area, either.

"So," he straightened his back and continued, "Gage's company was routed and turned back toward Braddock, a dozen miles behind. The French and the Indians pursued them and attacked Braddock before he could take up a defensive position. His men stood shoulder to shoulder, firing volley after volley, but they were exposed and did not last long. The General was killed, hundreds of his men lost, and the entire expedition destroyed.

"Today, we call it the Battle of the Wilderness. Young Washington, who had failed so miserably the year before, was hailed as a hero and promoted. For surviving another defeat!"

In the hushed silence that followed, I asked, "How many?"

"Some four hundred and fifty men killed and another four hundred wounded. Out of one thousand three hundred! It was a disaster."

"He built a damned fine road!" Jim chirped in.

Captain Walsh smiled wryly and finished his plate of

bacon and beans.

"So, how did the fort become British?" I asked.

"Well, there's the irony," he smirked. "Following two failed attempts, Washington came back again and took the fort in November of seventeen hundred fifty-eight. He promptly resigned from the Virginia regiment and became a gentleman farmer. The Army is better off, I can tell you. I hope he can cut tobacco better than he could cut down French!"

We all laughed at his small joke. It was good to lighten the mood after the grim story he had been telling us. Most of the men pulled out their rolls to settle down for a few hours' sleep, and we did the same.

Before I lay down, Walsh came over to my spot and squatted beside me.

"If I may, I want to offer a bit of advice as you head north," he said quietly. "You are no more a frontiersman than I, though I have been here a year now and still have my scalp. Heed my words. Never do anything, sleep, eat, or work, without one man on guard, and," he looked past my shoulder, "be damn sure that man isn't Morgan. I wish you well, Moorhead. Goodnight."

He patted me on the shoulder and went to check on his sentries.

CHAPTER 5
The Mill

May 6th, 1769
The Monongahela Valley, Pennsylvania

From the highest point of the mountain road, five weary travelers looked down on the gently rolling hills of the valley below. In the hazy distance, smoke rose from several homesteads.

"Those weren't there last time I passed this way," Jim said, a trace of disappointment in his voice. "We best find our land and claim it before this whole place gets filled up."

Sam laughed. "Jim, there's no more than twenty people as far as you can see. I believe we can find an empty acre or two. Let's go meet our neighbors."

It was a stretch calling anyone living in this valley a neighbor to our final destination, still sixty miles or more to the north. However, the sight of smoke rising from the thinly scattered cabins did make us feel a little closer to civilization than we might have imagined.

A couple hours of downhill hiking and two or three miles on gentle, forested land brought us to a well-built cabin alongside a wide creek. To our great surprise, not far from the cabin, a rough-hewn mill-wheel turned slowly in the stream.

Someone had built a grist mill in Indian territory!

"Hallo!" Jim shouted. "Friends come to visit!"

A man came to the cabin door, musket in hand, but pointed down in a non-threatening manner. Our guns were cradled loosely in our arms, as well.

"Howdy," the man called back, still not stepping clear of the doorframe. "Who are you, then?"

"My name's James Kelly, and these," he swept his arm to indicate all of us, "are my good friends and companions, bound for Fort Pitt and points north. We'd be obliged for a place to lay our rolls and maybe a drink if you have it."

The man rested his long gun against the doorframe and walked out to meet us. He was in his late thirties, a bit round and starting to go bald, but presenting a broad smile and a face that radiated friendliness.

"I'm Henry Beeson," he announced, and we shook hands all round. Indicating a small, pretty woman standing in the doorway, he said, "My wife, Mary."

Morgan, who up to this point had not said a word, pulled off his hat and bowed to the woman in an exaggerated manner. "Mrs. Beeson, it's a pleasure to meet such a fine lookin' woman so far from civilization."

Mrs. Beeson did not return the smile. She walked up to her husband and hooked her arm in his.

Beeson, somewhat piqued, said, "You're all welcome to sleep in the mill tonight. It's dry and comfortable once you get used to the noise of the wheel."

While this minor confrontation was playing out, Sam wandered off toward the mill. Beeson saw Sam standing on the side of the creek, staring up at the ten-foot diameter wheel, as if transfixed by its rotation. We all walked over to join Sam.

Beeson proudly said, "Tis a beauty, is it not?"

Without looking away from the mill, Sam said, "It is. I'd consider it an honor, sir, if you'd describe every plank and bolt in this wonderful machine."

I knew my brother had just fallen in love with a grand notion. It became a passion he would follow for many years.

Beeson waved his hand to indicate the stream running past his mill. "This here's Redstone Creek," he said with the pride of a new father. "I have never known it to go dry, so I believe it will be the perfect water source when I build my mill."

Sam looked puzzled. "What do you mean, sir? *When* you build it?"

"Ah," Beeson smiled. "You thought this was the mill. It's my first version to get things worked out, so to speak. A mill has more moving parts than you would think possible. In a year or two, I intend to build a two-story mill here with a pond up the hill and a proper flume to bring the water to the wheel. The water will turn the wheel from the top. This here's what's called an undershot wheel. It is using the water in the stream to move it."

"And water running over the top will provide much more power," Sam said, immediately grasping the concept.

"Indeed. The more waterpower, the faster the wheel turns, the better the grinding power. As more folk come to this country, they'll need a place to grind their corn. After a time, and more arrive, we intend to make flour."

"You built all of this so you could practice?" I asked.

He laughed. "Well, not only for practice. This grinds corn quite well. It will do until the big one gets built, and I have to transfer the stones."

Sam said, "I've been wondering about the stones. You have two of them. How on earth did you get them here?"

Beeson laughed at the memory. "That was harder than building the mill, I can tell you! I bought them at Fort Pitt, a Frenchy cut them twenty-odd years ago, and they never got used. Each one is four-foot in diameter and weighs nearly a ton! I was lucky to have a friend that could barge them up the Monongahela and then cart them from the Redstone."

He clapped Sam on the shoulder. "Want to see how it works?"

"Would I?" Sam blurted, and they both ducked under the low header and disappeared into the mill.

Sam and Beeson continued their discussion while I helped Mrs. Beeson pull a jug of cool hard cider from the spring-house at the base of the mill. Soon I was sitting comfortably on the streambank with my bare feet washing in the cold water. It was a beautiful place to spend the last of the day, and I thought how much Jane would like it here.

Henry and Mary, as they insisted we call them, were exceptional hosts. As evening fell, Henry invited us to join them for supper. Their four children, ranging from a baby in the cradle to a boy five years of age, sat quietly at one end of the sturdy wood-slab table that took up most of the cabin floor.

The children were well behaved; even the baby was quiet. I cannot say the same for a member of our group. Morgan had drunk more than his share of cider, and now that rum accompanied our supper, he became louder and more obnoxious.

He leaned against Travers while Mary spooned beans onto his plate. "I tell you," he said far too loudly, "that is a fine little woman, there."

"Shut your trap and eat," Travers hissed.

Morgan grinned and turned to leer at Mary as she went around the table.

"Fergus," Sam spoke up, trying to cover Morgan's rudeness, "you must see what this man has built. It's a wonder of science."

We all turned our attention to Sam, purposely ignoring Morgan.

"There'll soon be a need for more of these mills, I tell you," he went on. "I think we should consider this for our land. We wouldn't be a competition with you, Henry, not as far away as we'll be."

Beeson did not answer. He was still watching Morgan with a look I did not like. Morgan was oblivious to Henry's glare. He was shoveling beans in his mouth with one hand and drinking rum from the cup held in the other, his eyes never leaving Mary. I felt the need to break this tension, but before I could do anything, Mary made the mistake of leaning over Morgan's shoulder to deposit a slice of venison on his plate.

I watched the next seconds pass in slow motion before my eyes.

As Mary leaned in, Morgan reached back with his right hand and firmly grasped Mary's bottom. She straightened up with a yelp, dropping the plate on the table. Across from them, Beeson came to his feet with a roar. Mary pushed back from the table, breaking contact with Morgan's hand.

Before anyone could even move, with a flash of steel, Travers swung around on the bench and buried his hunting knife in Morgan's throat.

We all sat in shock at the suddenness of this horror. Morgan clutched at the knife, blood already flowing from his gaping mouth, and fell backward off the bench.

No one moved. A tableau of death painted in the dim candlelight. The only sound came from Morgan, gurgling on the floor.

Then Beeson's little girl screamed.

"You're still welcome to stay the night," Beeson said to us an hour or so later. His voice was soft, and his hands still shook.

"We appreciate that, "I said in an equally subdued tone. We stood in the darkness outside the cabin. No one felt ready to go back inside.

Travers and Sam had dragged Morgan's body to the edge of the woods. They promised to bury him in the morning if the wolves did not find him first. No one cared which. Then Travers went off and sat by himself beside the stream. Jim cleaned up what blood had not already soaked into the dirt floor. Then he cleared the table and stacked the dishes next to the barrel out back.

Mary had gathered up her children and retreated to the loft without a word. She never cried, but her face was white and hard as stone. After the first cry from the little girl, the children were quiet, their eyes huge.

It was not the murder but the suddenness of it that shocked us all. One moment Morgan was alive — the next, he was dead. In the space of a second. No one blamed Travers, nor were we saddened at the loss of that man. Travers only acted faster and did what Henry was preparing to do. I think Travers felt it was his responsibility for bringing Morgan into our company.

One by one, we quietly expressed our regret for disrupting Beeson's family this way and took up our rolls for the night. Inside the mill, it was pitch black. Beeson warned us not to strike a spark being that the fine dust filling the air was extremely flammable. We had to find our way to an empty corner in the dark to make our bed.

Travers did not join us. Henry said Travers sat by the steam all night, and in the morning, he was gone.

CHAPTER 6
Northward

May 7th, 1769
The Wilderness, Pennsylvania

We got sidetracked from Braddock's Road in our fateful visit with the Beeson's. Heading north from their cabin, we soon picked up the path again and followed it to the banks of the Youghiogheny River. Jim led us to a ford known as Stewart's Crossing. General Braddock's army crossed there in '55, so we figured we could do it, too.

The river was the first formidable waterway we had encountered. The crossing, where the bank had been beaten down years before, was easy to locate. Although the water ran fast and white over the shallow ford, we simply took off our boots and waded in, holding our guns high and dry. We stepped carefully, making sure to plant each foot before moving forward. It was more than 200 feet to the other side where we climbed up the slippery bank, wet up to our thighs.

Sitting down to rest and dry our feet, Jim voiced his concern.

"That may be the widest river we cross, but it won't be the deepest," he observed. "It was easy enough for us to wade — cattle and wagons is another thing altogether."

Sam was filling his canteen at the river's edge. I asked, "So do you have a plan, or do you intend to fall in that creek when you come to it?"

"Very funny. I don't have a plan. Part of our job is to find a ford and mark it clearly, so we don't have to hunt for it next time."

"But you've been here before," I said. "How'd you get over last year?"

Jim picked up a stone and threw it into the water next to where Sam was kneeling on the bank. It splashed Sam in the face. Not even bothering to look back, he shook his head like an exasperated parent.

"We waded or swam," Jim continued. "We weren't trying to stay with any particular trail. We just wanted to get there, see if it was all we heard it was."

"Braddock got an entire army across."

Jim nodded. "As I said, this ain't the one that bothers me. When we get to the next one, you'll see what I mean."

Ten miles north of the Youghiogheny, we reached a significant milestone — our last steps on Braddock's Road. What little evidence of a road we were able to follow was turning more and more to the northwest while our path lay to the northeast.

We camped alongside the trail that night beneath a lean-to of pine boughs and then turned away from it in the morning. No white man had yet raised smoke from a cabin in the land we now walked. This, indeed, was the wilderness.

Moving silently through the scattered woodlands, my mind kept going back to our visit at the Beeson place. None of us had spoken of what happened there. Travers was gone, so there was nothing we could do about the murder. I know the violence affected us all, but for me, it was not the death of that bastard Morgan; it was the sudden-ness of it. I know we were all ashamed for bringing such a man into the home of those generous people. There was no excuse for that.

This land was new and raw, and potential violence lurked around every bend in the road. It required men with strength and stamina — men who could stand up to the Morgans in this world and kill if necessary. Did I have that strength, I wondered? I shook my head to clear the cob-webs and tried to appreciate the beauty of the land sur-rounding me. Deep down inside, I knew this trip was no longer a young man's innocent adventure.

However, the one good thing that came out of our visit was Sam's interest in a grist mill. As we hiked and the hor-ror of the previous evening wore off, Sam talked of noth-ing else. He was convinced that was the business he wanted for himself. And, if Sam's anything at all, he's a man of conviction. He was determined to have his mill someday.

A day later, our intrepid band came to the banks of the Conemaugh River, and we understood Jim's concern.

We had forded Loyalhanna Creek, a mile or so to the east of what was soon to become Hanna's Town, without any problems. It was wide and shallow. The river we now looked down upon was narrow and deep. Birch and willow covered the steep banks. I could not see a way across, and neither could Jim.

" 'Tis too steep here to get big wagons over. We need to go further east," Jim declared, shaking his head. "The higher in the hills, the shallower it will be."

As usual, he was right. We hiked up the river three miles and came to a place where the water flowed over a rocky bottom, and the banks were low on both sides. This crossing was our last water obstacle of any size. Once again, we waded barefoot through the icy water and continued north.

The forest thinned noticeably, and soon we were making good time in open prairie, with a spattering of chestnut and oak groves. Here and there, walnut trees towered above the oak, looking like guardians of the forest.

When we came to a wide stream flowing out of the north, Jim stood with his hands on his hips and announced that he knew where he was. Encouraged and excited to be near the end of our journey, we followed the stream until it veered sharply to the east, and we turned west. A mile or so further on, Jim stopped dead in his tracks and leaned on his musket.

"We're here," he announced and threw down his pack.

I could not see what made this particular spot different from the hundreds of other worthy acres we had passed, but I took Jim at his word and collapsed onto a fallen tree.

We were now deep in what the old maps identified as Indian Territory, the land that would someday be called Indiana County.

May 11th, 1769
The Wilderness, Pennsylvania

Our thirteenth day. Jim and Sam and I sat on a knoll early in the morning and looked out on a wide field of tall grass. As the sun rose through the forest behind us, a heavy summer dew reflected the light off the grass like autumn frost. On the other side of the field, to the west, six whitetails raised their heads in our direction, suddenly aware that they were no longer alone.

"How do you know we're there?" Sam asked. We all spoke quietly, unwilling to disturb the tranquility of the scene before us.

Jim looked around as if trying to recognize a tree or bush. "I don't, tell you the truth, just that we're close. We'll search for the marker I built last year. Then we'll know for sure."

After a hurried breakfast, we set out to find the stone pile Jim had erected on this first trip. It would have been quicker for us to branch out in search of the cairn, but it was safer to stay together.

We often discussed the fact that we had encountered no Indians on our entire trek. Jim had run across a party in this area last year. They turned out to be friendly enough at the time. No telling if it still was true. As I came to know far too well, you cannot rely on a friendly Indian still being friendly the next time you meet. Their mood can change with the wind.

So, we stayed within sight of each other, carrying our muskets at all times. We made greater and greater diameter circles around a giant oak that was visible from any distance. On our third or fourth circumnavigation of the oak, Jim moved quickly past a stand of trees and then broke into a run. When we caught up to him, he was standing in a clear area, proudly resting his hand on a stone tower about four feet high. He beamed at us like a new father.

"I knew it," he said. "I wasn't off by half a mile. That's damn fine reckoning!"

Sam and I made appropriate sounds of appreciation and clapped him on the back. Though it was a minor celebration, I suddenly felt grounded in a vast world. I had a landmark, all a surveyor needs. From that marker, I could lay out any size plot of land we wished.

Sam leaned against the stack of stone with his arms crossed on his chest. "Jim, I got a ask you one question. Why here? We passed empty land that was as fine as this. Why this spot?"

Jim kind of chuckled as if letting us in on a long-held secret. "I wondered when someone would ask me that question," he said. "Someday, this particular spot of land 'll be an important crossroad. To the north's the Kittanning path. It runs east right past here, from the Allegheny River, all the way to Frankstown, and beyond. Anyone comin' from eastern New York 'll use that path. Then there's the Catawba trail we followed here from the south. That'll soon be a real road for people moving from Virginia to New York, or back. This land is high, there's good water, and it ain't swampy. And don't forget that we're not alone out here. There's a sizeable Delaware town to the north. For now, they're friendly and 'll want a trade. Might even be helpful as we get settled. I tell you, gentlemen, this spot's the future of our country!"

We all applauded and laughed heartily at his speech, feeling as proud of our success as he did. This was the land Jim had chosen, and this is where he intended to build.

First, however, we required a shelter strong enough to last our short time here. We got started right away, building the first cabin in this wilderness.

Not too far from the cairn, there was a stand of white pine growing tall and straight. We set to cutting and clearing and worked hard throughout the day. Taking turns cutting down trees, we more than once commented on how good it was to have old Mr. O'Conner's ax. It was worth every shilling.

By evening, there existed the semblance of a cabin ten feet on a side and five feet high with four standing pines holding up the corners. We took the boughs of all the pines we had cut down and layered them across stout poles to make a roughly thatched roof that would keep us dry if it did not rain too hard.

In one corner, we left a gap in the logs broad enough to crawl through. Inside, it was dry and fresh-smelling. In short order, we learned not to stand upright or our heads knocked against the rafters holding up the roof.

We dug a fire pit in the clearing and lashed thin poles to two pines to hang our gear and dry our clothes. During the day, we made so much noise that the deer I spotted early in the morning had moved away from us.

That evening, there was no fresh meat for supper when we finally settled down in front of our new home. We chewed on the dried venison Beeson had given us, tired and pleased with our day's work. By the time the stars came out, all three of us were snoring away. There was no watch that night.

CHAPTER 7
The Hatchet Survey

May 12th, 1769
The Wilderness, Pennsylvania

The next day, Jim announced that it was time to start work. I am not sure what he thought we had been doing up until then, but he was the leader, so we stood to.

"Now that I've done my part in getting us here, it's time for Fergus to haul his share of the load! We need to figure out where our homesteads are gonna be."

That hit me like a bucket of ice water. Our homesteads? That was not why I came on this trip. My job was to conduct a survey that the Penn council would accept as a valid claim. As Jane and I had discussed, we had no intention of moving from our farm. I know Jane did not think I planned to stake out a claim.

Sam noticed my stricken appearance. "What bit you?" he asked.

I looked around at the grasslands and the trees and the blue sky, absorbing how good it all felt. My mind reeled. I stood in the most beautiful piece of the country I had ever seen. It was green and plentiful and ready for the taking.

"I didn't intend to make a claim," I said, still shaken.

Sam snorted. "Well, what the hell'd you think we're

doing out here? I came to find land to call my own. I assumed you did, too."

Jim stood with his hands on his hips and looked at me like I'd suddenly gone stupid. "Don't matter why he's here, Sam," he said dismissively. "We know why we're here, and we're wasting time. Fergus!" he snapped at me. "Get your survey gear put together while Sam and I decide where our future lies!"

With that, he turned and marched out onto the open land. His head swiveled back and forth until he shouted at us. "I knew it when I first saw it. No need to go further. This is where I stake my claim. Let's get started!"

As my mind cleared and settled on the job at hand, I decided that this was an excellent investment opportunity, maybe even one that Jane would come to appreciate. I could always sell a land stake to someone, so I might as well go ahead and block one out.

The easiest way to work from our center point was to run four lines on each cardinal compass point. I could square the lines and create four equal plots of land. If Jim were correct, that someday this would be a real town, our first plots would form the basis for the settlers who follow.

Having work to do that I understood and loved helped me refocus and get started in an orderly manner. I sorted out my equipment from our packs, wiping each with a whale oil rag protected by a special leather pouch.

During our trek west, I carried the most important of our survey tools, the circumferentor. There was a new, more exact tool now used in England, called a theodolite, but it was far too expensive to bring on a journey like ours, even if I owned one. Which I did not.

The circumferentor would work well enough because, as I mentioned before, this was to be a relative survey based on Jim's central pillar. The tool consisted of an over-sized compass from which extends two movable wooden arms with cross-hair sights. The compass is set on a tripod, which we had to make. Then, the surveyor sights down the length of the wooden arms like a rifle. The surveyor either turns the arms and reads the bearing or sets a bearing and gives instructions to the poor soul whose job it is to march out the sighted line with the stadia rod.

I explained all of this to Jim as I assembled the gear. Sam was quite familiar with it already, having assisted me with my surveys around Chamber's Town. He found three thin poles and shaped them to exact lengths with his hatchet. Then he fit each leg into the tripod head we brought with us. I mounted the circumferentor on the head, and we were ready to start our training.

"The hardest part," I began, "is making a straight line and counting your paces. I didn't believe we'd have enough time to use a chain to measure our distances, so we're gonna count our paces, which we will practice."

Jim shook his head. "We're practicing walking?"

"Yes," I said in all seriousness, measuring three feet in the dirt with my tape. "We must be perfect at stepping from one end of this line to the other and doing that consistently through thick and thin."

We each took turns stepping off the distance until we established a comfortable, natural gait. Not too long, not too short.

"So how far do we have to go?" Sam asked after we mastered walking.

Our plan was to create four 300-acre plots, all sharing Jim's common corner point. The math was not difficult.

An acre is 43,560 square feet. If we accurately step out 3,600 feet, or 1,200 paces to a side, we will be very close to three hundred acres.

I showed them the calculations and sketch in my notebook. "One of you will carefully pace in the direction I will indicate. The other will clear his path and make a hatchet mark on a tree whenever possible. When we have extended out 1200 paces, we will erect another cairn benchmark and run at ninety degrees from there. Once we run four lines this way, guess where we should be."

"Back where we started!" my students chimed in together.

Jim was scratching his head, looking out across the rolling, wooded land. "What if we don't end up back at the starting point? Do we have to start over?"

"Yes," I said. "We have to start over since we won't know where the error was. The count could be off, or the angle could be wrong. Either way, if we don't close the box within, let's say twenty feet, everything else we do will be wrong."

Sam asked, "What if we run into a tree, or we can't see you?"

"In that case," I said, "we have to establish a temporary benchmark and move the circumferentor. I'll tell you now, it won't be easy."

Four hours of hard work found us soaked in sweat, filthy dirty, and in need of a rest. We had successfully established one line out of the twelve we needed to run. I think both of them had a new appreciation for the difficulties of my profession.

We soon realized that keeping a straight line and staying

in communication with each other was not our only challenge. Jim found the first timber rattlesnake within an hour. He shooed it back into the rocks with the barrel of his musket. Then, no more than twenty feet further, he found another, twice as long as the first.

"Snakes thick as thieves," he called back to me. "We must pay attention, won't do to get bit out here, I can tell you!"

We stepped over rock outcroppings and fallen trees with great care. By the end of the day, with merely two lines surveyed, we had killed or scared off eight good-size rattlers. A bite from any one of them would be the end of one of us.

Exhausted and a little discouraged with our lack of progress, we ate supper in silence and entered our mansion for the night. We were in for a rude awakening.

Sometime well after dark, Sam, awake for his turn as sentry, grabbed my arm. I was instantly conscious, so lightly did we sleep. Against the cabin wall came the unmistakable sound of an irritated rattlesnake. Our body heat had drawn the snake into the cabin, so I knew he sensed us, even if we could not see him. Nobody said a word.

Jim, now fully awake, struck a spark in a pinch of char cloth he placed on his dinner plate. He applied dry pine needles from the floor and quickly created a handheld bonfire that illuminated the interior of our abode.

The rattler was at least four feet long and thick as my arm. Luckily, it was only a foot or so inside the small opening we used as a door. Slowly, so as not to irritate the snake further, we pulled back to the opposite corner. Then Jim held out his dinner plate lantern and moved toward the snake.

The rattler shook its tail in warning, but it was obviously

bothered by the fire. Its triangular head pulled back until it looked like it would disappear inside its own coil, then in a snap, it ducked under the bottom log, out into the night.

Jim picked up the ax and ducked outside, the dinner plate illuminating the ground. Then we heard the ax chopping down hard.

"We'll have to work on that," he said, ducking back through the low door. "Need to build a berm around the base, keep those bastards out."

With that, Jim lay back down on his blanket and fell instantly asleep. My eyes remained open until the first light of dawn filled the forest.

By noon, we completed the final two legs of Jim's plot, and a miracle occurred. We returned to the central cairn within five feet! We congratulated each other for being able to walk a straight line and count at the same time.

The next two plots of 300 acres would be considerably easier with two lines and accurate corner markers from which to start.

We had progressed halfway down Sam's second line when I received the shock of my life. Sam and Jim were out in a clear area of grass, sixty rods from me when I looked up from a sighting into the face of an Indian!

He stood no more than ten feet from me, leaning casually on his musket. The man wore a hunting shirt and deer hide leggings with a breechcloth hanging down in front. His hair was cut short on the sides, and three feathers decorated the longer hair on top. His face bore no paint, which I hoped was a positive sign. I figured him to be a Delaware, and a handsome one at that.

We stood looking at each other for a moment before I

risked a glance out into the field. Jim and Sam were moving the stadia rod, oblivious to my potential demise.

The Indian followed my look and then turned back to me with his head tilted to the side.

"You make much noise," he said in English.

"We hope to live here someday," I said, trying not to stammer in my surprise.

"It is good land," he agreed.

His body did not move as he looked down at the stump where I had stuck my hatchet after clearing a spot for the circumferentor tripod. The shock of his sudden arrival may have made me slow, but I soon understood. I carefully extended my hand and dislodged the hatchet. Then I deliberately turned it, so the blade was in my hand and held it out to the Indian.

Without a word, he came forward and took the hatchet from me. He looked carefully at the blade, which was fine German steel, honed to a razor's edge. Nodding once, the Indian turned and disappeared into the forest.

I sat down hard on the stump. My first encounter with a native in the wilderness, and I lived to tell the tale!

Out in the field, Sam was waving his arms over his head to get my attention. They wanted to know why I had stopped giving them directions. I waved back and indicated that they should move a yard left. Another hour of work, and we gathered together at a corner of a plot to build a marker.

Did I have a story to tell!

Our ability to walk and count improved immeasurably as the week progressed. We finished the squares Jim and Sam identified as their claims. That meant that I had the choice of the two remaining quadrants. I already knew which one I wanted.

My land, as I already thought of it, was the southwest quadrant and bordered on Sam's and whomever we could get to buy the last parcel. Sam and Jim shared a common border.

It is worth noting that the land Sam chose was part of our quadrants, but it did not include a suitable stream on which he could build a mill. We discussed that, and he said he was satisfied with his lot, so to speak. Someday, he would buy more land and construct the best grist mill in the county. Maybe on the stream south of us, or he would go further north and see what that land was like.

As luck would have it, my quadrant gave us the most trouble, taking longer to finish than we hoped. Even with one established line, we failed to close the square by more than forty feet and had to start over. My land included a stand of oak and hickory, nearly one hundred acres of grassland, and two springs pumping out cold, clear water. The runoff from the springs and the surrounding fields all gathered in a broad stream flowing southwest toward the Conemaugh.

The day before, a thunderstorm with a pounding rain drove us back to our cabin for the remainder of the afternoon. It was while working our way across this stream the next morning that we lost our count. The creek was twice as wide as it had been before the storm, with rushing, muddy water all the way up the banks. We worked our way upstream and then tried to reestablish the line. It did not work. The delay added two extra days to our stay.

On our last day, Jim wondered aloud about the Indian I met and why he never returned. I, for one, was perfectly happy that we saw no more of him.

"Now that they know our intentions," Jim said, "I'm sure we'll see them again. Just keep hoping they stay friendly. It would be a good thing, having friendly Indians in the neighborhood."

"Why's that?" I asked, thinking it would be better not to have Indians in the neighborhood at all.

"Friendly Indians won't let other Indians bother us."

That made some kind of sense, I thought, even if it was not true.

Sam sat in front of our cabin for most of the morning, carefully writing up the deeds for our four claims. The deeds, complete with our names and the date, explained where the plots lay in relation to the sturdy central cairn. Then he made an exact copy of what he had written. He added a copy of my survey and wrapped them both in deer hide, creating a tight roll, the ends sealed with bear grease. Placing the documents in the cairn, he carved a deep X into a heavy, flat stone and laid it on the package, like an ancient tomb.

We had now done all that was required to legally claim this land when we returned to Chamber's Town and applied to the Land Office.

It was time to go home.

CHAPTER 8
The Return

May 31st, 1769
Chamber's Town, Pennsylvania

Our trip home was uneventful. We spent a night with the Beesons, who seemed pleased to see us, despite the murderous events of our previous visit. Beeson told us that a handful of people had come up the trail since, and none inquired of Morgan or Travers. As far as he was concerned, that sad day was in the past. On a lighter note, he and Sam talked long into the night about being a miller and the grand structure Sam intended to build someday.

The next day, we came upon some trappers heading east, with six pack-mules loaded with furs. They were five of the most disreputable-looking men I ever saw. Each sported a long beard, far bushier than the beards we three had grown in the past weeks, and a mass of tangled, greasy hair hung down to their shoulders. They were all dressed in buckskins stained with blood and sweat. Oddly enough, they were as friendly and cordial as you would want to find in the wilds of Pennsylvania and spoke with a refined British accent. They immediately invited us to join their supper while regaling us with accounts of far off Kentucky and Ohio, fighting Indians, and living off the land for more than a year. We thoroughly enjoyed their company, always trying to stay upwind.

Five days later, we climbed the last hill, and Chamber's Town spread out below us. It was a beautiful sight after thirty-three days away.

Jim's place came first. We shook hands all around, then Sam and I walked on alone until we reached the road to my cabin. It was a strange feeling to be going our separate ways, having been together for such a long time.

"We had an adventure, didn't we?" I offered quietly, anxious to get home to Jane yet somehow unwilling to break our bond.

"We did at that, Fergus," he replied. "It was nothing compared to what lies ahead. Now you have a job of explaining to Jane that she's moving into the wilderness."

My shoulders dropped. "Yeah. If you don't see me again, it was grand being your brother!"

Sam clapped me on the back and turned away. "I've got a strong feeling that woman of yours is up for anything," he called over his shoulder. "She'll be fine with the idea. Just wait and see!"

"Homestead!" Jane almost shouted at me. "Did ye lose yer mind out there, somewhere? When ye got this notion to walk off with that James Kelly, I told ye that it was a dangerous, godforsaken place, but ye had to go! Now ye think we're moving there? Bloody hell!"

I tried to stay on the opposite side of the table as she waved a dish in the air and then slammed it down on the table. Miraculously, it remained intact.

This was not going the way I had envisioned. The last two days on the road, I had considered every scenario I could think of to let Jane in on my plans. None of those scenarios included her murdering me, which she seemed ready to do.

"I tell you, Jane, "I said, trying to be reasonable in the face of a full-blown Scottish gale, "you won't believe how beautiful the land is out there. There're tall grass prairies, cold streams full of fish, and forests teeming with deer and turkeys."

"And Indians!"

I shrugged. "I met an Indian."

That stopped her. She stood staring at me with a blank look on her face.

"Ye met one?" she asked as if I was describing a new client for my surveying business.

The storm was passing, so I took the opportunity to sit at the table. It seemed more civilized, with less chance of being hit with a plate. "Sit down, love, let me tell you."

"Don't *love* me," she said, but sat down, nonetheless.

I took a deep breath and launched into the argument so carefully worked out on the road home. "I'll admit that I had no intention of claiming any land when I agreed to go with Sam and Jim."

That statement earned a skeptical "Hmph."

"Jim wanted to establish a *bona fide* claim, and I knew I could survey the land. Sam, too. He went with the idea of finding the right piece of land, and it's best if he's close to Jim. Which they are, by the way. Back to back neighbors. Anyway, I was only going along, honest.

"But then I watched the sun come up on a dewy grassland ringed with old-stand forest and, on the far side, six deer looking back at us without a fear in the world. It isn't like here, Jane. The hills are covered in hardwoods and pine, and the valleys are long and open with bright streams running through them."

She sat quietly while I talked, eventually leaning her elbows on the table, watching my face. I described our trek honestly, not glossing over any of the hard parts. I explained how the old Braddock Road fared well for us all the way to the other side of the mountains. I described the people we met, like Captain Walsh and the Beesons, whom I discussed without mentioning the death of Morgan. I told her of Sam's conviction that his future was in flour, which earned me a skeptical frown. I explained that the hardest part of the journey would be getting the wagons up the mountain passes and across four sizable creeks that hindered our way.

It grew dark while I talked, and Jane got up to feed Billy and Joe, who at least had made happy noises when I came in the door. She picked up the baby and held her on her lap.

"Tell me of the Indian ye say ye met."

She was fixated on the threat of savages, no doubt about that. "It was an extraordinary thing," I said and told her the story.

"Ye never felt threatened?" she asked, still unconvinced.

I shook my head. "No, not at all. As a matter of fact, I believe if we ever meet again, we might be friends."

"Hmph," she responded.

For the next few months, I let the subject lie. Jane had done an excellent job of maintaining the farm while I was out gallivanting around, as she put it, though there was a lengthy list of items that needed tending to. Between Jane's list and my surveying work, the days passed quickly.

Jim Kelly came over once or twice to sit and argue taxes and discuss the trouble that our merchant ships were having. The Royal Navy was stopping any ship they could and impressing the American seamen into their crews. It was getting so American ships were afraid to leave port. We carefully avoided mentioning our adventure or the land waiting for us in the west while Jane was within earshot.

The summer was pleasant, not too hot, and just enough rain. The corn grew high, and the wheat filled the valley below our cabin. Harvest time kept us busy and exhausted. The work never ended. It was early September before Jane or I raised the subject again.

After an exhausting day in the heat and dust, we sat on the porch as usual, looking west as the sun set. Neither of us spoke, enjoying the quiet and the companionship. The sun was huge and red as it settled behind the mountains. A sigh escaped me, and Jane turned in her chair to study my face in the gathering dusk.

"Tell me about the rivers again," she said without preamble. "How dangerous will they be to cross?"

PART TWO

The Wilderness
1772 to 1775

CHAPTER 9
Conestoga

May 8th, 1772
Fort Cumberland, Maryland

Three years later, nearly to the day from my first visit, a caravan of wagons descended into Fort Cumberland, tired and dusty from a week on the trail. We presented an impressive party consisting of six wagons with assorted livestock, either pulling or being dragged behind.

Of the six wagons, two were mighty Conestogas that the families had purchased together. They hauled most of the furniture, clothes, seed, and food we were taking with us. At sixteen feet in length, four feet wide, and wheels five feet high, they were monsters to maneuver. Both ends swept up like a ship's prow, and the arched bows holding the canvas cover in place added to the overall height. Four oxen, yoked two by two, pulled each Conestoga.

The driver walked or rode on the left side of the rig. We took turns driving, as it was demanding work, requiring constant attention to the road ahead and the innate orneriness of the oxen. With a blacksnake whip cracking in the air and the constant calling of 'gee' and 'haw,' a couple hours exhausted any man.

The other four wagons were open buckboards with

reinforced axles and wheels. Tightly lashed tarps kept the contents from bouncing out of the wagons while protecting them from the elements. The buckboards even had springs to lessen the jarring and banging that accompanied every mile. For the most part, it mattered not because everyone except the little ones walked alongside.

So, with the calling of the drivers and the crack of whips, the banging and jangling of pots and pans, and the chatter of the women and children, we wove our way down into the valley, a haze of dust marking our arrival.

I was amazed to see the town again. In the years since our last visit, it had grown considerably. Buildings now crowded the riverbank in each direction beneath the fort. We parked our wagons in a field outside of town already filled with half a dozen other parties. Most were headed south to the new Virginia territory. Conestogas littered the field like ships in a harbor.

We had to search for Mr. O'Connor's store. He was in a brand new, two-story building with his name prominently displayed above the wide front door. Five or six clerks worked feverishly within, and it took a few minutes before I could stop one long enough to ask for O'Connor. The young man said O'Conner spent all of his time upstairs working on the books.

The old man was stooped even more than the last time we met. He failed to remember us, but when I mentioned how he talked us into buying an ax we could scarcely afford, his face lit up in recognition.

"You're the only merchant we'd consider buying supplies from," I said, showing him our long list.

He smiled at us. "Glad to hear we have a repeat customer. Sad to say, many of my customers never return." He rubbed his face, lost in thought. "I hope it's not because they got themselves killed. I'd hate to think that, but many do, many do..."

Sensing that the old man was drifting into a poor mood, Sam said cheerfully, "We're back, and we brought more customers. I wouldn't be surprised if more follow us, neither."

O'Connor's smile returned, and he called on a clerk to start on our list. It would not be ready until the end of the next day, giving us an opportunity to repack and shuffle the loads. The week's travel taught us a lot regarding the wagons and the challenge of driving them. It also taught us about each other. We may be family and good friends, but there's nothing like a week on the road to really get to know someone.

A year earlier, Sam and Jim and I had started serious planning. We understood that we must take everything we would need and leave behind much that we loved. Lists of supplies and essentials wrestled with lists of comforts and heirlooms.

I will risk saying that it was hardest on the womenfolk. They knew what was needed for women's work, caring for the children, and tending the cabins. The hard part was being unable to take the things they had collected and held dear. So many of the niceties of our homes in Cumberland County got left behind. Grandfather's rocker, the family portrait, Sunday clothes, and more than we wished to consider were sorted again and again to whittle the load down to each family's allotted amount.

We decided early on to pool our resources. This included all the corn, oats, potatoes, and tools, as well as the purchase of the Conestogas. We also evenly distributed the loads in each wagon, regardless of who owned what. Once we arrived at our new homestead, the loads would be sorted again, with each family claiming their property. Brother Joseph was in charge of the bill of lading for each family to ensure there was no confusion or disagreement later. He took his responsibility seriously, making careful lists and ensuring that no one added anything without his knowledge.

We easily added members to our original crew of Sam, Jim, and me. Once word got out, it did not take long to assemble a caravan.

Sam was happy to be going even though he was a newlywed and an expectant father to boot. The year before, he had married Mary Elizabeth Lochry, fresh off the boat from Ireland. She was a dark-complected woman with hair as black as coal, nearly as tall as Sam, and announced she was pregnant as we prepared to leave. She was not coming with us, and Sam intended to return in the fall for the birth.

My younger brother Joseph married Mary Ann in '70, as I had so easily predicted. She was a slight, pretty girl with no hips. They still had no children, and with Joe being only twenty-two and Mary Ann not built for it, I thought that proper planning.

My brother-in-law, John White, made up the last of our party. He was a fine fellow, well-schooled with the idea of someday becoming a lawyer. He was married to Hannah, who was overly pregnant by the time of our leaving. Sam and I talked to him at length, but both Jane and Hannah thought it would be fine.

Joseph White, my father-in-law, and minister of our church in Chamber's Town, had died in '70. His death had a strong effect on Jane and her brother. Their mother moved in with their aunt and uncle, who recently arrived from Scotland. The siblings felt the pressure of caring for their mother lifted. This had a great deal to do with Jane's decision to move west.

Jim Kelly, his wife Sarah, and their two-year-old son Meek, who would someday marry my Janie, were among the few families in our group that I was confident could take care of themselves. Jim's tall, rangy frame made it easy for him to be seen anywhere on the trail, and once again, he was unanimously elected leader.

James and Mary Thompson had jumped at the fourth quadrant of our four-plot layout. A year or two younger than me, James was slow to get started but with boundless energy once motivated. He and Mary were an immense help in the early planning stages.

Then there was my herd. With four children, each a year apart, Jane had her hands full. We had been blessed with another son, Tommy, in '70. He was a frail boy and prone to colds, though a joy to be with. How I wish our time together had been longer...

As the time for our departure grew near, I learned Hannah would not be the only pregnant woman making the trip. Jane was due in October. She said nothing of this until we were ready to leave.

It came as a shock, although I had noticed a change in her figure without mentioning it. Typical of Jane, she did not want me to know until it was too late to change our plans. That woman has been running my life from the day I met her.

In addition to the families, a menagerie of oxen, cows, horses, chickens, pigs, and dogs was included in our caravan. Then there were the vast supplies of food needed to keep all the animals and people fed during our journey and for an unknown amount of time after. The seed to plant, the tools to clear the land and build our cabins…

There was no end to it.

Sixteen souls, plus two on the way, left their lives, their families, their work, and everything that was safe and secure, bound for the wilderness. We must have been crazy.

"You sure Conestogas been up this road before?"

"Stop complaining," I called up to James Thompson. "Course there's been Connies on this road. General Braddock built this road himself so he could get his wagons cross the mountains and attack Fort Duquesne."

James stood atop the high seat on Connie One, as we called it, hacking at low-hanging branches with his hatchet.

His wagon was the first Conestoga in line as we climbed the steep trail into the mountains. Jim, on his bay, and a lighter buckboard blazed the trail ahead. It was one obstacle after another west of Cumberland. Even though the road had seen several wagon caravans since we passed this way three years before, we still had to remove fallen trees and rocks along the entire length — all while keeping an eye out for rattlesnakes and Indians. Preventing the trees that overhung the road from tearing the wagon cover to pieces was a full-time job.

James threw another branch to the side of the overgrown path. "How did that go for the General?" he asked with a smirk on this face.

"How it went has nothing to do with how well he built this road. Been nigh on twenty years, James. You have to expect it to be a bit overgrown."

"Hmph," he said and threw another branch away.

Short stretches of the road were clear and wide, but the further we went up the mountain ridge, the worse it became. The last time I was on this road, the walking was not particularly difficult except for the occasional stream we had to wade across. However, as we hiked the trail back then, I have to admit that we never tended to look up. In the years since '55, when Braddock marched his army west, the trees had grown considerably and now enveloped us in a deep tunnel of foliage.

James managed to free the last of the limbs tangled in the wagon's cover and jumped down where several of us stood watching him work.

Jim Kelly, as usual, announced the solution from the back of his horse. "Right then, let's strike the covers. Pull 'em down into the rear of the wagons and then pull the bows."

I peered through the dense canopy of leaves at the sky visible to the north. It looked threatening to me.

"What if the rain comes?" I asked, thinking of the sacks of grain and other items that could not get wet. "It'll be considerable effort to put the canvas back up again."

"I don't care if it is extra work," Jim said. "Better than this constant cutting. If we think rain is comin', we'll all pitch in to get the canvas over the load. That's it. Get to it."

The canvas that stretched across each Conestoga was twenty feet long and felt like it weighed a ton. It took two men on each side to untie and fold the cloth back and settle it in the rear of the wagon. We pulled the hickory bows from their iron clips, reducing the overall height from twelve feet to a manageable six. Then we attacked Connie Two.

With a snap of his whip, James got his four oxen moving, bellowing and protesting with each step. He was doing an excellent job of driving them through this rough area, considering his limited training and experience.

Two weeks before we left Chamber's Town, James, Jim, Sam, and I were subjected to the cruelest treatment while learning to be teamsters. Although we acknowledged that James Thompson and Sam should be the primary Conestogas drivers, we all had to learn how to manage the beasts. There was some discussion of hiring professional teamsters, but everyone believed we could do the job ourselves.

Well, it was not easy. A Conestoga wagon with two pairs of oxen hitched to it is as unwieldy and clumsy as you can imagine. First of all, there are the oxen to deal with. I believe every part of their tiny brain is consumed with a deep hatred of their human masters. Especially the teamster driving them. They are slow, belligerent, stubborn, and smelly. They are also incredibly strong with amazing endurance.

The man driving the team usually walked along the left front corner of the wagon with a twelve-foot blacksnake whip in his hand. Learning to use the whip without putting out your eye, or the ox's, was another element of the training.

Then, once you get the entire mass moving forward with a loud whip-crack above their heads, you have to call out "gee" or "haw" to move the team right or left, respectively.

A sturdy brake handle controls the wagon and keeps it from overrunning the oxen on a downhill slope. This brake is easier to use if the driver jumps up on the lazy board and braces his back against the side of the wagon. A few hours driving and you were ready to hand the whip and reins over to another victim.

We went up to Lancaster to buy the wagons and receive our training. The man who sold them to us seemed to think we were foolhardy to try and learn to drive in two days. He took our money, though, and set to torturing us. In the end, he shook his head and said goodbye with a finality I did not appreciate.

CHAPTER 10
There's Indians

May 13th, 1772
Braddock's Road, Pennsylvania

By the end of our third day, a dirty and weary group of pioneers crossed the rolling highlands between the Allegheny and Laurel Hills. Travel through this open prairie was not particularly difficult. The road was clear of debris, and the temperature noticeably cooler. It was a welcome break after the hard climb over the first ridge of the Alleghenies.

During the day, most of the women and children took turns riding in the wagons. All except Jane's sister-in-law, Hannah. She waddled behind on our first day in an attempt to look self-reliant and rode from then on.

Now and then, Jim called a halt to the lead wagon while the rest caught up. He insisted that all the wagons stay within hailing distance of each other. Grumbling constantly, Jim rode his bay stallion up and down the line, urging the stragglers to keep up.

As the forest turned a deep purple and then disappeared in the night, we sat around our fire, the men too tired to talk while the women worked on supper. The children, who got fed first, soon ceased their chatter and settled down. They were holding up better than many of the adults. There were no real complaints, but the high spirits of the first few days had evaporated. Now it was simply hard work.

Jim, Sam, and I sat with our heads together, discussing the next part of the trip. Ahead rose the Laurel and Chestnut ridges, imposing mountain ranges that we had to cross before we could consider ourselves in the West. From our vast experience, we knew that the next days would be among the most difficult. From Fort Necessity, the last ridge and the final drop down into the Monongahela valley would tax everyone's reserves. We agreed to spend a day or two resting at the Beeson's place before turning north. It would be good to see Henry's friendly face again.

Suddenly, Joseph appeared out of the dark, his dog at this side. Joe's face was drawn and bright with sweat.

"There's something out there," he said in a hoarse whisper, kneeling at our fire. "I think there's Indians."

We always set a watch on the edge of our camps, a man on each side of the road, back along the tree line. Joseph's place this evening was on the north side of the trail. John was to the south.

Without a word, each man reached for his gun. There was no point in killing the fire. If Indians were out there, they had seen us already.

Jim gave quick and efficient orders to each man. The big Conestogas were parked side by side each night for such a possibility. We moved from the fire to the wagons and ordered the women, children, and dogs underneath. The only sound was the crackle of the fire and the shifting of the unsuspecting livestock on the picket line.

And then Hannah White screamed.

She cried out so frightfully, I thought she was being

scalped alive. Jane and two other women raced to her side as she cried out again.

Immediately, the forest came alive. From nearby, the most fearsome sound I ever heard pierced the night. At least half a dozen Indians answered Hannah's cry. The hair on my arms stood up.

"Quiet!" Jim hissed, but it was no use. Hannah moaned again, her face buried in her blanket.

Jane's face, white and frightened, turned toward us. "Her baby's coming!" she said as forcefully as she could under the circumstances.

John almost dropped his musket. "God, Almighty!" he swore. "Not now, wife!"

Several women kept the children close while the others tended to Hannah. They pulled her further under the wagon and covered her with blankets. Jane cradled Hannah's head in her arms, rocking slowly.

From the woods came another soul-piercing savage call. "Nobody fire!" Jim called out softly. "They might move on."

"Not if they're looking for scalps," Sam said, his voice stiff.

"They ain't," Jim said. "If they was, they'd of attacked us outright. Sit still, and don't shoot."

The women were working silently on Hannah. I chose not to look too closely. She had stopped making noises, and that was all that concerned me.

We stayed between the wagons for a half-hour more, guns pointed out from our makeshift fort. Then Hannah started up again. This time, however, no answer came from the woods.

She made one last full-bodied scream they must have heard back in Cumberland. It was followed immediately by the sound that makes every man go weak in the knees — the cry of a newborn baby.

The next morning we huddled around the fire, cold and damp from a long night of staring into the forest. John and Sam took down the Conestoga's tarps and made a tent between the wagons for Hannah and her baby. Jane had not left the new mother's side all night.

"We'll stay here today," Jim announced, looking from face to face. "First light tomorrow morning, we're moving out. I want us out of these hills in four days' time."

John, still vibrating with nerves, said, "I appreciate that, Jim. She'll be fine by the end of the day. Might have to ride, that's all."

"Course she'll ride. Case you hadn't noticed where your wife was, she already has a nest in the oat sacks."

A friendly laugh loosened the tension in the circle of men. We got stiffly to our feet and took up our job assignments. Sam and I worked greasing all the wagon wheels. Others fed the animals and hauled buckets of water from the stream. Still, others stood watching, muskets primed and ready resting in their arms.

We discussed the night's events, but no one could explain the Indian's behavior. Indians are unpredictable, was the general thought. If they were Shawnee, as Jim assumed, they had no quarrel with settlers in this area. Beeson told us three years before that he regularly traded with the Shawnee and Delaware and never had any issues.

Nonetheless, we kept a watch all day with a nervous eye on the forest that enveloped us.

Hannah was doing remarkably well, Jane said. The baby was a girl whom they named Margaret. Her tiny, pink face barely showed from the cocoon of blankets surrounding her and her mother. According to Hannah's counting, the baby came a couple of weeks early. Nothing like a good scare to bring on a baby.

Hannah and John's five-year-old son was quiet and solemn, keeping clear of his mother and sister, so Sam gave him the job of carrying the grease pot from wagon to wagon. After a while, the young fellow was so tired that he forgot the terror of the night and his jealousy and fell soundly asleep beside his new sister.

Now we were seventeen.

It soon became apparent that the Indians did not intend to leave us. At our first camp following the day of rest, Sam, our sentry to the north, reported he saw movement in the forest.

Within minutes, muskets and rifles were primed and half-cocked, hatchets and axes at the ready. As the main body faced the threat to the north, we did not forget to have two men watching our rear. If a fight came, I believe we could have held our own.

Darkness fell, and still, there was no sign of any hostiles. Then one, two, and finally, six Indians walked into the clearing. Each was bare-chested with streaks of paint on their cheeks. Their well-muscled arms sported beaded bands with hanging strings and feathers. They held their muskets casually to indicate they intended no harm.

One warrior stepped forward while the others stayed at the forest edge. The man had long gray hair and a weathered face indicating his advanced age. He raised his right hand from his musket and then held it out to us, palm up.

Jim stood up behind a buckboard wagon, his rifle also

laying in the crook of his arm. He held out his hand. The Indian nodded, and all six of them came forward a dozen paces.

Under his breath, Jim said to Sam, "Be casual but don't put your gun down. Stay on my left and come with me."

Together they strolled across the clearing, stopping a few paces from the Indians. Jim leaned on this rifle while Sam held his musket in the crook of his arm. The head Indian put the butt of his musket on the ground and rested his arms upon it. Everyone acted casual except for those of us hiding behind the wagons. We watched this play unfold in wide-eyed wonder.

Then, to our growing astonishment, Jim and the Indian war chief shook hands, like two English gentlemen meeting on a city street. Jim and Sam returned to us, and the Indians disappeared into the forest.

Sam exhaled a deep, shuddering breath once he was back in our line. "He speaks pretty good English," he said, picking up a water bag and taking a deep drink.

"What'd they say?" Joe asked for everyone. "What're their intentions?"

Jim answered. "The leader's name is Cornstalk. They're Shawnee, like I thought. I met him on my first trip out here in '67. Not sure, but he seemed to remember me. They're headed for Beeson's Mill. Old Cornstalk wanted to know if the woman was all right."

"Well, what do you know!" John exclaimed. "Why, we ought to invite them to supper, they're so civilized!"

"Hush, John," a voice came from a pile of blankets. "If we can be friends, we should be friends."

"Now, Hannah..." John, admonished for his aggression, settled down beside his wife and newborn, making little sounds at the baby.

The rest of the men turned back to the matter at hand.

"Do you believe them?" Sam asked.

"No reason not to. If they wanted our scalps, we'd be dead by now. They've no reason to be subtle."

"So, what do we do?"

Jim placed his rifle on top of the wagon and leaned his back against a wheel. "We go on," he said. "But first, we eat. I've worked up a sizable hunger!"

I went and sat with Jane and the children, who greeted me with round, frightened eyes. Billy, older than his five years, told me he had not been scared. Not a bit.

Jane handed me a plate of bacon and beans without a word. We ate silently and settled into our blankets under the wagon without talking. An hour after the camp quieted down, she raised up on an elbow, looking at me in the dim firelight. I waited, knowing what was coming.

"I told you, Mr. Moorhead. There's Indians."

CHAPTER 11
A Respite

May 20th, 1772
The Monongahela Valley, Pennsylvania

Seventeen days out of Chamber's Town, the wagons wound their way down the last rise of the Laurel Ridge. The Monongahela valley stretched into the green, hazy distance.

Jim rode ahead to announce our arrival, though it was no surprise. Henry Beeson said he had heard us coming all morning. To his credit, he welcomed us like long-lost friends. Not a word was spoken of the problems we created for him during our first visit.

"Welcome, welcome!" he shouted to each wagon as it stopped in the field next to his cabin. "*Hoko-les-qua* told us you were coming," Beeson said, indicating the Indian camp up on the hill. I took him to mean the man we knew as Cornstalk. "They came in yesterday. Brought us three months of venison in exchange for our cornmeal."

Now sporting a noticeable paunch and high forehead, Henry resembled a miller more than the first time we had met him. His friendly face beamed like a country squire welcoming dinner guests.

He had been busy. The new mill towered two and a half

stories, the huge wheel turning under a cascade of water from the pond up the hill. I looked at it in amazement and knew it would not take Sam long to disappear inside.

People introduced themselves right and left, shaking hands and wandering off to admire the mill.

"How long have you been out," Beeson's wife asked Jane, who was busy trying to round up our boys.

"Tell the truth," Jane said with a bright smile, "I've lost track of the days. Must be close to a year, I believe."

She and Mary laughed together, becoming instant friends. "I have a secret I'll share with you," Mary said in a conspiratory voice. "Up at the pond, there's a secluded place that you can take a real bath. I'll show you the way if you care to go."

I thought Jane was going to swoon.

"That would be grand!" she said, looking straight at me. "There's not a one of us that couldn't stand a bit of washing."

The secret got around, and several women climbed the steep path up to the millpond while the men worked on setting up camp. As soon as Mary discovered Hannah and her baby, she moved them both into the cabin. John was left standing in the field, looking lost and alone.

Sam, of course, got hold of Henry's arm, and they headed for the mill. I did not see him for an hour or more, and when he did return, you would have thought Sam just saw the most beautiful woman in the world instead of an old hunk of machinery.

Standing with a plate of mush in his hand and still looking at the mill, Sam said, "Course, mine'll be smaller. No need to build such a machine when there ain't even people to bring in grain. Beeson says he's taking care of everyone here in the valley, and some folk come down the river. He's busy all during harvest time. Especially now that the town is growing. Now he's thinking of expanding his cabin and opening a tavern."

"He's a hardworking man," I agreed.

"Hardworking?" Sam effused. He swept his arm out to indicate the flat land across the creek. "Henry owns most of that land and is partitioning it off piece by piece. He's already wealthier than anyone we know! And it all started with a mill! He intends to build a town..." Sam trailed off and wandered away, still lost in his dream.

It was not yet a town, but a dozen new cabins had sprung up since our last visit. I counted eight occupied cabins within sight, with others partially hidden by the forest on the far side of Redstone Creek. Folks were calling their settlement Beeson's Town. Today we call it Uniontown. (3)

A spirited and festive mood permeated the evening. We had crossed the Allegheny Mountains without a single mishap, yet people felt like they had been wandering in the desert for forty days. Without exception, this was further from home than any of our party had ever been in their lives.

Even the children were bouncing and noisy. Jim and James took a pack of them below the mill to a shallow spot in the creek and watched as they frolicked in the cold water, barefoot and fully dressed, washing two and half weeks of dust and grime away. Clothes and bodies got clean at the same time. Their happy squeals filled the valley.

An hour later, Jane returned to our wagon, a sly smile on her lips and a blush on her cheeks. Her hair was loose and hung in wet strands down her back. She was wearing a clean, dry skirt, but her shirt and bodice were wet and tight across her breasts. I looked around self-consciously to see if anyone noticed as she sidled up to me and ran an arm around my waist.

"You smell mighty fine," I stammered, unsure of her intentions. We were in public, after all.

"Um, do I?" she purred, smiling up into my face. I leaned down and kissed her and she pushed away, nose wrinkling, and took a step back. "I wanted to be sure ye had enough incentive to get up to the pond before it gets too dark. Ye won't be getting under any blankets with me until ye do, I can tell ye that. Now go. The day's a-wasting!"

I went.

We stayed two nights in the open land near Henry Beeson's mill. No one in our party indicated any urge to head north. Even Jim Kelly, usually astride his horse before the sun was up, seemed content to rest.

At dinner time the day after our arrival, we recreated an event now told in our schools from 150 years before. We sat down to eat with Indians, just like the Protestants that first landed in this county.

Hokolesqua, as the leader or sachem of the group was called, spoke English, though none of his warriors seemed to. We all sat on blankets, sharing cornmeal mush, fried venison, and apple-rhubarb pie. Mary Beeson acted like a hostess at a seated dinner party. She bustled about with a huge bowl of mush, spooning it onto any empty plate. Also, there was cold, fresh cider from the press inside Henry's mill.

Jim mentioned to me that Beeson clearly did not offer hard cider or rum to anyone. He explained that it was the best way to ensure the dinner came to a peaceful conclusion.

Ask anyone, and they will tell you that I do not have a prejudice bone in my body. However, over the years, I have observed the ill effect alcoholic drink has on Indians, and I can assure you it is not a stereotype. Perhaps, just as they had no defense against our diseases, their bodies absorb alcohol differently than ours, but there it is. Indians are an unpredictable people when sober. Drink of any kind is not a good idea.

Our dinner together passed without incident. Later, I tried to speak to Hokolesqua when our paths crossed. I asked the old man where his home was, and he raised his arm in a generally southern direction and said, "Two days." I took this to mean somewhere in the Virginia mountains. I had no reason to distrust any of them, but I was secretly pleased to know that we were going in opposite directions.

Our young ones could not take their eyes off the Shawnee warriors. Mothers shooed more than one curious child away, even though the Indians seemed happy to have them around.

Late in the afternoon, Jane came and sat beside me. "Well, I declare!" she said, puffing out her cheeks. "They're quite the proper gentlemen, are they not?"

"I've met Indians three times," I replied. "So far, they have all behaved well."

She wrinkled up her nose. "The smell is a bit on the strong side."

I had to agree. There was no getting past the pungent odor emanating from the warriors.

"I believe it's the smell of bear fat. It keeps the no-see-ums and mosquitos away. They rub it on their bodies and in their hair."

" 'Tis something we all must do, living out here in the

wilderness?"

"Don't you think you could get used to it?" I asked, laughing at the look she gave me.

"I'd rather have the bites, thank you very much."

As the sun set beyond the trees, I was shaken out of a comfortable slumber by loud shouts, or whoops, issuing from the throats of half a dozen warriors. Instinctively, I reached for my rifle before I noticed the band of Indians at the edge of the forest. They may have been calling good-bye, but it sounded like a warning to me.

CHAPTER 12
The Bear

May 25th, 1772
The Monongahela Valley, Pennsylvania

We crossed the Youghiogheny River at Stewart's Landing as easily as we had three years before. This was our first significant river crossing, and everyone was pleased that the water was low and there was a firm gravel bottom.

Jim kept the wagons moving, riding back and forth across the river with each one, shouting to the drivers to keep their animals straight. He was more concerned with the banks on each side than he was with the horses or oxen wading through the water.

The buckboards made it without a problem, but the big Conestogas required every adult to either push from behind or help drag the stubborn oxen up the far slope. Each wagon banged up from the river, threatening to tip over backward or spill its load into the water. Thank the Lord, we crossed without incident.

And then it started to rain.

Earlier, we had a day or two of passing thunderstorms while up in the high meadows of the Alleghenies, causing us to spend an uncomfortably wet night. Overall though, the weather had been perfect the entire trip.

The sky ahead grew more ominous as the morning progressed. The wind picked up steadily, cool and gusty out of the north. By dinner time, big wet splats were pockmarking the dust on the trail. Then, with a shuddering blast of chill wind, it started.

Fortunately, the Connies' covers were up, so the women and children piled onto the bags of grain and supplies. They pulled the tarp ends tight, forming a humid fortress against the weather.

The men slogged alongside the wagons, heads bowed to the wind, clutching our hats with one hand and muskets with the other. Jim and I put valuable rifles inside one of the wagons, loaded and primed in case the need arose. Despite the leather wraps, the other muskets were too wet to be of any immediate help.

The horses, cows, and oxen churned the ground into a sticky morass so that soon, ankle-deep mud threatened to suck our boots off. We slid and stumbled, soaked and cold, through the long afternoon.

James Thompson, usually strong and quiet, approached Jim with the idea of stopping early.

"If this rain keeps up," Jim explained, "we need to get to the next two rivers as soon as we can. If we wait, we could be held up for days."

"What about circling back to the mill?" John asked. "Hannah and the baby are feeling this damp, down to their bones."

Jim nodded in understanding but did not relent. Onward was his last word.

"I don't like this," Jim said to me at the end of our second day of rain. He leaned down from his saddle, water pouring from the front fold in his cocked hat. "The Conemaugh might not be too bad, we're still two days away from it, and we found a nice ford. With this weather, it's the Loyalhanna's got me worried."

I squinted up at him and spoke over the sound of the driving rain. "That was our easiest crossing," I was unsettled by the severe look on his face. "Do you believe it'll rise that much?"

He straightened up and looked at the northern sky. Suddenly, a tremendous bolt of blue lightning streaked from east to west, as if daring us to go on. It answered my question.

"She's coming down off Chestnut Ridge," he said. " 'Tis raining mighty hard up there." He paused and looked back down at me. "I'd like you and Sam to run ahead, see what it looks like. If our crossing ain't there, go east until you find one, then come find us. One way or the other, we'll stop at the river and wait for your report."

Well, that was a tall order. Except for hunting expeditions, none of us had ever separated from the party, and I was not sure I liked being selected. I found Sam already packing a kit for us both. His jaw was set in the way I knew meant business.

"What do you think?" I asked.

He handed me my roll, a powder horn, and a square of deer hide. "Wrap this around your breech and tie it tight," he said, ignoring my question. "It should keep your primer dry. And cork your barrel."

That sort of irritated me. "I know how to take care of my rifle, Sam. What I want to know is, did Jim order you to go, or did you volunteer."

He turned to face me and continued in a more conciliatory tone. "We need to find a place to cross, something we never searched for last time. You and me are the right choice for scouting ahead, so we go. One night out. Go tell Jane and come right back."

She was not pleased.

We trotted away from the caravan, heads down, but attentive and wary, the way we hunted together in our youth. Sam led as usual. Slipping and squishing, we ran on for several hours in the late afternoon gray light until we were six or seven miles ahead of the caravan.

Our biggest worry was crossing open areas in a lightning storm. The rain fell in hard slanting sheets, and occasionally a flash of lightning lit the sky. We pushed through high grass that maintained only a vague hint of a trail. My mind's eye spotted an Indian behind every bush and tree.

The pounding rain made so much noise that we came upon the creek without warning. A foreboding scene confronted us. The shallow stream we had crossed so easily three years before was now a deep, ugly brown torrent. It swirled and churned, bearing logs and debris from the mountains down to the Allegheny River.

There was nothing to say — we could not cross here. We turned east and faced the downpour. Beneath our feet, muddy streams streaked the forest floor, carrying away leaves and waterlogged soil.

As evening set in, we came to a hard bend in the creek. Beyond, the land flattened out and the banks dropped. Water filled the forest for fifty feet while the center of the stream raced over shallow rocks.

"It don't look good," Sam said. "Still, I believe we can get the wagons here without a lot of clearing. We'll work back some, then find a dry spot for the night."

I actually laughed out loud. "A dry spot?"

Rain dripped off Sam's hat and nose, but he smiled anyway. "Well, let's find a spot that ain't flooded. How's that?"

Moving away from the creek, back toward the caravan, we finally came to a gigantic oak recently uprooted by the storm. When it fell, it took ten feet of ground with it so that the trunk and the base formed a narrow shelter. We crawled into the tight space, shoulder to shoulder, and did our best to stretch out our tired legs. Our blankets, draped over our heads, provided a slight amount of relief from the constant beating of the rain.

Sam pulled a strip of jerky from his kit and sliced off thinner pieces with his hunting knife.

We chewed the salty meat until it could be swallowed without choking.

"Remember the first time you went hunting with Pa and me?" Sam asked. "You weren't more than eight or nine. We got caught in a rain like this, and Pa knew where there was an Indian Tree. Spent a couple hours packed in a hole this size."

I smiled at the memory. "Snug and dry. That was the first time Pa talked to me like I wasn't a child. Remember him telling us how Indians had hollowed out the tree so they could hide from other tribes if they were being chased?"

Sam laughed. "Then the real owner came back to his house! Weren't Indians made that hole at all. Just a big old porcupine had scratched the heart out of a dead tree. Mad as hell to find us there! You said you'd never believe another word Pa said."

We sat silently for a while, comfortable in each other's company.

Later, I said, "Ya know, Sam, there'll be hard years ahead. Do you ever question what we're doing out here?"

My brother shook his head in the dark. "Way I figure it, there's one man comfortable in his chair before his fire, a warm house around him. Then there's the man who sets out into the wild to settle a new world with only the belongings he can carry. One path is safe, the other dangerous as hell, and yet some men choose the danger."

"Is that how you see us?" I asked. "Explorers in the new, dangerous world?"

"I wasn't talking about us, Fergus," he said softly. "I was talking about our parents and all those who left Ireland and Scotland to come to America. But yes, that's how I see us."

The rain continued throughout the night, and by dawn, it had tapered off to a fine drizzle. We tried to sleep, though soaked hunting shirts and canvas trousers are not conducive to a good night's rest.

"Let's go find the wagons," Sam said, his mouth full of jerky. He began to rise from his cramped position and froze. A loud scraping noise came from the other side of the wall of dirt and roots framing our muddy hut.

Holding out a hand to stay me, Sam rose slowly and peered over the tree trunk.

What? I mouthed. My heart raced with the thought that Indians were stalking us.

Sam looked down where I sat in the wet leaves, his hand still held out toward me.

"Bear," he whispered, indicating the direction with his chin. "Redo your prime and then do mine."

I worked quickly and steadily on both guns, unwrapping the locks and blowing the old powder out of the pans. The blue jay feather I kept in the patchbox poked the vent holes as an extra precaution. I poured a pinch of powder from my horn, closed the frizzen, and checked the flint set. Both guns were already loaded, so I pulled the plug from the muzzle and handed Sam's musket up to him, halfcocked. Gradually, I raised my stiff body to stand beside my brother.

The creature on the other side of the root mass was a monstrous Black bear that looked to weigh at least 500 pounds. He was worrying the base of the tree, not more than twenty feet from us, probably looking for grubs or acorns. Every other scratch in the dirt, the bear lifted his massive head and sniffed the air with a muddy nose. I had to remember to tell Jane that being filthy, smelly, and wet can save your life, for the bear had no idea we were there.

Until he did.

Suddenly the beast stood up on his rear legs and looked directly at us. His beady, black eyes grew round in alarm, oddly out of place in such a broad head. Suddenly he bellowed so loudly my ears hurt. With years of practice, Sam and I cocked and raised our guns and fired as one.

The beast lurched back against a tree as the balls pounded into his chest. Bellowing in pain and anger, he shook his head, rose to all fours, and lumbered toward us.

"Run!" I shouted. We shot from our hiding place, tearing down the hill, away from the bear. Twenty paces on, I glanced over my shoulder to see what progress the bear was making. We both slide to a stop. There was no need to run.

The brute was sitting on his haunches, head hanging down, staring at us. He struggled to stand, took two steps, and crashed to the ground. We reloaded and watched as his breathing became more and more shallow and then stopped.

We did not move from our spot for another five

minutes. When it comes to bears, patience is a true virtue. More than one hunter has been killed by a bear he assumed to be dead. Eventually, it was over.

"Let's go find the caravan," Sam said. "We'll gather him up tomorrow."

CHAPTER 13
The River

May 28th, 1772
The Wilderness, Pennsylvania

Jim Kelly stood on the south bank of the Loyalhanna, hands on hips, staring down into the dirty brown water rushing west.

"You did fine," he said to Sam and me. "I'll tell you, though. I was afraid a this. It won't be easy."

Sam and I had been able to move quickly at an angle to the original trail. We intercepted the caravan before the wagons had to backtrack. Except for a log here or there, the forest floor, once we came to it, was open all the way to the flooded stream.

Although it stopped raining mid-morning, I could not see that the stream, or the flood attacking both banks, had diminished any. The water was moving awfully fast. The only saving grace was the way the bottom rose above the bend, providing a reasonably shallow ford.

Jim turned away from the stream and sloshed back to the wagons, where everyone waited for his decision.

"Right then," he called out so all could hear. "Listen up! We're crossing here cause we don't want to waste more time looking for a better place — "

"Why don't we camp for a day?" John interrupted. "Let the level go down."

Jim answered in a steady tone, like a father speaking to a child. " 'Tis a good question, John. My worry is, it could start raining any time now, and things'll get worse." Others nodded their heads and glanced at the threatening sky. "We still have the Conemaugh to deal with," he continued, "and that's deeper by far. The longer we wait, the deeper it gets. Now, here's how this will go…"

Jim announced the crossing order with the two Conestogas going first. They required undisturbed, solid ground under their wheels on both sides of the river. Entering the river was not too difficult, but the bank on the far side was steep with a quick drop beyond. We all feared the Connies could saddlebag on the hump if their wheels sank into mud churned up by the other wagons and their horses.

James Thompson was the driver of Connie One, with his wife, Jim's wife Sarah, and little Meek. Sam and I were on Connie Two, which held all of our earthly possessions in addition to my entire family.

Jim rode his bay out into the stream. The stallion was strong and steady, but as soon as the fast-moving water got to his belly, he started tossing his head and snorting. Jim gave him a crack on the rear, and the horse lunged toward a gravel shoal in the center of the stream.

Waving his hat, Jim called back at James on Connie One. "Move out!"

"Gee, gee!" James cried. His oxen bellowed, moving down the slight grade into the deep part of the stream. James laid on the brake, but the wagon still threatened to overrun the oxen. The water rose quickly to their sides, and their eyes showed white with panic. He kept them moving steadily with a firm hand and a cracking whip. When they reached the shallow island, Jim yelled for Sam to start over. I sat beside him on the wooden seat. Behind us, Jane and our children hung on for their lives.

The wagon rocked hard as the wheels slid off the bank and entered the stream, raising a yelp from the passengers in back. My throat was too dry to say anything.

On the far shore, James was starting up the slope. His oxen were doing well. They dug into the mud for a decent footing, slipped, and dug again. The two lead oxen crested the rise, disappeared beyond the edge, and then the wagon jolted from the river and practically shot up the bank. It lurched alarmingly at the top of the rise and then slid over the hump.

"Keep 'em moving! Keep 'em moving!" Jim shouted.

Our team had just pulled onto the shoal when a sudden cry of alarm sounded behind us. John's buckboard charged past our wagon on the downstream side. He was trying desperately to slow his horses, but they were completely out of control. As they came to the rise, the buckboard turned sideways in the stream and started to tip. Hannah's scream reached us above the sound of the water. Then the wagon tongue dropped and hit the river bottom. The horses lunged against the sudden snag, and the front wheels of John's wagon ripped completely off.

The wagon rolled over, dumping its entire load into the rushing water. Hannah and the baby catapulted over the side and disappeared. Still holding the reins, John followed the wheels and horses off the front of the wagon, flat on his belly.

Hannah surged to the surface, struggling to stand, and looked around in panic. "My baby!" she cried.

A chill hit me like an ice stake in the heart. John was trying to stop his horses and gain his feet, Jim was charging his stallion out in front to prevent them from running up-stream, and the baby was heading downstream.

No thought entered my mind. I crawled past Sam and leapt from the side of the Conestoga. Flailing as hard as I could, I used my arms to help propel me to the shallow area. Then running knee-deep to the end of the long gravel island, I threw my arms over my head and dove in after the baby.

The torrent threatened to suck me down as I spun in a circle, choking on a mouthful of muddy water. Panicked, I turned and came face to face with baby Margaret, head up, mouth closed, and eyes as big as dinner plates. I scooped her up with one arm and then looked for a way back to shore.

On the south bank, Joseph was charging downstream, splashing and slipping on the flooded ground. I fought against the current as Joseph uncoiled the rope he carried. He made a magnificent throw. The rope landed four feet in front of me, and I reached it with one hard kick. With Margaret in my right arm, I wrapped the line around my left and held tight.

Joseph dug his boots into the mud and heaved, hand over hand. I washed further downstream, eventually reaching slower water where I was able to stand and stagger to shore. My heart was pounding, and I realized I had forgotten to breathe. I handed the baby to Joseph and collapsed onto the flooded riverbank.

The baby smiled up at Joseph.

So I was a hero. That night, dressed in dry clothes for the first time in days, I sat beside a roaring fire, listening to the story from different perspectives, brushing off the praise and thanks. Everyone wanted to tell their version, and the exploit grew with each repeating.

Hannah and John were still shaking, but they were both all right. It was a miracle, we all agreed, that no one was hurt.

Jim had stopped the horses from charging off and got John untangled from the traces before he drowned. Jane had immediately climbed off our wagon to help Hannah and prevent her from chasing after her baby. Jane saw that I had safely reached shore with Joseph's help. She responded to our wave and calmed the terrified parents.

We returned the baby to her parents and then tracked down most of the supplies that had spilled from the wagon. Some were on the far bank tangled in low-lying branches, others grounded on the shallow island. Others were never seen again.

Sam got Connie Two over the north bank without incident, then he and James had raced back to help. The men all worked to right the broken wagon and drag it to shore.

Shaken and soaked, Jim called a halt for the day, and we made camp. No one complained about the lost time.

Escaping from the accolades, I found Jim standing by himself near the broken wagon. He did not look at me as I walked up beside him.

" 'Tis my fault," he said after a long silence.

I knelt down and examined the broken kingpin that had allowed the front wheel assembly to pull out. "I can't say it is, and I can't say it isn't, Jim. What I can say is you're our leader. Making decisions is a leader's job, and you made the choice you thought was right. That's all that matters."

"We should've made camp on the south side like John said."

"Maybe. We'll never know."

Jim rubbed his face and sighed deeply, putting it behind him. "We can replace the pin once it gets light. Won't take much time."

He turned and looked at me in the growing darkness. "That was quite a stunt, Fergus. That's twice you earned my praise in one day." He clapped me on the shoulder, and we walked back to the fire together.

Hannah was sitting on a log beside her husband, crying softly. Her head rested on John's shoulder, the baby cradled in her arms.

"What's the matter?" I asked, squatting down beside them.

" 'Tis foolish of me, I know," she said, turning a wet face in my direction. "Especially with what you did to save Maggie. That's all that really matters." She took a deep breath. "But we lost the Bible, Fergus. I can't believe it's gone. My father insisted we bring it. He said the future of our family would be made out here, and it should be recorded with the rest of the family's history."

Jane joined us and lightly rubbed Hannah's shoulder in sympathy.

Hannah sobbed again. "Six generations of marriages, births, and deaths. My whole family history lost..."

Jane put her arm around Hannah and spoke in a low motherly tone. "Ye remember many of the names, do ye not?"

Hannah sniffed and nodded.

"Well, yer our family now," Jane said, pulling her tight. "We'll re-create what we can in our Bible, and that's where yer history will be."

CHAPTER 14
Home

June 4th, 1772
The Pennsylvania Frontier

The Conemaugh was still high but nowhere near as dangerous to cross as the Loyalhanna had been. We came to the ford identified on our first trip and crossed without incident. No one even got their feet wet.

Jim led the party north, quiet and withdrawn. I tried again to talk him out of his despair. He knew he had made a bad decision and was beating himself relentlessly.

Unerringly, however, he found one of our outer corner markers and turned us toward the central cairn. Everyone expressed amazement in his pathfinding abilities, overdoing the praise a bit.

Standing with his hand atop the stone column, it reminded me of how proud he had looked the first time I saw him in that position. A smile crept across his face, and I knew he would be fine.

We had succeeded in a truly remarkable feat. Sixteen people, most of whom had never ventured more than a dozen miles from their birthplace, had walked, rode, and swam over 200 miles to an unknown wilderness — and we did not lose a soul. I am proud to say, we even gained one along the way.

Jim had a reason to be pleased. So did we all. However, there was no time to celebrate.

" 'Tis a beautiful spot, I agree," Jane said, standing with the rest of the party at the central marker of our new homesteads. She shifted Euphemia to the other hip and raised a hand to shade her eyes. "But why here?"

"That's not the first time that question's been asked," I laughed. "Jim chose it on his first trip out here, and nothing would sway him. This is where he built his marker, and this is where he intends to build his home. Sam and I just went along."

Jane cocked her head up to me. She was not ready for a joke. "Yer telling me that we left our homes, trudged four weeks through this Indian infested wilderness because ye *just went along* with that mad man!"

She was slowly building steam, and I tried to head it off. "Wait 'till you've walked on our parcel, love, you'll see how perfect it is."

"Don't you *love* me," she retorted. We stood silently for a while. The others were wandering around, looking at the trees and the fields as if trying to answer the same question for themselves. "All right, then. Show me this grand piece of earth worth coming all this way for."

I walked away from the center cairn, arms spread to indicate the adjoining lines of our 300 acres. Jane and the boys followed dutifully behind me.

"Imagine," I said, "from here stretching in each direction for three-quarters of a mile. There's two springs that I know of, open land for pasture and plenty of forest for logs." I pointed to a shallow vale where the grassland joined the forest. "Our cabin will be there, far enough from the others to have our privacy and close enough to be neighborly."

"And safer," Jane added.

"Within hollerin' distance," I agreed.

"Well then," she said, turning back to the wagons, "let's get ourselves settled in. The day's a-wasting."

Despite being tired, we got started on our fort right away

Now, to hear the word 'fort' used to describe a log cabin in the woods may seem farfetched, but its purpose was twofold. First of all, working together, we built a large enough structure, so we all had a place to sleep at night. Eventually, as other cabins were completed, families would move to their own homes.

Secondly, the fort served as our place of refuge in case of an Indian attack. The cabins would be constructed close enough together so that everyone could retreat back to the fort if need be.

It was only a matter of time before the Indians discovered us. The question on everyone's mind was, how would they receive their new neighbors? While the fort was under construction, we gathered the wagons together as they had been on our journey out. We still slept outdoors, either in or under a wagon for security.

After the fort, we would work together to build the next cabin, and so on. The four cabins in the original quadrant would be built first. In this way, the tools, oxen, and manpower were evenly distributed, and construction of the last cabin would not fall to one man.

We decided my brother Joseph and his wife, Mary Ann,

and Sam would live with us for a while. This meant that, when the time came, my cabin needed to be more extensive until we could build their cabins.

The party was in high spirits as the men began felling pine trees for the walls. We knew pine was not the best choice, but we had to work quickly, and pine is much easier to cut than any of the hardwoods growing close by.

Whether at work, rest, or sleep, at least one man was always on guard during the entire day. We took turns, musket and rifle loaded and primed, watching over the families. If it was necessary to go further afield in search of the perfect tree, someone with a musket went along.

Everyone had a task. Sam and I drew a twenty by twenty-foot square for the first logs to be rolled into place and pinned. The few inches of ground slope was eliminated by digging out on one side and placing heavy fieldstone at each corner. It would be many years before any of us had hardwood floors.

Each log rolled from the forest had to be trimmed and a simple saddle-notch cut to receive the adjacent log. Cabins built later would be of hardwood split down the middle and carefully notched to eliminate gaps. We were in a hurry.

One of the hardest parts of constructing a cabin was the extremely labor-intensive and backbreaking work of making shake shingles. We cut and rolled eighteen-inch oak and hickory blocks back to the worksite. Then James, our best carpenter, used his frow and mallet to split out the shakes. He shaped them with a deadly-sharp drawknife, forming a perfect wedge. In six days, he and Joseph produced enough rough shingles to cover our fort.

As the walls rose, several women and the three oldest boys took the chips from the shingle production and wedged them into the cracks between the uneven logs. Then they made daubing by mixing dirt from the floor excavation with handfuls of finely chopped grass. Eventually, all of the spaces between the logs were filled. It was dirty work but necessary to keep our fort dry and safe from wildlife. The boys thought it was great fun for the first hour, then it became a muddy chore.

By the end of the week, we had the roof beam and rafters in place so that the sleepers and shingles could be laid in an orderly, overlapping fashion.

The fort had no windows. Nor was there hearth. All the cooking took place outdoors. The door hung from leather hinges in a hardwood frame, and a stout crossbar held the door securely closed. Two narrow loopholes on each wall allowed enough maneuvering room for a musket to protect that side.

We all agreed it was a wondrous structure. The first night sleeping indoors was a memorable experience after so much time in the open. However, it was tight, with each family holding down a space where they placed their blankets. Stacks of baskets and boxes created an inadequate privacy wall. For the first time, I was aware of the sounds of fifteen people sleeping in close proximity to each other. James Thompson could wake the dead with his snoring, and his wife was no better.

Despite the constant rumbling, I slept well, comfortable in the secret that no rattlers would disturb our sleep due to the excellent job of packing the seams.

While the fort was under construction, we did not neglect the livestock or the need to get the planting in. The cows and oxen stayed loose in the grassland until split rails pens could be built. As long as there was food, they did not wander off. The horses were in use all day long, dragging logs and hoisting beams. At night, the tired beasts stayed in roughly constructed corrals.

The pigs and chickens roamed free and seemed content to stay near, waiting impatiently for any scraps tossed their way.

Planting was a high priority. It soon became apparent that stones were the most abundant building material available to us. It was impossible to push a spade into the ground without hitting a sizeable rock, and they littered the forest and grasslands.

Cutting a tract of land for the communal garden required more effort than we thought possible. Once an area was cleared and the topsoil turned, the boys were put to work picking stones. Then, it was the women's job to get our corn and potatoes started. The soil between all the stones was fertile, and a month after our arrival, everyone was pleased to see bright green corn sprouts emerging from the ground.

As the summer progressed, so did the size of Jane's belly. Her ability to help with the heavy chores diminished until finally, she was assigned the job of full-time cook for the entire community. I tried to lend a hand as much as possible, but my work was cut out for me, too.

My job, as you might expect, was that of official community surveyor. Each time a foundation or a fence needed to be straight and square, my skills with the circumferentor were called upon. Soon, John White and Joseph had their plots of land established. Fence lines went up everywhere. I am proud to say that we experienced few boundary disputes.

Joseph's skill at shingle making soon branched out to include furniture crafting. He was continually presenting an appreciative family with a new three-legged stool or nicely turned wooden pins. The pins could be pushed through the cracks between the logs to support shelves or hold the headboard of a rope and slat bed.

By the end of July, two cabins were finished. The White and Kelly families moved out of the fort. Those left behind spread out and enjoyed the extra room. In the case of an emergency, however, everyone would return to the fort. It did not take long.

On the first day of August, the Indians came.

CHAPTER 15
Fall

August 1st, 1772
The Pennsylvania Frontier

The first warning came from the horses working a field on Jim Kelly's property. His old bay and the workhorse borrowed from James Thompson stopped dead in their tracks and refused to pull the log further. The workhorse raised his head and whinnied into the warm summer breeze.

Jim left them standing in the field and walked casually to the tree his rifle leaned against. Bear was the thought that came to him first. We had killed two since our arrival in June. The more we planted, cooked, and ate, the more interested the bears were in our activities.

The horses became more anxious when Jim walked away from them. Even his bay started to shiver. Jim stood quietly against the tree, rifle cocked, ready for anything that might come out of the forest.

Ten Indians stepped out of the cut line without a sound, the same way they had that night on Braddock's Road.

Fortunately, James was coming to retrieve his horse. He entered the clearing, saw the Indians, saw Jim, and slowly walked out into the field to his horse. Jim joined him, and with hearts in their throats, they led the two horses back to the fort.

I saw them coming and realized it was an unusual way to end the day. I picked up my rifle, checked the pan, and strolled out to meet them.

"There's ten or so," Jim said as we came together. "Best get the women and children into the fort, then we'll go meet them."

I walked back to Jane, where she was stirring a copper pot slung from a tripod above the fire.

"Gather the children and everyone you see and head for the fort. Be quiet and be quick. Don't let anyone run."

Her eyes grew round, but she did not question. Within a minute or two, most of our party was either standing in the central area or inside the fort. Three muskets poked from the loopholes, aimed in our direction.

"What do we do?" I asked Jim without thinking. It revealed my nervous state because we always expected Indians, and I knew what to do. Joe, Sam, and John had the task of defending the fort, while Jim, James, and I acted as ambassadors.

"We wait," Jim said.

We did not wait long. Four of the Indians walked toward us while the others stayed along the edge of the forest. They walked naturally, muskets in the crook of their arms, not exactly threatening; not at ease, either.

With a start, I realized that one of the Indians was the same man I had met three years earlier — the warrior to whom I had given my hatchet.

Emboldened, I stepped forward a pace and said, "We are sorry to make so much noise."

My companions stared at me as if I had lost my mind. The man I addressed cocked his head in that familiar way, looking closely at me. I held out my hand and indicated the hatchet stuck in his belt.

He glanced down at the hatchet and then quickly back at me, recognition in his eyes.

"This is good land," he said with a slight smile. "Many deer."

"It is," I agreed. I then indicated the pot that Jane was tending. "We'd be pleased if you would share our meal."

The warrior did not answer me directly. He raised his musket and called out alarmingly loud in his language. The other Indians came across the field, still showing no signs of aggression. One spoke to my Indian friend and indicated the fort where musket barrels still projected.

My friend looked at me and said, "I speak the British language. My father was a Frenchman. I speak the French language, Algonquian, some of the Seneca." He tilted his head again. "How many do you speak?"

I choked back a laugh behind my hand. "I'm sorry to say I only speak English. My compliments on a fine education."

He held out his hand, indicating the long gun barrels aimed in his direction. "We also live on this land. We do not point muskets at you."

Chagrined, I waved to the fort, and Jim also indicated that they were to withdraw their guns.

"My name is Fergus," I said. "What may I call you?

The warrior proudly puffed up his chest. "I am called *Gele-le-mend*. My father's father is the great *Neta-wat-wees*, sachem of the Turtle Clan. He came to this land many years ago from the east. Now my family lives beyond the *Wel-hik-heny* river and north of your land."

Needless to say, we were all appropriately impressed. Sitting before us was an important man of the Delaware, or Lenape people. What we did not know then was how important he would also be in our lives. Our paths would cross again.

It is time for me to insert a comment regarding the Indian manner of speech depicted in my narrative. In my vast experience, Indians who speak the King's English to some degree or another do so in a rather loud, guttural voice, as if continually irritated with you for being so slow. I have witnessed white men doing the same to foreigners who they believe will better understand them if they apply extra volume.

The Indian often speaks in flowery metaphors that do not always translate into English. So, I shall always endeavor to present what my Indian acquaintances were trying to express in intent and feeling instead of the exact words they may have used. Thankfully, as I learned more and more of their language, the communication became quieter in both directions.

Together, we sat around the fire and ate the venison that Jane had cooked to a tender, succulent stew. She had included new potatoes, onions, and carrots, that had recently sprouted in our garden.

No one spoke while we ate, but occasionally a warrior would make a sound that obviously showed appreciation for Jane's skill. She and Jim's wife, Sarah, served while the rest of our group and all the children stayed inside the fort. The Indians did not seem to care.

When everyone had finished this somewhat edgy repast, Gelelemend stood. Each warrior handed Jane their plate, gathered up their muskets, and walked away without a word.

"For this feast," Gelelemend said, addressing the men

119

still sitting at the fire, "I thank you." Then he followed his warriors.

At the forest edge, he looked back at our settlement. He raised no hand in farewell nor shouted a goodbye. He was there, and then he was not.

"My Lord," Jane said as we all looked out across the empty field. "They do come and go most abruptly!"

That, I thought, is the problem.

CHAPTER 16
The First Winter

November 14th, 1772
The Frontier, Pennsylvania

I have another son! Samuel came in October as we finished the last of the harvest. Jane had grown so ponderous that we joked twins might be in our future. Though he was a hefty baby, Jane did well. However, it took her longer to get back on her feet than with the previous four.

So Samuel was the first child born in Indiana County, as we know it today.

Our cabin progressed as fall chilled the air. By November, we seven, plus Joseph and Mary Ann, finally moved out of the fort. Sam and several others were finishing his cabin half a mile away.

During that time, we saw no more of the Indians who had visited us in the fall. However, as the weather grew colder, a new visitor to our settlement created a problem.

A scream pierced the crisp autumn night, waking me from a deep sleep. It was immediately followed by the howl of frightened dogs. Every man within hearing reached for his gun and hurried to the common area.

Sam and I scrambled from our cabin and met Jim coming across the field. John joined us from the fort.

"Indians?" I asked the group in general.

Jim held his rifle at the ready. "I think it was a pig," he said. His breath showed in the moonlight. We were all breathing hard. "Two by two, let's head for the pens. Shut those dogs up!"

Sam and I went in one direction while Jim and John slide down the side of the fort toward the pig pens. A couple of boys grabbed the three whimpering dogs and dragged them into the fort. I took a deep breath. If the dogs were scared, so was I.

As we turned the corner of the fort, the answer became clear. Six of our pigs cowered in a corner of the pen, loudly squealing a frightful challenge at the looming shape near the center of the pen.

A gray wolf, at least two feet at the shoulders, was tearing chunks from a dead sow. As I raised my rifle, Sam touched my arm and pointed toward the edge of the forest. In the shadows, beyond the pens, three sets of yellow eyes glowed in the moonlight.

The wolf in the pigpen had stopped its desecration and was staring directly at us, its bloody lips curled back to expose long, glistening teeth. A deep, menacing growl escaped its throat. The wolves on the tree line responded with a chorus of howls that made the hair on my neck stand straight up.

"Don't move," Sam whispered needlessly. I froze in place, my rifle half raised to my shoulder.

He looked behind him where Jim and John stood against the side of the fort. Sam pointed at me and then at the wolf in the pen. He then looked at the two men and then at the line of shining eyes at the edge of the forest.

Jim nodded in understanding, and they both raised their guns.

Sam held up one hand and swiped it down in a sharp motion. Instantly, our three guns flashed and split the night with a deafening roar. My shot took the wolf in the pen through the heart, and it collapsed on its kill.

The wolves on the forest edge shrieked in terror and bolted, leaving one of their fellows kicking out the last of its life in the frosted leaves.

Jim and John joined us at the pen. We looked over the fence at the wolf lying atop our poor dead sow. It was a she-wolf, maybe eighty pounds by the look of her.

"They must be getting plenty hungry to venture into an area like this," Jim observed.

"I don't know," I responded, looking at the dead wolf. "It's early. Hard to believe they can't find a deer to bring down. I'm thinking they chose easy prey."

"That ain't good," Jim said, shaking his head.

We were all familiar with wolves. Back home, they had been trapped or hunted to the point where they no longer posed much of a threat. However, you never knew when a pack would pass through the valley. Hunters had to be constantly wary.

Starving wolves, like a starving bear, were a particular problem. They would attack anything if it looked like food. That included us. We would have to make all the pens more secure.

The tension seeped from my shoulders and I shivered in the night air, realizing that I wore only breeches and a nightshirt. Jim and John dragged the she-wolf to the edge of the forest and left it with its dead companion. Then they pulled the poor old sow out of the pen and threw a bucket of mash in the trough to give the other pigs something else to think about.

"We'll hang her up when it gets light," Jim said in his usual calm voice. "Wolves won't be back tonight." Then he smiled at us. "Looks like Christmas dinner's come early."

Not long after the incident with the wolves, a troop of soldiers hailed us from the far meadow and crossed to the settlement. They were from Fort Pitt, having gone upriver to Fort Kittanning and walked east from there.

A grizzled veteran named Captain Frasier led the troop. I thought he was too old to still be in the army, but he was solidly built with a ruddy face of a Scot beneath a gray beard.

He brought amazing news.

Given all of the time and effort the British Army had expended capturing Fort Duquesne from the French, they abandoned it to a militia force. Frasier said that as far as he knew, it was all about money. Fort Pitt was the westernmost outpost of the British Army. It was simply too expensive to maintain troops so far from civilization.

The captain also brought some unwelcome news that affected us more than anything that happened in Fort Pitt.

Ohio Seneca had attacked the settlements west of the Allegheny River. A family of five had been murdered, and their cabin burned to the ground. The others, the captain said, retreated to Fort Pitt for protection. The far western homesteads, built on land officially recognized as Indian Territory, were being abandoned.

After Frasier relayed the story of the massacre, Sam told him of his intent to return to Chamber's Town for the winter. Sam's wife, Mary Elizabeth, was still there, and the baby due very soon.

124

Frasier listened with some trepidation. "That's a hard decision," he said. "I believe the number you have here makes you safer in case of attack. And, the hostiles are less likely to be away from their villages during the winter. They tend to hunker down. Until they run out of food, of course."

We all sat close to the cook fire, huddled against the sharp wind. Frasier had ridden in on a swaybacked mare, thirty soldiers walking morosely behind, and set up camp in the field beyond our fort. It was evident from their appearance that their march had already been difficult and tiring. There was still a long way to go.

Frasier said that most of his troops were career soldiers and would be redeployed. However, a few of the soldier's enlistments were up. They would either be returning to England or back to homes somewhere in the colonies.

"How long have you been in these parts?" I asked, handing Frasier a hot cider. He smiled appreciatively and held it between his hands for warmth.

"I came out with General Forbes in '58 as a young ensign. We took Fort Pitt from the French."

I was impressed with his longevity. "Fourteen years! All this time in Fort Pitt?"

"No, no," he said, shaking his head wearily. "I was down at Fort Ligonier for most of Pontiac's uprising. We protected the entire frontier in those days."

"We had problems of our own back then," Sam interjected. "A group of men caused problems along the Conococheague River until James Smith and his boys put a stop to the illegal trade with the Indians." (4)

The captain frowned deeply. "That was bad all round. I met Lieutenant Grant when I was at Fort Loudoun for a while. He was an ass, if you'll excuse me. He got what he

deserved for dealing guns to the Indians. More than anything, I wish there hadn't been a cause for you settlers to
take things into your own hands."

"Wasn't us," Sam said, bristling at the comparison. "We
didn't even know Smith. Every man here is a loyal subject
and respects the Army."

Frasier held out a placating hand. "I meant no insinua-
tion, sir. The work you settlers do, moving the frontier
west, is a tribute to the Crown. Every man Jack under colours thanks you for your work and sacrifice."

Sam dipped his chin, accepting the apology. He was not
one to easily rowel, but once stirred up, Sam was formidable and intimidating.

"If I might suggest," Frasier said, trying to move the
conversation ahead, "if you're planning on going east, you
should come along with us. We're marching for Hunting-
don. Fort Shirley is not much beyond that. From Shirley,
you simply head south and pick up the Conococheague.
It's a shorter route than the old Braddock, I can tell you
from experience."

Out of nowhere, Joseph said, "I'm going with you!"

Mary Ann, tending the fire nearby, squeaked as if she
had stepped on a rattler.

"What are you saying?" she cried. "You can't go!"

"I need to," he said, moving closer to her. "Sam is coming back with Mary Elizabeth and a baby, we hope. He
can't do that by himself. We can bring supplies, maybe
some more people, too."

He turned to his brother. "Ain't that right, Sam? You
shouldn't be alone."

Sam shrugged his broad shoulders, unwilling to be
dragged into the argument.

"Good. It's settled," Frasier announced. He stood and

126

bowed to the women and turned to Sam. "I'm sure you can be ready by first light."

Mary Ann squealed again.

Sitting around the fire, Sam, Joseph, and I discussed the trip with the others. There was much to consider. We always knew Sam intended to be with his wife for the birth of his first child. However, with the news Captain Frasier brought regarding the marauding Indians, we had to consider the loss of two guns.

There was also the grim reality that we would need supplies by spring. In addition, at least two men would have to go to Kiskiminetas, or Beeson's Mill, before winter set in to have our corn ground. Every man who left the community put it more at risk.

Following much discussion, we agreed that Sam and Joseph should travel with the soldiers. Those staying at the settlement needed to be more vigilant but, we believed, safe enough without the support of their muskets.

As the sunlight streaked the open field, we stood and watched the troops break camp. Captain Frasier was already mounted and quietly calling out commands to his troops. Sam, mounted on John's gelding, and Joseph on his own mare, joined him. They looked rather proud marching off with the soldiers and we all cheered and waved goodbye and watched until they were out of sight. Mary Ann was still crying when Jane gathered her up and went to make breakfast.

CHAPTER 17
Spring

April 9th, 1773
The Pennsylvania Frontier

In the years to come, we would suffer winters harsh enough to freeze a man's soul. Winters so long that the snow came in October and stayed until March. Winters so cold that pine trees in the forest exploded during the night.

However, our first winter in the wilderness was less severe than it could have been. Little snow fell until January, and there was not a freezing rain until the end of the month. To make up for the lack of snow, it rained almost every day.

Cold and wet was how we spent the winter. The creeks flooded the fields. The livestock pens became a swamp. The horses suffered the most and huddled together in the lean-to built beside the fort.

We were pleased that our new cabins withheld the weather and stayed warm when the wind did not blow. Each new cabin had a hearth so cooking could be done indoors. However, when the wind blew hard, the warm air in the cabin went right up the chimney. Another consequence of indoor cooking was that we saw less and less of our neighbors in the long, dark evenings.

By the first of February, supplies were getting low. By the end of the month, we had eaten all of the cornmeal so laboriously carried back from Kiskiminetas in the fall. We slaughtered all of the non-breeding pigs and chickens, knowing that even the breeders might have to be sacrificed soon. The horses, oxen, and milk cows were too valuable to eat.

One evening, Jane's brother John announced that he and his wife were considering returning to Chamber's Town with their baby. It would only be until spring, he said, then they would return. Most of the men argued against it, trying to get John to understand the danger. No one else was willing to go, and with all the rain, the best way home was to take the shorter, more mountainous Forbes Road. John, however, had never been on it.

That night, John confided in me that it was only Hannah who wanted to go home and that he was determined to talk her out of it. She sulked for a week or so, but in the end, they stayed.

My job became full-time hunter. Each expedition required that I go further and further from the settlement as the deer became warier. No longer did a herd graze casually each morning in the fields beyond our cabins.

Hunting alone was dangerous yet necessary. In addition to the deer, I had to keep an eye out for the occasional bear — and Indian. Usually, I built a blind and waited for the deer to come to me. Staying in one place was much safer rather than stalking through the forest.

On a frosty morning in early March, I came across the carcass of a recently butchered buck. It was clearly the work of man. I estimated the kill had been made earlier in the day because it was not yet completely frozen. As quietly as possible, I backtracked to the settlement, leaving the deer where I found it. That night we keep an extra watch, but no one threatened us.

The first week of April, a dog's joyous barking far to the south surprised us all. It was such a natural thing to hear that it took several moments to realize it was not coming from our hounds.

Moments later, a long-legged hunting dog bounded into the common area, barking and jumping in happy circles. Then a 'halo' sounded from the open field to the south and three Conestogas rolled up the trail.

Sam and Joseph were home!

More dogs barked, children yelled, women cried. It was quite the scene. Joseph ran ahead of the wagons, spotted his wife in the gathering crowd, and swept her into his arms.

Then he stepped back from her, a look of pure terror on his face. Mary Ann blushed bright pink, patting her rounded belly.

"Welcome home, husband," she said with a smile as broad as the Allegheny. "I've been busy while you were gone!"

Joseph was speechless. He gave me a bear hug, kissed Jane, and disappeared with his wife before the wagons came to a stop.

Sam drove the first wagon. He climbed down and took a bundle from Mary Elizabeth. She hopped off the wagon without assistance and retrieved her baby. The two of them could not stop smiling. They were proud parents and happy to have successfully made the journey.

"You've lost weight," Sam said, crushing me to his chest.

"Things were getting desperate," I replied.

His arm waved toward the wagons. "Well, tonight, you feast! We brought you a horn o' plenty!"

"Food is welcome," I said in all seriousness, "and you more so. We've missed you."

I looked back as the other two wagons disgorged their occupants. The first face I recognized. It was Will Simpson, our old friend and neighbor in Cumberland County. His wife, Sarah, and his two young children and Andy, a handsome young man of fourteen, came forward to join the celebration.

The other family was new to me. Their name was McCreary. Sam met them at Fort Cumberland and convinced them to come to our area of the country instead of going south to western Virginia. They brought a pack of six children, from a baby on up.

Our little community was suddenly much noisier.

That evening members of our original party came to my cabin for a feast and to hear the news from back home. The new arrivals settled into the old fort. Sam was quiet for a time, watching with concern as we devoured a chicken, potatoes, and corn cakes. He understood then that the food and supplies had arrived just in time.

Jane, Mary Ann, and Mary Elizabeth chatted happily as they cooked our supper. They were all friends and had a lot of catching up to do. It turned out that Sam arrived back in Chamber's Town on the exact day Mary Elizabeth went into labor. It was a homecoming to remember, he said.

We men sat at the rough plank table, sharing a most welcome jug of rare and expensive Barbados rum — Sam's present to us all.

"Tell us of your trip," I said as the jug made its rounds. "Mary Elizabeth said you were on the road a mere twenty days. That's remarkable."

Sam set his mug on the table. "The road is getting better all the time, Fergus. Others have used it since we came out last year. Nowhere did we have to move any stones or clear trees off the path."

"And the river crossings?" Jim wanted to know. "Been raining here all winter."

"Back east, also," Sam continued, somewhat embarrassed to be the center of attention. "The rivers were high and running, but we knew where to cross and had no incidents."

"Lucky," Jim said, thinking back, perhaps, to his turn as wagon leader and our near disaster.

"How are mother and father?" I asked.

Sam smiled. "They're fine, Fergus. I spent an entire evening telling Pa of our trip and what it's like out here. He wants to join us."

"He'd be welcome," I laughed, "though I can't see Mother agreeing to it."

We all sat quietly, each reflecting on the families we left behind. This was the lot of a pioneer. You have to leave behind much of what you love. In my parent's case, they were looking for a better life when they boarded a ship for America. And they found it. Whether we had come to a better place was yet to be seen.

"So tell us what news you bring," James chimed in, breaking the mood.

Sam hung his head, gathering his thoughts. "Well, I'll tell you what I saw. Folks back home may not realize it cause they're living it day to day, but all they talk of is how they're mistreated."

"Who by?" I asked.

"By the legislature."

Sam meant the Colonial government. The Penn dynasty ruled our Colony with no sign of releasing their control. Although they claimed to have the colonist's best interest in mind, they were loyal to the King.

The most common complaint was that the Colonial legislatures were allowed no real say in the governance of their colonies. With no members in parliament, we in the colonies had no choice. We had to follow the dictates from England.

"That's hasn't changed," John White put in. "Ever since the Proclamation, people have been grumbling that they don't have a say in their own lives. Well, we wouldn't be in this part of the country if we didn't have a say. The Proclamation forbid us from coming here, yet here we are!"

Sam nodded in agreement. "That's true, the Fort Stanwix Treaty opened up this land, and it was the people of New York that got that done."

As we talked, the red glow from the hearth and the smoke from clay pipes gave the room a conspiratory air. The children were all in the loft, pretending to sleep, and the women moved closer to listen.

John was not finished. "We mustn't forget," he said with pride in his voice, "that we are British citizens, even if we are thousands of miles away."

"Bollocks!" Jim Kelly exploded. "We're not British citizens, were British *subjects*. We're at the will of the British government and have no say in what they proclaim." He dumped his pipe on the floor and stamped on the glowing embers. "Sugar, paper, land, anything at all that they think is taxable, we get taxed. And who stands up to them?"

"No one should stand up to them," John said, his voice rising. "If we are subjects, as you agree, we do what we are told. Parliament may not always do what is best for us, but they are the Parliament! We owe our allegiance to them and to King George."

"Of course we do," interjected Sam. "Still, we need a say in how we're treated. Every man in England has a representative. We have none. That's all I'm saying."

John shifted in his seat, uncomfortable to be holding the solitary Loyalist position in the room. "Look, all *I'm* saying is that the King is our king, and we must do our duty. This talk is dangerous. It's a good thing we're so far away, or someone might construe such talk as sedition."

Sam sadly shook his head. "We may be far from it for now, John, but our families are in the thick of things back home. Taxes are increasing every year just to line the pockets of the politicians. Why, our neighbors are even forced to billet soldiers with no compensation. Let's not forget what happened three years ago in Boston. They called it a massacre even though only five men got killed. The point is, the Army fired on civilians."

"Who were defying the rule of law and attacked the soldiers!" John shouted.

Hannah moved to stand behind her husband as he became more animated. She placed a hand on his shoulder. "We're all family, John," she said quietly. It had a calming effect on us all.

"At least there hasn't been any more violence," I said, adding my thoughts for the first time.

"That's not exactly true," Sam said, looking from face to face. "There's been an incident in Rhode Island."

Jim snorted. "Those Yankees are gonna get us all hung."

"What happened?" I asked Sam.

"It's old news back home. Happened right after we left. A British customs schooner named *Gaspee* ran aground trying to chase down a packet ship for some reason. Seemed the *Gaspee* suspected the other ship of not paying enough dues. Anyway, she ran aground, and a group of Providence men boarded her, shot and wounded the captain, took the crew captive, and burnt the ship."

"Bloody hell," John said under his breath.

"Was there a reprisal?" I asked.

"Not exactly. The men were charged with treason, but no one officially identified them. The case simply fell apart."

"So no harm done, no real violence," Jim said.

"No harm done?" John exploded, coming to his feet. "They destroyed a Royal Navy ship doing its legitimate duty and shot the captain!"

"That's probably the end of it," said Jim, trying to sound calm and moderate.

"No!" John said, heading for the door. "I tell you, it's only the beginning!"

And he was right.

PART THREE

War Drums
1775 to 1777

CHAPTER 18
Rebellion

June 9th, 1775
The Pennsylvania Frontier

Two years passed in a blur of activity. Our community grew as settlers arrived from Virginia, New York, and back home. Sometimes it seemed that most of Cumberland County was relocating to Westmoreland County as our part of Pennsylvania became designated in '73.

The county seat was in Hanna's Town, a long day's ride to the south. We elected Jim Kelly to go to the first council meeting and represent the county's northernmost settlement interests. The main topic of discussion was the role of the Independent Militia in protecting the settlements springing up throughout the area. And our community was, after all, only a handful of miles from the treaty line. Beyond that line was Indian Territory.

As the settlement grew and more supplies came in with the new arrivals, we were able to make improvements on our land. Soon the communal livestock pens were replaced with corrals and barns at each homestead. Fields were plowed for corn and wheat, and gardens sprung up everywhere. People were scattered so widely that I could no longer see the smoke from all of the cabins.

The fort was rebuilt with stone and it became our community center and meeting place. James and Mary Thompson built a proper cabin on their land, having lived in the old rotting fort for two years.

And our families grew. Jane seemed to spend most of her time pregnant. Beautiful little Peggy came in '74. There were now eight of us in the original cabin. It was still tight despite my brothers having places of their own. During the summer of '74, I added two rooms with actual plank flooring, and we moved the kitchen in from the cook shed.

We worked hard all day, every day. Even Sundays could not be considered a day of rest. The horses and cows and the rest of our livestock did not stop eating or requiring attention, so we could not stop either. It was hard, though overall, we were content and proud of what we had accomplished.

Winters were the hardest, of course, and they seemed to grow progressively more severe as the years passed. Following the somewhat mild weather of our first winter, we did not expect the amount of snow, sometimes three or four feet, that covered the land from November to March. Then in the spring, we dealt with the hordes of no-see-ums, mosquitoes, and bloodsucking horseflies that infested the lowlands.

But with it all, we so loved this beautiful, difficult land.

Sam, however, was not as fortunate. After his return in '73 with Mary Elizabeth and his baby, the idea of building a mill absorbed his every waking moment. From the time he first saw Beeson's grist mill, he talked of building one near our settlement. He claimed a piece of land on Stony Run at the juncture with Two Lick Creek, where the stream ran high, even in late summer.

The same year, William Bracken built a mill fifteen miles south on Blacklick Creek, which was a great convenience to us. It was closer than trekking all the way to Kiskiminetas, and a new community soon grew up around it. Two of our old neighbors from Franklin County, John Stewart and Joseph McCartney, settled there.

Once Bracken had opened his mill, Sam was more determined than ever. He and Joseph worked off and on during the summer and fall. I joined them from time to time, happily sweating alongside my brothers. We formed a pond and built a sluice that funneled water to a moderately-sized vertical water wheel. Lighter than Beeson's, his grinding wheels were supposed to come down from New York to Kittanning. The wheels never arrived, and the mill was never finished.

In the fall, the Indians attacked the frontier.

We learned of these troubles from a group of passing militiamen ordered to re-establish the old fort at Kittanning. According to them, it was all the fault of the Shawnee and Seneca living in Ohio and western Virginia. These Indians did not accept the validity of the 1768 Treaty of Fort Stanwix that purchased the land west of the Alleghenies and opened it for settlement. The Shawnee and the Ohio Seneca claimed the Iroquois did not speak for them. There had always been attacks along the frontier, but things got worse toward the end of '73.

In October, down in the section of Virginia called Kentucky, two frontiersmen named Daniel Boone and William Russel had tried to establish a western settlement. A band of Shawnee and Delaware captured a son of each man and killed them most horribly. Boone, who would be famous one day, and his entire party, went back to North Carolina for a few years.

Learning of the atrocities in Virginia, a group of Fort Pitt militiamen attacked an Indian town north of the Ohio and killed the family of an Ohio Seneca sachem. No longer content with minor raids, the Seneca and the Shawnee went on the warpath.

It pleased me to learn that the Shawnee chief Cornstalk was doing what he could to keep the peace. Cornstalk was the warrior we had met at Beeson's Mill on our journey here. Although his history included many atrocities against settlers, he wanted no part of the war threatening to envelop us all.

More settlements north of Fort Pitt were attacked, and we knew it was just a matter of time before the fight came to us. We set extra watches, and one or two of the new, outlying families came into the fort for protection. When we worked on the cabins or in the fields, two men stood guard, muskets at the ready. Construction on Sam's mill came to a standstill while all of this was transpiring.

Then one evening, shortly after sunset, fire illuminated the sky to the south. There were no cabins in that direction, so we all knew it could only be one thing. The next day, a well-armed party ventured out and found Sam's mill burned to the ground. My brother, uncharacteristically withdrawn for days, swore to rebuild once things calmed down.

Calm was not seen again until Lord Dunmore, governor of Virginia, launched a campaign against the Shawnee and Seneca. The militia and Indians fought a fierce battle at a place we now call Point Pleasant along the Ohio. In the end, the Indians lost, as they always do. The new year brought a feeling of relief, although the Shawnee never officially surrendered, and we never let our guard down.

By April of '75, the Virginia militia withdrew from Ohio and Pennsylvania, going back to their homes and farms. With the Indians subdued, and the army gone, we began to believe life could return to normal.

Then news came that the Yankees had gone to war.

Massachusetts was in open rebellion. There was no other way to say it — we were now in a shooting war with the British.

A new family to our settlement brought news of a minor skirmish fought between Massachusetts militiamen and the British Army in the farm town of Lexington on April 19th. Another battle was fought the same day in a place called Concord.

The militia did not fare well at Lexington. However, they held their own at Concord, forcing the British redcoats into a full retreat back to Boston.

The militia immediately cut off all access to Boston, and the city was now under siege. An American city, occupied by the British Army and surrounded by rebels!

Then the quickly formed Massachusetts Congress authorized their militia, led by Colonel Benedict Arnold, to attack Fort Ticonderoga. He was helped by a Connecticut militia calling themselves the Green Mountain Boys under the command of Ethan Allen. And to make matters worse, Fort Ticonderoga is in New York! They captured the fort in May.

In June, the British attempted to break the siege of Boston, and they fought a bloody battle above the city on Bunker Hill. Our new neighbors told us of the battle with a mixture of horror and pride. The regular army suffered massive losses. The British took the hill, then withdrew back to the city under intense fire. Last they heard, a stalemate existed.

"Here's the best part!" Sam exclaimed as he sat at our table to relay the news. "There's now a Continental Army. Can you believe that?"

"No more militias?" I asked.

"I don't know. I believe the militias are still standing, especially on the frontier, but they're being absorbed into the new army. You'll never believe who's in command…"

I shook my head, waiting for him to go on.

"Washington! George Washington, the same man who failed to capture Fort Duquesne two times and surrendered at Fort Necessity? Don't you remember the story that Army captain told us on our first trip out here?"

I did remember. Young Captain Walsh was a friendly and, I believed, honorable soldier. He told us of George Washington's first attempt to take Fort Duquesne and then again, his failure with General Braddock. On his third attempt, Washington captured the fort for the British. As I remembered, the Captain held no love for Colonel Washington.

And now Washington was Commander in Chief of the entire army. What was this world coming to?

We were also amazed to learn that the Colonial Legislatures had formed a Continental Congress. That they could agree on anything was news. The First Congress met in Philadelphia a year earlier, the Second in May. Men whose names we knew — Franklin, Handcock, Jefferson, and Adams were all representatives. They were surely placing their necks in the noose.

By authorizing the formation of a standing army, the

colonies were firmly announcing their intent for Home Rule. For years, there had been a wave of sentiment pushing hard for independence, while others, like myself, still hoped for recognition as a self-governing colony. Who would win out was yet to be determined.

Sam, who once described himself as the King's Most Loyal Subject, was now adamantly in favor of full independence from Britain.

The summer passed without much news, and the Indians were quiet. Fighting had progressed from New England down the seaboard to North Carolina with the Patriots, as we were now called, going back and forth with the British Army. During that time, General Arnold had failed in his attempt to attack Quebec. Why we wanted Quebec, no one could explain. I was not even certain where it was.

As winter settled in, heavy snow shut down all work on cabin building, and the menfolk spent more time at the fort, grumbling and arguing about where this was all headed.

The fort was also our tavern, now. Rough benches lined three walls with a high-top serving bar against the fourth. If a man went missing, his wife knew where to find him.

The women, for their part, spent the cold, dreary days together at one cabin or another. I learned more about the community and the outside world when Jane came home from a sewing circle than I ever did at the tavern.

A week before Christmas, the realities of the discontent in the east came home. A group of Pennsylvania militia officers arrived from Fort Pitt. They were going from settlement to settlement with orders from Governor Penn and the newly formed General Assembly. Every man between the age of sixteen and fifty was now in the Militia. You had no real choice. You volunteered, or you would be fined!

They told us to have a long gun, powder, and shot ready at all times — which made us all laugh, wondering where they thought they were.

We were also required to elect a local militia commander. After a quick meeting and a unanimous vote, Sam was elected. He was commissioned as a Captain and ordered to form a company of forty men and march to Fort Kittanning in the spring.

CHAPTER 19
The Indians

May 19th, 1776
The Pennsylvania Frontier

The winter of '76 was long and harsh, and we struggled to find enough food for our families and livestock. I spent most of my time hunting. Even the deer seemed to be in hiding. The few I managed to shoot were thin and made poor stew, though, before long, we were thankful even for that.

It snowed for six days without stopping in late January and buried us in drifts so deep we had to dig tunnels to reach the barn. The animals were shut in for weeks, the children grew restless, and the adults snapped at each other.

Samuel received orders to go to Kittanning at the earliest possible time, but he could not move from our settlement until late March, when the snow finally melted. He took John White and three others from our area and rounded up more from outlying settlements. Samuel's wife and children moved in with Jim Thompson's family. Hannah and her two children stayed with us.

Around the same time, news came that the British had been expelled from Boston. This led folks to believe that the Continental Army was more victorious than they actually were. Prayers that the fighting would soon be over were on everyone's lips. That was far too optimistic.

Also, there was a new Indian Affairs agent at Fort Pitt named George Morgan. His job was to ensure that the Shawnee, Ohio Seneca, and Delaware remained neutral as the fighting with the British intensified in New York and North Carolina.

His efforts failed. By April, the Ohio Seneca were raiding up and down the Allegheny River once more. In New York, there was growing concern that the Iroquois nation was being enticed to fight for the British despite American efforts to keep them out of the war. The British were more effective in their dealings with the Indians, primarily because of the gifts they offered. They promised items that the Indians valued, whereas the Americans were mostly poor and undersupplied as it was. Consequently, the British won the Iroquois to their side, while the Americans, for the most part, failed in their attempts to keep them neutral.

Trouble came to our settlement late on a warm spring evening at the end of May. As news of attacks to the west became more frequent, we kept a nightly watch and had a warning system in place. Until then, there had been no cause to use it.

Most of the families had settled in for the night, the fires banked, and the lanterns extinguished. In the stables and pens, the livestock was already sleeping peacefully.

Will McCreary was the watchman for the early part of the night. He was almost taken unawares, so quietly did they come from the forest.

I had just dozed off when three sharp raps on the door jolted me wide awake.

"Indians!" came the harsh whisper from beyond the

door, and then he was gone to warn the next cabin.

Jane was awake and out of bed in an instant.

"Bring the boys in," I whispered to her, lifting my rifle from the pegs above the door. She went to the side rooms and quietly roused the boys, and hurried them to join their sisters in the loft. Hannah and her children joined them.

Billy, now a tall nine-year-old, followed me to the window. His job was to load my long rifle and old musket if I needed to keep up a steady fire. We had practiced this many times, and he was a brave, steady lad.

Along the valley, Will was raising the alarm with much risk to his own scalp. If we had more warning, we planned to gather at the fort. These Indians had entered our settlement unannounced, so we would have to defend ourselves cabin by cabin, every man for himself.

Jane joined me at the window, and we both peered through the slats into the moonlit night.

Suddenly she grasped my arm. "There's fire!" she cried, pointing west. Newly arrived families had built in that direction, and I guessed the fire came from the Bennett place.

My scalp contracted in horror as the distant sound of a woman's scream carried to us. Bennett's cabin was more than half a mile from ours, but we could hear her in the stillness of the night. As suddenly as it started, the cry stopped. We could see the glow from their cabin reflecting in the sky.

Then a volley of shots rang out nearby. I reached out to Billy and gave his shoulder a reassuring squeeze. "Just do what we've practiced, son," I said. "We'll be okay if we can keep them away from the cabin."

His eyes were huge and luminous in the dark. "Yes, Pa," he said in a high yet confident voice.

Jane stood on my other side, still holding my arm. "My God, Fergus," she whispered. "Do ye think — "

"There's no good in thinking on that," I cut her off. "We need to be ready. It's all we can do."

Together we stared out of the thin gap in the window slats, waiting. Suddenly there was movement to the right side of the cabin. I raised my rifle and pushed the end of the muzzle through the loophole.

"Fergus!" came a voice from outside the door. "It's Will. Let me in!"

I took a deep breath. "Open the door," I said to Jane.

Will quickly slipped inside, and Jane slammed the door shut, replacing the heavy bar in its holds.

Will's face shined with sweat. His voice trembled as he relayed his efforts to warn the settlement.

"My dog heard 'em first," he said. "She's a smart one, didn't make a sound, and came up in full alert. Then I saw the movement beyond the field. I think there's six of them."

"What about Bennett," I asked.

Will hung his head. "They was in the wrong direction, Fergus."

"You did good," I assured him as more shots came from Kelly's and Thomson's direction. We heard a few whoops, but for the most part, the night was still; the quiet pierced now and then with a shot or two. The only sound after a while was Hannah talking low and soothingly to the children in the loft.

Then, there they were. Two warriors, stripped to the waist, war paint gleaming, charged our cabin. One was holding a flaming pine torch high over his head. Jane gasped and moved back from the window to give me room to maneuver the rifle. The warriors came straight on, evidently failing to see the loophole and the death that stared them down.

The Indian with the torch advanced as the other stopped in the pathway and let loose a terrifying death cry. In the same instant, I shot the warrior holding the torch in the chest. His forward progress halted as his legs left the ground, and he rocked backward into the dirt. The torch fell across his legs, but he made no effort to remove it.

Without looking, I handed Billy my rifle, and he replaced it with the loaded musket. Even though a musket is not as accurate as a long rifle, I believed the second Indian was within range. He stood looking at our cabin as if the devil himself had suddenly appeared. I confess, my hands were shaking a bit when I fired. The ball hit the warrior in the thigh, and he spun in a circle while keeping to his feet. He whooped again, much less fiercely, and hobbled back down the path, leaving his companion lying in the dirt, the torch sputtering out.

"I think they may be leaving," I ventured to those behind me when several minutes had passed in relative quiet.

"You killed 'em, Pa," Billy said with hushed wonder in his voice as he peered at the dead warrior lying in the path — the only man I ever killed.

The reality of that act settled on me slowly. I shook my head to clear the thought and concentrate on the immediate threat. I was somewhat surprised that I could shrug it off so easily.

Billy was staring at me with wide eyes. I turned back to the window without responding. Together, like every other cabin in the settlement, we stood watch the rest of the long night.

The next day we dealt with the first deaths in our settlement.

At first light, several of the men ventured out to determine the damage. The warrior I shot was still lying in our path, so Will and I dragged him to the woods for the wolves, or his comrades if they cared to retrieve him.

Then we went to see to the Bennetts.

The remains of their cabin still burned as the morning sun cut through the ground mist. The smoke trailed away from us as we approached, so the smell was not evident until we stood beside the ruins.

John Bennett lay face down in front of his cabin. He had been scalped, and his long gun was missing. His wife's body was in the collapsed doorway, charred and smoking. We never found the body of his son and never saw him again, either.

A mile from our cabin, a beautiful stand of white pines stood on a steeply banked hill. The pines overlooked a stream where other cabins had been built in the last few years. We carried John and Mary Bennett there in the evening and laid them in the first graves of our new cemetery.

The peepers were loud in the valley below while Jane read a passage from the Bible. Being the daughter of a minister, Jane sometimes led prayer groups, and families often turned to her in times of need.

The distraught group of fifteen or so were moved to tears. Some of the tears were shed for the Bennetts, whom we had only recently got to know, but some of the tears were for ourselves, as well. This was our first fatal encounter with the Indians, and we feared it would not be our last.

CHAPTER 20
Independence

August 29th, 1776
The Pennsylvania Frontier

In late summer, a rider came into the settlement and called for us to all come to the fort. He said he had the most portentous news. My boys, William and Joe, came running to find me in the cornfield where I was clearing weeds.

Along with most of the neighbors, I made my way to the fort. Streaked with dust, the man said he was from the county seat in Hanna's Town. He stood on the front porch beside a black horse that was still breathing hard.

We gathered together, everyone talking at once and asking the man what had happened. He stood stoically, not saying a word until the last straggler came up the road.

"Is that all of ya?" he asked, seemingly disappointed that he did not draw a larger audience. I figured the man arrived to announce the outcome of a decisive battle until he deliberately unrolled an oversized sheet of paper and began to read. (5)

A hush fell upon the gathering, and we heard these words for the first time: "*In Congress, July Fourth, 1776. A Declaration by the Representatives of the United States of America*

— "

And that's all the further he got. The cheer that went up, I believe they heard at Fort Pitt. There was no doubt in anyone's mind what those words meant. All the meetings, the arguments, the attempts to satisfy the British peacefully had fallen by the wayside. They had thrown the Olive Branch back in our faces. Now, we were declaring our independence!

The man waited for the clamor to reside, cleared his throat, and continued. "Ah-hem. *'When in the course of human events, it becomes necessary for one people to dissolve the political bands which have connected them with another, and to assume among the powers of the earth, the separate and equal station to which the laws of nature and of nature's God entitle them, a decent respect to the opinions of mankind requires that they should declare the causes which impel them to the separation.'*"

The man paused and peered at the gathering over the top of the document as if he knew the effect his next words would have.

"*'We hold these truths to be self-evident, that all men are created equal* — '"

The second round of cheering was louder than the first. Thinking back on it chills me to this day. In time, the crowd settled down to hear the rest. Men and women listened with unnoticed tears blurring their vision. The children looked on in confusion and then wandered off, but every adult in the settlement stood in the hot afternoon sun and heard the document read through to the end.

The words we heard — the grievances against our King and his government and the promises of freedom and righteousness — expressed the thoughts and the arguments that had consumed us for years. These were the words we wanted to hear, that we had waited for, that we

154

were willing to fight and die for. These were the words that would impact our future and the future of our country.

"I'm worried about John," Jane expressed to me a month or so later. "He's strong-headed."

"He's a White," I responded.

John was still in Kittanning with Samuel. We did not know how he would respond to this Declaration of Independence, as it was being called. He had always expressed Loyalist views, so I shared Jane's concern.

"John's an intelligent man," I said, keeping the conversation light. "He may have a different opinion, but we're on a course that cannot be changed."

"Except by defeat."

"True," I agreed. "Except if we lose."

Jane finished putting plates on the table and turned to look at me. "Do ye think there will be fighting out here?"

"We have our own problems," I said, putting an arm around her. I hugged her close, something I did far too seldom. "I don't believe we'll see an army this far west. The Indians, though, they'll be more of a problem. Of that, I'm sure."

Word had arrived the previous month of more trouble in New York, especially along the Mohawk River. The Iroquois were burning homesteads and forcing settlers back east.

"Will they come south?" she asked, still leaning against me.

"I don't know," I answered truthfully. "I wouldn't be surprised if they do. The Mingo are already on the warpath, as we've seen. So far, only the Delaware are staying out of the war. We have to hope that continues."

Jane looked into my face. Her eyes were ready to over-flow. "If there's fighting, ye'll have to go, then, won't ye?"

"I'm in the militia, like everyone else."

She buried her face against my chest, and we held each other until the boys came in for supper. They did not ask why the front of my shirt was wet.

The summer progressed, with very little good news from the east. In late August, the British defeated General Washington at the Battle of Long Island. It was a complete rout, but Washington, lucky once again, managed to with-draw his entire army before it could be captured. The Brit-ish now held the city of New York.

Somewhat better news arrived at the end of September. Washington had regrouped and held off a British attack at a place called Harlem Heights on the island of Manhattan. It was the first real success Washington and our new army could claim. Morale improved considerably, and there was actually talk of victory.

Late in October, as we settled for the night, "Halo the house!" brought us to the cabin door. Two men stood at the far end of our path, hidden by the shadows. Each was holding the reins of a weary horse, and it took me a second to realize it was John and Samuel. They were leaning against each other in a troubling way.

"Samuel!" I shouted and started toward them, Jane close behind.

"Stay back!" Samuel called, holding up a hand to stop us. "We're sick. Don't come closer."

I held out my arm to stop Jane from running past me. "What's happened, Sam?"

"We've got the smallpox," he said. "We need your help.

156

Where's Mary? She's not at our place."

"She's with the Thompsons," I said, moving closer until I could see Samuel more clearly. Ugly blisters covered most of his face and his lips were puffy and cracked. John did not look as bad, but he, too, was obviously sick and weak.

"I don't want anyone to come near us," John said. "We need to rest. We'll stay in Sam's barn, so we don't spread it."

Jane stepped closer. "Ye don't scare me, bràthair," she said with her usual conviction. "Yer both going to our barn, where I can keep a proper eye on ye. Now go!"

"She's right," I said, stopping their protest. I turned to Jane. "Find Hannah and Mary Elizabeth. I'll get them settled in."

Jane hesitated, trying to decide who could be of more help. Then, she got hold of William and told him to find Hannah while she went for Mary Elizabeth.

Smallpox was a mystery to us all. It killed many of those infected, though many unaccountably survived. It seemed to have more to do with God's will than any care you could provide the stricken. I remembered hearing stories of a Puritan minister back east claiming that infusing a drop of the puss from a smallpox eruption into a healthy person's vein prevented that person from getting a bad case of the disease.

That sounded like witchcraft to me. The one thing I knew about smallpox was to avoid touching the sick person or anything they touched. As I settled Samuel and John in a corner of our barn, I made sure that everything nearby could be burned. None of the animals would come in contact with the straw on which they made their beds.

Smallpox had hit numerous settlements during the last year but, until now, we had no cases. Yet. I was determined to care for my brother and brother-in-law and not endanger the rest of the community.

I brought the sick men a bucket of clean spring water. They attacked it with the ferocity of a man lost in the desert.

"How do you think this happened," I asked after they had quenched their thirst and settled back on the piled-up straw. Both of them were exhausted.

"I know how it happened," Sam replied through broken lips. "Six traders came downriver three weeks ago from the Indian Territory. One was sick, so we made him stay in a cabin by himself. He died next day. The other men traded pelts with the men at the fort and then went on their way. Wasn't long before I got the fever."

John spoke up. "I got sick the same time, but it hasn't hit me so hard as Sam. Can't explain that. Other men in the fort who've seen the pox before said we could still make others sick."

"Were there others?" I asked.

Both men nodded, and Sam said, "Six men got sick the same time as us. All have gone back to their families."

Hannah interrupted us, flying into the barn, face red, and streaked with tears. She saw John laying back in the straw and rushed for him with a cry of anguish. I scooped her up as she tried to push past me. "You can care for him," I said, holding her tight, "just don't touch him."

"John!" she cried, the tears now in full flood.

Jane and Mary Elizabeth were right behind her. Jane took Hannah from my arms and tried to calm her.

"What can we do for you?" Mary Elizabeth asked her husband in a level, tight voice. Her eyes also overflowed, but she maintained a calm we had come to expect, even as she gazed on his ravaged face.

Sam tiredly shook his head. "I'd like more water and a bowl of mush," he said, sounding very much like my youngest boy.

Over the next week, Jane and I watched their children while the men's wives became nursemaids. John had a much milder case of the disease and was able to walk outside within a week.

Samuel, however, languished in abject misery for days. The pustules became more pronounced and then broke as his fever returned. Mary Elizabeth practically lived in our barn. Day and night, we saw her going to the spring or back to her house to make more food. She never grew weary and never stopped praying for Sam's recovery.

During one visit, Samuel told me that he wanted me to go to Kittanning.

"I won't be able to return for a long time, Fergus," he said. "I can't abandon my company, and right now, there's only Sergeant Culpepper to maintain order, and he's more interested in his own welfare. I need you to go."

"I'm not an officer," I protested.

A weak smile crossed his face. "*I* am," Sam said, "and I can give you my warrant. From this moment on, you're Captain Fergus Moorhead, Tenth Company, Mackay's Battalion."

Well, when he put it that way, how could I refuse?

CHAPTER 21
Militiaman

December 21st, 1776
Kittanning, Pennsylvania

Fort Kittanning was a miserable place.

The poorly built stockade stood on flat land beside the mighty Allegheny. It was surrounded by a scattering of cabins and lean-tos that looked like they could wash away with the first heavy rain. Mud and more mud — that was my first impression.

The river, however, was a sight to see. In all the time I had lived in this land, I never made it as far as the river. At this point, the Allegheny was 350 yards wide. A sparsely wooded island stood near the western shore covered in scrub and bare trees.

From the hill, the winter sun reflected off the water in a dazzling array of colors. Up close, the surface of the water rippled a deep brown.

"It's beautiful," I said as we worked our way down to the fort.

"It's hell on earth," John responded, looking up at the light snow beginning to fall. "At least there won't be mosquitoes."

We had ridden the twenty-five miles from our settlement to Kittanning as soon as John was strong enough to sit his horse.

Samuel, however, was not going anywhere for a long time to come. He was no longer contagious, so he had moved back to his cabin. We all thanked God for his deliverance.

Sam insisted that John return with me. My warrant to command Sam's company was legal, but John was needed as a witness. They both agreed that Colonel Mackay would be highly skeptical if a man simply rode up to the fort and announced he was in command of a company. Even if his name was Moorhead.

I expressed my concerns about never leading a group of men before.

"Never had I," Sam said, waving a dismissing hand. "There's nothing to it. Just act like you're in charge, and they'll believe it. I'll write a letter to Mackay. He'll be pleased to have you, you'll see."

With those words of encouragement, I prepared to leave.

As I packed a kit, Jane stood silently, watching me from the doorway. Then we walked out to where John and my horse stood waiting, our breath showing in the frosty air.

She pulled me down for a quick kiss. We had said our farewells the previous night. "Ye will promise to be careful, then." she said, not really asking a question.

"There're more than four hundred men at the fort," I said with a smile. "How could anything happen?"

She smiled in return and was still smiling when I looked back from the road. Jane raised her hand goodbye. With a tug at my heart, I realized that this was the first time we had been separated from each other in many years — not since my first venture to this land in '69. I waved back and turned onto the road west.

Jane stood in the cold afternoon sun until we were gone from her sight, a sliver of ice in her heart.

A sentry challenged our approach to the gate, even though we had passed other men working outside the fort. The guard read over Sam's letter and told us to go to the Commander's office attached to one side of the stockade. Barracks and supply buildings filled the remaining walls. In the open central area, dozens of men were busy loading supply wagons.

Colonel Aeneas Mackay was short and round, pushing fifty, with the ruddy complexion of a Highlander. However, compared to many of his countrymen, he did not look much like a fighting man, and I did not think he looked happy.

"I'm mighty glad yer here, lad," he said, placing Sam's letter on his wood slab desk. "Ye'll be needed. We've received orders to march for New Jersey and save General Washington."

I was shocked speechless. He must have read the look on my face. "Don't worry, lad," he said with a gruff laugh. "We need a company to stay here and guard the stores while we're away. Now, yer freshly arrived and new to our command, so I'm appointing you."

"How do you intend to get all these men to New Jersey?" I asked, still not believing what I was hearing.

"We'll march, of course," Mackay said with conviction. He sat down behind his desk with an expulsion of air. "As soon as we can get ourselves organized, we'll head for

162

Hanna's Town and then east on the road over the mountains. Maybe next week." He looked out the window at the thickening snow and shook his head. "Find yer men, Captain. That'll be all."

Sergeant Culpepper was an enormous man who looked as if he could singlehandedly consume the majority of our meager supplies. With a bulging stomach, a full black beard, and a dark scowl, he looked me up and down as if appraising a new horse and none too happy with what he found.

"Gather the men," I said without any preamble. Culpepper made no indication that he heard me. "Now, Sergeant!"

"Yes, sir," he grumbled and lumbered off.

I looked at John for support. He only shrugged. "Don't take it too hard. Wasn't any better with Sam."

My first job was to work with Quartermaster Douglas to assess the amount of food and ammunition the departing battalion intended to leave behind. Both were practically nonexistent. Douglas was less pleased with the impending march than his commander.

"I ain't leavn' you much," he said to me one day, "but it's more than we can carry, so be pleased with that."

"Why leave anything?" I wanted to know. Keeping a company at the fort simply to guard a few dozen barrels of powder and dried beef seemed like a waste of manpower to me. Then again, I was happy not to be marching with them.

Douglas took his pipe from his mouth and looked at me for a minute before answering. "It is all political," he said with a slow Virginia drawl. "There's men who live nearby, and they have the ear of the committee in Hanna's

Town. One is a Mr. William Lochry, the other's John Moore. Important men, it seems. Their letter woke the devil, but Mackay has his orders. So, to placate those gentlemen, you'll stay behind to show the flag, so to speak." (6)

"Do we have a flag?" I asked.

"Course we don't have a flag, you idiot! We don't even have any food!" And with that, he turned back to his paperwork, dismissing me from all thought.

Sergeant Culpepper told me in no uncertain terms that the forty men remaining at the fort could not make it to March without replenishment from Fort Pitt.

"When is that expected?" I asked.

"When the river thaws," was his answer.

"When does the river thaw?"

"When it thaws," he said and walked away from me. Discipline was a serious problem.

Mackay and his second, Lieutenant Colonel George Wilson, did their best to gather supplies from the countryside. They sent men who could be trusted to return to the settlements for food and ammunition. Some returned, some did not.

The men were extremely unhappy to learn that they were facing a march of more than 300 miles in the dead of winter. They had 'volunteered' to be in the militia to protect the frontier and their homesteads. Never had they foreseen conscription into the Continental Army.

Christmas came and went without acknowledgment. Nor did anyone celebrate the new year. Then on January 6th, 1777, 420 men assembled in the parade ground, buffeted by a driving, wet snow blowing straight off the river.

Mackay and Wilson rode to the front of the battalion. Mackay sat for a while, looking at his men as if trying to decide what to say. In the end, he turned to Wilson and quietly ordered, "By company, march!"

Ill-equipped and in the middle of winter, the battalion marched southeast to Hanna's Town, where they managed to gather a few supplies. Then they took Braddock's Road east all the way to Quibbletown, New Jersey.

With only twelve horses to drag the wagons, no tents, and dwindling reserves, they trudged through a brutal month of snow and freezing rain. Dozens died and even more deserted.

The ragged battalion struggled into Washington's camp in dire condition. History records their winter march as a truly epic story of the War. Both Mackay and George Wilson, his second in command, died of pneumonia shortly after arriving in New Jersey.

General Washington accepted the battalion into the Continental Army and commissioned them as the 8th Pennsylvania, but they shall forever be remembered as Mackay's Battalion.

CHAPTER 22
The Captains Moorhead

February 21st to March 16th, 1777
Kittanning, Pennsylvania

Three weeks after my commission as a Captain in the militia, I found myself the Commanding Officer of Fort Kittanning with a complement of forty men. The frontier was safe now!

I made John my adjutant and promoted an apparently intelligent man to sergeant so that the company could divide into two platoons. Culpepper was not pleased with my decision.

A week following the battalion's departure, I discovered that our stores were even more depleted than expected. Then I observed three men coming back to the fort with an armful of beaver pelts. I summoned Culpepper.

"Sergeant, what do you believe is our objective?" I asked the big man standing at attention in front of me.

"Objective, sir?"

"Yes," I said patiently. "What are we expected to accomplish here?"

The sergeant stood staring at me for a second. "Why, fight the Indians!" he finally responded.

I pointed to the lean-tos propped against the side of the

fort. "Those Indians?" I asked. On a dry piece of land, four warriors and two squaws sat in the sun with their backs against the rough timbers.

"Why, no sir," Culpepper scoffed. "Them's Delaware from upriver. They're friendly. Come once a month to trade pelts for food."

"The same food that you and your men are running out of, even as we speak?"

The sergeant shuffled his feet. "Well, sir, it's how we get paid. If it weren't for the Indians bringing us pelts, we'd have nothing to show for our time when we go home."

Standing in the freezing wind, it was my turn to stare at the sergeant. This, I realized, was a fundamental problem of keeping a standing army instead of militiamen, who were called up only when required. The need to keep men on station in a remote location was self-defeating.

"Sergeant Culpepper," I said with a firm voice, "you will cease this trade at once. Now that I know what's going on, I'll be keeping an eye on you and the men. Is that understood? We must keep what food we have. Your pay will be coming when we're relieved."

Culpepper looked skeptical. "When will that be?"

"When will that be. *Sir.*"

"When will that be, sir?"

"When the river thaws."

The outpost was intended to protect the growing settlements scattered along the riverbank in each direction. Only twenty or so people now lived in the village of Kittanning. It had once been a thriving Indian town.

The fort also provided an advance warning for the militia contingent at Fort Pitt. We possessed a small-bore cannon that could fire on any hostiles coming downriver — supposing there was enough powder to fire it and assuming the men could hit a canoe in the middle of the river. They had never practiced.

I seriously doubted that I could make any substantial changes in the way the men did business. We mustered each morning, practiced the required military drills, and did our best to be professional.

I established hunting parties to try and replenish our failing supplies, and, in early February, I sent a letter to Hanna's Town explaining how desperate things were. I received no reply.

So it went. Winter grew fierce, and I gave serious consideration to abandoning the fort and sending everyone home. In truth, I was surprised each morning at roll call to find any men remaining at all.

Then, on February 14th, Samuel rode into the fort.

That night, Sam, John, and I sat in the Commanding Officer's cramped quarters, sharing the warmth of a fire and each other's company.

Sam was still exceedingly weak, and his face would show the scars of his sickness for the rest of his life.

"You shouldn't have come," I said. "We're doing all right. You need to get your strength back."

He pulled the blanket more securely around his shoulders and puffed on his pipe. "I had to come, Fergus. When I heard you were here all alone, I couldn't stay away. This post is now my responsibility. So tell me what you've been up to."

We talked well into the night. I told him of my troubles with Culpepper, and he was not the least bit surprised. I wanted to know how Jane and my children were faring and did they miss me.

It was wonderful to have him back.

We spent a month together at Fort Kittanning, the two Captain Moorheads and Lieutenant White. Although I maintained my rank, no one doubted that Sam was the Commanding Officer. Even Sergeant Culpepper's attitude improved with the weather.

The constant snow of January and February subsided suddenly at the start of March and the temperature rose. Within a week, the ground was clear except in the deep shadows and where the drifts had piled up against the hills.

The river, which had been solid enough to walk on at Christmas time, was now cracking in an alarmingly loud way, echoing across the valley like cannon shots. In the middle of the night, I would snap awake to a particularly loud explosion and listen for the sentry's cry of an attack. None came, for it was only the ice breaking.

At last, on March 16th, it was time for me to head home. A young man from our settlement named Andrew Simpson was to accompany me part of the way. He carried letters to the committee in Hanna's Town, once again begging for more supplies.

I knew Andrew and his parents quite well and looked forward to the company. I said my goodbyes to the men. Even Sergeant Culpepper shook my hand and wished me well.

Sam gave me a hearty hug. "We'll be relieved soon, Fergus," he said as I mounted my horse. "Tell everyone to look for us in a month or so."

"I will," I said.

Andrew and I rode out the gate and gave a wave while the sentries snapped to attention, almost like real soldiers. As we passed, I saw that the group of Indians always squatting in the sun near the gate was no longer there. A half-formed thought left my mind as we turned uphill on the road home.

PART FOUR

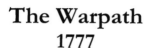

The Warpath
1777

CHAPTER 23
Blanket Hill

Sunday, March 16th, 1777
The Kittanning Path, Pennsylvania

The ground was sloppy under the horse's feet, so we progressed at a leisurely pace. With the warm sun on our faces, we discussed how quickly spring was approaching.

I felt pleased with myself. My time at Fort Kittanning had been uneventful, which is sometimes the most you can hope for in the army. The company accomplished some important work, setting things in order after the hasty departure of the battalion. We produced accurate records of everything that remained, and I put an end to the beaver pelt trade that was depleting our stores. Why, even Sergeant Culpepper had started to treat me like a legitimate officer.

I rode beside Andrew, perhaps with a slight smile on my face. Off to the left of the path, a robin whistled, always a dependable sign of the coming spring.

Andrew seemed as comfortable as me, riding in the warm morning sun. I asked him, "Will you be coming back to the settlement when you deliver the letters?" I knew Andrew was homesick. He had recently married Bill Lowry's daughter, Sarah, only to leave for the Kittanning post.

"Not sure, Captain. They may have a response that your brother would require right away."

"Well, if you do," I said, smiling at the young man, "I want you and Sarah and your folks for Sunday dinner soon."

"We'd appreciate that, Captain. Thank you."

"I'm not a captain anymore, Andrew. You can call me Fergus."

"Thank you," he said with a smile, "Mr. Moorhead."

Suddenly a crashing sound off to our left, north of the trail, caused us both to pull up. The foliage shook ahead, and a ten-point buck burst onto the path. The beast stopped in the clearing, seeing us for the first time, dipped his head, and then bolted. In a heartbeat, he was there and gone again.

My pulse surged with the first sound, and it brought me back to the reality of our situation. I had been foolish not to be on guard at all times. We were in the wilderness, riding alone, with unknown dangers lurking in every shadow. I thought back to the fort, the fact that the Indians had not been there this morning.

"Andrew," I said, "I want you to be exceptionally careful going south. It's a long thirty miles to Hanna's Town." The plan was for us to go our separate ways seven miles out of Kittanning, where Andrew would ride south, and I would continue to the settlement.

Andrew sensed the seriousness of my voice. "Of course, Mr. Moorhead," he replied.

"Used to be, the further south you go, the safer it was," I continued, "but things are changing out here. The tribes we thought were our friends are being influenced by the British. They're all turning against us."

"Not the Delaware," Andrew said. "They all seem

174

happy when they come to the fort."

"Well, that may have changed when I stopped the men trading for pelts. There's fighting in Virginia, somewhere south of Hanna's Town. The more of us there is, and the more we push the Indians west, the more they'll fight us. Truth is, Indians are unpredictable. Remember that."

Andrew nodded his head. "Yes, sir."

He was a smart lad and deserved a long life.

I looked around to get my bearings. "Tell me," I said, trying to lighten the mood, "do you know why they call this Blanket Hill?"

Andrew shook his head. "I know there was a massacre here, but I don't know what happened. Please…"

Making myself comfortable in the saddle yet eyeing the forest as we rode, I quietly told Andrew the story of Colonel John Armstrong and his destruction of the Indian town at Kittanning back in '57. There had been a massacre, all right, just not where we now rode.

"After camping near here, Armstrong and most of his force continued to Kittanning. He left twelve men behind under a Lieutenant named Hogg with orders to attack a smaller group of Indians that the scouts had spotted. Hogg's men left all their blanket rolls and packs and set out to attack the Indians in the morning.

"Hogg attacked the war party only to discover it was much bigger than expected. He lost half his men in the fight. Hogg, himself was gravely wounded and died on the way to Kittanning to meet up with Armstrong. All their blankets and packs were abandoned at the top of that hill," I said, pointing at the steep rise ahead. "That's why it's called Blanket Hill."

Young Andrew sat up tall in his saddle and peered at the deep undergrowth on each side of the trail.

"It is easy to see how those savages could hide in a forest as thick as this," he observed.

Right then, I should have noticed that the robins were no longer singing.

"I wonder what happened to all the blankets?" Andrew asked.

It was the last thing he ever said.

An explosion of musket shots splintered the still air.

A mist of blood blew out of the side of Andrew's head, and he and his horse crashed to the ground as one. Piercing war-whoops came from the side of the trail, curdling my blood.

I dug in my heels and the old mare surged forward, as frightened by the suddenness of the attack as I. Mud flew from her hooves. I ducked low beside her neck to make as small a target as possible. She only made four strides.

Another volley of musket fire sounded behind me. I felt a ball pass my cheek, and another carved a line across my thigh. My mare screamed and pitched headfirst onto the path. There was no time to step clear.

Crushed beneath the weight of the horse, I tried frantically to free my rifle from its leather case. I pushed with one foot against her back, but the old girl had pinned the gun and my right leg. She was dead, and I was about to be.

I pushed and squirmed and freed my leg and rose to my feet as three warriors surrounded me. One held a tomahawk in a most threatening manner, and the others aimed muskets at me even though I suspected they were no longer loaded.

In a matter of moments, another half dozen warriors came out of the forest. All blazoned with war paint and decorated with feathers.

An Indian approached and shoved me hard on the shoulder. I fell back against the body of my mare and looked up at the face I thought would be the last I ever saw.

With a start, I recognized the leader as Gelelemend, the man still carrying my hatchet. He was equally surprised to see me. His lips curled in an unfriendly way.

"Our paths cross again," he said.

"Why have you attacked us?" I asked as a large warrior secured my wrists with hide strips. "We have always been friends with the Delaware."

Without a word, Gelelemend turned and walked back down the trail. Two warriors hauled me to my feet, and another pulled the saddle and rifle from my poor mare. He thrust the saddle at me and indicated I should follow Gelelemend.

He kept my precious long rifle. Pa's rifle.

Pushed and shoved, I stumbled back to the point where we were attacked. To my horror, a warrior was scalping poor Andrew. He held the bloody mess in the air and shouted his death cry. My own hair stood on end, believing it was not to be mine for long.

Gelelemend was searching the bag Andrew carried on his chest. He pulled the letters out, broke the seal, and scanned them quickly. So, I realized he also could read as well as speak perfect English. Then, to my surprise, Gelelemend sat on Andrew's dead horse, pulled a pencil from the pouch, and began to write on the back of the letter!

While this was happening, while I stood in shock at the speed my life had changed, two warriors stripped Andrew naked. They bundled his clothes and boots and added them to a pack by the side of the path.

A warrior threw a pair of moccasins at my chest. He pointed at my feet and shoved me down into the mud. Struggling with bound wrists, I pulled my boots off and replaced them with the old deer-hide moccasins. I understood the Indians did not want my boots leaving a trail that would-be rescuers could identify as belonging to a white man. With relief, I realized that I would live for a while longer.

Gelelemend finished his note and carefully placed it inside Andrew's saddle. He then propped the saddle against a tree near the mutilated body of that gentle lad.

He smiled at me. "You wonder what I write," he said, indicating the saddle and letter. "It is a warning to the other white men. You will be remembered."

That did not sound good. "Why are you doing this," I tried again. "Why am I being spared."

"Three times, we shoot and miss. The Father permits three strikes with musket or tomahawk, then you must live. For now."

I tried another tack. "I thought we were friends."

"You are alive," he replied and walked away.

With a gruff order to his warriors, we left the trail and headed directly north.

To Indian Territory.

In a single file, we moved at a fast pace, eventually coming to a clearing where twenty more warriors waited. With this group were five white prisoners — two young women, two boys no more than eight or nine years old, and a man about my age.

I was led to the spot where the prisoners sat in a circle. They were all dirty and wide-eyed but unhurt, for the most part. A purple mass closed the man's right eye. None of them spoke as a warrior threw me to the ground and tied my hands to the line that connected all of them. An Indian took the saddle I had carried from the Kittanning path.

The children looked like brothers. They sat side by side, heads bowed, dirt-covered faces streaked with tears. The women were just as abject. One was a redhead. Her dress was torn and tied together with cloth strips. Her bruised arms showed the trauma she had suffered. She never looked at me and clung to the arm of the other girl.

The second girl was a pretty brunette of nineteen. She was nowhere as damaged looking or dirty as her companion, who held her so tightly. She looked at me and smiled grimly, as if ashamed to be meeting like this.

With a shout, a warrior yanked on the deer hide strap holding us all bound together. We struggled to our feet as well as we could with our hands tied and dutifully followed.

As we walked deeper into the vast forest, I tried to talk to the man and ask him if he knew where we were headed or what our fate might be. In gruff, short sentences, he told me his name was John Tanner and that he was from Fort Pitt. He refused to say anything more, so I decided to bide my time and watch for a possible chance to escape.

Through the long day, we marched in single file, hungry and wet, slipping and sliding on the cold ground, covered in mud and tears, toward a doubtful future.

CHAPTER 24
The Great Shamokin Path

March 20th, 1777
Punxsutawney, Pennsylvania

I spent my first night in captivity curled against a towering oak tree. We prisoners were spaced around the base of the tree, still tied together. A warrior sat on my saddle with his back against another tree, the hide rope secure in his hands. If we so much as stretched our legs, his eyes popped open.

I sat beside the young brunette. In whispered tones, she said her name was Rebecca. She had been taken from a settlement on the west bank of the Allegheny and did not know the fate of her family. She was far from her cabin getting water at a stream when a war party came out of the forest. They moved so fast she had no time to scream.

Rebecca said the other girl's name was Mary, and the boys were Mary's brothers, Robert and Ryan. They had been captives for a week or more, also captured near Fort Pitt. Mary spoke little, even to Rebecca, but she learned that the Indians had burned Mary's cabin and killed her parents in front of her and her brothers. Indians had attacked other cabins in the settlement at the same time. Mary and her brothers were the only ones not killed and scalped.

"The boys won't talk to me, just to her. I think those Indians may have *touched* her," Rebecca said under her breath and shuddered in the night air. "Please, sir," she whispered after a short silence, "allow me to lean against you for warmth."

Without waiting for a response, she shifted her position. The Indian guard was instantly awake. He gave the tether a sharp snap but did not interfere. Rebecca moved against my side and leaned her head on my shoulder. She wore a thin homespun dress with no shawl nor bonnet to keep her warm.

I placed my arm across her thin shoulders, and we fell asleep for an hour or so. It was definitely warmer.

At first light, we were dragged to our feet. Our guard threw the saddle at me and indicated I was to resume the burden. Immediately, the Indians set out, and we soon came onto a broad, clear path running east and west. I knew of an Indian trail that crossed half of Pennsylvania, but I did not know of anyone who had ever been on it. In the east, they called it the Great Shamokin Path. It ran 150 miles from Kittanning all the way to Shamokin on the Susquehanna. It would have been an excellent road for settlers moving west except for the fact that it passed through Indian Territory.

Later, our captors stopped at a creek so we could drink a handful of water, my first since the ambush. Flinging the hated saddle aside, I dropped face down in the icy water. I thought I might drown, I drank so much.

And soon, another problem arose. Pitiful cries from Rebecca forced the Indians to stop, despite vicious yanks on the tether that held us.

Tanner and I turned our backs and made our water as the women squatted in the bushes as far away as the tether allowed. The Indians ignored them completely. With some concern, I observed that neither boy relieved himself.

We had not eaten anything, and the Indians did not seem to care. I tried to get the attention of Gelelemend to complain about the treatment of the women and the young boys. He refused to acknowledge my existence.

Although Tanner would still not converse, he was willing to help the young women and the boys along the trail. We assisted the women in crossing streams, hampered as they were by long skirts. I tried to leave the saddle behind twice, but our guard insisted I continue lugging it along.

Traveling on this open trail that crossed meadows and dived through deep forested valleys offered me a chance to observe our captors more closely. Twenty-four Delaware made up the party, and my 'friend' Gelelemend was their leader. He now carried my long rifle.

The warriors were still dressed in their winter clothes. Deer hide leggings with heavy hunting shirts were the most common attire. One or two wore beaver pelt cloaks around their shoulders. Their heads were either completely bald or plucked clean on the sides with a stiffened tuft on top. Each warrior sported frightful streaks of red, yellow, and blue paint upon their faces, decorations meant to put the fear of God in anyone who saw them. It worked, let me tell you.

As evening approached, we came to a well-established village with a dozen or more poorly constructed cabins and lean-tos scattered haphazardly about. There was no stockade to provide any security. I believed it to be Punxsutawney, the closest Delaware village to our settlement.

We drew the attention of the inhabitants who crawled from their hovels as we approached. They were a scroungy lot, mostly old men and women, and poked at us in an unfriendly manner. A few of the warriors in our party greeted the old folks in pleasant tones, and I assumed they were family members.

As on the previous night, we were all tied to a tree. However, this time, an old woman was permitted to give us water and a strip of dried venison for our supper. I sucked mine until it was soft enough to chew and watched Rebecca try to entice Mary and the boys to eat some. They were suffering so that I feared for their lives. The Indians did not keep sickly captives alive for long.

Soon we came to regret the fact that spring was coming early. The weather may have been improving, and the snow melting from the dark forest shadows, but it brought another misery. As the sun sank lower in the west, the no-see-ums swarmed us like smoke from a fire.

There was no fighting them off. They bit every part of our exposed skin, flew up our noses and into our ears. For once, the Indians had the advantage. The bear grease they applied so liberally to their hair and skin was as repellent to the midges as it was to us.

Gelelemend seemed to notice us only when he could relish in our despair. He laughed as we slapped at the horrible little creatures.

"The Lenape people have lived in this place for fifty years," he said, looking down at me with a curl in his lip. "Why, I do not know. We call this place *Punk-wsu-tènay*."

He laughed without mirth as I waved a midge away from my face. "Now you know what it means — the place of the living ash! Eat your meat, Moorhead. Tomorrow we go to *Chin-glaca-mouche*, the great town of the *Lenni Lenape* people. Then we will see if you live another day."

We slept poorly that night, and the morning light found us exhausted, swollen, and pox-marked. As I roused myself for the continuation of the march, Mary broke the morning stillness with a cry of anguish and despair. Her youngest brother Ryan had died during the night.

With no regret, we left the miserable village behind us and walked a day and a night without sleep. Mary and her brother sobbed and stumbled in their grief. Tanner and I had buried the boy in a shallow grave we scratched out with our bare hands. The surviving siblings were inconsolable. The more they cried, the more viciously the warrior leading us pulled on the tether. At one point, Mary fell to the ground and refused to move despite the whipping she received.

To stop her torture, I stepped in front of the warrior wielding the strap as bravely as I could manage. He stopped hitting the girl and stared menacingly at me, then he simply turned and walked away. Rebecca and I pulled Mary to her feet, rearranged her tattered dress, and urged her on with gentle words. Head down and tears flowing, she followed after us.

On the morning of the second day, we stood on the banks of a deep river that seemed to flow north. Further in the distance, smoke rose from dozens of cooking fires in a large village.

Our captors forced us to sit on the muddy riverbank while four of them proceeded downstream to announce our arrival. Soon we heard a piercing cry, and shots rang out. A handful of dugout canoes shoved off from the far bank and paddled our way. Each canoe was eight or ten feet long, paddled by three men.

When the boats reached our position, we were untied and forced to squat in the center of the boats. As tired and frightened as I was, I could not help but admire the craftsmanship and time it took to create such lightweight boats from a single tree.

With long, steady strokes, the paddlers swung the dugouts into the swiftly moving stream. In minutes, our party shot downstream and across the river to a sandy beach where a hundred Indians awaited us.

We had come to the town of Chinglacamouche, named for the branch of the Susquehanna that 'almost joins.'

CHAPTER 25
The Gauntlet

March, 1777
Delaware Territory, Pennsylvania

The village was well situated on a spit of land surrounded on three sides by the river. The name Chinglacamouche referred to how the river made a sharp loop, almost coming together to form an island. The village could only be approached by land on its southern border where a stout stockade wall, more than ten feet high, provided protection.

Warriors, women, and children had all responded to the scalp whoops from our captors. The terrifying screams and the gunfire brought half the village down to the riverbank. As our boats grounded, unknown warriors reached out to drag us up the beach.

Fists waved in our faces and struck our bodies. Sticks and handfuls of sand pelted us. The shouts were deafening, further heightened by the handful of scrawny dogs that yelped and danced around us. I anticipated being torn to pieces and eaten on the spot.

An old woman came at me with a chunk of driftwood and made to strike until the warrior holding my restraint shouted at the harpy. I searched for my companions, but they were lost in the melee until Gelelemend ordered us all gathered together again.

The village itself came into view as we crested the steep rise from the beach. I had expected to see longhouses, as the Iroquois were once famous for, but it was not the case.

A broad dirt street stretched from the river to the stockade wall at the far end. On each side, thirty or more squat, irregularly shaped cabins lined the way. Not in straight lines and tightly packed as one would expect to find in Philadelphia, or even Chamber's Town for that matter. Instead, these log cabins sat at odd angles as if uncaringly placed by their builders. Smoke rose from a hole in the roof of some, while others utilized fire pits outside on gravel courtyards.

The comparison to our European communities was enhanced by the sight of extensive clearings for gardens and cornfields. Squaws who had not come to the beach stopped chopping at the dirt with their stone hoes to watch us pass.

The Indians deposited us in an enclosed corral that might have held cattle at one time. A five-foot-high fence of stout, sharp sticks formed one side, and a foul hut leaned against the southern stockade wall. A stinking ditch ran down the center of the corral.

While I struggled to make sense of my new situation, Rebecca led Mary and the boy to a dry area, where they collapsed in each other's arms. Tanner sat with them.

A face appeared at the entrance to the lean-to, and a scrawny, filthy, bearded creature emerged and limped toward me. So we were not the only prisoners. Though we all bleed from scratches and scrapes, we looked downright healthy compared to the man greeting us.

He was a gray skeleton, barefoot and covered in welts and bleeding sores. Tattered remnants of clothes hung on his thin shoulders like a death shroud.

"Do you have food?" the man asked without preamble. "Anything?"

I shook my head, stepping back from his outstretched claw-like hand. "I'm sorry," I said. "They've given us nothing."

The man looked like he would burst into tears. He turned and shambled back to his hovel without another word. I joined my party, as far away from the man as possible.

We sat together, huddled with our backs against each other through the rest of the day. Mary sobbed quietly, and Rebecca had her arm around Robert, who seemed unaware of his surroundings. Tanner sat by himself, head hung low between his knees, and acted as if the rest of us did not exist.

As the sun set and a cold dampness rose from the river, a crowd of warriors and squaws gathered outside our pen. They shouted and gestured in the most threatening manner, waving sticks, clubs, and thorny branches in the air. Soon, at least fifty Indians had formed two lines, one on each side of the street, leaving a space roughly six feet wide between the rows.

I then realized that Gelelemend was standing at the corral gate. He motioned to two warriors who entered our space and roughly pulled Tanner to his feet, and cut the bindings that held his wrists. When I looked to the other captive for an explanation, he was nowhere to be seen, evidently cowering in his lean-to.

One of them grasped Tanner's arms, pinning them behind his back while the other ripped his shirt and trousers from his body. Completely naked, he stood shaking and crying, trying to cover himself.

"No! No!" he wailed as they dragged him to the front of the double line. The Indians were in a frenzy. They hooted and shouted in their language, gesturing for Tanner to come forward. One warrior stepped behind Tanner and gave him a vicious shove. Tanner pitched forward onto his knees. Fear etched his face, and I could see his trembling from where I stood.

The other prisoner joined me at the barrier. Rebecca had Mary and the boy in a corner, wrapped in her arms, heads down. They, at least, did not see Tanner's shame.

"What is this?" I cried. "Why do they treat us this way?"

The man could not take his eyes off Tanner, who was hauled to his feet and pushed once more toward the line.

"This is their way of saying howdy," he said in a voice barely heard above the din of the horde. "We call it 'running the gauntlet.' It's an old-fashioned way of determining a man's worth."

"His worth?" I asked, appalled at what I was seeing.

"Or of executing him," the man shrugged. "If a man survives and shows that he has the proper mettle, they may let him live. I ran it and survived. My companion, my friend of ten years, did not."

Horrified, I watched Tanner as he staggered down the line, past the first warriors and squaws. He raised one hand to protect his face while clutching himself with the other. Blow after blow rained down upon him, and he staggered from one side of the line to the other, reeling from each successive strike. Already, he was bleeding on his back and shoulders.

Suddenly, he did the most unexpected thing. With his head down, Tanner screamed at the top of his lungs and charged a squaw who was brandishing a thorn encrusted club. So unexpected was his move that the woman fell back in surprise, creating a gap in the line of tormentors.

Tanner shot through the space the woman had vacated and, still yelling, ran for his life in the direction of the river. A few dogs pursued him, happy with the new sport.

The Indians forming the gauntlet line were so shocked that, for a heartbeat, no one moved. Then a mighty whoop came from a dozen throats, and they took after him, brandishing clubs and tomahawks in the air.

From where I stood behind the corral fence, I could see Tanner fling himself into the river like a man possessed. Water sprayed in all directions as he stroked frantically for the far shore. Several Indians charged into the river and quickly overtook the poor man.

Within minutes, an unconscious Tanner was dragged back to the waiting mob. A piece of his scalp hung loose, and blood covered his face.

Gelelemend turned to face me. "Now, you will see what happens to men when they try to escape." The sneer on his lips was as frightening as what they were preparing to do to Tanner.

Two stout tree limbs tied at the top formed a cross on the ground. They laid Tanner on the crossed section and secured his arms above his head. Then they raised him upright and braced the cross, so it stood on its own. Squaws came running with armloads of kindling, and within seconds, a fire blazed beneath the poor man's feet. It was then that Tanner regained consciousness, despite my prayer to God that he be already dead.

At first, Tanner did not realize what was happening until the growing flames drew his attention. Still uncomprehending, he stared at his bare feet as they began to smoke. Then he screamed, his body twisting frantically to break free. I turned away and fell to the ground, covering my ears, but it did not help. I can hear it, still.

The horrors of that night were just beginning. The crowd's attention soon refocused on the corral, where I sat in the mud, rocking back and forth in fear and praying to God for strength. Could I be brave enough to face what was coming? My sanity threatened to disappear as two warriors yanked me to my feet and ripped off my tattered clothes. My nakedness reflected the firelight from what had once been John Tanner.

The lines reformed. I knew that I must make it to the end of that bloody gauntlet as quickly as possible to have any chance of survival. If I did, would they let me live, or was it better to attack with my bare hands and hope for a quick end?

Trembling, trying to control my bladder, I looked at Gelelemend, the question clear on my face.

He gave me a curt nod. "If you reach the end, you will live."

At least that was something. I stepped slowly up to the front of the line and steeled myself for the inevitable.

Behind me, the other prisoner called out, "Run as fast as you can and protect your head. The men go for the head, the women go for your bollocks!"

I took a tentative step, and the noise rose to a fever pitch. Down the line, fierce determination showed on the faces of the warriors. On the faces of the squaws, I saw a leering hatred for everything a white man represented. The warriors may try to kill me, but the squaws were determined to inflict the most pain.

Without giving any warning, I rushed the line, making it past five or six on each side before anyone could strike me. As each person swung their weapon, I ducked toward the opposite side. I kept both hands about my head and sacrificed the rest of my body. A particularly vicious blow struck me between the legs, and I gasped, nearly falling to the ground. The absurd idea that I might have no more children flashed into my brain, pushing out the logical thought that I was being murdered.

An inhuman sound came from my throat like the moan of a wounded deer when you miss the kill shot. As they struck me, blood filled my right eye, so I could not judge the attacks from that side. My head reeled, my breath came in gasps.

I tripped and went down on one knee, and as I started to rise, some coward cast a handful of dirt in my face. Blind, I staggered on, the end of the line seen only as a dim light that drew me forward.

And then I was out.

Not even realizing I was no longer being struck, I collapsed face-first on the ground. I cried out and tried to struggle away as hands picked me up bodily. The single thought that came to me was that I would soon face as hideous a death as Tanner had. Then merciful darkness enveloped me, and I knew no more. (7)

CHAPTER 26
Cornplanter

March, 1777
Delaware Territory, Pennsylvania

Light seeped into my eyes as I slowly came alive. Voices whispered near me. My head buzzed, and my stomach heaved, and I tried to focus.

"He lives," a voice said.

I tried to sit up, but my back and shoulder refused to move. Two small hands restrained me.

"Stay, you need to stay still," a soft voice said.

Bit by bit, my encrusted eyes adjusted to the light, and relief flushed through me like a shot of whiskey. My darling Jane leaned over me, her forehead scrunched in concern, her black hair falling loose…

No, that was not right. I blinked again and concentrated on the woman sitting beside me. A sob of disappointment may have escaped my lips as I recognized Rebecca. Behind her, an Indian peered around her shoulder.

"Where…" croaked from my throat. I realized I was inside a log cabin, and my hands established that I lay on a pallet of corn husks, wrapped in a bear rug.

"You're all right, Fergus," Rebecca said quietly. She held a gourd to my lips, and I sipped a mouthful of water. "Lie back. Right now, you need to sleep."

I relaxed back onto the pallet and closed my eyes. "How long?" I managed to ask.

"Two days," I heard Rebecca say, and then I fell back asleep.

By noon on the third day following my ordeal, I could sit up and eat a spoonful of soup. My wounds were deep and plentiful, but everyone seemed to agree I would live.

Rebecca had neatly stitched a deep gash on my left shoulder and one above my right eye. The rest she had covered with cornstarch poultices. Realizing I was naked as a babe, I carefully explored under the bearskin cover and was relieved with what I found.

"How did we end up in here?" I asked after the soup had soothed my throat. Though my head still buzzed like an enraged hornet nest, I was thinking more clearly.

Rebecca said she had been with me from the time Ge-lelemend's warriors dragged me to this cabin. She convinced an Indian who brought food to the corral that she was my woman. He believed her, even though we had shown no apparent familiarity during our trek to this village.

Suddenly the hide door flew open, and an Indian entered. He was dressed differently than any Delaware I had seen so far, almost European, with a cloak over his shoulders and a wool cap pulled down to his oddly pierced and extended ear lobes. Wide-set gray eyes and full lips complimented a handsome and intelligent face.

Rebecca immediately dropped her head and scooted away from me. She already knew to show a squaw's deference to a warrior.

The Indian stood a moment looking down on me. Then he plopped down cross-legged beside my pallet. "You look much better, Moorhead," he said with a slight smile. "I did not believe you would live through the first night."

My mouth must have been hanging open because the man laughed aloud, not something an Indian is inclined to do.

"Why are white men always so surprised to hear our people speak English?" He laughed again. "My English is good, and my Dutch is better. My name is John Abeel. You may call me *Ki-ant-wa-chia*!"

I continued to stare, finally responding in an equally gentlemanly manner. "I am pleased to make your acquaintance," I said. "You know my name?"

Kiantwachia nodded toward Rebecca. "Your woman and I have had many conversations while you slept. She has been very devoted to you."

"She's not my —" I began to say when Rebecca forcefully interrupted.

"That's enough talk for now! You need to rest."

I did need to rest. The food and the conversation had sapped my strength. I lay back on the pallet.

"You are welcome to stay in my house," Kiantwachia said as he rose to his feet. "It is much safer than that stinking pit in which these *Lenape* dogs held you."

That confused me further. "You're not Delaware?" I asked.

He laughed sharply. "I am Kiantwachia, sachem of the Seneca people, first son of the Wolf Clan, and I am a captive like you!"

With that pronouncement, Kiantwachia strode from the cabin. I understood him to mean that he was an important Seneca chief. In fact, I was the guest of the man history would know as Cornplanter, greatest of the Seneca sachems. (8)

Over the next several days, Cornplanter, as I shall refer to him, told me of his situation among the Delaware. The Seneca are one of the six tribes that comprise the Iroquois Confederacy, also known as the Six Nations. The Delaware, an equally noble people originally from the eastern parts of the country, are not members of the Confederacy. It was with the Delaware that William Penn made the first treaty to establish our colony of Pennsylvania. Over time, the growing number of Europeans pushed them west of the Alleghenies.

The Iroquois occupied most of New York, and the Seneca are the most western tribe of the Six Nations. The other tribes included the Mohawk, Cayuga, Oneida, Onondaga, and the late joining Tuscarora. (9)

"Why not the Delaware?" I asked one evening after Cornplanter finished his history lesson. We sat together on a log outside his cabin. I was wrapped in the bear rug, wearing only deer hide trousers that Cornplanter had provided. My upper body was still too bruised and sore to tolerate a hunting shirt.

"The Lenape are subjects of the Iroquois," he responded haughtily. "They are women who owe us allegiance. Often, we find ourselves fighting on opposite sides. The Shawnee and Lenape are fighting for the British. I was returning from a council fire at Fort Pitt, and these dogs surrounded me on the road. They believe they can sell me back to my people."

"For a prisoner, you seem to have great liberty," I observed.

Cornplanter shook his head and tapped his pipe on the edge of the log. "I say I am a prisoner because I cannot leave. I have given my *parole*, as the French call it — my word of honor that I will not try to escape. So, for now, I am an 'honored guest.'"

"Does that mean you will never try to escape?" I asked, somewhat let down by the thought yet terrified at the consequence of failure.

"What is the word of a sachem to women?" he responded with a sly smile.

The use of the term 'women' confused me. "Why do you call the Delaware women?" I asked.

Cornplanter's mouth twitched contemptuously. "In truth, that time has passed. Once, the Lenape could not go to war or make decisions without approval from the Five Nations. Now, they do what they wish. It does not change how we warriors of the Seneca feel. They are dogs."

Rebecca brought us bowls of mush to eat while we talked. She was fitting easily into the role of a squaw, caring for my broken body, cleaning the cabin, and making our food. She did anything that kept her far from the filthy corral in which we had first found ourselves. We heard no news regarding Mary and her brother or the unknown prisoner who had instructed me how to survive the gauntlet.

When asked, Cornplanter casually stated that they had been given to a warrior as slaves. He doubted that the lone prisoner still lived.

"That man had no food," Cornplanter said. "He was kept so they could watch him die. The woman and boy will live."

We were far more fortunate than others. Sometime during my convalescence, two white men were brought to the village and forced to run the gauntlet. I knew what was

197

happening from the commotion at the stockade and refused to leave the cabin. Cornplanter went to watch and
reported that neither man survived.

I shrugged with indifference. I found it more and more
difficult to have any feelings or concerns for the welfare of
outsiders. At this point, my primary intention was to keep
myself, and Rebecca if possible, alive.

Rebecca and I were blessed that Cornplanter held a different view. He had generously taken us in and shared his
cabin and his food. It was not until much later that he revealed his ulterior motives for adopting us.

After our threatening welcome, the rest of the villagers
paid us little attention for the most part. We wandered anywhere we cared to go, except for the beach where the canoes sat on the sand. I met Gelelemend only once, and he
turned his head away as if offended by the sight of me.
After capturing me and dragging us to this place, he
showed no further interest in our lives. So much the better,
I thought.

When I asked Cornplanter what he thought would happen to us, he was vague and said that the Great Father decided the fate of all mankind, and it was not our place to
know. The plan of the Delaware, however, was clear. They
intended to sell us back to our people. Or to other tribes.

In this lazy manner, three weeks passed. I was now
strong enough to help with the chores and work in the new
garden next to our cabin. Cornplanter never did any actual
work and scoffed at me for assisting Rebecca. It was wom-
en's work, he would say, and walk away puffing on his pipe.
He also encouraged me to pluck my whiskers as he and the
other Indians did. I refused. My beard was growing full,

and I kept it as a sign of my station in the Indian town.

Rebecca seemed as happy as she could under the circumstances. As her dress disintegrated, a squaw living near our cabin gave Rebecca a roughly woven skirt and blouse to wear. Seeing her with braided hair and dressed in native garb for the first time, I told Rebecca that any more sun on her face and she could pass as a real squaw. She did not seem to appreciate my humor.

I will say, however, that our sleeping arrangements were slightly awkward because Cornplanter was under the impression that she was my woman. I did not want to dissuade him from that belief — I was determined to protect Rebecca, and acting as her mate was the best way to do that. Cornplanter showed no interest in her other than the work she performed.

At night, she and I slept on the same pallet, under the heavy bearskin rug. It was not always easy for either of us. We dressed and undressed with as much modesty as we could manage. Occasionally, we were escorted to the river to bathe, keeping our backs to each other and trying to ignore the Indian standing guard.

The truth is, however, she was a beautiful young woman. There was no denying that, and she was desperate for a promise of protection.

As we lay one night, Rebecca and me on one side of the cabin floor, and Cornplanter on the opposite, I felt her shift under the covers. Then a slim arm slipped across my shoulders.

"Are you awake?" she whispered against my back.

I nodded, suddenly too numb to speak.

"Are you going to escape?"

"No!" I answered decisively. "Our only hope is to be rescued or sold. You saw what happens to anyone who runs."

She shifted closer until I could feel the heat of her naked body against my back. "Cornplanter is becoming suspicious that I'm not really your woman. If he learns the truth, he'll take me for his. Or sell me."

I did not know what to say, so I stayed quiet.

"Fergus," she continued softly. "I will be your woman if you promise to keep me safe."

I carefully reached up, gently patted her arm on my shoulder, and spoke without moving my quickly overheating body. "Don't worry. I promise to keep you safe. I do. But I will not break my marriage bond. We don't have to be together like that for me to protect you. If Cornplanter or any other questions our relationship, I shall stand up for you."

In a while, I realized Rebecca was crying silently. Having made the first overture and been rejected, she rolled away from me in shame. I could feel her sobbing in the dark. I felt like a real bastard, not knowing how to make it better.

You may roll your eyes in disbelief at this, but my soul belonged to another. God tests us by throwing temptation in our path. As attractive and vulnerable as Rebecca was and tempted though I may have been, I would not break my vows, and I never have.

Somewhere, many miles to my south, a woman waited for me with the same convictions. I knew it in my heart.

CHAPTER 27
Meanwhile…

From the Journal of Samuel Moorhead
Tuesday, March 18th, 1777
The Kittanning Path, Pennsylvania

It was an unusually warm spring day when three men arrived from Fort Pitt with new orders. I was to leave my post in Kittanning and ride with the mounted militiamen to Indiana and then south to Hanna's Town. At each settlement along the way, I was to enlist as many able-bodied men as I could find to reform the garrison at Fort Kittanning. It was to be called the Independent Pennsylvania Militia.

I thought it poor timing. I had arrived only days before, and my brother, Fergus, had departed on Sunday. But orders were orders, even the illogical ones.

I left John in charge of the remaining men and followed the path east toward my home. I rode with the three militiamen and Corporal Smyth.

The day was bright after a light shower the night before. It pleased me to see that the forest was starting to show signs of spring. Skunk cabbage heads were popping up in the wet areas along the path, and tiny buds showed on the pussy willow.

My companions and I rode quietly, watching the edge of the woods at all times. The Delaware who usually camped at the fort had disappeared two days before, the same day Fergus had started home. I was uneasy despite the wonderful weather.

About noon, my men and I rode up a steep grade. Ahead, a group of crows suddenly took flight, settling on the nearby trees. I pulled my horse up short, and the men stopped with me.

"Eyes open!" I hissed, apprehension tightening my shoulders. We sat still, listening intently for any sound or movement. Our heads moved from side to side. Even the horses, ears pricked, made no sound.

"Slowly," I said, pulling my long gun free. We walked our horses up the grade and into the shadows where the trees arched over the path. We held our muskets at the ready.

The smell warned me before the horror met my eyes.

"Oh my God," one of my men exclaimed before I silenced him with a raised hand.

The bloated body of a dead horse lay on its side in the middle of the path. Beside it was a man's body. Though he was naked and face down, it was clear that the man had been scalped.

"It's Simpson," whispered Corporal Smyth. "Where's Captain Fergus?"

I looked for signs of my brother, my heart pounding in my chest, my head buzzing. I forced my nervous mount past the first dead horse to where the second one lay. There was no body.

"Dismount and search the bushes," I quietly ordered. "He may be wounded and crawled off."

The men searched the area in vain. We observed moccasin tracks and the deeper markings of boots. Then another man found where the Indians had waited in ambush. The trail continued north from there, but we saw no more boot prints.

"Look here, Captain," Corporal Smyth called out. He pointed to a saddle propped against a tree. When I picked up the saddle, a folded piece of paper fell to the ground. (10)

"It says that this is a warning to others," I read out loud. I looked around in frustration. "The day is getting late. We need to continue on. Fergus may have made it home. We must look for him there before

202

we try to follow the trail."

The men gathered branches to cover Andrew Simpson's body to protect it from animals. Not having an extra horse and wanting to travel quickly, we agreed to return the next day to retrieve him and search for Fergus, if necessary.

As the sun set, we rode up the path to Fergus' cabin. My nephew heard us coming and alerted his mother, who rushed to the door expecting to see her husband.

"Fergus?" she said, the confusion evident in her voice.

"He's not here?" I asked, my fears deepening further.

Jane leaned against the doorframe, hand clutching her chest. "What's happened?"

"We can't jump to conclusions," I said, dismounting and taking Jane by the shoulders. "We don't know where he's at, that's all."

I tried to explain what we had seen, keeping the story as free of details as possible. Jane sat numbly at the table, unsure how to deal with this news. Fergus hadn't been killed at the ambush site, and there was no evidence of him further up the trail, so the only conclusion we could reach was that he had been taken captive. This, at least, gave her hope while also chilling her bones to the marrow. Everyone knew the fate of Indian captives.

"First light," I said, exhausted with worry, "we'll return to Blanket Hill and follow the trail north. I promise, Jane, we'll find him."

The next day and night, me and two of the best men followed the trail north of the ambush site. It led to an area where the forest floor was matted and heavily marked. Many warriors had waited here for the ambush party's return. Nowhere did we see signs of a white man's boot prints. We were surprised to identify the footprints of at least two women and two children among the many Indian tracks.

I realized that we were following a war party with far too many warriors for my ill-equipped group. With a heavy heart, I abandoned *the search.*

Corporal Smyth carried Andrew Simpson home to his parents with the news that the Delaware were on the warpath. I returned to Kittanning, intending to gather my militia and follow my brother.

Before I could mount an expedition, a newly arrived Captain relieved me of command. He ordered me to continue with my recruitment efforts. I was prepared to disobey those orders, torn between my duty as an officer and my duty as a brother. Several of my men agreed and were willing to go with me. However, fate stepped in before I could act.

Two days after my arrival, the new commanding officer suddenly abandoned Fort Kittanning, allowing all of the men to return to their settlements. All attempts at recruitment ended, and what force I might have commanded simply faded away. I had no choice but to return to Indiana. The protection of the frontier now fell to the men at each settlement.

No one could rely on the militia any longer.

CHAPTER 28
Escape

April, 1777
Delaware Territory, Pennsylvania

A rough hand across my mouth startled me awake. "It is time," Cornplanter whispered. "We leave now."

"What?" I blurted. "I'm not going anywhere! I've seen what they do to anyone who tries to escape." I could not believe what I was hearing. Cornplanter had shown no indications that he wanted to escape. In fact, he had always given the impression that he rather enjoyed his position of 'honored guest,' despite the restrictions.

He punched me hard in the shoulder. "Get up! We go!"

Rebecca raised her head from the other side of the pallet. "What is it?" she asked, voice groggy with sleep.

Cornplanter punched me again. "Get up. I have been walking the village all night. No one will see us."

With growing concern, I realized that he was serious. "What makes you think we can get away? What about the sentries?" I referred to the Indians who wandered the town during the night. They were not true sentries with assigned posts or routes, but they served the same purpose.

"Tonight, there is one," he said calmly. "We can cross the river unseen. Now get up!"

I still resisted. "Why do you think we can escape? They will track us down and burn us alive."

"My people are near."

"How can you possibly know that?" I asked, starting to think the man had lost his mind.

"I heard their calls. They are on the north side of the river, not many miles away. We can reach them before the Lenape run us down." Then in a most threatening manner, he again told me to get dressed.

Unsure of my intentions, I nonetheless obeyed his instructions. I began pulling on my leggings, shirt. and moccasins. "Get dressed," I said to Rebecca, who was standing beside me, clutching the bearskin cover around her thin body.

Cornplanter turned from where he was packing cornbread and dried meat into a bag. "Not her!" he hissed.

In the dim light, I could see Rebecca's eyes widen in shock. "Fergus!" she pleaded.

I looked steadily at Cornplanter and said, "She goes, or I don't."

He came at me so menacingly that I took a step backward. "The squaw stays here!" he said, his face inches from mine.

"If I'm to escape, Rebecca must come also. She's my woman; I will not leave her."

"She is not your *woman*," Cornplanter sneered. "Do you think me dull? She can cook and clean. That is the only reason I did not sell her to another."

I stood my ground, despite the surprise that Cornplanter was on to our deception. I pulled her close. "We escape together!" I announced as firmly as I could.

A low chuckle came from deep in his throat. "You are not *escaping*, white man, I am *stealing* you!"

"What?"

"You will be treated better among my people than with these dogs until we decide what to do with you. You are now *my* prisoner!" He grasped my forearm in a crushing grip and pulled me toward the doorway. I yanked my arm from his hand.

"Not without her," I said, speaking each word clearly. Stepping back against the wall, I pulled Rebecca to me. "She comes, or I sound the alarm, and no one goes anywhere."

Cornplanter stood silently, weighing his options. "Get dressed," he finally said and turned back to his packing.

Rebecca pulled on her clothes and moccasins as I finished lacing up my leggings. We followed Cornplanter from the cabin and down the main thoroughfare. It was still the middle of the night. The moon was gone, and the dogs were asleep. One sentry passed close by as we crouched against the side of a cabin. We held our breath, and he continued on.

At the beach, Cornplanter whispered for me to grab one end of a canoe, and together, we slid it over the sandy beach to the rushing stream.

Rebecca stepped in as we held the dugout steady. She knew to squat down low in the center. As I climbed in the far end, a shout came from the bank above us. The silhouette of a Delaware warrior stood out against the night sky. We were in deep shadows, but he had seen us. With a howl of alarm, he charged down the bank, tomahawk in his hand.

Cornplanter turned and ran toward the man without hesitation. He dipped his head to avoid the swinging tomahawk and came up behind the other man, one arm encircling the warrior's neck. The Delaware collapsed to the sand, blood welling from a slit throat.

Sounds of alarm spread through the village. We were out of time. Cornplanter ran to the canoe, gave it one mighty shove, and leapt aboard the boat as it took to the stream.

I grabbed one of the short paddles lying in the bottom of the canoe and sliced into the water. With a couple of strokes, Cornplanter and I found our rhythm. The center of the stream was moving fast enough to quickly carry us away from the beach.

With my heart pounding, I bent to the task of paddling. I risked a quick backward glance in time to see four canoes entering the water. Then we raced past the river's bend and away from that miserable place.

A mile downstream, Cornplanter indicated a gap in the left bank where a shallow creek joined the river. We aimed our canoe in that direction and managed to run aground on the rocky spillway with a few deep strokes.

I stepped ashore, holding tightly to the dugout to prevent it from washing away while Rebecca climbed out. Cornplanter climbed over the side, knee-deep in the water. He pushed the canoe away and watched as it spun in the current and continue downriver.

"Up the stream! Stay in the water!" he ordered, speaking just loud enough to be heard above the water rushing down the slippery rocks.

Rebecca took one look at the wet, moss-covered rocks and pulled the front of her skirt up to her knees. She tucked the hem beneath her hide belt, exposing more shapely leg than is proper. Without hesitation, she followed Cornplanter up the steep causeway and into the forest.

The water rushing downhill to the river was cold and fast-moving. We climbed as best we could, trying not to disturb the rocks or muddy banks on either side. If we could get away from the river quickly enough, the pursuing warriors might miss our landing area and continue around the river bend. Once they discovered their error, it would be a hard paddle back upstream.

Half a mile up the creek, we came to an area where the bank was low and covered in stones. Cornplanter helped us out of the water, carefully stepping from water to dry bank without disturbing the beach.

A hundred yards on, he stopped and leaned against a tree. We all gasped for breath. My heart pounded in my chest, and I assumed Rebecca was equally exhausted from the climb. However, when Cornplanter called for us to move, she did not complain.

We walked quickly within the uncluttered forest on reasonably level ground for another half hour. Then a war cry echoed through the woods. The Delaware were on our trail.

"Run!" Cornplanter ordered.

We raced on, thankful that there was only minor undergrowth to block our way. As we moved further north, the delicate ash trees along the river gave way to pine, providing a soft path beneath our feet.

I ran behind Rebecca, ready to lend a hand if she faltered, but it was never necessary. My thirty-five-year-old heart was no match for her youthfulness.

At another shallow stream, Cornplanter entered the water, and we plunged in after him. This creek was deeper than the first, and we struggled to make headway. A hundred yards upstream, we again exited upon a gravel beach and stopped to rest.

No one spoke. Cornplanter sniffed the air and tilted his head from side to side like a dog searching for a rabbit.

"Not much further," he announced, and we dutifully fell in behind him.

We covered the next half mile at a much calmer pace until Cornplanter suddenly dropped to a knee. Rebecca and I stood against a pine tree, holding our breath.

Without a sound, four warriors appeared in the dim morning light, beginning to penetrate the forest. Rebecca gave an involuntary gasp, and I held her shoulders tight.

Cornplanter stood and approached the men. They spoke in their language a moment and then clasped each other's arms in greeting.

"Come," Cornplanter said to us, motioning with this arm. "We are safe. These men are Seneca of the Wolf clan. We are family."

CHAPTER 29
Keepers of the Western Door

April and May, 1777
Seneca Territory, New York

Our trek north of one hundred miles was uneventful and exhausting. The Seneca party we joined consisted of twenty warriors who had been searching for Cornplanter since his capture.

To my eye, they were indistinguishable from the Delaware from whom we had just escaped. Most shaved or plucked the sides of their heads bald and used bear grease to stiffen the center section so that it stood up in a tuft. They all tied feathers in their hair. A number carried muskets, and others only a bow with a quiver of arrows across their backs. With great remorse, I accepted the fact that my long rifle was gone forever. With a very un-Christian thought, I hoped someone killed Gelelemend for it.

Rebecca held up remarkably well the entire trip. The warriors seemed genuinely fond of her, partially for her beauty but also her stamina. Of course, when we camped, she was responsible for making the fire and the cooking. I often saw a warrior help her with a small chore. One would bring her an armful of firewood; another would cut pine boughs for her bed at night. She always responded with a bright smile, and much to my amusement, they smiled shyly in return.

One night I commented on how she had wooed the war party, and she took it as a compliment. Anything to stay alive, she said, even if it meant being your woman in name only. That stung, so I stopped talking.

We moved at a steady pace through dense forest most of the way, either along a stream bank or on well-worn paths. Then we crossed several deep creeks and dropped steeply from high ground to the Allegheny River. The Seneca called this river the *Ohi-yo*, as we knew it below Fort Pitt.

Six days after our escape from the Delaware, we arrived at a Seneca village called Salamanca on the northernmost turn of the Allegheny River. We were no longer in Pennsylvania, I believed. It was the first time I ever set foot outside my home colony.

The village of Salamanca (11) was compact and remarkably clean. It fit snugly in the lowland between the hills on the south and the river on the north. It had the look of a temporary hunting camp, more than a village. I saw no indications of farming, or stockades, or children for that matter.

We stayed in Salamanca for two nights while the warriors replenished their stock of dried venison and cornmeal. The twenty or more Indians living in the village seemed happy to provide whatever they could. It was good to be in a safe place, if just for a day or two.

The second evening in the village, I found my way to a rise that provided a view of the river. A dozen birchbark canoes rested on the bank below me. With a deep sigh, I looked to the west, where the river made a long curve south, back toward Pennsylvania, and eventually, all the way to Kittanning. I had traveled many miles to return to the same waterway I rode away from in March.

Cornplanter appeared without a sound, as he enjoyed doing purely to impress me. We stood looking at the water as a deep bronze from the setting sun reflected across the land, perhaps giving us the appearance of ancient statues standing guard over the village.

"If you run," he said quietly, "we will catch you. There is no escape."

"I wasn't thinking of running," I lied. "I understand that for now, I belong to you." I turned to face him full on. "But not forever."

"That is yet to be seen. I do not know the Great Father's plan for you."

For a while longer, neither of us spoke. The sun disappeared beyond the forest, the red and gold faded from the sky.

"Tomorrow we leave," Cornplanter said. "Five more days to my home. You will be treated well. My people are nothing like the Lenape dogs who captured us. We are a peaceful nation."

How different history would be if that were only true.

I will not bother with the rest of the journey except to say that it taxed Rebecca and me to the end of our reserves. The Seneca set an exhausting pace.

We walked quickly from sunup until a break was allowed at high noon. Then, with an hour's rest, and a bite to eat, we set off again. We stopped before dusk settled in each evening, allowing enough time to build a fire and a few lean-tos to ward off the chill.

In this way, we walked for ten hours, covering fifteen to twenty miles a day for five days straight. Cornplanter said he was taking a more leisurely pace believing that neither Rebecca nor I could keep up. We were thankful for that kindness, even if it did gall a bit.

We moved in a general northeast direction until we picked up the Genesee River. With the deep river gorge twisting on our right, we turned more to the north. After a camp at Silver Lake, the land flattened out, and our walking became easier by far.

Eventually, exhausted and filthy and ready for a long rest, we looked across gently rolling land to an Indian town that rivaled Chamber's Town for its size.

Ca-na-wau-gus was a more substantial version of Chinglacamouche, with more than 200 cabins, numerous stockades and corrals, and acres of cultivated fields. The Genesee River protected the eastern side of the town, and a swampy moat encircled the rest. I could only see one road in. A British fort provided no better protection.

Cornplanter stopped on a grassy rise above the village. "My father and his father lived here much of their lives," he said with pride in his voice. "I own many cabins and much land that produces corn and squash. If I ever went to England, like that whore's son, Brant, they would call me a lord!"

He did think highly of himself, no getting around that. I did not wish to encourage him further, so I asked nothing of whom he spoke. I let it go, but there would be a time when I, too, would curse the name of Joseph Brant.

As we approached the village, the warriors in our party

fired their muskets and let out scalp whoops. Hundreds of Indians turned out to meet us and celebrate Cornplanter's return. They plucked at my sleeves and patted Rebecca on the arm, but no one threatened us or threw anything. I was becoming confident that I would not have to run the gauntlet again.

Cornplanter thanked his warriors, and we followed him to a newly built cabin at the edge of the village. It was tidier than most others we had seen, here or in the Delaware town. There were no piles of discarded skins nor rotting food to be seen. To my surprise, a colorful flowerbed decorated the path to the door.

Cornplanter stopped outside and called out in English, "*Deh-he-wä-nis!* I have brought you a guest!" This was quite different from his usual approach of barging into any cabin he cared to enter.

There was a shuffling within, and a dark-haired, middle-aged woman pushed the hide door aside and squinted into the bright sunlight. She was dressed in a deer hide skirt and ornate linen blouse. Her long hair was braided to frame a round, intelligent face with light blue eyes.

The woman who greeted us was white!

She spoke to Cornplanter in the Seneca language. He responded in the same tongue. Then she turned to Rebecca and me.

"Welcome to Canawaugus," she said in English. "My name is Mary Jemison."

We stood with our mouths hanging open in an inconsiderate way long enough for Mary to take Rebecca by the arm.

"Come," she said in a soft voice with a trace of an Irish brogue. "You're exhausted, my dear. Come inside."

Rebecca turned to me, apprehension evident in her

215

eyes. We had not been apart for many weeks.

"Come," Mary said again, and together they disappeared into the cabin.

Cornplanter continued walking down the road, and I hurried to catch up, somewhat unsure how I felt having Rebecca taken from me like that. She had been my responsibility for so long that I took it for granted she would remain under my care.

"It is best she stays with Dehhewänis," he said. "She will care for your woman." Then he laughed out loud. "Perhaps a warrior will buy her from me and treat her properly!"

"Who is that woman?" I wanted to know. I had heard stories, but I was still surprised to find a white woman living as an Indian.

Cornplanter did not look at me as he continued to stride on, greeting fellow Indians along the way. Everyone seemed pleased that he had returned.

"Dehhewänis has lived among us for many years," he said after a time. "Her husband went north and is believed to be dead. She will teach the woman the duties of a Seneca squaw."

As events unfolded in our lives, Rebecca and I were fortunate that Mary lived in that village when we arrived. She took Rebecca under her wing, and no one challenged her authority. I accepted the fact that Rebecca was no longer my 'woman.' Cornplanter laughed heartily when I told him that.

He directed me to a low, run-down log cabin near the corrals. Two other white men lived there as 'honored guests,' as I was also labeled. We had the same basic freedoms allowed during my captivity in Pennsylvania — with much less threat of imminent death.

I slept for two days straight, tucked beneath a coarse

blanket in the corner, until hunger and thirst overcame me. I raised my aching body from the corn husk pallet and joined the world of the living.

CHAPTER 30
Canawaugus

June and July, 1777
Seneca Territory, New York

My first action was to shave my beard. I had been without a razor for so long that my face hid behind five inches of thick, tangled black hair.

My new cabin-mate, Alexander Stewart, lent me his skinning knife, which he had been allowed to keep. With nothing but water, I worked at the whiskers until my face was red and sore. For the first time in months, I was back to looking like myself.

The other man sharing the cabin was William Booker. Where Stewart was thin and wiry, Booker was broad and lumbering. I felt fortunate that both men were friendly and willing to share their meager belongings. Stewart gave me a hunting shirt that did not stink, a vast improvement over the stained and shredded garment I threw in the fire pit.

Both men were fur traders who had wandered into the wrong part of the country. They were from the Mohawk River valley, where the Iroquois were making periodic raids on the settlements, especially German Flatts and the surrounding countryside. Both men spoke the Mohawk and Seneca languages, but Booker said little. On the other hand, Stewart, obviously the sharper of the two, never stopped talking.

When I asked about the war, he explained that the Mohawk were actively supporting the British in the east. Their leader, Joseph Brant, whom Cornplanter had mentioned in our discussions, had recently returned from England. Stewart said that Brant actually had an audience with old King George! That's a new one — the King of England meeting with an Indian!

Stewart spat a tobacco wad in the dirt. "So, you can imagine," he said, biting off another chunk and working it into his cheek, "that Brant's all cocksure and acting as if he speaks for the entire Mohawk people."

"Does he?"

"Well, that's to be seen. He does have a loyal following, and the other Mohawk sachems don't seem inclined to stand up to him."

"Cornplanter says the Seneca intend staying out of the war," I said. "If they don't want to get involved, why then are they keeping us?"

Wiping his chin on the back of his sleeve, Stewart said, "Way I figure, Cornplanter and the other sachems are hedging their bets, so to speak. They ain't truly involved, but they're playing along with the other Nations. For now, the Mohawk are carrying the load and doing most of the fighting. The Ohio Seneca will be in it sooner or later, and then we're of more value."

"So, you think the Seneca will fight for the British?" I asked.

"There's this fella named *Sa-goye-watha*, comes and goes all the time. He is a talker. Always standing up at the council fire. Goes on and on. Speaks good American, though I'm able to understand most of what he says in Seneca. He says this is a family feud, and the Iroquois should stay out of it."

I hoped it was true. If all the Iroquois Nations came in on the side of the British, we stood no chance at all of winning this war.

Taking advantage of my relative liberty and considerable free time, I spent most of my day exploring the village. It was a noisy, sprawling metropolis. More than 600 people lived within the walls and moat, with more living in cabins scattered in the surrounding farmland.

While most of the structures in the village were log or plank cabins, there was one longhouse in the center of an open grassy area. This was the Great House, the meeting place for the chiefs and heads of the clans. The lawn often saw a gathering of several hundred Indians who listened to speeches or heard the decisions of the elders. These assemblies happened rather frequently. The Seneca loved to debate every issue.

Along the river, on the upstream side, there was a thin, sandy area the squaws used for washing and drawing water. A paddock with a fence extending a dozen feet into the water on the downstream side allowed the few scrawny cows and pigs access.

I soon discovered that the town's location on the Genesee River had one drawback. Occasionally, when the wind was out of the east, a most obnoxious smell emanated from the land across the river. Gunpowder came to my mind, but Stewart informed me that the smell rose from the sulfur springs on that side. During special ceremonies, the Seneca sometimes drank the foul water flowing from the springs. I wanted nothing to do with that devil's brew.

From time to time, I stood on the bank of the river, looking at the birch canoes pulled up on the muddy bank, and evaluated my chance of escape. Naturally, I was heartsick to be away from Jane and my family for so long. But, on the other hand, the thought of being burned alive haunted me still.

Cornplanter often made it clear that I was a captive, even though he was friendly toward me. If I tried to escape, he told me sternly one day, the same fate awaited me as had befallen poor Tanner. And then, he would sell Rebecca to a warrior as a slave.

No, I decided, best to bide my time and hope to be sold to the British or the Americans. So I waited, and the months went by.

For the most part, everyone ignored me. If I found a group of warriors squatting at a fire, passing a pipe, or enjoying a communal pot of stew, they always refused to include me. They never even acknowledged me. So after a while, I determined that the friendliest path for me to follow was over to Mary's cabin.

The first time Rebecca saw me without my beard, she squealed in delight and kissed me on both cheeks.

"I didn't recognize you!" she said, taking my arm and leading me to the log bench near Mary's garden.

I noticed a change in Rebecca, too. Her face had filled out, erasing the line of hardship that marred her beauty during our long trek to Canawaugus. She seemed genuinely happy.

"Oh, Mary is so wonderful!" she effused. "She put me in charge of the garden. We're growing corn in the back, beans up front, and pumpkins for the fall!" She pointed to each area of her garden as she explained the layout. I watched her expressive face and marveled at the resilience of youth.

One lazy afternoon, Mary joined us in the shade of the cabin wall, and she told me more her story. For most of her life, she had spoken Shawnee and Seneca. However, her English, slightly halting from lack of use, still had an unmistakable lilt. Listening to her talk, I often sighed, thinking of my redhead back in Pennsylvania.

"Mary has lived with the Indians all her life," Rebecca explained. "Tell him, Mary."

Mary smiled at the girl's enthusiasm. "It is a long story, Fergus, as is yours, I'm sure. If you survive at all in this country, you have a long story to tell. No one lives a simple life on the frontier."

She studied the lush garden, gathering her thoughts, and told us her story.

In April of '58, when Mary was twelve, Shawnee attacked her family homestead in central Pennsylvania. She and her parents and a brother and sister were captured. At Fort Duquesne, she was sold to the Seneca, who carried her down the Ohio to their village. There, they took her name, they said, and all of her clothes, and threw them in the river. From then on, her name was Dehhewänis, Handsome Girl.

"When I was considered old enough, I married a Seneca warrior who treated me kindly. I came to love him, and in time, we had a little girl — she died. Then we had a boy named Thomas, after my father.

"When the French war ended, we walked many hundreds of miles to this land. Before we arrived my husband became terrible sick. I tried to care for him, but he died."

"You loved him very much," Rebecca said, laying her

hand on top of the woman's.

"As time went on," Mary continued following a reflective pause, "I married another man, a member of the Wolf clan."

"Where is he now?" I asked.

Mary gave us a slight shrug. "No one knows. He and my son, Thomas, and a few other warriors went north many months ago to join the Mohawk. I believe he is alive, but I know no more than that." (12)

Rebecca cooed softly and patted Mary's hand again. They were obviously comfortable together, and I was happy for them.

Early in July, a year after the declaration of our independence from Britain, word came to Canawaugus of a great council fire that was to take place. At first, there was talk of meeting at Niagara. Stewart, who always tried to hang around the Great House whenever there was a meeting, said no, now they intend to go to Fort Ontario, at Oswego.

"You need to come listen to this," he said. "There will be another meeting tonight."

"I won't understand a word," I protested.

"I'll tell you what they say. Will, says my English ain't very refined, but I speak good Indian. Ain't that so, Will?"

"Very good," Will replied loquaciously.

So, along with a hundred or more warriors and squaws, we gathered at the Great House. I saw Mary and Rebecca standing together on the far side of the field. It was so crowded I could not get close enough to speak to them. It was a hot and sticky evening, having rained most of the day, and the bodies pressed together in the spacious grass yard were damp and musty smelling.

Cornplanter and the other elders stood in the Great House doorway. The gathered Indians were quiet and stood very still, unlike how large crowds of white men behaved. Cornplanter raised his right hand and began to speak.

Stewart and I stood near the back. After one or two sentences, he quietly translated what Cornplanter was saying.

"Today, my brother *Sgan-yo-daiyo* comes with news of a great council fire to be held at Oswego. All of the Nations are to attend. My brother will speak to us."

It was easy to see that Cornplanter and the man he called his brother were indeed related. Sganyodaiyo, whom I shall call by his English name of Handsome Lake, possessed the same intelligent, wide-set eyes and full lips of his brother. He was older, but standing side by side, each exuded power and authority in equal measure.

Handsome Lake spoke for a long time in that somewhat flamboyant manner I now expected from all of the Indian orators. They never went straight to the point.

"The Mohawk Nation sends greetings to their brothers, the Seneca," Stewart was saying. "The Mohawk sachem, Captain Brant, has crossed the sea and met with our great white father" — meaning King George — "and his chiefs. Captain Brant brings the words of the white father, who promises that the Seneca people will keep their land and their water forever if his rebellious children are defeated.

"Our council has spoken many times of the white man's war. We believe this war is between our white father and his children and has nothing to do with us. However, Captain Brant warns that we will lose our land if the rebels win the war, so we must help our white father. Captain Brant asks us to come to the great council fire with open ears and listen to the British."

A murmur passed through the crowd, and I gathered that this was not a popular idea. They did not like what they heard, but even more so, they did not like that the message came from Captain Brant.

Cornplanter held up his hand again, and the group grew silent. "My brother speaks the words of the Mohawk sachem. He does not speak for the Seneca. We will go to Oswego and listen to the Redcoats and the other Nations. We will speak for the Seneca — they will speak for their people. Then we will decide."

And with that pronouncement, the four men turned and re-entered the Great House. The meeting was over. Stewart smiled at me in the early dusk as we found the way back to our cabin.

"Looks like I was right. We're going to Oswego."

"Why would we go?" I asked, appalled at the prospect of another wilderness trek.

"Because," Stewart said, smacking me on the back, "just like I said. The Seneca are hedging their bets. And we, my friend, are the bargaining chips."

CHAPTER 31
Birchbark

July 1777
Irondequoit Bay, New York

The next morning, I witnessed firsthand the power of women in this matriarchal society. Cornplanter gathered Stewart, Booker, and me for the trip. He tied us together — just as a precaution, he said, until we got underway. Dogs on a leash, we all trooped over to Mary's cabin.

"She is staying with me," Mary stated once Cornplanter explained his intention to take us all to Oswego and the great council fire.

Stewart translated as we stood in the background and listened to the exchange. Rebecca hovered in the cabin doorway, her eyes wide, hand covering her mouth in despair.

"If she stays," Cornplanter was saying, "then you must buy her. She is my property."

Mary folded her arms across her thin chest and smiled up at Cornplanter. He stood and stared at her.

"I have given her my food. I have given her my clothes. Now the woman belongs to me." She swept her right arm in a quick motion level with the ground.

Stewart snorted. "It's over," he said. "Mary has ended

the discussion. Once an Indian swings that arm, there's no more talking. Ain't that so, Will?"

Will nodded. "Done talking."

Cornplanter towered above the small woman, his face dark with anger. Then he turned, snatched up our lead, and started down the road. Before he could get up any momentum, I dug in my heels and dragged everyone to a stop.

"Let me say goodbye," I demanded.

Eyes blazing, Cornplanter threw the leash in the dirt and turned his back on us. I led my companions back to the cabin path, and Rebecca flew into my arms.

"Fergus! No!" she cried, tears streaming down her sun-tanned face. "You can't go!"

Awkwardly aware of the others standing right behind me, I held Rebecca at arm's length. "You know this is for the best," I said, trying to sound confident. "Cornplanter intends to sell us to the British. Who knows how they'll treat us?"

"Not too damn good," Stewart offered from behind my back.

"But I want to be with you," she whispered, looking down at her feet. "I love you."

I took a deep breath. "And I love you, too," I said, knowing that Jane would forgive me. "You'll be better off here with Mary. When I can, I'll find your people and come back for you."

She looked at me with such trust in her eyes that I cursed myself for making a promise I knew I could not keep.

"Goodbye, darling," I said and turned away before I started to blubber.

Cornplanter grunted in disgust, and we followed him down the road.

"That was just lovely," Stewart said quietly, wiping a grubby sleeve under his nose, "weren't it, Will?"

For once, Booker had no reply.

In the end, I failed miserably in my promise to return and never heard of Rebecca again. I regret that to this day.

An enormous party of 200 warriors and 50 squaws, packed with supplies, headed north. An easy trail ran along the twisting Genesee River and then across flat land toward Irondequoit Bay. The river was passable in a canoe down to the falls, but Cornplanter and the other war chiefs decided to march our party instead.

The Indians made leisurely progress so that it took until noon the next day before we came to the first cataract and turned east toward the bay.

We made camp on the shore, and in short order, everyone was hard at work. In an unusual display of equality, the warriors and the squaws worked together to build a series of lean-tos. There was little conversation, yet everyone was in fine spirits. For them, a council fire was similar to our barn-raisings or county fairs, something to look forward to during the long winter nights.

Once the temporary shelters were built, the men attacked the birch trees in the surrounding forest. Someone had determined that twelve canoes would be necessary to carry the delegates, a few women, and three 'honored guests' the sixty-some miles to Oswego. Half of the people in our party had come to help build the canoes and would return to Canawaugus when the boats were completed.

We white men were set to chopping down birch trees. No one trusted our skill enough to have us strip the bark or make spruce-root stitching. That was critical work, and

Indians followed behind us, carefully removing wide slabs of the pliable bark.

"Have you ever built a canoe?" Stewart asked as we both stood aside to let our tree crash to the ground.

"No," I replied. "I've cleared a great deal of land, though."

Branches and leaves filled the air before the dust settled. A dozen trees away from us, another fell. The Indians carefully selected which trees to cut and which were to remain in the forest for future use. Despite using this forest to build canoes for hundreds of years, the trees were plentiful, strong, and straight.

"It ain't that hard. We're going a fair piece on the lake and need big canoes."

"Why not walk to Oswego?" I asked. "We walk everywhere else."

"It's a hard trail round this lake, and this ain't a war party that can travel fast and light," he replied. "We have women and supplies to take with us. Best to go by water. Weather out there can be tricky, so the boats gotta be big and sturdy. What we're building here is called a *rabaska*. Means 'big canoe.' Never can tell what kind of storm will kick up on the lake. Ain't that right, Will?"

"Almost drowned once," Booker injected, then returned to carefully slicing a deep line into the trunk of the tree with a tomahawk.

"True enough," Stewart agreed, leaning on his ax. "That was a time, I'll tell you. We was headed for Mississauga with a load of pelts when the wind came up without warning. Hit us so hard the canoe rolled right over. Eh, Will?"

Booker bobbed his head enthusiastically. "Almost drowned."

"Did you right the canoe?" I asked.

Stewart laughed. "Nope, it was too big for us. We lost everything. Had to straddle the damn boat upside-down and paddle it to shore with our hands. Took two days, sitting on the bottom of the boat. Ha!" he laughed again. "That was a good time. Eh, Will?"

They both smiled at the fond memory. I could only shake my head.

For three days, the woods rang with the steady crack of axes and hatchets. Steam rose from pots of boiling water and gum sap. It was an amazing enterprise. The process is lengthy and detailed, but to provide an idea of how much work we accomplished in a short amount of time, consider:

As the trees are felled and stripped of their bark, the squaws gather and boil spruce roots for stitching. Before the bark can dry, it is bent to a framework of stakes using boiling water to ease it into the proper shape.

Finally, the long, thin root stitching joins sections of bark together, eventually lashing pre-formed ribs to the bark hull. Opposed to European-style boat building, the Iroquois construct their canoes from the outside in — first the skin, or hull, then the ribs.

The last step involves turning the canoe upside down and applying a thick layer of hot tree-sap to all the stitched seams. Each of the finished canoes is unique, although they are all twenty-four feet long and wide enough for two men to sit side by side and paddle.

I have to disagree with Stewart on how hard it was to make a canoe. All of us, including the Indians, were dirty and tired at the end of each day.

When the task was completed, most of the squaws and sixty or seventy warriors packed up and walked back to

Canawaugus. The rest of us loaded supplies in the center of each canoe and took our assigned places. We pushed off, our armada bound for Fort Ontario.

The early morning sun reflected brightly on the milky green water lapping against the thin hulls. It was a beautiful day. If we were lucky, this weather would hold. According to Stewart, we would not make Oswego until nightfall.

My two companions were in separate boats. They, and all the Seneca, fell into a rhythm before I got the hang of paddling. The pace was quick and steady. Before long, a sharp pain developed between my shoulder blades.

We paddled for three hours and then rested for a spell. The warrior behind me tapped my shoulder and handed me a hard johnnycake. I broke off a bite and passed it on, then scooped up handfuls of water from the lake to wash the dry cake down my parched throat.

Refreshed and fortified, we stroked on through the sweltering summer day. By the second rest period, the blisters on my hands had burst. Stewart told me to tear strips from my shirt and wrap my hands, but I hated to ruin the only shirt I possessed and hesitated to do it. A warrior noted my dilemma and threw me a piece of beaver pelt to make a sort of mitten. It made all the difference in the world. I offered my thanks, and he ignored me.

Their broad backs glistening, shoulders working, stroke after stroke, hour after hour, the Indians never seemed to tire. As the evening progressed, I was ready to collapse in the bottom of the canoe. My breath came in rasping gasps, and my shoulders had long since lost any feeling.

The sun was a giant red ball when it sank into the lake behind us. As dusk settled in, a chill breeze came up across the water. We paddled on as the darkness grew. I lost sight of the other boats, but I could hear the relentless rhythm of each stroke. Then a whoop sounded from the lead boat, and it was answered by a man in each boat down the line.

Soon, I could discern a light in the distance. A large fire burned on the shore, several miles ahead. It was a beacon for any canoes still on the water and a welcome one, I can tell you.

Much relieved and with trembling legs, I stepped onto the rough stone beach at Oswego beneath the walls of Fort Ontario.

CHAPTER 32
The Great Council Fire

July 18th, 1777
Oswego, New York

Fort Ontario was an impressive wood and earth structure standing proudly atop a high bluff between the lake
and the Oswego River. It was a five-pointed star with a
scattering of buildings visible inside and a wicked *fraise* of
sharpened stakes embedded beneath the outer parapet.
The fort looked well protected to my untrained eye.

We were among the last to arrive. More than 2,000 Indians encamped in the wide grassy area east of the fort.
Campfires and lean-tos stretched as far as I could see.

Cornplanter spoke to his half-brother, Handsome Lake,
and our party split into two groups, each going in search of
unoccupied ground. The three captives, back on our
leashes, went with Cornplanter.

I felt like I had sat down on an anthill. Everywhere I
looked, there were hundreds of Indians. They crouched at
cook fires, or traded wampum beads spread on blankets,
or lounged in the grass while the squaws tended to their
needs.

Cornplanter called out instructions to the squaws once
he found an acceptable area. Immediately, the women

began erecting squat tents with the blankets and poles they had carried with them.

"You sleep under the sky tonight," Cornplanter told us. "Tomorrow, you and the squaws will build lean-tos and fire pits." He stood with his arms folded, inspecting the camps nearby. "This will be a good council. All the Nations are here."

I was more than content to lay down on a blanket and go to sleep while the squaws busied themselves setting up a fire and boiling a stew for our late supper.

By the time the food was ready, I was sound asleep and missed out altogether. The sun was breaking on the eastern horizon when I next raised my head.

I awoke stiff and sore and soaked from the dew. As usual, the women were already busy frying corn mush for our breakfast. Smoke from hundreds of cook fires wafted along the ground, held down by the damp morning air.

Tethered as we were, Stewart, Booker, and I were forced to coordinate each move — even our trip to the latrine on the far side of the encampment. We got along, so with minor adjustments, we each knew our position in line. We ate thick mush and sassafras tea sweetened with maple syrup, and bit by bit, my body began to move smoothly again. My hands, however, would be sore for days.

Near the wall of the fort, a gigantic bonfire was flaring up. Bare-chested warriors attended it, adding logs and brush, a task that was usually the job of a squaw. Soon, a series of whoops passed through the encampment, each noticeably different than its predecessor. As one, the mass of humanity moved toward the roaring fire.

"Now we start," Stewart said as our guard led us forward. Another warrior from our party motioned us back and spoke to our guard in Seneca. "We're forbidden to be too close," Stewart translated, "though they don't mind if we sit back here and listen."

We found an open space and made ourselves comfortable in the damp grass. The guard holding the end of our tether spread a blanket and sat behind us. The leather leash that the Indians used to lead us was purely for show. It was tight and secure about our wrists, but we could have worked free at any time. As I have said, however, I had no intention of trying to escape, and the leash showed the other warriors that we belonged to Cornplanter.

A buzz of anticipation rippled across the field as twenty men approached the fire. They all took places on sections of logs draped with blankets. I admit I felt like a youngster waiting for the medicine man to start his show. The energy was palpable.

"Those are the sachems from each Nation," Stewart said.

"How can you tell them apart?" I asked. Every Indian looked much like another to me. None of the sachems wore face paint since this was intended to be a friendly meeting. One old man caught my attention. He wore a British redcoat with the sleeves cut off like a gentlemen's waistcoat.

Stewart chuckled. "Telling them apart is a true art. Ain't that so, Will?"

Booker answered with a nod, as he always did. "They wear hats," he said knowingly.

I noticed that every sachem did, in fact, wear a headpiece, but again, I saw no discernible difference. Each was a strange skull cap embellished with feathers and trinkets.

"So, here's how it works," Stewart explained. "Our Seneca sachems, like Cornplanter and Handsome Lake up there, got a feather in his hat stuck straight up. Deer Hunter, an Oneida chief I ran across once or twice, has two feathers up and one to the side."

"You're not serious," I scoffed. "They have coded hats?" The three of us wore salvaged felt cocked hats that showed more than minor wear.

"It's a fact, eh, Will?" I did not bother looking to see if Booker agreed. By now, I took it as a given.

"Then there's your Mohawk, don't know him, with three feathers up. Tall Oak from the Cayuga, fella with the red coat, he's got one to the side. Over there, with one up and two to the side, is an Onondaga. The only tribe I don't see is the Tuscarora; they got no feathers in their caps."

"Why not? They don't rate a feather?"

Stewart shook his head. "Tuscarora come late to the party, you might say. The Iroquois Confederacy had five Nations for a couple hundred years. Then, few years back, they let the Tuscarora join. So Tuskies don't get a feather."

He and Booker laughed uproariously as if this were a colossal joke. I failed to see the humor and let it go.

So, now that I could identify each sachem, I settled in for a long day of speeches and debate. I have already mentioned how Indians go on and on when they are before an appreciative crowd or pontificating in front of other sachems. The first sachem to speak represented the Onondaga Nation, the official Keepers of the Council Flame.

As the morning wore on and each man stood to address the council, Stewart translated for me. He said that at council meetings, all of the sachems speak Mohawk, their

236

common language. Before long, however, I begged him to stop and just give me the abridged version. For the most part, each sachem welcomed the others to the council fire as if it had been their idea to have a meeting.

The man I understood to be the real council host, Joseph Brant, was nowhere to be seen. Stewart thought that was peculiar.

I must have dozed for a while because Stewart jabbed my side and told me it was impolite to snore while the sachems were giving their speeches. I sat up straighter and tried to pay attention.

Cornplanter was standing with a colorful blanket draped over his shoulders and speaking to the seated chiefs. He spoke for all of the Seneca, who, as the most western nation, were identified as the Keepers of the Western Door. Stewart reported that Cornplanter said everyone was here to establish two important points with the British.

First, would the Iroquois participate in the white man's war as the British wished, or remain neutral as the American's wanted? Second, either way, the British must agree that there will be no more incursion into Iroquois land.

All of the other sachems were in agreement, so at least the fundamental reason for the council was established. I closed my eyes again and let the warm sunshine lull me back to sleep. These people made decisions as slow as growing grass.

Late in the afternoon, all eyes turned to the fort as the heavy gate swung open. An armed escort of four soldiers marched out with a civilian leading the way. The soldiers were dressed in clean red coats and black cocked hats. They carried their muskets with fixed bayonets on their shoulders. Bright, newly clayed belts crossed their chests. Their knee-high boots shined with fresh blacking. These boys had turned out for a show.

The man they escorted was not as imposing as the soldiers marching behind him. He was thick around the middle and wore a civilian green suit that could have used a proper brushing. He had the appearance of an eastern gentleman recently returned from a long journey.

As the man approached the council fire, all of the sachems rose to their feet to greet him. More slowly, the hundreds of Indians in the audience stood also. The man walked up to the sachems, swept his hat from his head, and bowed deeply.

In English, he loudly proclaimed, "Great chiefs of the Six Nations, I, Colonel John Butler, Commissioner of Indian Affairs, appointed by His Majesty, King George, welcome you to Fort Ontario."

I gathered that Butler was likely to be as long-winded as the others, so I sat back down.

"I am sent by our father, the King," Butler continued, "because of the alliance that our people and the people of the Six Nations have shared for many years. We are bound to each other, and that binding is strong. Now, our American brothers have become disobedient to our father, the King. They do not listen to his words, so there is war between the white brothers. Our father, the King, now asks that the Six Nations join him in punishing his American children who are disobedient to his word."

There was a great deal more, but you get the gist. Soon Butler came to the part all of the Indians were waiting to hear — what presents were the British offering for help against the Americans? Butler described the copper pots, scalping knives and tomahawks, the muskets, and all of the great presents that would be theirs. Most importantly, he said that the rum would be as plentiful as the water of the lake. The Americans, he pointed out truthfully enough, do not have presents to give. They are poor and expect the Indians to stay in their cabins and hide like women.

He spoke forcefully, his words flowing smoothly. Butler was used to this kind of speech-making, and he had quite an impact on the gathering. Having an armed escort standing at attention during the entire long speech added to the overall importance of his words. When he finished speaking, he faced the fort and held out an arm. On command, the gate swung open, and a cart, drawn by four soldiers, rumbled across the grass to the council fire. It was loaded with two barrels.

"Now, we're in for it," Stewart said, shaking his head. "Can't have a council fire without rum. We best move on back to our camp." He spoke to our Indian guard, who was against the idea of leaving now that the party was getting underway. Stewart started toward our camp, and we had no option but to follow.

"We don't want any part of this," he said as we wound our way past the mass of people advancing on the rum barrels. "Things might get nasty, and case you ain't noticed, we're the only white men without guns."

CHAPTER 33
Captain Brant

July 19th, 1777
Oswego, New York

It was well past noon the next day before anything much happened in the camp. The revelers were slow to get up, and no one seemed in a hurry to start the meeting again.

Cornplanter, however, was up early and in a foul mood. He went around his camp, kicking at his warriors and telling them to get up. For the most part, everyone completely ignored him. We stayed away from him all day long.

The smoldering fire was rekindled at dusk, and it looked like this would be a short, uneventful meeting. Most of the warriors had been shamed into sobriety by this time. A crowd slowly gathered to hear a speech by an old Oneida chief named Shenandoah, who argued that the Iroquois should honor the previous agreement made with the Americans and stay out of the war.

Cornplanter took this as an opportunity to voice his support for that position. He stood boldly before the council, his body glistening in the firelight.

"My brother speaks with wisdom," Cornplanter began, raising an acknowledging hand to the old sachem. "The Americans say we should not raise our tomahawks for either side. There are none among us who can say for certain why the Americans have chosen to be disobedient. If we do not know the reasons, we may make a mistake if we join one side. I say this to my people and the people of the other Nations — War is war, death is death, and a fight is a very hard business."

A murmur of agreement rolled through the assembly, and the other sachems nodded their heads. Cornplanter had made several important points. I thought he had swayed the council in favor of neutrality until a loud shout arose from the woods beyond the open field.

The call was picked up by other Indians in the audience. With growing alarm, I saw knives and tomahawks pumping in the air everywhere I looked. The noise grew and grew until a group of Indians entered the field.

Like Moses parting the sea, seven warriors strode toward the council fire. Their faces and gleaming, bare torsos were striped with war paint. They whooped and shouted, holding a spear in one hand and a tomahawk in the other. No one stood in their way.

"Ah," said Stewart with mixed emotions, "he does like to make an entrance."

"Is that Brant?" I asked.

"None other," he responded. "Now we'll see which way the wind blows."

The man in the center of the war party, for there was no question that it was, walked like a general assuming command of his army. He was tall with broad shoulders, and his round head was bald and painted red. I have to admit that Joseph Brant cut a rather handsome figure. (13)

As he entered the council circle, I noted that in skin color and facial features, he could have passed for a white man. He had dark, intelligent eyes, a strong brow, and the typical full lips of the Mohawk people.

Joseph Brant, first sachem of the Mohawk Nation, stopped in front of the seated sachems and looked at each one in turn. Then he faced Cornplanter, who still stood near the fire where he had been speaking. With a single violent motion, Brant flung his spear to the ground at Cornplanter's feet.

Cornplanter did not move, refusing to recognize the challenge. Brant turned toward the assembled crowd, all of whom were on their feet, and raised his arms to them. Eventually, the whooping died down and a semblance of order restored.

I noted that Handsome Lake, sitting at his place in the circle, was frowning deeply. So were one or two other sachems. Warriors from our Seneca party grumbled among themselves. Brant may have many of the Indians behind him, but he was not popular with everyone.

Without looking back at Cornplanter, Brant spoke in Mohawk, and the field of onlookers buzzed in alarm.

"What's he saying?" I asked Stewart.

Stewart's face was tight, and he rubbed his hand over his bearded chin. "Brant just called Cornplanter 'Nephew.'"

"Is that bad?"

"They're both the same age," Stewart said, his voice reflecting the seriousness of the moment. "It's like me calling you a bastard. You wouldn't take it too kindly. Now it's getting ugly."

"There are warriors in the Six Nations," Brant was saying, "and there are squaws. My brother from the Seneca Nation is a coward if he does not want to fight as a warrior is meant to fight. No warrior should listen to his words. I bring three hundred men — true warriors! They have the scalp belts to prove their bravery! Um, um, um." The last words were Stewart's as he finished translating.

The Seneca in the audience, including those in our group from Canawaugus, raised their tomahawks as one and shouted that they were not cowards. Seeing the sudden change in the audience, Cornplanter deflated before our eyes. He looked back at the other sachems who had spoken for peace, and they sadly shook their heads.

In one fell swoop, Brant had arrived and completely dominated the council. They were going to war.

Our guard yanked on our leash and quickly led us back to the Seneca camp. It was not a happy group. On the one hand, they were excited at the prospect of war. On the other hand, however, their leader had been grievously insulted. Cornplanter ignored everyone when he returned to the camp. He ducked into his lean-to, and his squaws busied themselves bringing him food.

Things calmed down after an hour or so, and we told our guard we needed the privy. He was unhappy with the idea but led us to the edge of the camp to do our business. The latrine was nothing more than a long trench dug in the woods at the edge of the encampment. Someone was thoughtful enough to dig it downwind of the camps.

I was lacing up my breeches when three mean-looking Indians joined us. Stewart's translation was not required to understand that what they said to our guard was not a pleasant greeting.

"They're Mohawk," Stewart whispered. "Don't look 'em in the eye."

Our guard was a fierce young man, and to his credit, he tried to step past the three men blocking our path. As he attempted to lead us away, one of the Mohawk warriors leapt forward and, with a startlingly loud whoop, struck Booker on the head with his tomahawk.

Poor Will hit the ground like a rock, nearly dragging Stewart and me down with him. Our guard cried out in anger and astonishment, pulled his knife from his belt, and threw himself at the Mohawk attacker.

The two men crashed together, each trying to grapple for the other's weapon. Before I could make a move, they lurched against me, the Mohawk's back hitting my shoulder. Instinctively, I reached for the man, momentarily pinning his right arm. He fought to free himself from my grasp, and in doing so, released the Seneca's knife hand. It was enough. There was a blur of steel, a scream, and our attacker fell to the dirt, blood gushing from his throat.

Without thinking, I snatched up the fallen tomahawk and stepped beside our guard. In one smooth movement, he reached out and slashed my leather restraints. We turned as one and faced the other assailants who had not yet made a move.

Realizing their attack had not gone as planned, the two Mohawk warriors turned and fled back to their camp.

Our guard looked at me without the slightest trace of emotion on his face. He held out his empty hand, indicating the bloody tomahawk I still grasped and nodded once. His meaning was clear. I handed it over and turned to my fallen companions. Only seconds had passed since Booker had been wounded.

"Will! Will!" cried Stewart, kneeling beside his friend. Booker's face was a mask of blood. A hunk of hair hung down on his forehead, and his eyes were open and round in shock.

"That hurt," he said, sitting up and feeling for the loose piece of skin. "Alex! I'm scalpt!"

Four Seneca warriors rushed to our aid, apparently hearing the fight. Our guard quickly explained what had transpired, and they helped pull Booker to his feet. Stewart rummaged a bandana from inside his shirt and placed it on Will's head in a feeble attempt to slow the bleeding. Head wounds bleed terribly, and this one showed no signs of stopping anytime soon.

We all limped back to the camp, leaving the dead Mohawk lying beside the stinking pit.

Cornplanter sat cross-legged before our lean-to, his face severe and drawn. "Brant is to blame for this," he said, gesturing toward Booker, now with a corn plaster holding his loose scalp in place. "He believes that he speaks for all of the Iroquois, and his warriors do not follow the laws of the council fire. We are here to talk, not fight."

"I'm not so sure he doesn't speak for all the Iroquois," I ventured. "Last night, he had a strong effect on the meeting. I believe the Nations are ready to follow him to war."

Cornplanter shook his head. "There are always troublemakers. Brant told me he had no knowledge of the attack before it happened and assured me it was not of his making."

I raised an eyebrow.

"No one believes him," he continued. "You have my thanks, Moorhead, for standing with my nephew last night."

"Nephew?" I said with surprise, glancing at Stewart. "I thought that was a bad word."

A smile passed briefly over Cornplanter's face and then disappeared as quickly. "The words of Brant were used to insult me, make me look less important than he, but *Te-*

kay-e-tu is my sister's son. He *is* my nephew. He tells me that you stood shoulder to shoulder against the Mohawks, and for that, I thank you."

With this, Cornplanter held out a small beaded wampum belt. I took it with both hands and admired it appropriately. I wrapped it around my wrist and let Stewart tie the string ends. Giving me wampum was more than a cash reward — wearing Seneca colors was a tribute. I glanced at the young warrior, and he nodded his head. That was as much of a thank you as I could expect.

Over the ensuing years, this young man, Tekayetu, would go by many names as his reputation and position among the Seneca grew. Today, he is the well-known sachem we call Blacksnake. (14) However, back then, he was a young, hot-tempered warrior of twenty-three wanting nothing more than to bloody his scalping knife.

CHAPTER 34
St. Leger

July 25th, 1777
Oswego, New York

Word of the attack spread quickly. I heard that the other sachems admonished their people to avoid any conflict. There were no more incidents that I knew of.

I also learned that the majority of the sachems were leaning strongly in favor of Brant and support of the British. Two groups of sachems, representatives of the Oneida and the Tuscarora, held out for the Americans, and that led to heated discussions and no resolution.

Early on the seventh day of the council fire, a booming noise went up from the fort and most of the Indians, and we three 'honored guests' gathered to see what was happening. Until now, the fort had ignored most of the Indian's activities.

With drums beating, a troop of fifty or more soldiers marched from the fort, flags waving in the stiff morning breeze. They circled past the river side of the fort and down to the beach, where they formed up in columns and faced the lake.

In the distance, gorgeously lit by the rising sun behind us, we could see an armada of boats rowing toward the shore. These boats, called by their French name, *bateau*, were usually thirty feet long and six feet wide with flat bottoms, that is, no keel. Due to their design, they carried more men and supplies than canoes, and they could be carried or dragged cross-country if a portage was required. Each boat held up to thirty-nine men, twelve of whom were rowing.

The boats squared up, and one rode the swell onto the beach. It was impossible to make out any faces from where I stood, but the first man ashore was clearly a high-ranking officer. The gold trim on his red coat reflected in the sun.

A cacophony of cheers went up from the Indians on the hill above, and musket fire filled the air. John Butler and the fort's commanding officer stood on the beach, waiting to greet the arriving officer. Off to the side stood Brant with his Mohawk honor guard. The commanding officer shook hands with the new arrivals. Then they all waited as each bateau landed and discharged the soldiers it carried. As each boat emptied, the rowers pulled away from the beach and moored in the calmer waters of the river.

Each arriving division formed up on the beach behind the officer. Then with high precision and perfect form, they all marched back up to the fort, flags impressively displayed.

It was all great theater, and the Indians loved it. More powder was wasted that morning than used in many a battle, I would think.

An hour later, soldiers re-emerged from the fort and marched to the council fire. Butler introduced the officer to the sachems, and each shook his hand in turn. The officer was a slight man with a narrow face and a prominent nose. He had that scrunched-up face that British nobles tend to affect as if smelling something unpleasant.

Brigadier General Barrimore Matthew St. Leger had arrived in Oswego. (15)

I did not like him.

Young Blacksnake was still responsible for us prisoners, but he wanted to hear what the Brigadier had to say. He worked his way toward the front of the crowd, and we followed on our tether, shoved and kicked by those we annoyed.

St. Leger spoke no Mohawk, so for once, I did not require Stewart's interpretation. However, even though the sachems all spoke some amount of English, Brant stood beside the Brigadier and translated the speech into Mohawk. These two men were cut from the same cloth.

In a high, stilted voice, St. Leger expressed how pleased he was at the size of the council. He came to Oswego, he said, to begin a most critical mission. He wanted the help of the Iroquois in transporting his army down the Mohawk River, where the rebels had possession of a fort.

"Do not worry," he said to the gathered warriors, "you will not be asked to do any fighting. I ask you to come and watch as the mighty British Army removes the rebels from the King's fort."

Well, after the last few days of doing everything possible to incite this rabble, that was *not* the shrewdest thing to say. At this point, fighting was all they wanted to do.

Brant turned to St. Leger, whom he seemed to know well, and spoke in a muffled voice. St. Leger, obviously irritated to be interrupted in such a familiar manner, stepped away from Brant to continue addressing the sachems.

"I bring many presents for the children of our King," he announced, and a young subaltern lifted a bolt of scarlet cloth and pulled off a yard or two with a grand flourish. Another junior officer held up copper kettles and handfuls of beads.

"Trinkets!" Stewart said dismissively and spat tobacco juice in the dirt.

St. Leger continued, "I promise more presents are now coming across the lake — rum, sugar, and powder. And," he paused for added effect, "the warriors who accompany me will be allowed into the fort once it falls. Anything they want is theirs."

There was a general murmur of appreciation at this, but he was not finished. St. Leger paused a moment and then stood straighter. He spoke loudly, so even the Indians in the back row could hear the words that many later questioned his authority to speak.

"I also promise," the Brigadier called out, "our King will pay for every scalp that his children take from the rebels!"

That did it. The mob whooped and cried out ferocious war calls and once more fired muskets into the air. I had to hand it to St. Leger, he knew how to work the crowd, and he knew what they wanted. Many of the warriors, like our young guard Blacksnake, had not yet bloodied their scalping knives. St. Leger had just signed the death warrant for every Patriot in the fort.

Beside me, Stewart tsk, tsk-ed, and Will gently touched the plaster on the top of this head.

There were more speeches from other sachems while St. Leger stayed at the council fire. Then they voted, like we do, by raising a hand. Cornplanter agreed to the overall consensus and committed 150 Seneca to join the 300 Mohawk Brant controlled. The Onondaga and Cayuga offered a handful of warriors, but the Oneida and Tuscarora said they would not participate and walked away from the fire.

The other sachems did not take this news well. For the first time in the 500-year history of the Iroquois Confederacy, the policy agreed upon at the council fire was not unanimously accepted.

A post, about head-high, was erected near the council fire. One after the other, the remaining sachems, and then the minor war-chiefs, danced around the post and struck it with their tomahawks to signify their willingness to go to war. As they attacked the post, each sung a haunting tune that rose and fell in time with their dancing. No storyteller has ever adequately described the savagery of this primitive scene. Bodies glistening with bear fat and sweat reflecting the red glow of the fire, the guttural, unintelligible singing, wood chips flying, and the moon shining down on it all. It was beautiful.

Soon the post was reduced to chips, and the sachems turned to the dying embers of the council fire. Together, they took two old, wet blankets and laid them on the coals. The great council fire of Oswego was extinguished. The meeting was over.

Within minutes, another barrel of rum magically appeared from the fort, and the party resumed.

That evening, the Oneida and Tuscarora camps packed up and quietly departed.

Sitting close to the front of the audience, I became aware of a British officer staring right at me. I looked back at him, and his face lit up.

"Moorhead?" he shouted. "Good Heavens, man, is that you?"

Then recognition hit me. I was dumbstruck. Hundreds of miles and many years had passed since I last saw Captain

William Walsh. He was the soldier who had welcomed Sam and Jim and me at his camp at Fort Necessity during our first trek west of the Alleghenies. I noted that he was now a Major.

"Walsh!" I cried, stretching as far as my leash allowed. "For God's sake, you've got to help me!"

Walsh looked at the tether held by Blacksnake and spoke to him in Mohawk. Blacksnake answered curtly and turned his head away.

"It seems you're the property of a powerful sachem who wishes to sell you."

Tears of frustration filled my eyes. My fear of being sold to the British, who had a poor reputation, at best, when it came to the treatment of rebel prisoners, vanished in an instant. If Cornplanter sold me to Walsh, I knew I would be well treated, maybe even exchanged, so I could return to Jane. Suddenly, my world focused on that British officer. My mind reeled with the possibility of going home.

"Buy me, Walsh!" I pleaded. "I know you're an honorable man. I'll go with you. You won't let anything bad happen." I was blubbering.

Walsh pursed his lips in thought. "We are forbidden to buy prisoners, personally," he said. "I will go to the Brigadier. He has the authority."

My heart raced at the thought of being with civilized men again. "Please, Walsh!"

"I'll do what I can." He spoke to Blacksnake again, and we followed Walsh toward the gathered officers. Brant was still there, of course, and so was Cornplanter. Blacksnake spoke to Cornplanter, evidently explaining the prospect of a sale.

St. Leger frowned at Walsh. "What's this, then, Major?" he asked in a high, nasally voice.

"Sir," Walsh began, "these men have been captives of the Seneca for many months. They belong to this chief. He is willing to sell them to us."

The fucking prig refused to so much as look at us. "We are here to kill rebels, Major," he said, "not buy them. It would be best if you remember that. We are going into battle, sir. Concentrate your energy on that."

"Please, General," I said, stepping up, "we aren't rebels. I'm a loyal Pennsylvania settler. My home's on the Allegheny frontier."

"Humph!" St. Leger snorted. "Loyal Pennsylvanian, indeed! As if there were such a creature."

Then he turned his back on us and walked away!

I stood staring at him, my mouth hanging open.

"Walsh!" I cried. "Isn't there something you can do?"

Walsh sadly shook his head. "I am sorry, my friend. I shall try to talk to him again before we leave tomorrow. I'll see what I can do. I promise," he said, patting me on the shoulder. Then he followed his general back to the fort. I was devastated. Stewart and Booker, mouths gaping, looked as stunned as I.

Cornplanter, who had been listening carefully to the exchange, hung his head. His two missions at Oswego — convince the Nations to stay neutral and sell his captives — had failed.

Our eyes met, sharing the disappointment each felt, albeit for vastly different reasons. A shudder passed through me as I read the look on his face.

My value had just severely depreciated.

CHAPTER 35
Fort Stanwix

July 27th to August 4th, 1777
The Mohawk Valley, New York

I had to keep reminding myself that I was traveling with the enemy, and they were on their way to attack my fellow Patriots. Sometimes that fact got lost in the effort to move St. Leger's army from Oswego to Fort Stanwix. It was fifty miles as the crow flies, but our path was much longer.

The main body consisted of no more than 350 regulars — small detachments of the British 8th and 34th Foot, and part of the German Hesse-Hanau Jäger Corps, the skirmishers and sharpshooters. The British soldiers were in high spirits, believing themselves on an easy expedition to wipe out the American rebels. The Germans were a surly group, speaking no English and staying to themselves.

There were also Loyalist troops from Sir John Johnson's Royal Regiment of New York, calling themselves the Royal Greens. Then there were close to 700 Indians, led by Brant. Cornplanter's Seneca made up a majority of the contingent, yet he was now clearly subordinate to Brant.

All of St. Leger's bateaux and dozens of canoes were dragged above the first Oswego River falls and then loaded with men and supplies. Four of the bateaux carried a light cannon lashed to the thwarts in the center of the boat.

Many of our Indians took to their canoes. Stewart, Booker, and I went on foot with a party of Seneca, meeting up with the boats at each night's camp.

You may wonder why the Seneca still kept us as prisoners, seeing as how Cornplanter had failed to sell us to the British. I have no answer for that, except that Indians are patient people. Cornplanter had kept us this long, and he would not simply let us go. And, thank God, he lacked the will to kill us.

As we progressed, the Loyalists explained that our role in this campaign was just one leg of a major operation planned by General John Burgoyne. The General's grand scheme was to cut a line through the colonies, separating New England from New York and the southern states.

The plan was sound. Burgoyne was moving his army from Montreal to Albany on Lake Champlain while St. Leger moved his forces from Lake Ontario east and, eventually, down the Mohawk River. Along the way, St. Leger was to capture Fort Stanwix, thought to be held by an insignificant garrison of Patriots. At the same time, General Howe's army was supposed to move up the Hudson. All three armies would converge on Albany, and the rebellion would be over.

Funny how things do not always work out as planned.

The first leg, thirty miles up the Oswego River, was not all that difficult, though the longboats were crowded and uncomfortable. The men rowing and poling did the hardest work. In places, they had to wade ashore and use ropes to drag the boats over shallows or a series of rapids. From time to time, our shore party was ordered to help, but overall, walking through the forest was easier than being in the boats.

Eventually, the river widened out, and the boats made better time up to Lake Oneida, a beautiful body of water stretching twenty miles from west to east. Those of us on foot circled it in one long, exhausting day while the boats rowed straight across.

On the eastern side of the lake, it took longer than expected to find the entrance to Wood Creek, the stream that would lead us to the Mohawk River carry.

When it was finally located within the reed-infested marsh, the boats only progressed half a mile before coming to an impassable log jam. Freshly felled trees crisscrossed the stream for a hundred yards, forming a perfect abatis. Stewart believed it had been set by the men from the fort, no more than a day before. The boats could go no further.

St. Leger stomped and swore and then assigned a group of Indians and a handful of Loyalists to start cutting a trail. Stewart, Booker, and I worked alongside our enemies while others labored to clear the creek.

It was difficult work due to the thick undergrowth beneath the trees. St. Leger pushed us to make the remaining sixteen miles to Fort Stanwix in three days. We did not quite make that, but it was not for lack of effort. I vented my anger and frustration on the forest. Every time I spied St. Leger, my blood boiled, and I swung my ax all the harder.

Of course, the troops hauling the four small cannons, mortars, and supplies did not have it so easy, either. As hard as we worked, stumps and logs interfered with their every step. Each cannon required twelve men to move it, pushing and pulling, lurching and bumping along the rough-hewn trail.

In the afternoon of August 3rd, the echoes of musket fire identified our destination long before the fort came into view. We knew nothing of it at the time, but St. Leger had sent an advance party ahead as soon as the boats stopped at the log jam.

The skirmishers had arrived on the 2nd and were already sniping at the fort and taking fierce fire in return. The first thing I noticed as we exited the forest was the pile of bodies awaiting burial. The unpleasant sounds of injured men emanated from a hastily erected tent near the top of the rise.

Behind us, soldiers poured from the trail we had labored so hard to clear. Company after company took up positions along the ridge above the fort. Pleased to stay away from the mounting confusion, we were tied to a tree along the forest edge.

While working on the trail, we captives were free of the ever-present tether. Young Blacksnake was no longer assigned to us, having gone with the sachems in the canoes. Instead, a muscular and remarkably morose warrior had replaced him when we first departed Oswego.

Our new guard hated his duty and showed it by roughly leading us like cattle when we were not free to work. I never learned his name, and he never attempted to speak to us. Now, sitting in the mud and rain, he looked even more depressed than usual. He hung his head between his legs, using his knees to block the relentless barrage from his ears.

Puffs of smoke bloomed from the top of the fort's stout ramparts, immediately followed by the high-pitched crack of a small-bore cannon. To make matters worse, musket balls splattered the mud only a hundred feet in front of us.

No one seemed interested in what we did, so I sat with my companions and studied the massive structure we had come so far to capture. Our position afforded a perfect view of Fort Stanwix and the deploying British Army.

Sitting on a lonely stretch of the Mohawk River, the value of Fort Stanwix was not immediately evident. However, as Stewart explained, it was critical to controlling the Mohawk Valley. We were in his old stomping grounds, so he understood its importance.

The sixteen miles of wilderness we had labored so hard to clear included an open section known as the Oneida Carry. The portage connected two great waterways. On one side of the Carry, the Mohawk River allowed transport east to Albany and then to the Atlantic by way of the Hudson. By crossing Lake Oneida on the other side, boats could go down to Oswego and Lake Ontario in the west. From Ontario, it was again possible to reach the Atlantic by the Saint Laurence River. Fort Stanwix strategically defended the portage, and thereby, travel in both directions.

The fort was an immense square earthwork with triangular bastions at the corners. Each side measured 330 feet, point to point. A dry, wide ditch protected walls higher than two men. By comparison, Fort Ontario was only a log cabin.

As I considered the fort, Stewart commented that the structure before us was vastly improved since the last time he passed this way. A twenty-eight-year-old colonel named Peter Gansevoort, and the men of the 3rd New York, had done a masterful job rebuilding the fort. I was amazed that such a fortification existed in the middle of this wilderness.

"You know," Stewart said, "you wouldn't have your homestead if it weren't for this fort."

I must have looked skeptical because he continued, "It's true. Back in '68, the Iroquois signed a treaty right here, allowing settlements in Pennsylvania west of the Alleghenies and in the western parts of New York. They gave up a whole lot of land so you folks could move west. I'm thinking they might be regretting that about now."

Now that he said it, I did remember Jim Kelly explaining the importance of the Treaty of Fort Stanwix. In '69, we were the very first to take advantage of the newly opened land. It felt like a lifetime ago. How many more had made the trek since we braved those mountains? Our new country was growing quickly. I wondered if it would survive.

Eventually, the cannon brigade made it up the trail and positioned their guns about 600 yards northeast of the fort on higher ground. The Loyalists and Indians were ordered to make their camp west of the river's bend in low, swampy ground. Stewart observed that St. Leger wished our smelly bodies to be far from his tent.

Fort Stanwix was soon effectively besieged by a loose triangle of men and artillery. St. Leger was still optimistic, strutting here and there, pointing with his sword to direct the cannon emplacements or the line of sharpshooters. If he was surprised by the unexpected size and condition of the fort, he never showed it.

The Brigadier, however, would not have been so cocky if he possessed one additional piece of information — something that would have a significant impact on the siege in the days to come.

Just hours before St. Leger's advance party arrived, 200 New York militia reinforced the main body of Patriots within the fort. They brought enough food, rum, ammunition, and powder to outlast any length of siege St. Leger could front.

He now faced a well-fortified and supplied army of 800 men inside a fort he had viewed as a minor irritation on his march east. St. Leger's campaign to quickly meet up with General Burgoyne at Albany was doomed.

I tried to get some sleep before the intermittent rain returned, but Stewart nudged me sharply in the ribs. "Look here," he said, motioning with this chin. "They're going to *parlez*."

Indeed, St. Leger intended to talk before fighting. Two officers and two flag bearers walked down the hill toward the fort. The soldiers held a white flag alongside the King's Colours. I saw Captain Gil Tice, whom I had spoken to a few times during our march. The other officer was my old acquaintance, Major William Walsh.

They stopped before the main gate and stood at attention while the Patriots on the walls silently stared down at them. After an insultingly prolonged period, the six-foot-wide gate swung open, and the four men disappeared inside.

We sat and watched the fort like children waiting for a play to begin. Nothing happened for an hour, and then the gate opened once more, and the British marched out, flags still held high. However, this time the men on the wall were not quiet. As the officers walked stoically back to our line, jeers and insults followed them. From their drawn faces, I knew the *parlez* had not gone well.

Then a remarkable event occurred. On the southeast bastion, a handful of men raised a short pole with a ragged piece of cloth attached. As we watched, a slight wind ruffled the heavy, unwieldy material. I could see that it was mostly red and blue, and I figured they were raising the British flag upside down — as a further insult to the retreating officers. Then the wind came up, and the flag snapped out stiff in the breeze.

Stewart let his breath out in surprise, and I stared, my heart in my throat. The flag looked like it was made from old shirts roughly sewn together. It consisted of a series of alternating red, white, and blue stripes. Thirteen stripes, to be exact.

A roar of voices came from within the fort as 800 men shouted and cheered, and a cannon fired into the wind. For the first time in history, a version of Old Glory stood proud and waved defiantly above an American fort. (16)

Tears still come to my eyes when I think back on that day when I stood in the rain on the muddy banks of the Mohawk River and hailed my country's flag.

CHAPTER 36
The Siege

August 4th and 5th, 1777
The Mohawk Valley, New York

St. Leger did not wait for Tice and Walsh to report. The flag flying over the fort was evidence enough that his offer for surrender was rejected.

I practically jumped out of my skin when the line of cannons on the hill behind me fired. They were not big guns, but even a six-pound iron ball can do a great deal of damage. And it makes a hell of a lot of noise. Across the field, the crows that had gathered together exploded into the air with cries of alarm.

We three huddled together in the rain, somewhere between the cannons firing nonstop behind us and the musket fire coming from the fort. This was my first initiation to an artillery barrage, and I am glad to say it was my last.

Within an hour, I could hear nothing Stewart was saying. He sat cross-legged, water dripping from his nose, smiling like a drunk man, and occasionally pointing out a particularly well-placed cannon shot to Will. Booker would nod in agreement, and they would both laugh. I was too miserable to join in their merriment.

As I watched the bombardment, I was impressed, once

again, by the size and strength of the fort. The walls seemed to easily accept the punishment St. Leger's artillery was meting out. Each ball caused a geyser of mud to spray upwards, yet the earthen parapet absorbed every shot. Occasionally, a piece of the timber palisade shattered, sending deadly splinters in every direction. When this happened, faces showed from behind the walls, and the jeering echoed louder than the guns. Not once did I observe a cannonball land within the redoubt.

It was soon apparent to me, a man utterly ignorant of siege warfare, that the British Army would never breach the walls of Fort Stanwix — not by a frontal attack nor with artillery. Amazingly, this observation did not seem as apparent to the Brigadier as it was to me.

If the siege was to succeed, the only means would be to starve the Patriots out. And that was not happening any time soon — the fort had been resupplied just hours before we arrived.

Brant's Mohawks and the German sharpshooters kept up a continuous barrage of their own. They were not as well protected as those firing at them and suffered for it. I witnessed two or three Indians hit during the afternoon, but the British and Germans took the brunt of the fire. At least ten men were killed or wounded within our view alone. God knows how many died that day.

At precisely eight o'clock that night, the rain stopped, and with it, the artillery barrage ceased as suddenly as it had commenced. The silence was unnerving. My ears continued to ring for an hour more.

Like civilized men in every war, the cannon fire and the sniping on both sides paused for supper.

Our guard was dragging us back to the Seneca camp when I spotted Walsh walking with Tice toward their tents. I pulled sharply on the tether and brought the Indian up short. He growled and glared menacingly but did not resist.

"Walsh!" I called. "It's me, Fergus!"

The Major walked up to our group. Shaking his head, he said, "You aren't looking any better, Moorhead. But at least you're still alive. Eh, what?" His tired face betrayed the small attempt at levity.

"Have you spoken to St. Leger?" I asked, trying to keep the desperation from my voice.

Walsh shook his head again. "The day has not lent itself to the disposition of rebel prisoners, Moorhead. We are more interested in those still behind the walls." He raised a hand and pointed unnecessarily at the fort.

"They seem to have no intention of surrendering," I ventured.

"So it would appear."

"Can you tell me what they said?" I asked, curiosity overcoming my own plight.

Walsh hesitated before answering. "Colonel Gansevoort, himself, said he intended to defend his fort to the last extremity, on behalf of the United American States." Walsh laughed ironically. "The United States! Whoever heard of such arrogance?"

Walsh turned to walk away. He stopped and looked back at me and sadly shook his head before continuing to his tent. I watched him go, thinking about what he had said.

The United States.

I liked how that sounded.

When we arrived at the Seneca camp, Cornplanter,

Blacksnake, and Joseph Brant were standing around a blazing campfire. Not knowing what to do with us, our guard stopped beside the fire to warm himself. No one seemed to care as their attention was fixed on a middle-aged woman talking to Brant in a low, firm voice.

The woman was dressed in European clothes but with long braids and a dark complexion that suggested she was Indian. Also, she was speaking Mohawk to the men.

Stewart crept up behind me and whispered in my ear, "That's Brant's sister, Molly. Lives down the river some. She's telling them soldiers are coming to defend the fort."

"Who do you think's coming?" I whispered back.

"Only militia anywhere near here would be from German Flatts, below the falls. Herkimer's my guess."

Stewart said the last part too loudly, and the Indians stopped talking and looked at us.

Joseph Brant approached Stewart. "What do you know of this militia?" he demanded.

To his credit, Stewart hesitated long enough to show that he was not intimidated. "I doubt I know more than you, Captain," he said. Both men called the Mohawk Valley home.

Brant cocked his head to the side, as Indians tend to do, and said, "We scattered Herkimer's militia last winter. We burnt all the forts and houses. He has nothing left."

Stewart wagged his head from side to side. "Well," he said with a slight grin, "then you ain't got nothing to worry about."

Brant spoke sharply to Cornplanter and turned and strode away, his sister at his side.

"You come with us," Cornplanter ordered. Although our guard understood no English, his leader's meaning was clear. We all hustled to catch up to Brant, who was marching quickly toward St. Leger's tent.

"What the hell?" I sputtered, but Stewart only shrugged.

Brant snapped at the young soldier standing beside a luxuriously large white tent and barged in without waiting to be announced. Following him inside, I saw an impressive tableau spread before us.

Brigadier General St. Leger, Colonel Butler, Colonel Tice, and Sir John Johnson sat at a camp table enjoying their supper. Real wax candles sat on the table, illuminating the officers' faces and sparkling off the crystal wine glasses like a painting by an old Dutch master.

"Captain Brant!" St. Leger barked, coming to his feet. "What is the meaning of this?"

Showing no sign of contrition, Brant spoke right up, "You have heard of my sister, Molly. She lives above German Flatts. She has seen many militiamen gathering down the river. It may be General Herkimer's Tryon County Regiment."

The officers looked at each other in shock.

"I was told Herkimer's militia was defeated last year," St. Leger said, his voice rising in pitch and volume. "Tice! Weren't we told that?"

"Indeed we were, sir," Tice agreed. "Perhaps the situation has changed. How many men do you believe Herkimer could muster, Brant?"

"My sister says she counted more than five hundred, all armed. Also, they have Oneida with them."

"Oneida!" St. Leger practically squeaked. "Bloody hell, Butler! That was your job!"

By this, St. Leger was referring to the recent council fire that Butler had organized to sway the Iroquois to their cause. Everyone knew the Oneida and the Tuscarora had gone their own way at the end of the meeting. No one knew, however, that they had decided against neutrality, after all. It seems they intended to fight alongside the Americans and against their Iroquois brothers.

St. Leger seemed to notice the three mud-encrusted men standing inside his tent for the first time.

"Who the devil is this?" he demanded, raising a hand in our direction.

Brant indicated Stewart, and our guard pushed him forward. Will and I had no choice but to follow.

"This man is from the lower valley," Brant said. "He knows Herkimer and the men fighting for him. He can verify what my sister says."

Stewart stood stiffly at attention, his chin thrust out. "I ain't got nothing to say," he said.

St. Leger looked Stewart up and down in obvious disgust. "How long have you been a captive?" he asked.

"Ain't sure," Stewart chuckled. "What's the date?"

"The date, sir, is the fifth of August."

"Well, then," he answered with a note of surprise in his voice, "I've been with these fine gentlemen for a year! Fancy that!" Then he spat a wad of tobacco juice on the ground.

Sitting back down at this place, St. Leger studied Stewart before addressing Brant. "Frankly, Captain, I do not believe this man has any information that we can use. However, I do believe you, and you believe your sister. Indeed, Sir John has spoken of her often. So, we shall send a detachment downriver to reconnoiter."

"And if we find them?" Brant asked with an air of disdain in his voice.

"Then, you shall observe and report or engage and

destroy. It shall be Colonel Butler's decision."

Choking down his mouthful of beans, Butler looked around the table as if only now aware of the conversation. "You're sending me? With what? What forces are you giving me?"

"They're farmers, Colonel. I'm sure you can deal with them. You can have sixty men from the Jäger detachment, Sir John's Royals, and Brant's Mohawks. As many as he can scrape together."

Butler was counting in his head. "That's not enough. I want the Seneca, too," he said, indicating Cornplanter. "And these men," he pointed at us. "I think one of them knows more than he is saying."

Waving his hand in dismissal, St. Leger said, "That is between you and Captain Brant. I expect you to be on your way before daylight."

CHAPTER 37
Oriskany Creek

Wednesday, August 6th, 1777
The Mohawk Valley, New York

"Observe and report, my arse," Stewart said as we stumbled through the darkness. "These bastards is ready for a fight, and they're damn well gonna make it happen."

When Stewart failed to ask Booker his opinion, I knew he was truly upset.

We were moving slowly on a wide trail on the south bank of the Mohawk. Dawn was beginning to lighten the sky ahead of us, and the tiny crescent moon had set long before. Even the birds were still asleep, so the forest was still and silent. The only sound came from the soft crunch of moccasins and boots and the jangle of swords, muskets, and tomahawks.

It had required most of the night to round up the men and armament that Butler and Brant insisted on taking with them. Our role in the upcoming event was not clear to me at all. Our laconic guard did not seem to know, either. He located a position near the rally point and sat in his usual manner, head between his legs, staring at the ground.

Then, at four in the morning, the ragtag company of 450 Germans, Loyalists, Regulars, and Iroquois set off on the narrow wagon road that led down to German Flatts. Our position was at the head of the column, along with Cornplanter, Brant, Blacksnake, and the two colonels, Butler and Sir John.

To this day, I could not say who was actually in command. Sir John was the senior officer, but Butler gave all the orders to the small group of white soldiers. The vast majority of our company was comprised of Brant's Mohawks and Cornplanter's Seneca. There was no question about the Indian leadership, however. Brant was in command, and Cornplanter was not.

At first, there was a lot of talking among the men. They had been roused from their evening meal and told to be ready for action. Typical of every military operation I ever witnessed, the men were ready, and the companies formed long before the order to march came. The grumbling and general discontent was audible.

Now, however, after six miles of marching, the group was silent. Only Stewart's endless whispering disturbed the forest. No one paid any attention nor admonished us to be quiet. Butler received word from a scout that Herkimer was still miles away.

The shadowy form of Stewart on my left said, "I ain't going into any battle with these men. We must get away before the shooting starts. What do you think, Will?"

"We ain't important," Will said.

I could not agree more. For months, one Indian or another had dragged us from location to location. We were whipped, beaten, and generally abused at every opportunity. My wrists were raw from the leather straps, my moccasins were worn through, and my shirt hung like a rag across my shoulders. With all of that, this was the first time I felt genuinely concerned for our lives. We were of no value, so why take us? I knew that the chill deep in my bones was not from the pre-dawn air. Was this how a steer led to slaughter felt?

It was time to end this ordeal regardless of the risk of recapture. Stewart had no information to provide, and I certainly could be of no service. Cornplanter, now realizing we had no further value, might decide to simply have us killed.

It was time. I had to try to get back home, back to Jane and my children — at any cost.

"What's the plan?" I whispered back.

Gesturing at the lumbering Indian leading us, Stewart said, "My grandmother is more likely to get in a fight than that jackass. Once we get where we's going, he'll tie us to a tree and hunker down. If there's shooting, as I figure they're planning, then we can try to overpower him and make our escape in the confusion."

I thought that sounded somewhat optimistic but figured it was our best hope. If there was to be a battle, we would be the closest to our compatriots we had ever been. Our goal was to avoid getting shot by either side.

The forest was emerging from the shadows when Brant raised a hand and led us off the trail. We halted above a thickly wooded, narrow ravine. Its sides dipped steeply to a marshy, overgrown stream meandering northward to the Mohawk. From our vantage point, I could see the road we had recently abandoned circling down from the hill beyond. A shallow section of the stream afforded a crossing, and then the road climbed up the hill on the far side. It was the perfect place for an ambush.

Butler immediately began issuing orders. "I want the Germans and Royals over there," he said, pointing at the far hill. "They will provide the first contact."

He turned to Brant and continued, "Captain Brant, I want your warriors well-hidden on both sides of the ravine. Under no circumstances are you to open fire until the entire column is in the ravine. Is that clear?"

"Of course," Brant responded with a slight smile. Like his warriors, Brant was bare-chested, his body and face painted blood red with yellow and black stripes. The colors of war. "My warriors are ready to take many scalps. They will not fail."

"Good, I expect nothing less."

Brant turned to give orders to Cornplanter and Blacksnake when he noticed us standing nearby.

"What is your name?" he asked me in a mockingly friendly tone as if sitting down for a beer.

"Fergus Moorhead," I replied warily.

"I understand that Colonel St. Leger refused to buy you from Kiantwachia. You are of no value. Why are you still with him?"

I could not answer that, though I did notice that Brant used St. Leger's actual rank and not the title of Brigadier, with which he was brevetted for this campaign. Brant was full of insults.

"Chief Kiantwachia and I are friends," I offered. "We have seen much together."

Brant barked a mean laugh and looked at Cornplanter. "When you are dead, they will entertain my squaws."

Cornplanter stepped up to Brant and spoke to him in Mohawk. Brant laughed again and walked away, calling out instructions to his warriors.

Without a word, Cornplanter started positioning his men as Brant had ordered. He did not look happy.

"What did he say to Brant?" I asked Stewart.

Stewart had an amused look on his face. "Cornplanter

told the bastard to watch his own back and not worry about him. Those two gonna get into it one day, ain't that right, Will?"

"Country ain't got room for 'em both," Will replied with remarkable insight.

As Stewart predicted, we sat on the ground, tied securely to a pine tree five yards back from the edge of the ravine. It was a perfect seat for whatever was to happen.

"Can't we warn them?" I asked no one in particular.

Trying to make himself more comfortable in the pine needles, Stewart simply grunted. "You could stand up and holler at the top of your lungs as soon as you see someone, though you'd die before the sound reached Herkimer's ears."

"But it could save all of those men," I protested weakly.

"True. Don't let me hold you back."

I leaned my head against the rough bark of the tree in frustration. I was in a position to save hundreds of lives. Did I have the courage to do it? That was the question.

Stewart was right. The retribution would be swift and final. Overpowering these thoughts, the face of a beautiful redhead crept into my mind, and ashamed as I am to admit it, I offered no word of warning.

Mosquitos discovered us within half an hour and refused to go away, even as the morning wore on. The humidity increased with the sun's arc, thick clouds hung low and menacing, and we sat and waited, sweating and itching. Looking around the forest on each side of the ravine, you would never have believed that 300 Indians lurked in the shadows. Of Sir John's soldiers in the valley below, nothing whatsoever was evident.

A bird called out sharply in the distance, and Stewart's head snapped up. So did our otherwise lethargic guard's. I looked at Stewart, the question clear on my face. His eyes were wide, and he nodded to me. They were coming.

Brigadier General Nicholas Herkimer was a round, plump man on a big horse. At forty-eight, he was known as a competent leader and had, in the past, inspired confidence in his men.

As it turned out, however, this attempt to reach Fort Stanwix had not gone well from the start. They had left Fort Dayton two days before with 800 men and 400 oxcarts full of supplies. Several of his officers disagreed with the slow pace Herkimer set for the advance. They felt he was too timid and said so to his face.

Today, he rode his old white mare at the front of the column with his most loyal officers by his side. His army spread out a mile behind him, with the oxcarts far in the rear.

Aware of their officer's growing dissatisfaction with Herkimer, the ranks showed a general lack of discipline. The first group of militiamen coming over the rise walked two abreast, muskets in crossed arms or clubbed, upside down on their shoulders. They were not an organized unit.

At the sight of cool water crossing the gravel ford, a dozen men rushed from the column and threw themselves down to drink. They discarded their muskets and packs on the road, creating even more confusion for those who followed.

Herkimer was looking down the length of the ravine, probably thinking the same thing that we were — what a perfect place for an ambush.

"Get those men up!" I heard him hiss loudly. "Get them back in line. This is no place to stop!"

His officers pushed their agitated horses forward, demanding that the men reform. By then, another dozen men arrived, falling into the stream. There was chaos before the first shot.

I actually opened my mouth and drew in a breath before a sharp look from Stewart reawakened the survival instinct within me.

The hundreds of Iroquois hidden among the trees looked down upon their prey and smiled. Before them, 400 white men were exposed and unsuspecting. It was more than any warrior could stand.

It was ten o'clock in the morning when a single shot rang out, echoing across the valley.

General Herkimer raised his head in alarm.

And the Indians opened fire.

CHAPTER 38
The Place of Great Sadness

Wednesday, August 6th, 1777
The Mohawk Valley, New York

The first volley shattered the silence. Three hundred muskets fired from the forest surrounding the ravine. I was looking right at General Herkimer when the guns went off. His horse screamed and reared, falling to the side, taking the General with her.

The men in the stream flailed forward and backward as musket balls tore into them from every direction. In an instant of time, half of Herkimer's army was dead or wounded.

A thick wall of white smoke filled the air, blinding me for a moment. I could not see, but the war cries that issued from 300 throats, and the cries of agony from the valley below, came clearly to my ears.

With minimal effect, some of the officers were trying to form the men into a firing line. In horror, I saw a squad aim directly at our position and fire. Pine needles and bark rained down upon us as the balls ripped through the trees.

Just feet from me, two Indians spun away from the trees meant to protect them and fell to the ground. One of them tried to crawl toward my hiding place, a hole in his shoulder pumping blood into the pine needles. He did not make it.

As soon as the militiamen started to reload, dozens of warriors rushed down the hill and attacked the poor men with tomahawk and knife. They whooped as they ran at the frantic militiamen and killed with little resistance.

Two men pulled General Herkimer from beneath his horse and dragged him to a nearby tree. Blood coated his left leg, disturbingly bright against the white uniform trousers. The General, propped up against the huge beech, continued to issue orders even as one officer wrapped a scarf around the shattered leg, and the battle raged on.

I ducked low as another volley sliced over our hiding place. Stewart was face-down, his body pressed flat on the forest floor. I looked for Booker. He had his back up against the same tree as me, unharmed as well.

The same, however, could not be said of our guard. He sat on the ground in his usual position, head down and between his knees. Blood dripped steadily from the end of his nose.

"Stewart!" I shouted above the maelstrom.

When I had his attention, I pointed at the dead Indian. Stewart's eyes almost bugged out of his head. He reached as far back as he could with one leg and managed to push against the side of the Indian. The body rolled toward me.

Another volley erupted from the surrounding Indians, cloaking us in powder smoke.

"Get his knife!" Stewart shouted without fear of being heard more than a few feet away.

I pulled against my restraints and managed to hook a finger in the dead Indian's knife belt. I dragged him closer, extracted his scalping knife, and sliced my straps. I was free. Stewart and Booker quickly followed.

We squatted at the base of our tree and tried to

determine the safest route to freedom. The Indians close to us were intent on firing into the valley. They had no interest in us.

"We have to go round, get clear of this fight!" Stewart shouted and immediately moved off to our right. Keeping low and moving as fast as possible, we ducked and scrabbled from tree to tree while the noise, the smoke, the war cries, and the screams filled the world.

On every side, Indians were firing their muskets or rushing down the hill, shrieking wildly. At Herkimer's direction, the militia tried a new tactic to survive. As one man fired and reloaded, another man shot the Indian rushing at them. It was proving effective.

Another volley pummeled the forest around us, and Booker cried out and fell to the ground.

We threw ourselves down beside him. Blood welled from between the fingers that clutched his calf.

"Bloody hell, Will!" Stewart yelled close to his friend's face. "What'd you do that for?"

"I'm shot," Booker said.

"I see that. Well, there's nothing for it. You're just gonna have to run on it."

Booker grimaced as we helped him to his feet. We intended to go south of the fighting and find the rear of the relief column, but somehow we slipped down a steep gully and came face to face with another part of the raging battle. The Loyalists had joined in the hand-to-hand fighting. It was nearly impossible to tell friend from foe. Indians and white men fought side by side against their brothers.

It is a sad fact that most of the participants in this battle were Americans — Patriots and allied Oneidas fought against Loyalists and allied Seneca and Mohawk. The German and British regulars kept to the sidelines, sniping where they could.

At the time, I was too busy trying to avoid being killed by either side to appreciate the historical significance. (17)

We dodged men rolling on the ground while others bounced off of us, embraced in a deadly dance. To one side, a clear path opened among the combatants. Stewart turned and ran that way with Booker's arm over his shoulder.

A guttural sound made me look back in the direction of the fighting, and there was the young warrior, Blacksnake, grappling hand to hand with a man whose face glistened with blood. With a final twist, the white man fell backward, and Blacksnake sank his knife into the man's chest.

I was suddenly aware of a militiaman beside me as he raised his musket and took aim at Blacksnake.

Then a series of events happened in slow motion.

Blacksnake stood up from his kill, bloody knife in hand, and looked straight at the man aiming the musket.

Unthinking, I shoved my fellow Patriot with all of my strength. He staggered sideways and fell into the bushes, his musket discharging harmlessly in the air.

And Blacksnake charged at me.

I turned to follow Stewart and Booker, now a hundred feet away — and ran full stride into an Oneida warrior.

The warrior grabbed me by the throat and let out a scalp cry. My own death reflected in his bloodshot eyes as his tomahawk swung toward my head.

The rain woke me. My head throbbed, and my right eye was full of blood. I tried not to move as I assessed my body and determined that most of it was in working condition. I was alive, and that was not what I had expected.

Bit by bit, the world returned, and I realized that I could no longer hear the battle. Other than pitiful cries for help somewhere in the distance, the only sound was the driving rain and the relentless flash and explosion of nature's artillery.

Blacksnake called out in Seneca, and Cornplanter knelt at my side.

"Once again, you stand by my nephew," he said, a sad smile on his face, rain dripping from his nose.

I pushed myself up on an elbow and looked between the two Indians. To say the least, my emotions were conflicted. Technically, these men were my enemies, sworn at the council fire to fight against the Americans. On the other hand, we had been together for a long time and had gone through a great deal. I could not help seeing them as friends.

"I acted out of instinct," I said. "I didn't want your nephew to get shot. I'm afraid I may have caused a fellow patriot's death."

Blacksnake spoke again, and Cornplanter translated. "Tekayetu says that the man who tried to shoot him survived — at least at that moment. The Oneida who tried to kill you was not so fortunate."

Probing at the lump on the side of my head, I asked how long I had been unconscious.

"My nephew and another carried you to this spot as the rain started. No more than one hour has passed."

That was hard to believe. The first volley on the column was at mid-morning, and now, Cornplanter said, it was noon. Only two hours?

Each side had agreed it was too difficult to continue a battle in the middle of a pounding thunderstorm and withdrew to protective cover. As the storm raged, skirmishers took occasional shots at the other side just to ensure they stayed put. Both parties needed this respite to lick their wounds. Dead and wounded littered the valley floor.

Carefully moving my head, I looked around for my companions. The last I saw of them, they were running east as fast as Booker's damaged leg allowed.

"What happened to Stewart and Booker?" I asked Cornplanter.

Cornplanter spoke to Blacksnake. His response was brief. "My nephew did not see them die."

Well, at least that was something, I thought. Those two were survivors. I did not doubt that they would find a way out of this hell. I silently wished them Godspeed.

Decades later, I ran into Alexander Stewart during a lull in the uprisings along the Miami River. He was no longer traveling with his old friend but had settled down and making a good living selling supplies to settlers heading for the Northwest Territory. We had a couple drinks for auld lang syne and said goodbye.

The storm passed quickly, as summer rains are apt to do. Thunder rumbled in the distance, and the pines dripped onto our soaked skin. For a long moment, the world was silent and peaceful. Then Joseph Brant stepped to the edge of the embankment, held his tomahawk high overhead and uttered a piercing war cry. Hundreds of voices answered on both sides of the valley, and the fight was back on.

I sat on the hill and watched, still dazed from the vicious blow to my skull. The Oneida warrior had opened a ragged wound that would not stop bleeding.

Irregular musket fire obscured my view from time to

time, though I witnessed the worst of it. The fighting was hand to hand as the combatants staggered and tripped over fallen men and the thick entanglement of the forest growth. There was no respite. One side would withdraw to regroup, and then attack again. I could not determine who was winning the battle.

Cornplanter and Blacksnake left me completely unguarded, but where was I to go? My head throbbed and my vision narrowed down to a pinhole every time I moved. The best I could do was drag myself behind a low-lying rock and keep down. Occasionally a round of musket fire shattered the trees near me, but for the most part, I was safe.

Hours passed, and the fighting raged on, eventually becoming more and more sporadic. Late in the afternoon, rough hands shook me awake. I do not know when I passed out.

Cornplanter squatted beside me, his face, torso, and arms streaked with blood. He looked like a fiend from Dante's hell.

"We go," he said with simple finality. "We have won this day at great cost. The fort sends more men."

A warrior dragged me to my feet. I swayed with dizziness, barely managing to follow the Indians as they started through the woods. Nearby, dozens of prisoners stumbled in obvious confusion, trying to keep up. Every man was bloodied, some shot and others with knife wounds, but they were alive.

The Battle of Oriskany, as it came to be called, was finally over. It was hard-fought on both sides. Due to the British forces leaving the field first, the Americans considered the battle a victory, despite suffering the most casualties. The Patriots carried General Herkimer from the battlefield. He died ten days later after his leg was amputated.

When we returned to our camp near the fort, more than 400 men, dead or dying, remained on the forest floor behind us. The Patriots lost almost their entire army, while the combined loss to the Loyalists, British, and Iroquois was seventy-five killed. However, sixty of those dead were Iroquois warriors, and that was a loss the Indians could not comprehend.

As we marched back to Fort Stanwix, tears were on the faces of many a warrior. They walked with their heads hung low in sorrow. You would not have thought that they had thoroughly defeated an army twice their size. No one celebrated.

Forever, the Seneca called this forlorn wooded valley The Place of Great Sadness.

And that was not the end of their despair.

As we approached the British camp, a company of Loyalist intercepted us. They brought bad news.

Earlier in the afternoon, St. Leger had become aware of the concentrated firing to the east. He ordered a detachment to reinforce the men fighting a pitched battle at Oriskany Creek.

Soon after the British departed their camp, Colonel Gansevoort sent a raiding party out from the fort to plunder and destroy the Indian camp. Right under St. Leger's nose, the raiders succeeded in carrying off most of the items promised to the Iroquois for their efforts in the campaign. What they did not steal, they destroyed.

The exhausted warriors could only stare in disbelief at what remained of their camp. Their lean-tos and blankets still smoldered, sending a rancid smoke into the air. The gifts from Butler and St. Leger, the pots and cooking utensils, the knives, beads, and mirrors, were all gone.

Butler and Brant stood off to the side, arguing loudly with Cornplanter. Observing how the Indians were mistreating the new Patriot prisoners, I decided I would be safer close to Cornplanter. Brant saw me walking across the littered field and ordered a warrior to bind my hands and keep me back. I could hear the argument that raged between them.

Butler was furious. "You gave your word at the fire!" he shouted at Cornplanter in English. "You held the wampum belt and gave your word to fight with us." His face was red with anger. I understood what was happening. Cornplanter was devastated by the loss of so many warriors. The destruction of the camp was the final blow.

Brant spoke to him in Mohawk, and Cornplanter shook his head. I could see tears on his face. This was not a decision he took lightly.

Suddenly Brant reached out and shoved Cornplanter in the chest. Cornplanter took a step back, and his muscles tightened, but he did not retaliate.

"You are the coward I always knew you to be," Brant said in English. "Go back to your squaws." He gestured toward a group of Seneca observing the confrontation. "And take those women with you! We, of the Mohawk, will honor our pledge to our British father. The Seneca are not needed here."

Brant turned and marched off, leaving Butler staring at Cornplanter. Butler sadly shook his head and then followed Brant. They went to tell Brigadier St. Leger that half his Iroquois force was leaving.

I sat with Blacksnake and Cornplanter in a ruined lean-to, sharing a pot of tea someone had stolen from the British camp. I enjoyed the warmth. Much had happened since I last tasted tea. The strange circumstance of our tea party was not lost on me.

No one spoke for some time, then Cornplanter looked me in the eyes. "You have been my property for many months, Moorhead," he said softly. "It is time for us to return to Conawagus. I spoke to the Redcoat officer who knows you. He gave me this musket." Cornplanter patted the army Brown Bess by his side. "You are now the property of the British."

I was stunned. After everything we had experienced together, after standing with Blacksnake at the council fire, after saving his damn life! Now they had traded like an old horse.

Even if Walsh was an honorable man, I was still conflicted about being the property of the British. From everything I heard, the Seneca treated me far better than the British treated their prisoners.

"My wish," I said evenly, "is to return with you. I am of no value. You can simply let me go. From Conawagus, I will find my way back to Pennsylvania."

Cornplanter shook his head. "It is done. The Redcoat gave me a musket. It is a fair trade." He picked up the new muzzleloader, and we all stood. Blacksnake offered his hand, and I shook it with little enthusiasm. Then he simply walked away. Cornplanter started to follow but stopped and turned back to me.

"When I sit at my fire and tell the tale of this sad time, I will speak of you, Moorhead," he said with a slight smile.

I inclined my head in the Indian manner.

"I will say that I have never owned anything else that I called friend. *Eh-sgo-ge-hae*!"

I will see you again, he said and walked away.

And so I became a British prisoner of war and learned that you are the friend of an Indian only as long as he wants you to be.

CHAPTER 39
Meanwhile…

From the Diary of Dr. Robert Penrose
Wednesday, August 20th, 1777
Indiana, Pennsylvania

At thirty-two, Jane Moorhead was still a beautiful woman. The frontier had hardened the lines around her eyes and mouth, and wisps of gray hid within her dark red hair. And despite having borne six children, her figure had withstood the test of time. Maybe a little broader in the hips and fuller in the bust, she still turned heads at our spring dance.

On this day, sweat beaded her forehead and soaked her nightshirt. Her hair hung in wet strands. She tried not to cry out, but the pain was sharp and deep within her body.

"One more, Janie!" her sister-in-law, Mary Elizabeth, begged. "Just one more, and it's over."

Jane bore down as ordered, and the scream erupted from her throat as the baby slid into its aunt's waiting hands.

Bending over Mary Elizabeth's shoulder to examine the results of our morning labor, I could see that all was well. If nothing goes awry, my job in a birthing is to observe and stay out of the women's way.

"That's fine," I pronounced. "Not much bleeding and a fine little boy to show for all your effort."

The other sister-in-law, Mary Ann, pried her hand from Jane's grasp and wiped the sweat from the new mother's brow. Mary Ann couldn't stop smiling, even with the painful thought that this was Jane's sixth child, and still just one for her and Joseph. I had to admire that.

"You did real good, Janie," Mary Ann said. Jane smiled up at her, the strain etching deep lines on her face.

"What is it?" she whispered.

"Just like I said it would be, a perfect boy."

Jane let out a long sigh, and tears welled in her eyes. No doubt, she was thinking of her long-lost husband. Mary Ann, perceptive as always, patted Jane on the shoulder.

"He'll be home soon, Janie. I know he will."

Mary Elizabeth nestled the cleaned and swaddled baby boy in Jane's waiting arms.

"Well," I cleared my throat and interrupted the moment. "I need to get to the patients really needing my skill. It is proving to be a long day, and you women have this well in hand."

I gathered up my hat and bag and headed for the door. Turning back to the women huddled beside the mother and new baby, I said, "Don't worry, Jane. We're taking fine care of Thomas and the others. You feed that little one and get strong. I haven't lost a patient to smallpox yet, and your son won't be my first."

Smallpox had invaded the settlement two weeks ago with four adults and three children stricken immediately. I quarantined all of the patients in the shed behind my cabin. So far, no one else had fallen sick.

Sarah acted as my assistant, caring for the sick while I dealt with other emergencies and the occasional birth. As I sat down wearily at the table and told her of the new addition to the Moorhead family, she burst into tears.

"Oh, Robert," my wife cried. "Today has been a blessing and a curse."

A chill ran down my spine, and I took her hand in mine. "What has happened?"

All Sarah could do was sob.

I had been correct. Five-year-old Thomas Moorhead wasn't the first patient I would lose to smallpox. He was the second.

From the Journal of Samuel Moorhead
Friday, August 22nd, 1777
Indiana, Pennsylvania

Jane named her new son Fergus. He was born on a hot summer day and never knew the brother who died a few hours earlier.

The trial of a difficult birth and the loss of her son had edged Jane into a black mood that caused us all great concern. She insisted on attending the burial on the tree-covered hill west of the growing community. Ten more families had arrived in the years since she and Fergus and others of our family had first built a cabin. Most of them gathered to lay Thomas in the ground. The day before, we had buried the little McCreary girl.

Holding Fergus on her lap and surrounded by her children, Jane stared blankly into the distance as I drove the wagon to the gravesite. She barely acknowledged the helping hands, speaking only when asked a direct question.

"I'm worried," Mary Elizabeth told me that evening. "This isn't like her at all. Jane is the strongest woman I know."

"You're the strongest woman I know," I corrected, taking her hand. "This is a lot to go through. She'll be fine. Just needs time, that's all."

Mary Elizabeth sat quietly, playing with the remains of supper on her plate. Finally, she looked me in the eye.

"Sam," she said in a faint voice, "we need to go back home."

I knew this was coming, yet I was unwilling to face it. I stood abruptly and went for a mug of water before allowing myself to say

289

anything.

"This is home," I said. How could we leave? How could we abandon all that we had built—not to mention my responsibility to the militia?

In my heart, I knew she was right

Fergus' capture was well known on the frontier, but then, every settlement west of the Alleghenies had a horror story of their own. During the spring and early summer many communities had worked themselves into a full panic. News of Indian abductions and atrocities were an everyday occurrence.

In April, two trappers headed for Kentucky stopped at the garrison in Kittanning. They said the Seneca at the top of the Allegheny River held men and women from our area. Among them were two young boys and a girl. The news caused further alarm. This was the first time that Pennsylvania Seneca had been named in any disturbances.

The Delaware and the Ohio Seneca had been on the warpath for months, attacking homesteads along the river. In response, one by one, most of the militia under my command deserted and returned to their families. I couldn't blame them.

In July, the new western militia commander at Fort Pitt, General Edward Hand, sent me on another recruiting mission. It was a complete failure.

Everywhere I went, I was greeted with empty cabins or wagonloads of families heading east. Even the threat of a fine would not deter the men from leaving.

Strong, brave men admitted that they feared for the lives of their families. The men said they weren't sure they could provide protection at home, let alone if they were away with the militia. Between the fighting in the east and the Indian raids on the frontier, people were unsure if any place was safe. At least their odds were better back east with their families. That's where you should be, too, they told me more than once.

290

From the Journal of Samuel Moorhead
Saturday, September 6th, 1777
Indiana, Pennsylvania

By late August, the western frontier was as thinly populated as it had been five years before. Without any explanation, I was relieved of all duty, and the Kittanning outpost abandoned. (18)

Upon my return to Indiana, I was pleased with the news that Jane had worked her way out of the slump she had fallen into. However, I was distressed to learn that James and Mary Thompson left with another group the week before.

"I never thought I'd see James give up," I said to my old friend Jim Kelly one night as we sat together on my porch. The settlement was quiet except for the shrill mating call of locusts in the forest.

Jim, ever the stoic, sipped his beer and didn't respond.

"So when are you leaving?" I asked after several moments passed in silence.

Jim drained his mug and placed it on the table between us. "We have no prospects but desolation and destruction," he said, looking me square in the eyes. "We came here together, Sam. We need to leave together. It's time to bury what we can't take with us and pack up what we can."

Inside the cabin, Mary Elizabeth laid her head on the table and wept.

PART FIVE

The British
1777 to 1778

CHAPTER 40
The Retreat

August 7th to August 28th, 1777
Oswego, New York

Brigadier General Barry St. Leger was in a panic, and his army in full retreat. A month earlier, St. Leger had confidently advanced on Fort Stanwix with 1,200 fighting men. By the time we slogged back to the shore of Lake Ontario, no more than 200 remained.

Butler had taken his men of the 34th, most of Sir John's Royal Greens, and Bird's 8th, a day before we left Fort Stanwix. He said he was returning to Fort Niagara, where there was heavier artillery. His intention, so he claimed, was to return and resume the siege. It never happened.

We arrived at Fort Ontario in a driving rain, totally exhausted and totally defeated. To our surprise, and St. Leger's horror, the fort gates stood open. Butler had told the fort's commander about the relief force General Arnold was bringing up the valley. The commander wisely decided to join Butler and withdrew his men to the better-protected fort at Niagara.

This was just another of the many disappointments St. Leger and his army had faced in recent days. There was no time to lose. Everyone knew that Arnold was right behind us. St. Leger ordered a dozen men to search the fort for supplies. There was nothing to be found.

Both sides claimed victory at Oriskany. The Americans believed they won despite horrendous losses due to the British abandoning the field. The British thought they won due to the minor casualties they suffered and the fact that they stopped the relief column from reaching Fort Stanwix.

I had to go with the British view on this issue. However, the glow of victory was soon dimmed by the constant rain of August and the incessant fire from Fort Stanwix.

There is no need to describe the monotonous details of the siege. It was a siege. Every day was the same as the next. The cannons fired impotently at the walls, the sharp-shooters picked off an exposed Patriot now and then, and the Patriots shot back, doing far more damage.

St. Leger continued with the determination of a dog worrying an old bone. By now, even he had to see as clearly as his subordinates that the fort would not fall. Yet, defying all logic and military experience, he did not give up.

For two weeks following the battle in that small valley, the British continued to take heavy casualties from the well protected men inside the fort. The Patriots had three small cannons, and they used them effectively, firing grapeshot at the British sappers trying to dig assault trenches. The soldiers continued to dig closer and closer to the redoubt, all the while dragging wounded and dead back to the surgery tent.

I spent most of that time in a stockade built on the southwest side of the river with sixty other prisoners of war.

Prisoner of War. There is a term I sorely misuse. The British made it clear that we were prisoners, period. At the beginning of the conflict in '75, King George declared the colonies to be in revolt and that any man raising a hand against the Crown was a Traitor. So any Patriot captured by the British had no rights as a combatant. My earlier concern of being treated worse by the British than I had been by the Indians soon proved well-founded.

Except, that is, for the remaining Indians assigned to guard us. They were in a foul mood.

The day after the battle, a group of the Mohawks wishing to revenge their losses pulled four men from our ranks. They stripped them naked and made the poor fellows run the gauntlet. It was extremely brutal, and none survived. I did not watch.

Then there was the rain. Our stockade and all the land surrounding the fort was churned into a sea of knee-deep mud. With no lean-tos or tents, we prisoners were forced to huddle together under a stack of pine boughs against the rough-cut stake walls.

Despite our confinement away from the main camp, rumors were widespread. I cannot say how my fellow prisoners discovered the things they did, but somehow we knew what was happening in the British camp as if we lived there.

Each day, a soldier marched a prisoner up to the high ground to retrieve a pot of stew. One small pot intended to feed all the men in the stockade. The man always came back with a tidbit of news along with our meager rations. The men lined up and took two spoonsful of stew from the pot, then passed the spoon to the man behind him. There was never enough. Woe is the last man in line who only got to swipe the pot with his filthy finger.

At one point, during a short truce, Colonel Gansevoort

297

managed to get six of his men out of the fort and avoid the British lines. They carried reports to the Northern Department Commander, Major General Philip Schuyler. To his credit, General Schuyler immediately ordered General Benedict Arnold to march his Continental battalion to relieve the siege. Why no one from Herkimer's defeated militia had reported the fort's desperate situation is a question for the ages.

Then one night, a strange thing happened. Somehow, a man came into St. Leger's camp and spread rumors of Arnold's impending advance. The man, they said, was not very bright. Still, his defection seemed genuine. He was considered too stupid to lie, so the story he brought of a 3,000-man army marching up the Mohawk to destroy St. Leger chilled every British officer to the bone.

St. Leger believed the rumors and panicked. He announced that we were withdrawing back to Fort Ontario at Oswego.

It was a ruse! The report was not true! The man was not as stupid as he acted and managed to pull off a convincing lie. Arnold was coming, all right, with a mere 800 men, a force the British could have faced and probably defeated.

On the night of August 23rd, after twenty-one days of unproductive siege, several of us were forced to dig pits near the cannon emplacements. The British soldiers rolled their guns to the edge of the muddy hole and tipped them in. We buried all of the cannons and shot, gathered what supplies we could, and prepared to run for our boats still sitting on the beach at Lake Oneida. I looked for every opportunity to get left behind in the confusion, but it was not to be.

Brant insisted on taking his Mohawks to assist General Burgoyne on the Hudson. From a distance, I witnessed a confrontation between St. Leger and Joseph Brant as the war chief explained his plan to go east. St. Leger's face was as red as any man's could ever be. He shouted words I could not make out. Typical of Brant, he simply turned and walked away. All of the Mohawk followed.

At Lake Oneida, it became clear that we had insufficient crew to man all of the boats. We abandoned eight of the bateaux in Wood Creek.

Then, we prisoners and every able-bodied soldier rowed across the lake and down the Oswego River. Luckily, the rains had swollen the lake, and the river ran hard and fast. Except for the small falls, we did not need to portage past the rapids; instead, we rode over them, one harrowing drop after another. A day and a half later, we were back at Oswego.

In a panic.

As the scavengers searched for supplies in the empty fort, two exhausted men from St. Leger's rear guard entered the fort and collapsed in the mud. General Arnold, they reported once their breath returned, had skirmishers out in front of his main force. They were almost upon us.

Orders were shouted, the drummers beat retreat, and the men ran for the boats, frantically pushing the lumbering crafts into the river. The strong current swung the boats into the lake and away from Oswego.

My boat was the last to clear the river's mouth. I ducked involuntarily as musket fire sounded from the edge of the forest. Lead balls splashed the water, barely distinguishable from the raindrops pelting the lake. We pulled hard, and in a matter of minutes, Fort Ontario vanished in the whiteness of the torrential rain.

That is how it ended. The critical western arm of General Burgoyne's three-pronged Saratoga Campaign to end the rebellion had failed miserably. Burgoyne was on his own.

And we were headed for Montreal.

CHAPTER 41
The Bateaux

August 29th to September 1st, 1777
Saint Laurence River, Canada

"A man could get lost in here," Rolf, the man rowing beside me, observed for the third time.

"We follow the boat ahead of us," said our coxswain, a bear of a Highlander with hair as red as my Jane's. He was known simply as Mac and shouted everything he said, especially the profanity which laced most of his sentences. "He's a *riverman* and knows where he's fookin' going. If we lose him, don't worry yer pretty little heads, cause I know where *I'm* going."

I tried to watch the boat ahead to see if he showed any special knowledge we were unaware of.

"Pay attention to your fookin' oar!" Mac hissed at me. The portion of the river upon which we now floated contained more than a thousand islands. To me, it looked like an infinite number of possible paths. Water flowed in every direction. I could see no particular route that was better than another, yet we kept moving on.

The fifty miles from Oswego to Wolfe Island at the

entrance to the Saint Laurence had nearly killed us all. Already exhausted when we reached Fort Ontario, the trauma of our sudden departure drained us further. Then we rowed through the rain and gloom for hours without rest. My hands, white and wrinkled from the constant wetting, blistered and peeled. We all held pieces of beaver pelt against the hard oars to ease the pain. Even the soldiers, slightly better fed than us prisoners, collapsed on their oars when the rain stopped late in the day and we ran up on the beach.

Thankfully, St. Leger allowed us to have campfires and warm our bones. We heated water and ate dry biscuits for supper before settling down on the wet sand to sleep. The night felt as if it would never pass as we tried to ignore the sand fleas and mosquitoes enjoying a meal at our expense.

Early the next morning, we pushed off before the sun broke the horizon. By noon, the river current had us, and our rowing became far more precise. Mac showed that he did indeed know the river. Everywhere I looked, there was another grassy hump of land rearing its head from the fast-moving water that required a quick course correction.

"Larboard, pull!" Mac would call out, and the six men on my side of the boat pulled as hard as we could. Then, satisfied with this adjustment, he would yell, "Ship oars!" and we quickly pulled our oars into the boat, barely in time to avoid ramming a rock or grass-covered hummock. The next moment it was the starboard crew's turn to pull. Rarely did we have to work together, so quickly did the river carry us downstream.

That evening, as dusk settled in, and we thought our arms would fall from our bodies, lights showed on the right bank. Someone from the lead boat was waving a lantern to get our attention and guide us in. We came about sharply, rowed upstream, and landed in a stone harbor protected from the river current. Behind us, three more boats came in.

Above the rocky shore, more lights glowed behind a low stockade wall. Amazingly, people lived in this desolate land.

"*Fort de la Presentation*," Rolf announced with a passable French accent. He said it as if I should be impressed, though it did not look like much to me. While we rowed, Rolf assumed Stewart's old job of providing a running commentary. I suspected he made most of it up as we went along. I did not mind the chatter. Rolf was a broad-shouldered and compact Huguenot with a ready smile, despite our situation. I doubted he knew much about the Saint Laurence River, seeing as how he was from the Mohawk.

As it turned out, he was incorrect in the name of this place. True, the French had named the fort *Presentation*, but the British had renamed it for the confluence of the river it guarded — the *Oswegatchie*.

Tiny Fort Oswegatchie consisted of a square redoubt with towers on each corner. It had no earthen work or embrasures. My vast knowledge of fortifications and siege warfare told me it was not at all defensible. It did, however, have food and, surprisingly, women.

A meager garrison of twenty soldiers manned this remote garrison, and for some unknown reason, their wives accompanied them. We were not invited into the fort, and soon a group of soldiers and five women came down the path to the beach where our boats landed. They brought bread loaves and honey and a beef stew containing fresh meat.

We considered it a feast, although divided among all the soldiers and prisoners, it amounted to little. Again, beach fires were permitted. St. Leger and his officers felt more comfortable now that they were safely back in Canada. Before long, the soldiers started singing. They found a keg of rum, as soldiers often do — even in the Canadian wilderness.

Watching the soldier's wives pass food and cider among the men made me realize how much I missed a woman's soft voice. How much I missed my wife. How long had it been? A woman about my age told me the date as she handed me a bowl of stew and a hunk of fresh bread. I sat and stared at my food, lost in thought, as my emotions overwhelmed me.

"If you don't intend to eat that, hand it over," Rolf said. I peered at him through a haze of memory and saw his face take on a look of compassion. I wondered what he thought of my condition, seeing my beard hiding a face deeply browned by the sun and ground-in dirt, tangled hair to my shoulders, rags hanging on a too-thin frame. He had been captured at Oriskany and looked no worse off than a farmer at the end of a long day in the field.

"Come, now," he said quietly. "Eat. Might be the last you have for a spell. Never know."

I sniffed my tears away and dipped the hunk of bread in the stew. It was possibly the finest meal I ever ate.

"Now listen up!" Mac shouted at us. "Ahead of us is the worst this river has to offer. I need ye all to listen for my calls and obey smartly. If I call for ye to pull, pull like your fookin' life depends on it, cause it do. If I call for ye to back, watch the men around ye and don't get yer oars fouled! We go broadside cause ye fooked up, we all die."

We rode on a narrow, slow-moving section of the river

surrounded by innumerable grass-covered islands. Our boat was at the front of the column because our tillerman knew this stretch of the river. St. Leger and various officers were in the boat directly behind us.

After days and days of relentless rain, the sky was finally clear and deep blue. Every man was soaked in sweat — from the hot sun blistering our arms and faces, as well as the thought of what lay ahead.

The first set of rapids, a few miles downriver from Fort Oswegatchie, were actually exciting, if you can believe it. The boats picked up speed and flew across the hard water without us dipping an oar. Up to that point, I do not think I ever moved faster in my entire life. Incredibly, that speed was soon bested.

Ahead, the river disappeared into the swirling mist where the rift dropped forty feet. Beyond, Mac told us, there was a place where we could catch our breath before the next set of rapids. Within a four-mile stretch, the river fell a hundred feet in elevation.

The rapids were loud and threatening, even where we backed our boat against the pull of the water, waiting for the column to form up. As a surveyor, I was interested to see how the land fractured and dropped, creating this change in elevation, but there was no time to appreciate it.

St. Leger stood in the stern of his boat and shouted at the others resting near him. Although I could not hear what he said, I knew he was instructing them to watch us shoot the rapids. Our boat was to find the best path through the deeper water and past the rocks — at least the rocks that showed their head above the churning mass of white rushing water. If we succeeded, the others would follow.

A wave from St. Leger and Mac shouted for us to

straighten the boat and move toward the first set of rocks. My mouth was suddenly dry as sand, yet I dared not dip a hand in the river. We quickly picked up speed, and Mac leaned on the tiller to center us on the rapids. His jaw was set, and a crease furrowed his forehead, but he showed no fear. For once, I was glad I faced the stern of the boat and could not see what was coming.

We kept our oars outboard, just skimming the water, ready for a call from Mac. It came sooner than I expected.

"All, toss oars!" he bellowed as the first rocks rushed toward us. An admiral's barge crew might have been sharper, but at least we got all the oars up before they snagged on a rock. Holding an oar out of the water while desperately fighting to keep your seat in a pitching boat is a formidable task. Each time we hauled our oars in, they usually ended up resting on the shoulder of the man seated beside you. More than one man took a hard smack to the side of the head that day.

On both sides, wet boulders scraped against the hull. There was a sudden drop, the boat rose up in the bow and then dipped like a bucking stallion. Water sprayed over the boat and drenched us all. I licked my lips — all thought of my dry throat had vanished.

Two hundred yards behind us, St. Leger's boat entered the rapids. They were attempting to precisely follow our path.

"Let fall an' prepare to row for yer fookin' lives," Mac shouted, and we lowered our oars level with the water. Suddenly he changed his mind, "Larboard, hold!" he ordered, and my side dropped our oars into the churning water, fighting with all our strength to hold them rigid. The action worked like a wagon brake. From my perspective, Mac, in the stern, swung off to my right as our boat went past another rock. The order to toss followed, and once again, the oars were out of the water.

Then Mac's eyes widened in alarm, and I almost dared a glance back to see if I should prepare to swim for my life.

"All, pull! Pull!"

Mac required more steerage to control the boat and maneuver it to the side of the channel he had selected. Twelve oars hit the water in perfect unison, and we gave way together, making the boat move even faster in the wild torrent.

The boat dipped alarmingly as the trough of a standing wave cascaded over the bow. The soldiers hunkered down between the rowers and began bailing water past our faces in an attempt to lighten the boat. Another wave tumbled in and made their work meaningless. Most of them simply tried to hold on as we bucked and slewed, totally out of control.

Because I faced the stern, the bow reared up, and we shot clear of the first section of rapids with no warning.

Mac did not need to order us to bring our oars in and rest. Every man collapsed across his oar, chest heaving. We were still moving downstream rather quickly, but at least there was a moment's respite.

In a matter of minutes, we had gone a mile through the most treacherous water I had ever seen. St. Leger's boat soon joined us, and then another, before we had drifted toward the next cataract.

"Get this fookin' water out," Mac shouted, pointing at the brown water sloshing around our calves. We rowers were too tired to move from the thwarts, so the soldiers in the center of the boat used their hats and the single bilge scoop to bail. The boat needed to be as light as possible for the next portion of the river.

"How did you ever get up these rapids?" I asked a young soldier bailing near my bench.

"Emptied 'em out and carried 'em up the shore," he answered, pointing his jaw at the far bank. It did look calmer than what we had recently traversed. "The rest is much easier," he continued with a mean smile. "You'll see."

"Don't fret, lassies," Mac interrupted, is brogue thicker than usual. "The next part 'tisn't so bad."

Thank the Lord he was right. The second section of this drop in the river was longer than the first though not as precipitous. Consequently, the water did not move as fast or as confusingly. There were no standing waves or whirlpools to avoid. In twenty minutes, we cleared the rapids and rowed easily onto Lake Saint Francis.

CHAPTER 42
The Great Carry

September 2nd, 1777
Saint Laurence River, Canada

"Now for a different kind of work," Mac said as our bateau glided against the riverbank. "Everyone out!"

We climbed over the sides as the boats pulled onto a protected shale beach on the south side of the river. To the north was Grande Ile, the wide, flat island that divided the Saint Laurence a mile or so above Montreal.

We had rowed across Lake Saint Francis to this spot in a matter of hours. A trail called the Beauharnois Carry led away from the beach. This was to be our first portage.

We unloaded our boat and stacked the meager supplies on the dry bank. The soldiers added their packs and muskets and returned to the water's edge to help pull the boats up.

"I hope this trail is not too long," Rolf said with a touch of humor in his voice, "I enjoy our time on the water."

"Ye'll get another chance," Mac said lightly before bellowing a new set of orders. "I know every man here has carried a canoe at one point in yer miserable lives," he shouted over the roar of the rapids, "and this ain't no different. They're just heavier! Every man'll get a chance to prove how strong he is. Who was with us going up? Raise a hand."

Half the men from each boat raised an unenthusiastic hand. Mac, taking command of the portage, nodded. St. Leger and his officers stood to the side, content to let him direct the operation.

Mac continued, "Y'men will take the first carry and show the rest of these bastards how to pick up a fookin' boat!"

"Just like a canoe," Rolf said as the first boat was overturned and smoothly hefted to the shoulders of the men assigned to carry it the first leg of our portage.

I thought it would be easier to drag the big boats. Rolf assured me it was too far. "Drag 'em couple hundred feet, that would be fine," he said. "But you got to carry a boat this far." Then he laughed. "It is called a 'carry,' not a 'drag!'"

Those of us not struggling under a boat picked up a bundle of supplies and followed our vessel.

"How far you think it is?" I asked the men nearest me.

One of the soldiers loaded down with three muskets gave me a blank stare. "You'll know when we get to the other side," he said helpfully.

It was not far. The first group carried the boats a quarter-mile before gratefully passing them to the second group, which included me. Each of the replacements stepped in and took the load without setting the boat down.

Thankfully, the men with me were either soldiers or recently captured Patriots. I was not ashamed to let them shoulder most of the load. What little strength my failing body had was back on the river.

We stumbled along the trail, mostly downhill until the river reappeared before us. One more change of porters brought us to the bank of Lake Saint Louis.

The boats were set down at the water's edge and reloaded. Then it was a pleasant fifteen miles to the next set of rapids, the infamous Lachine Fall. Running more than three miles, this set of rapids was so strong that it effectively stopped all shipping from going further up the Saint Laurence River. Montreal became a crucial trading post because of these rapids.

Our portage around this set was much longer than the Beauharnois Carry, and thankfully, we did not have to carry the boats.

A group of men and boys met us at the top of the carry, smiling and agreeable, eager to help. They were local farmers supplementing their income by using their horses and oxen to drag boats on the four-mile path. St. Leger must have told them to apply to the army for payment because the smiles disappeared, and heads began to shake.

Before St. Leger could declare martial law, Mac spoke to the farmers. I do not know what he promised, but soon our boats were being carried on roughly built carts to the far side of the Lachine Fall. We followed, happily walking on solid ground without a load to carry. Irritated that a riverman had more sway with the locals than he did, St. Leger ordered the soldiers to form up and march as if on parade.

In the distance, the island of Montreal, with Mount Royal towering beyond it, glowed in the setting sun. The lake overflowed with sailing ships of every size and purpose. A Packet and two Man-of-War loomed above us as we rowed the last distance to the city walls. Cutters and barges ran from ship to shore and back, finishing the day's business. It was an impressive show of Imperial might. I was in the very heart of the British hold on North America.

"Major Walsh!"

"Sir!"

St. Leger looked down at the remains of his army, all eight boatloads, sitting exhausted against the quay wall. Walsh had not yet climbed up the stone steps to the street above.

"Take all of our men to the barracks. See that they are well fed. There will be no leave. I expect to be underway again in four days."

Walsh looked skeptical, and all of the men in the boats groaned audibly. "Four days, sir?"

"I intend to resupply, add more men, and relieve General Burgoyne as we originally intended. Have the prisoners escorted to the stockade," he added. "Do not let them mix in with other traitors. We are taking them with us to Lake Champlain."

Walsh saluted in acknowledgment, if not in agreement, and Brigadier St. Leger and Sir John went to find the commanding officer and report the disaster of their campaign. Neither man looked particularly strong or confident. Their uniforms were stained and tattered, and, somewhere during the retreat, St. Leger had lost his sword. An empty scabbard flapped sadly at his side.

We rowed the boats half a mile further and dragged them onto a landing area in front of the sally port. Stone steps led up from the riverbank to the towering walls. The soldiers pushed and shoved us past the gate and into the city. They were none too happy to hear the Brigadier's orders.

Immediately, incredible smells and sounds of an old port assailed our senses. The streets were growing dark, but the occasional lantern provided enough light to see our way. People filled the streets, completing their day's business and heading home or to a tavern, of which there were many. Overall, the citizens of Montreal seemed well-fed and happy. They knew that General Burgoyne had gone to crush the rebellion and had no fears. That was about to change.

Walsh told the sergeant in charge at the stockade that Brigadier General St. Leger wished to keep his prisoners separate from the general population. The sergeant had a problem with that until Walsh explained that we were from Fort Stanwix. The soldier seemed to think that was significant, though for the wrong reasons. News of the British defeat on the Mohawk had not yet reached the city.

The iron gate closed behind us with discouraging firmness. A vast space blocked off with iron gratings was separated into cages of sorts. From where our group of sixty prisoners stood, I could make out another 200 men huddled in the gloom.

Every one of them was starving to death.

CHAPTER 43
The Prison Yard

September, 1777
Montreal, Canada

We did not leave in four days. Instead, I sat in that hell hole for more than two weeks while St. Leger and Sir John beat the bushes for additional troops.

General Burgoyne had seriously depleted the garrison in July, and few reinforcements had arrived since. Every ship that stopped at Quebec on its way up the river to Montreal was bound to lose most of its complement of fresh soldiers. Quebec had an insatiable demand for more men. So we sat.

More than 200 Americans were confined within the stockade. Many had been prisoners since Arnold's failed attempt to capture Quebec in '75. Those men kept to themselves in the far corner of the courtyard that held us all. The sixty prisoners from Fort Stanwix were locked together, separate from the other unfortunate souls.

In one respect, luck was with us. The next day was Friday and every group in the compound received their twice-weekly allotment of food.

Compared to what I had been eating for the past few months, it was a feast. But for the rest of the men in the stockade, men held in captivity for months or years, it was not enough to live on.

Each man received a half-pound of pork, a half-pound of hard biscuit, a half-pint of dried peas, and an ounce of butter. It was doled out to us in the same way the navy has a mess cook responsible for his table. Cook fires were permitted only three times a week. All of the meat was boiled in a pot until it fell apart and was scooped out. Then the peas boiled for hours in the broth to make soup.

Rolf, whom I took a liking to, was our mess cook for the first two days. He was honest and careful with the division of the food. Because our group was kept separate from the rest, and we had been together for a long time, problems resolved themselves more quickly than they did among the other groups. Fights and arguments plagued the compound, while our group stayed relatively friendly.

In the rest of the compound, a man rarely received his food allowance. Somehow, it always got divided up according to rank and general meanness. I suppose that is as true in nature as it is in prison. The biggest, meanest man gets whatever he wants

Looking around the compound at the men squatting in the mud and shit, eating their meager meal, it was clear that most would not live through the winter. Each had a beard and hair reaching to their shoulders. Their clothes, like mine, were rags, and most went barefoot.

One afternoon, Rolf and I sat with our backs up against the bars separating us from another group. On the other side was a boy not much more than seventeen years of age talking to some men. His name was John and he had arrived that day with news.

"I tell you it's true," he said to a skeptical audience.

"They say old Gentleman Johnny Burgoyne is

surrounded down by Saratoga and fighting for his life."

More prisoners gathered close to hear John's report. We were all behind on the news. An older man limped over, supporting his weight on a makeshift crutch.

"I was at Ticonderoga in July when St. Clair abandoned the fort," he offered. "The entire company went down to Skenesboro in every boat they could find. What a mess!"

"How did you get caught?" I asked.

"Cause a my leg, me and a handful a boys got left behind. Then they sent me and some others up here to Canada."

Rolf said, "I'm surprised to hear Burgoyne's in trouble. Last I heard, he outnumbered the Continentals and was moving south to Albany."

John nodded in agreement. "That were true until poor Miss McCrea got herself scalpt."

A general uproar sounded among those listening.

"Jane McCrea? Dead?" someone asked in pained disbelief. Other men shared the lamentation. Young John looked embarrassed at all the attention.

" 'Tis a sad story," John began. "She was up near Fort Edward, on her way to meet her fiancée Dave Jones, who's with Burgoyne. Some a you know Dave." A murmur of agreement came from the group. "Well, she was staying with her friend Sara McNeil when Gentleman Johnny heard they was close and sent couple a scouts to fetch them back to camp."

John paused to take a sip of cloudy water.

"What happened?" several impatient voices asked at once.

"So, the scouts got to arguing over the women, and somehow Jane and Sara was separated. No one knows how, exactly, but Jane got murdered. They say, couple days

316

after, Sara spotted Jane's long hair on a buck's lance and nearly died, herself, right then and there."

It surprised me somewhat that so many men knew this woman. They were genuinely shocked, and more than one wiped away tears.

Voices grew in volume as the news spread within the compound. Shouts of 'damn Burgoyne' and 'damn the British' and 'damn all Indians' erupted.

British troops hurried onto the parapet.

"Quiet in the ranks!" a sergeant bellowed. "Quiet! Or I'll fire into you!"

The shouting died down to a low rumble, but the dissension and anger were palpable. If this story affected these poor men so strongly, I could only imagine what it would do to the colonists around Albany and Saratoga.

And what an effect it had. News of the murder and mutilation of Jane McCrea enraged the settlements like a forest fire in August. She was known for her beauty as well as her willingness to help her neighbors. Many families, once staunch Loyalists, were outraged that Burgoyne could let a thing like that happen. Up and down the Hudson, allegiances shifted, and the ranks of the Continental Army swelled. (19)

By mid-September, Burgoyne was forced into battle at a place called Freeman's Farm. His 7,000 faced more than 9,000 infuriated Americans led by General Horatio Gates and Major General Benedict Arnold, freshly returned from Fort Stanwix. Even though Burgoyne managed to hold the field, British casualties were enormous. The Patriots were fired up, and Burgoyne was in trouble.

Soon a rumor circulated that St. Leger was ordered to Fort Ticonderoga to support Burgoyne's rear. And we were to go with him.

"Why would he want to take prisoners?" a man in our group, called Isaac, asked.

"To trade," Rolf replied, but it was more of a question.

"That don't make sense," Isaac persisted with a backwoods twang. " 'Tis been clear for some time, Washington don't want no exchanges." He barked a short laugh. "Why look at us! We ain't fit to fart, let alone fight!"

That elicited a welcome laugh from our group. I agreed. What value did we have? In truth, I was damned tired of being dragged from place to place for no apparent reason. My only hope was that, eventually, I would find myself in a location where I could make my escape.

Three days later, still unsure of the reasoning, we camped at Fort Saint-Jean on the Richelieu River.

St. Leger and Sir John had worked magic, rounding up more than 300 men. They supplemented Sir John's Royal Yorkers and the 34th Foot with a scattering of men from different divisions. They then added us sixty prisoners as galley slaves. Barges ferried us across the Saint Laurence to the south shore, where we formed columns and marched fifteen miles on a solid road to Fort Saint-Jean.

The British had recently increased the size of the fort and built a shipyard on the banks of the Richelieu. This river emptied Lake Champlain into the Saint Laurence and was of significant military importance. The shipyard constructed all of the bateau needed to reach Fort Ticonderoga.

St. Leger left two companies at Saint-Jean to guard the river while we took up our oars once again and began the journey to Fort Ticonderoga. To save General Burgoyne.

CHAPTER 44
Fort Ticonderoga

September 25th to October 7th, 1777
Lake Champlain, New York

They told me it was only twenty miles from Fort Saint-Jean to the calmer waters of Lake Champlain. I do not believe it.

My condition and those of my fellow prisoners deteriorated each day. We were already in extremely poor health. During the two weeks in the Montreal stockade, I developed a nasty cough, like so many others. For some, the minor sickness proved fatal. Each day we said goodbye to two or three inmates. I believe it was a concerted effort to waste away the American prisoners and discourage exchanges. We were slaves, nothing more, and that is why we were on this trip. St. Leger intended to make the prisoners do all of the rowing to save the soldier's strength.

Rowing upstream on the Richelieu was much more exhausting than coming down the Saint Laurence had been. My hands, which had begun to heal during the time in Montreal, blistered and peeled within the first hour. I had no beaver pelts to protect them as before, so I pulled my shirt apart and used the rags.

"Bloody hell!" one of the Redcoats in the center of our

boat protested. "These men stink!"

That was not all. We were all infested with lice, picked up in the Montreal stockade. They crawled in my beard and my hair, driving me insane with the need to scratch.

I was in the lead boat with St. Leger, Captain Tice, and Major Walsh. Major Gray, now in command of the St. Leger's 34th Foot, rode in the boat directly behind us. Twelve boats — filled to the top of the gunnels with supplies, ammunition, and scratching men.

St Leger sat in the sternsheets with the coxswain, providing me an opportunity to observe the remarkable changes in the man. The fluffed-up peacock I had watched come ashore at Oswego was gone. A morose, withdrawn and defeated shell of an officer who believed his career was over sat in his place. He rarely looked up, and when he did, I could see his red-rimmed and exhausted eyes. From time to time, he pulled a flask from his coat and drank deeply, not caring if his officers saw.

The change in the water was also evident as we came out of the Richelieu River and entered Lake Champlain. Dozens of islands in a very narrow channel marked the end of the lake, and it was on a larger one that we pulled in for the night.

The soldiers were so irritated with our smell and lice infestation that they marched the sixty of us into the lake, clothes and all. My shirt had been torn to rags, so I shivered, bare-chested throughout the night. I may have been cleaner, but the lice were still tenacious.

The following days were much the same except that the further south we went, the more gutted stone buildings and abandoned or destroyed cabins we passed. Each night we camped ashore in large, recently cleared areas in the forest. Months earlier, Burgoyne's mighty army had spent the night there.

Above the Narrows, we pulled into the shallow cove near the hamlet of Essex. Again, no one came out to greet us from the half dozen cabins scattered beyond the tree line. I overheard the officers discussing the frosty reception they were receiving. I think they were starting to realize that more foe than friend surrounded this lake. I thought back to the story of Jane McCrea, wondering how one death out of the thousands in this war could have such an impact.

Mid-day of our fifth on the water found us beneath the guns of Fort Ticonderoga. We had come a hundred miles to protect General Burgoyne's escape route.

The fort sat on a windy bluff above the lake like a medieval castle. Timber parapets protected two-story buildings and a high tower within the redoubt. From the water, the fort looked impregnable, looming over the lake and the strategic carrying place it defended.

All of the walls, including the outer parapet, were studded with embrasures. The dark mouths of twenty-four pounders could be seen protruding from each gap.

"Now that's a fort," Rolf whispered as we rowed up to the beach. Our boats slid silently onto the soft sand landing beside dozens of other bateaux. Two small frigates rode on their anchors a hundred yards offshore. We jumped out to hold the boats steady while the soldiers disembarked.

Securing the boats to posts driven in the landing, we handed out the supplies and ammunition and began the long climb to the fort.

I dropped my load, the third I had carried up the steep path, and sat on the box of biscuits, trying to slow my heart. The man unloading our bateau had some pity and handed down the lighter boxes for me to carry. Still, three trips did me in. I had no intention of climbing back down for another crate, even if they shot me where I sat.

The view was breathtaking. From my vantage point, the lower part of Lake Champlain stretched off to my left as far as I could see. The well-fortified Mount Independence loomed on the eastern side, beyond the ruins of a floating bridge.

To my right, and far below, was the LaChute River. The little three-mile-long river was choked with white rapids and waterfalls. It dropped 200 feet from the foot of Lake George to Lake Champlain and was impassable in a boat or canoe. This furious waterway explained both the need for a carrying place to portage boats and the military importance of the fort. No one was coming north into Lake Champlain without falling under the deadly firepower of Fort Ticonderoga.

A soldier walked up to me with his long gun slung casually and kicked at my foot. "All right, you, that's enough lollygagging. Move that box to the larder."

I picked up the load and shuffled off in the direction of the kitchen. The smells coming from the stone blockhouse were enough to make me cry. Fresh bread was baking in the ovens, an aroma I had almost forgotten.

At the door to the storeroom, another soldier directed us to stack the crates among the other supplies. The larder was full of boxes. I was sure the armory was equally full of shot and powder. Ticonderoga was ready for a siege if it were to come.

Then the soldier told us to line up beside the kitchen once we deposited our load. To our wonderment, a young mess cook with a serving tray went down the line, handing each man a hunk of steaming bread dripping with honey butter. The bread disappeared in two bites, despite burning my tongue. It was manna from Heaven and only succeeded in making me hungrier.

Indian scouts coming north brought news that General John Burgoyne was in real trouble. Since the last battle on September 17th, his army had been stalemated, making no move to attack or withdraw.

Now Burgoyne was surrounded. Many of the prisoners believed it was only a matter of time before he withdrew back to Canada, which explained why we were there.

"Way I hear it," Rolf confided to a small group a few nights after our arrival, "St. Leger never intended to go past Ticonderoga. Anyway, what can a measly three hundred men do that Burgoyne can't do with six thousand?"

That, I thought, was a good point. "So why bring us all the way down here?"

"Ain't it obvious?" Rolf snorted. "Barry St. Leger's trying to save his reputation. He was supposed to meet up with Burgoyne by going down the Mohawk. Well, we damn well stopped that! Ain't I right, boys?"

A chorus of cheers from the men listening to our discussion pronounced their agreement. "Damn right, we did!" someone added.

"So, now that St. Leger's failed to reach Burgoyne as intended," Rolf continued, "the best he can do is pretend he was trying to get to him any way he could. Not his fault Powell's making him stay here."

"This is all for nothing?" I asked.

"Not for nothin'. If Burgoyne has to retreat, this fort will protect his rear. Didn't you notice that our bateaux ain't being carried to Lake George? No one intends to go south on the lake, least of all St. Leger. He's content to wait right here."

This news was a great disappointment. So far, I was pleased that the British Army was taking me south, away from Canada and closer to Pennsylvania. In my daydreams, I even hoped we might go as far south as New York. The closer to home, the closer to freedom, and the closer to Jane.

"So we're here to stay," I said, the grief clear in my voice.

"Not necessarily," Rolf said quietly. "Not necessarily."

CHAPTER 45
Escape

October 21st, 1777
Fort Ticonderoga, New York

On the 20th of October, while I was working on the outer parapet wall, a small contingent of soldiers arrived with news that sent a shock wave through the fort. Within an hour, every soldier and prisoner had heard the story.

General Burgoyne had surrendered his army!

The officers huddled together in one section of the fort, the soldiers in groups here and there around the parade grounds. No one knew the details except that on October 7th, the Continental Army had destroyed the British at a place called Bemis Heights. Then, on the 17th, General Gates accepted Burgoyne's surrender with full military honors, even returning his sword, which I thought was nice. Burgoyne gave Gates 6,000 prisoners in return.

The grand plan to separate the colonies had failed. We were all optimistic that the end of the war was just over the horizon.

The prisoners tried to celebrate, but the British were in a foul mood and shut down our attempts at revelry with extra work details.

So far, my time at Fort Ticonderoga had gone well. I put on weight, the work was none too strenuous, and I possessed a new shirt. That is not to say we were treated well — far from it. The food was deplorable and infrequent, our holding area in the abandoned armory was moldy and damp, and the slightest infraction of the rules resulted in a beating.

Most of our guards were Germans. These Brunswickers accounted for maybe half of Powell's command, the rest being the 53rd Foot and St. Leger's men. They kept to themselves, and we tried to avoid them, as well. One day, however, a hulking sergeant beat a man to death with the butt of this musket.

The guard received a reprimand that did not curtail the abuse. As far as the British were concerned, we were traitors to everything they fought to uphold and would eventually hang anyway. The British officers turned a blind eye and left the Germans alone.

The bulk of our work involved rebuilding the parapet on the western outer wall. Our task was to clear the stones down to a solid base and then help the mason set them back in proper order.

During a rest break, a grizzled old prisoner sitting with us chuckled to himself and said, "We sure got terrible timing."

Rolf looked skeptically at the man. "Why, in particular?"

The old man laughed with a thick throaty sound. "I was talking to the mason. He says this here portion of the wall was knocked down by Colonel John Brown's men. They fired the Brit's own twelve-pounders from up on Mount Defiance, there."

He waved a hand in the general direction of the massive

hill that dominated the skyline to our southwest. Fortifications were visible along the top ridge.

"Brown attacked the landings over on Lake George," the man continued, "and captured a passel of soldiers and freed a hundred or more Americans."

"He didn't take the fort," I stated obviously. "What happened?"

"Company a Brunswickers showed up, and Brown skedaddled back up Lake George. But not before he scar't the piss out a old Henry Powell, I can tell you."

Rolf and I looked at each other.

"When was this?" I asked, dumbstruck.

"Hah!" laughed the old man. "They call that irony. Just a month back! If we'd arrived ten days earlier, we'd be free men!"

"I have an idea," Rolf said to me as we rolled another stone block into place. The wall was waist-high, and the mason had orders to complete it as quickly as possible. He was pushing us hard to fill the gap before the end of the day.

The gap was what gave Rolf his idea.

It was near suppertime, the sun low in the west. We were high above the lake and could see for miles across the tops of the forest as the last of the sun lit the orange and red leaves in a dazzling display of fall colors.

Without warning, Rolf gave our block a push, and it slipped out from under my hands, tumbling down the embankment. With a jarring crash, it came up against a tree some thirty feet down the hill, making the maple leaves fall in a crimson shower.

"Bloody hell!" shouted the mason, drawing the

attention of our guard. They both peered over the edge to where the block leaned precariously against the tree.

"You'll bloody well go fetch it," the mason said. "That's the last stone for this course."

The Redcoat guard looked at the last of the setting sun. "We're finished for the day, Smith," he said to the mason.

"It was an accident," Rolf said. "We'll go get it."

The mason grumbled that he would finish tomorrow and stomped off.

The soldier stared blankly at us for a few seconds before saying, "Well, if you're going to go get it, move your arses!"

"Right away, Corporal!" Rolf replied. "Come, Fergus. We can roll it back up together."

The hairs on the back of my neck were standing up. Rolf was up to something.

We stumbled down the embankment, slipping on the damp grass until we rested against the tree holding the stone from rolling all the way down the hill. Below us, the trees and brush grew thick. Above, there was nothing but grass all the way up to where the soldier waited impatiently.

"Are you ready?" Rolf asked, getting his weight under the stone.

I leaned in and positioned my feet to take the load.

Rolf looked at me and grinned. "Ready? One, two…*Run*!" And with that, Rolf heaved the stone off the tree. I jumped as it slid past me and started rolling down the hill. The stone was sixteen inches square and weighed more than I did, so it cleared a sizeable path as it bounced and careened from bush to hummock. Rolf and I flew after it, arms flapping wildly in an attempt to keep our balance. Completely out of control, we leapt over bushes and broken saplings, following the trail of destruction left by the bouncing stone.

Suddenly realizing something was amiss, the corporal cried, "Here! What's this?" A shot rang out, the ball shredding the leaves to my left. Accepting that he had not hit us, the soldier ran for help, and we ran for our lives.

The stone finished its flight down the hill buried in a marshy stream. Rolf splashed down the stream, ducking low under the overhanging branches.

"Rolf!" I cried. "Where are we going?"

"Lake George!" he called back without turning. "Canoes!"

Then I understood his plan. The men who brought the news of Burgoyne's surrender came with half a dozen Mohawk. They had come down Lake George from Fort Edward, leaving their canoes at the top of the portage.

The stream emptied into the rocky mouth of the LaChute River. We splashed across, stumbling on hidden rocks, running dangerously close to disaster. As we neared the center of the river, a musket ball ricocheted off a rock beside me and whined overhead. The crack of musket fire reached my ears half a second later.

Taking that as a cue, Rolf cut sharply to the right, and I followed, pushing hard against the strong current surging to my waist.

Another shot splashed water in front of us, and I risked a glance back at the shore we had just vacated. Three soldiers and an officer came to a halt on the edge of the river. Although more than a hundred yards away, they seemed awfully damn close.

"Moorhead!" the officer called. "Stop now!"

It was Major Walsh.

"Rolf!" I cried.

"I see them. Just keep going, Fergus."

Reaching the far side, I slipped and scrambled up the

muddy bank. I stood in the grass, chest heaving, trying to catch my breath. On the far shore, the three Redcoats raised their muskets. It was a long shot, but we were still within range. My shoulders hunched in anticipation of the imminent volley.

Walsh called out again, "Moorhead! Stop!"

The order to fire did not come. Walsh stood there as if expecting us to obey. Then, in the last of the dying light, I saw my old friend place his hand on the closest musket barrel and push it down. The other soldiers looked at him in confusion but lowered their guns, all the same.

Walsh watched as we ran for the woods, then he turned and slowly walked back up to the fort.

It was three miles from the bottom of the river, around Mount Defiance, to the foot of Lake George. Uphill all the way. We covered it in exemplary time, considering the condition of our health.

Whitewater roared down the steep drop on our right, tightly confined by high banks along the wooded trail. Soon a louder sound announced the presence of a massive, rocky waterfall. The mist from the water cascading twenty or thirty feet glowed in the darkness. Then we turned away from the river and followed the trail to the landing.

By the time we flailed onto the beach, my heart was pounding in my ears, and I could taste blood in the back of my throat. Off to our right, I could make out the remains of the armory and sawmill destroyed by Colonel Brown a month earlier. A dim light glowed within the small sentry hut, but no one was about.

Most importantly, four birchbark canoes sat high on the landing beside the burned hulks of a dozen bateau.

Rolf gave me a self-congratulatory smile, and we each grabbed the end of the smallest canoe. Rolf climbed in while I pushed the boat out until it floated free. Careful to not overturn the flimsy craft, I lowered myself in the stern. Rolf was already paddling, digging in as hard as he could. I found a paddle on the bottom of the boat and matched his strokes. Together, we moved into the lake, away from Fort Ticonderoga, away from captivity, toward freedom.

CHAPTER 46
Freedom

October, 1777
Lake George, New York

My mind reeled with the reality of it. I was free! For more than seven months, I had been a prisoner, and now I was free. I was heading south — back to Jane, back to my life.

We paddled hard down the eastern shore, straight across the shallow bays, keeping clear of the main channel. We did not know if the Indians, from whom we had just stolen a canoe, might be hunting us or not. Also, we wanted to avoid any other British coming north. It would be hard to explain why we were out in a canoe, looking like we did.

"That was your friend Walsh," Rolf commented after we backed our efforts to a steady rhythm.

I could not say why Walsh had prevented the soldiers from firing at us. Although we had a long history, he never showed me any real friendship. True, he did buy me from Cornplanter for a musket and might have considered me his property. Who other than a friend would do that for you?

"He let us go," I answered simply. "I can't say why."

"Well," Rolf said, "maybe he figured we're of little value, anyways. Maybe he's tired of this whole damn thing. Know I am."

We paddled on, and I took a moment to consider Lake George. A half-moon peeked through scuttling clouds, giving the lake an icy, white chill and making us far too visible. Ahead, the lake stretched on forever.

"How far can we go on this lake?" I asked.

Rolf sat up straight and rested his paddle on the gunnel. "Lake's thirty miles long. I figure to go all the way to old Fort William Henry, then set out for home on foot. You'll come with me."

I knew Rolf was from German Flatts, the same town where General Herkimer had gathered his doomed militia army to relieve Fort Stanwix. He was with Herkimer at Oriskany and lucky enough to get captured. His brother-in-law had been killed fighting right beside him.

It was hard to realize that I could decide which direction I would go next. It had been a long time since a choice like that was mine to make.

"I don't know, Rolf," I said softly. "I've got four hundred miles ahead of me."

"I believe things have calmed down along the Mohawk. You could spend the winter, get strong, then head home."

I shook my head, even though he could not see it. "No, I need to keep moving. I truly do appreciate the offer, though."

Keep moving. Keep moving south. That was all my mind could picture. Just keep moving.

We paddled for hours without seeing another living soul. Twice we passed cabins sitting back from the shore, windows glowing dimly from the hearth fire within. As the chill of the night overcame the heat of our exertion, the warmth of a cabin was very inviting. But we did not stop until the early dawn brightened the lake.

"Best be pulling in," Rolf said. "We'll head for that cove and find a stream. Drag the boat under the trees."

The cove Rolf selected was well protected, with the steep mountain rising behind. A flat area allowed us to drag the canoe a dozen feet up a cold, rushing creek. It was not exactly hidden, but no one would see us unless they were looking.

Rolf stretched out in the canoe in one direction and me in the other. Sunlight filtered through the red and yellow leaves above us with the promise of a crisp, clear day. A beautiful day to be out on a lake, I thought before sleep and exhaustion pulled me under.

I slept the sleep of the innocent. It was late afternoon before I stirred. Climbing out of the canoe, I realized how much my body hurt. Every joint ached and cracked as I worked my muscles loose. Still, I felt rested and ready to go. That was the most important thing.

Except I was as hungry as a bear. It had been nigh on suppertime when we made our escape, many hours past. We needed to find food soon, or this wonderful rest would have been for naught.

Rolf agreed. "We got nothing to hunt with," he said after a search of the canoe proved it was as empty as our stomach. "I think we'll have to rely on the kindness of the folks in those cabins."

He was pointing at two cabins on the far side of the lake that we had failed to notice that morning. Smoke rose from each cabin. Someone was cooking an early supper.

We waited until dusk and then crossed the lake, keeping

low and paddling smoothly. As we pulled the canoe up the beach, a terrible thought occurred to me. "What if they're Loyalists, Rolf?" I whispered.

He stood still, thinking. "There's a good chance they once was. I'm willing to bet they changed their tune, now that the news of poor Miss McCrea has got around."

"It's a big bet," I said.

"Less you have a better idea…"

I did not. I was hungry enough to risk it. "We must try," I said.

We followed the path up to the cabins and approached the closest one. As we came to the clearing, a dog howled inside the house, sounding the alarm. The front door opened, and a heavyset man emerged. He held a musket in our general direction.

"State your business," he called in a none too friendly voice. An old hunting dog growled menacingly from behind his legs.

We both stopped and raised our hands in front of us.

"We mean you no harm, friend," Rolf said. "We're militiamen escaped from Ticonderoga trying to make our way home. We'd appreciate a bit of cheese and bread if you can spare it. We've had nothing for a long time."

The man looked us over, trying to make up his mind. We presented a sorry picture, I am sure.

"So you're Patriots, then?" he asked.

Rolf and I looked at each other and answered at the same time. "Yes, sir, we are, and proud of it."

"How is it you weren't with Brown?" he asked. "Couple hundred or more men went up the lake a few weeks back."

"Bad timing," Rolf said.

The man smiled and rested his musket on the ground. "Then you're welcome," he said. "Come on in."

Our new friend was alone, his wife having gone to Skenesboro to stay with her sister while the west was in such turmoil. Unlike some of his neighbors, Owen Pitt was a Patriot and had been from the start.

Once he got going, Owen was eager to talk. Except for his old dog, he had little company. He possessed a ready laugh but turned serious when we mentioned the murder of Jane McCrea. He agreed with Rolf that the news of her death had changed many people's opinions of the British. However, he said, there were still those on the lake and down to Fort Edward maintaining their loyalty. We must be careful.

So, stomachs full for the first time in months, we continued south. At our feet was half a roasted chicken and a jug of cider. We were free and considered ourselves fortunate.

Sometime later, the moon came up, and Rolf abruptly ceased paddling. He sat quietly, peering intently into the distance, and then whispered, "Head for that cove, someone's coming!"

Paddling carefully so as not to splash, we moved our canoe under a group of overhanging willow trees. I grasped a handful of the wispy branches to steady the canoe. I could hear the soft splash of half a dozen paddles stroking through the calm water. I held my breath.

Two fast-moving canoes swept past us, not more than a hundred feet away. As they passed, I could tell that Indians were doing the paddling, digging hard, while two British soldiers sat in the center of each canoe. At least two of the white men were officers, probably conveying news to Powell and St. Leger at Ticonderoga.

We waited until they were far down the lake before continuing our journey south.

"Those are excellent eyes you've got," I said to Rolf.

Rolf grunted. "Last thing we want is to run into Redcoats asking too many questions."

"I don't care to run into any Continentals, either," I added. "Last thing *I* need is to be conscripted into the damn army!"

"So we keep to ourselves," Rolf agreed.

Around midnight, the wind picked up, coming up the lake behind us. It had a sharp edge to it, and soon, a misting rain began to fall. The wind helped us along until a chop developed. From then on, paddling was like sitting on a wagon going down a washboard road.

Hours later, long after the moon had set, we passed Diamond Island. Campfires and torches indicated that a British force still held the tiny island.

Since Ticonderoga, we had been following closely on the heels of Colonel Brown. His force had unsuccessfully attacked the island depot before burning their boats and heading overland to Skenesboro. Staying as far east as possible to avoid detection, we soon came to the southern end of Lake George.

Above us, looming darker than the sky, were the ruins of Fort William Henry. A quarter of a mile to the east, on a small rise, several fires were visible. Rolf said that must be the British depot optimistically called Fort George. In reality, it was nothing more than a single stone wall.

We sat for a while, watching the shore for signs of life. No lights showed in the ruins before us, nor was there a patrol on the beach.

We pulled the canoe in, gathered our bounty, and then shoved the boat back onto the lake. The canoe sat in the choppy water, as if not wanting to leave us, and then slowly bobbed off to the west.

The misting rain turned into a real downpour as we climbed the soggy bank up to the remains of the fort. Charred and rotten timbers lay in heaps where the parapet once stood. We carefully stooped under a section of the wall leaning in toward what used to be a parade ground. It provided meager shelter from the rain, but we crowded in anyway.

"Hope there's no rattlers," Rolf said, looking at the moldy pile. "I don't like rattlers."

I laughed at that. "No one likes rattlers, Rolf."

Cold, wet, and tired, we waited for daylight while water constantly dripped upon us.

"Suppose a fire's out of the question?" I ventured, arms wrapped around my chest, teeth chattering in the dampness.

"Would be nice," Rolf said. He scratched at the debris we were sitting on. "Could dig a fire pit, though everything's soaked. I'm scared we would announce our presence with a smoky fire."

I had to agree. So, with nothing to do but wait and unable to sleep, I peered out from our hiding place and pictured the fort as it once was.

William Henry was notorious, even to a Pennsylvanian like me. In the previous war, the French laid siege to the fort and nearly destroyed it before the British surrendered. The French General Montcalm promised the British Colonel Monroe safe passage for his men and their women.

In that war, the Iroquois and the Huron fought on the side of the French. The Indians did not honor the surrender terms. The Huron attacked as the British marched across a valley not far from the fort, slaughtering a hundred men and women. The fighting was hand to hand. Finally, the French called off the Indians, allowing the survivors to stagger the last ten miles to Fort Edward. (20)

After the siege, the French destroyed the fort. No one had bothered to rebuild it in the twenty years since.

Rolf cleared his throat, interrupting my thoughts. The low clouds brightened slightly, and the rain tapered off, but the temperature was dropping.

"Something we need to discuss," Rolf said in a somber voice.

"I know," I said. "It's going to snow."

My friend gave a short snort. "If you're determined not to come home with me, then our paths lie in different directions," he said. "You know my offer stands. You can come back to German Flatts. Spend the winter."

I sighed deeply. It was so tempting — crawl into a warm bed in a cabin, let the snow pile up, and try to forget the last seven months of my life.

"No, Rolf," I sighed again. "I'm going home. To Jane."

Rolf unwrapped the cheesecloth from the half chicken Pitt had given us and tore it in half again. Then he split the cloth and handed me my share.

"Can't split the cider," he chuckled, "so I suggest we drink up."

So we drank the half-gallon of hard cider in quiet companionship, waiting for the dawn.

After a while, Rolf stood, looking at the small depot to our east. "We should be getting on before those fellas in the fort up there decide to send out a patrol."

Flurries drifted in the air as we climbed out of our hiding place. Rolf pointed to the south. "Fort Edward's that way," he said. "You'll hit the Hudson first. Flows east in this area. Cross as soon as you can. Stay away from the fort, it's most likely still be British. For that matter, stay away from the Americans too. Then you need to find a boat. It's a long way to New York, so you'll need to resupply somewhere — "

"Rolf," I interrupted, laying a hand on his shoulder. "I'll be fine."

Rolf screwed up his mouth. "Guess I'll be seeing you," he said with a coarseness in his voice, looking straight at me. Then he turned and walked away.

I stood watching until Rolf cut left into the trees and disappeared. That was the last I ever saw of him.

CHAPTER 47
On My Own

October, 1777
The Hudson River, New York

Before I reached the Hudson, the snow was falling in big wet flakes. I desperately needed to find warmer clothes. All I wore was the shirt the cook gave me back at Ticonderoga, worn-out deerskin britches from Conawagus, and moccasins that let a toe show.

I was alone, unarmed, underfed, poorly clothed, and heading through enemy territory as one of the worst winters in memory began to leave its mark on the land.

I was also feeling a bit lonely. A man can walk many miles and have only one friend like Rolf. He was so friendly and full of life that his departure left a hole in the world. Over the years, I have often thought of him, wondering how he made out.

And, as he had predicted, I came to the upper reaches of the Hudson River with just a short hike. The low rumble of a waterfall drew me to where an immense stone island split the river in two. Water raged over a jumble of boulders on either side of the island. Five cabins sat on the north side of the river.

I waited in the tree line until convinced that the cabins

were empty. It seemed strange to me how many settlements emptied out as the fighting circled around them instead of defending themselves. I knew my people back in Indiana would never abandon their homes.

Silently approaching a cabin, I listened for any sounds from within. The door opened easily. Inside, I detected no scent of recent human habitation. Only a few pieces of handmade furniture remained. Two mice ran for cover, a further indication that no one had been here for a long time.

The first rule of wilderness survival is to seek shelter. I looked longingly at the hearth and the cold embers, thinking how good a day's rest in front of a roaring fire would feel. But I was determined to keep moving. Who could say how much snow there would soon be?

The second rule was to be adequately clothed. Searching the room, I found a worn blanket so full of holes that the owner had tossed it away. I shook out the dust and mouse droppings and pulled it over my shoulders, Indian style. It would help.

The cabin had nothing else to offer. It was time to move on. I made a quick inspection of one more cabin and found it just as empty except for a broom used to sweep the last dirt out the door as the owners fled. Though the enemy might be coming down the road, you dare not leave the house a mess. I smiled at the thought as I broke the handle off to make a walking stick.

My plan required that I avoid both the British and the Americans. To do this, I had to cross to the other side of the Hudson, skirt Fort Edward as widely as possible, and then cross back to the east side of the river. According to

Rolf, and what we had discovered at Ticonderoga, Burgoyne surrendered at Fort Hardy, near the town of Saratoga. So it reasoned that any British or Loyalist stragglers, and most of the Continental Army, would be on the west side.

I climbed down on one of the more substantial boulders in the rapids and spotted another that I thought I could reach. Steeling myself and getting a sound footing in the wet snow, I took two running steps, bounded across the white water, landing face down on the next rock. From there, it was an easy jump to the rock island.

The other side of the island was closer to shore, and I cleared the distance in two leaps.

Then I stopped and looked back at the river, back to the north. Crossing the Hudson was a milestone for me. Canada was now far away, and I was heading home.

Facing south, I pulled my shoulders back and entered the deep pine forest. The land was flat, and walking was easy. I soon came upon a well-used trail running north and south. The light snow continued, drifting down through the pines with a soft whisper.

I was forced to scurry off the trail twice during the day and hide as a group of British soldiers passed by, heading north. They looked dejected and defeated, but the twenty soldiers marched in two orderly columns, muskets on their shoulders, true to British army discipline. They must have been some of Burgoyne's men who slipped past the Continentals.

I finally stopped for the night north of Fort Hardy. Far ahead, smoke rose from hundreds of campfires. I could go no further on this side of the river.

A frigid night under a snow-laden pine tree convinced me it was time to find a boat and speed my progress south. I remembered a series of rapids I had passed the day before and backtracked to that point. Below the falls, a small wooded island sat in the center of the river, a few lean-tos scattered about. A flat-bottomed rowboat rested on the riverbank. I thanked the Lord and apologized to the owner, and pushed off into the current. The sky was leaden, but the snow had stopped. I was feeling optimistic about being back on the water and heading south at an excellent rate.

My only job was to keep the bow aimed downstream while the current did the rest. As I approached Fort Hardy on my right, I veered the stolen craft as far as possible toward the left bank. No alarm came from the fort, although I spotted men on the ramparts watching me pass. After that, I never saw another soul until I came to Stillwater.

My quarter of the chicken had only succeeded in making me hungrier. Food — the third rule of survival — was becoming particularly important. I backed water to slow my approach to a low, weathered pier. Several well-built clapboard houses sat on the high bank beyond. The settlement did not look like a military occupation, so I decided to risk a foraging expedition.

Before I reached the pier, a stooped-over old man came partway down its length. He watched me approach with neither suspicion nor welcome on his craggy face. As I got closer, however, his eyes scrunch up as he assessed my poor condition.

"Can I help you, friend?" he asked with a heavy German accent. My boat bumped against the rotted pilings, and I held it in the current.

The man was not being hostile, just wary. I decided to throw caution to the wind.

"My name's Fergus Moorhead from Pennsylvania. I've been a captive of the British and recently made my escape. If you can spare it, a bite of food would be most appreciated."

The man did not move or offer to tie my boat to the pier. "Why didn't you stop at Fort Hardy? I hear General Gates has plenty a new mouths to feed. Won't mind one more."

I humbly bowed my head, not to mislead the man, but because he had a point. Some would think I should be trying to help my county further its cause. Instead, I was doing my best to avoid any conflict and make my way home. I was in an indefensible position.

"You speak the truth, sir," I said. "To be honest, I feel I've done my part. I was at Fort Stanwix and saw the massacre of General Herkimer's militia. I was a prisoner in Montreal and Fort Ticonderoga. I've seen a great deal. I only want to go home."

"Tie your boat," the old man said. "You can come along with me."

Yon Snell was the dockmaster for the town of Stillwater. His job, he explained as we walked to his crumbling hut at the foot of the pier, was to keep riff-raff like me from abusing the town's hospitality. Turned out, many lost men were moving up or down the river.

His life was a lonely one, and Yon, a widower, was happy to talk. I told him most of my story as he prepared a wonderful supper of johnnycakes, chicken, and potatoes. He was an excellent cook.

"If you plan to go down the river and not draw attention to yourself," he advised, "you might want to clean up some."

I laughed out loud. "I've become attached to these clothes."

"The clothes, I think," Yon chuckled, "have become attached to you!"

He went to a chest in the corner and pulled forth a pair of canvas britches. "These will do. A shirt, I cannot spare a shirt, though. Your old one will have to do."

"I appreciate it, Mr. Snell. You wouldn't have a razor, would you?"

An hour later, I relaxed with a full stomach, a new pair of trousers, and my beard back to a civilized length. I even chopped off part of my hair so that it no longer hung below my shoulders. I felt like a new man.

Yon took my old deer hide trousers and the rotten blanket and threw them in the river.

We sat at his table, a warm fire burning in the hearth. Outside, snow was falling again in a fine layer that would vanish as soon as the sun came up. An enormous yawn escaped me.

"If you care to," Yon said, "there is a blanket. You are welcome to sleep in front of the fire."

"I appreciate that," I said, relieved that he was not throwing me out in the winter night. But what of tomorrow? So I asked, "What's the river like downstream?"

Yon scratched at his beard, looking at me for a quiet moment. Then he said, "Below Stillwater, there is a stretch of rough water. Your little flat bottom will ride it if you can steer past the rocks."

I smiled at that. Maneuvering a boat through rapids was a skill with which I had a great deal of recent experience.

Yon continued, "Before noon, you will pass Albany. Might be Continentals there, so stay on the left bank. Then there is not much until you reach the Highlands, seventy miles or so below Albany. That must be the end of your river journey."

"Why's that?"

"Below Poughkeepsie, the British control everything. They use the river, the roads, they swarm like mosquitoes. There, you must not go."

"How will I know when I'm approaching the Highlands?"

Yon smiled, "You will know. Leave the river when you see the mountains."

I was underway before the sun came up the next morning. Between my feet were the remains of last night's roasted chicken, a loaf of bread, and a jug of milk. Yon's old blanket draped my shoulders, and another protected my feet.

The old man stood on the pier and watched me pull away. He gave a short wave and turned back to his hut and the warmth of a fire I would not know for many months.

Yon was correct in the distance I needed to cover. The current quickly increased, and I soon rode comfortably down a series of shallow rapids. For a man who had conquered the Saint Laurence, these minor disturbances proved to be no challenge. My boat was easy to steer, and I avoided the rocks like the skilled oarsman I was.

Five miles on, I passed the mouth of the Mohawk, roaring down to join the Hudson. Albany was busy, the piers packed with boats. I saw a few soldiers and figured that most of the army was still north, dealing with the thousands of British prisoners.

Then, there was nothing except the occasional cabin

sitting on its own above the riverbank for mile after mile. That night, I found a deep cove, protected by a jumble of overhanging limbs. It was cold, and I sleep poorly. Then, when I finally did sleep, I woke with the sun already up. Angry at myself for losing valuable rowing time, I pushed off and continued south.

I rowed and I rested, I rowed and I rested. That was my lot for that day and the next. Soon, despite the food Yon had given me, my strength started to fade. The dampness attacked my feet and hands, and my back ached incessantly.

The evening of the third day after leaving Stillwater, I suddenly snapped awake, realizing that I had come close to falling out of the boat. This scared me because I did not even know I had been asleep. I desperately needed to rest.

Looking for a spot to pull in, I found a low area near the entrance to a small creek on the right bank. Far ahead, downstream, I could make out the remains of a string of houses along the riverbank. Smoke rose from two large buildings further on.

Do not get any closer, I thought numbly and paddled the boat toward the creek. I climbed into the mud and managed to pull the boat onto dry land. Then, exhausted beyond my years, I lay down in the bottom of the boat and fell instantly and deeply asleep.

"What do you think it is, Sergeant?"

"I think it's a fucking deserter, 'ats what I think. Drag 'es arse up out a there."

The voices floated in my head while still asleep before the rough hands reached down to haul me out of the boat. Two soldiers held me by my elbows in front of a leering sergeant. Strangely, I could not quite understand what was happening. Convinced I was dreaming, I stared stupidly at the Redcoats surrounding me.

"Stand 'em against that tree."

My mind came back to me as the two soldiers dragged me to a massive oak and slammed my back against the rough bark. Three other soldiers formed up twenty feet away. They intended to shoot me!

"Wait!" I cried. "I'm not a deserter. I've never been in the army! Indians captured me, and I escaped!" Even as I spoke the words, I recognized how incredulous it must sound.

"My arse," the sergeant laughed. "You're a fucking deserter, an don't matter which army. If you ain't a deserter, you're a traitor. We shoot 'em all."

The sergeant stood aside, and the two soldiers let go of my arms.

"Ready!"

I could not believe this! A deserter was the one thing no one could accuse me of. True, I had become an accomplished thief, but I was not a deserter. Looking around in desperation, I realized that neither running nor begging was an option. I squeezed my eyes closed, knowing in my heart that I breathed my last.

"Aim!"

The next words I heard were the sweetest I ever knew.

"Hold, Sergeant!"

My eyes sprang open to see a baby-faced lieutenant mounted on a black Friesian that impatiently stomped the ground. The officer was resplendent in a new, bright red coat, white powdered wig, and a black cocked hat with a white feather in it! This was not an officer running from General Gates — we were in his territory.

"Sir?"

"Who is this man?" the lieutenant asked, turning up his nose and pointing with his riding crop.

The sergeant stiffened. "'E's a deserter, sir! Caught 'em in that boat, trying to escape. I was about to shoot 'em, sir. What 'e deserves!"

The lieutenant looked me over. "If he's a deserter, then he is our prisoner, Sergeant. Put him with the rest."

"But, sir —" the sergeant began to protest.

"General Clinton's orders are clear — prisoners are to be sent to New York."

The sergeant still did not move. He looked at me and then back up at his lieutenant like a child deprived of a toy.

"With the rest, Sergeant! Now! We're moving out."

Before I could plead my cause, the lieutenant turned his horse and trotted to the front of the line. Thirty or forty soldiers and half a dozen wagons waited on a narrow road only yards from my hiding place.

The soldiers threw me bodily into the back of a flatbed wagon holding six other men. None of the prisoners said a word of welcome and avoided looking at me for the most part. It may be hard to believe, but I was in better condition than any of them.

Most of the men had bloody bandages on an arm or leg, and one looked like he would not live to see the next day.

"Where are we going?" I asked the man next to me.

"Going?" he said, an edge of hysteria in his voice. "Going? Brother, we're going to hell. To a place no one survives — a prison ship in New York."

He turned his head to look at me, desperation showing in his red, tear-filled eyes.

"Brother, we're all dead men."

Four days later, I knew he was right.

CHAPTER 48
The Prison Ship

November, 1777
Wallabout Bay, New York

The smell of death greeted us before the ships came into view. Death, and death in the making.

Wet snowflakes drifted out of the night sky as four Royal Navy sailors rowed our jollyboat to the farthest of the looming hulks. The coxswain sat in the stern sheets, buried in his cloak, and a soldier leaned against the gunnel.

Four ships hung on their anchors in Wallabout Bay, off the west shore of Long Island. Our destination was a dismasted, battered old sixty-four once known as HMS *Scorpion*.

In place of masts, a spindly derrick had been erected to lift supplies aboard. It had the unsettling appearance of a gallows.

Suddenly, a man behind me started to moan and thrash violently in his restraints.

"Deal with that," the coxswain growled. The soldier raised his musket and soundly smacked the poor man on the back of the head. He slumped forward, unconscious.

"Enjoy the ride, gentlemen," the coxswain called out merrily, "because this is the last one you will ever take.

'Lasciate ogne speranza, voi ch'intrate,'" he quoted in remarkably good Italian and laughed at his own oft-repeated joke. "I don't imagine any of you are educated enough to understand that, are you? Well, you'll learn soon enough."

Abandon all hope, ye who enter here — the inscription written above the gates of hell in Dante's *Inferno*, a book I read in English some years back. I do not recommend it.

The coxswain did not seem to be the kind of man to quote Dante. At the time, I was as ignorant of its meaning as everyone else in the boat. However, the coxswain was correct — as I soon learned.

Indeed, my hopes sank deeper the closer we got to the ship. Dull lanterns partially illuminated the deck and the landing platform floating alongside. Three men stood on the platform, two holding muskets at the ready, while the third raised his oil lantern to watch us approach.

"How many?" the man with the lantern asked.

"Twelve," the coxswain called back. "One might be dead, though."

The sailors shipped oars in proper navy manner, and we bumped against the platform. A man at each end of the boat jumped out to hold us fast.

"All ye traitors! Out!"

One at a time, the eleven conscious prisoners were unshackled and stepped onto the floating platform. The man lying in the bottom of the boat was still, his head covered in blood. The soldier kicked the man in the stomach, but he did not respond.

"He's dead," the soldier said without a trace of emotion.

"Well, toss him on the float," the man with the lantern said. "We'll bury him tomorrow with the rest."

As the jollyboat pulled away, the man with the lantern turned to us. He was dressed in an oilskin coat and cocked hat. A thick wool muffler encircled his neck.

"My name is Lieutenant Hughes," he said. "Aboard this ship, you will address me and all other loyal servants of the Crown, as sir. We are Army, not fucking Navy, so you say 'Yes, sir!' when addressed. We have few rules. You will speak only when spoken to by one of us. There is no escape, so set aside any thoughts you may have in that direction. Below deck, it is every man for himself. I don't give a damn what goes on down there so long as you turn out when ordered. Now, up the ladder!"

And with those words of welcome, I was introduced to my new home.

We climbed the swaying wood and rope ladder to the main deck, where more men stood waiting for us. Silent as a specter, a soldier pointed to the main hatch with his musket. Another soldier leaned on a pulley rope to raise the cover. The smell that assaulted my senses was so foul that I believed it must be visible in the daylight.

"There's two decks below," Hughes said as he joined us. "American traitors can stay on the gun deck, foreigners down to the orlop. You will be turned out at eight in the morning for four hours, rain, snow, or sun. That's all I care to say except, know this — any man who causes a problem or disobeys an order will be shot on the spot."

He moved away from the opening as we filed past, groping for the rungs of the ladder hidden in the blackness below. One man slipped and fell to the deck. His cry of pain elicited angry curses.

As soon as my feet touched something substantial, the hatch cover slammed shut, and we were immediately lost in a Stygian blackness.

It was so dark that colors flashed before my eyes as they desperately tried to adjust. I gagged at the horrendous smell that floated about us like a living thing. It was worse than falling into an outhouse well.

Even though we had never been friendly, the eleven new arrivals huddled together at the foot of the ladder. No lantern or candles were permitted below deck for fear of fire. Touch was the only method for finding your way in this horrible place.

"What are we supposed to do?" someone asked in a plaintive whisper.

"You have to find a place to make your own," another whispered. Moans and cries of men mingled with harsh whispers. I felt we were in mortal danger from the other prisoners.

Forward of where we stood, I could make out the slightest glimmer of light. In truth, it was only less darkness, coming from what I assumed was a covered gunport. Hands out in front of me, I crept cautiously in that direction. I have explored deep caverns that presented more light.

Shuffling my feet along the deck, I received more than one oath from a body lying in my path. I reached the meager light source and came upon several men crowding a gap in the gunport lid.

"Clear out!" said one ghostly form.

"These spaces are claimed," another hissed.

"Move on!" said a third, roughly pushing me away.

Staggering back, I tripped over another body lying on the deck and fell across his legs.

"I'm sorry," I cried, panic and desperation in my voice. My mind threatened to run from my head, all sanity escaping into the foul air. What was I to do? Oh God, I thought, what has happened to me?

I sat still next to the pair of legs I had fallen over, and a prayer came to me. Quietly, barely moving my lips, I prayed for strength, I prayed for my soul, now lost in the bowels of a floating hell, this *valley of the shadow of death...*

After an eternity had passed, or perhaps a minute, a hand took hold of my shirt and pulled me forward. "Come here," a young voice whispered. "There's a space here."

My heart warmed with gratitude. I climbed past the young man, guided by his hand on my sleeve. Moving slowly up the rounded hull, I recoiled in horror as my groping hands discovered another body. This one was stiff and cold.

"He's dead!" I squeaked.

"It's all right," the young man said. "He died a couple hours ago. You can have his place."

The coxswain had been correct. Surely, this was the hell Dante imagined. I was trapped in a lunatic world with no escape.

"What do I do with him?" I whispered.

"At turn out, you have to carry him up on deck. I'll help you."

"What did he die of?"

The young man laughed ironically. "What didn't he die of?"

I pushed the corpse away from me until another voice complained, and then I settled down on the deck next to my new friend. The deck was covered with stinking straw that felt damp and rotten.

"My name's Kit," the young man said. "Christopher Hawkins, actually, but everyone calls me Kit."

"I'm Fergus Moorhead," I said, foolishly holding out my hand. Kit did not attempt to find it.

The voice sounded incredibly young. "How old are you, Kit?"

Kit laughed again, "In years, I'm seventeen. In body, I must be close to fifty."

"How long have you been here?" I wanted to know, trying to judge how long I might expect to survive.

Kit said, "Three months, though I've been a prisoner for longer. It wasn't until I escaped the last time that they decided to send me here. No one has ever escaped from these ships. Least, not yet."

He chuckled to himself, and I felt a surge of confidence. His optimism made me think of Rolf. I liked him from the start.

"How 'bout you, Fergus? How long you been a prisoner?"

I had to think hard, unsure of the date. My only sure feeling was that we were still in November.

"Indians captured me near the Allegheny River back in March. So eight months, I figure. I got sold to the British, went to Montreal and Ticonderoga, escaped, and then made it down the Hudson on my own before getting caught again."

"That sounds like a story," Kit said with a note of appreciation in his voice. "Tell me what happened."

We talked for hours, lying in the dark, shoulder to shoulder for warmth as the body behind me grew colder.

Christopher Hawkins also had a remarkable story to tell. He went to sea at fourteen and was captured not long after. Within a month, he escaped from a prison on Long Island and signed aboard another raider. When that ship was sunk off the coast of Nantucket, Kit was sent to New York and put aboard this hulk.

With great conviction, Kit vowed to escape in the not

too distant future. If you stayed, he told me, you died. It was as simple as that.

"So I don't intend to stay," he assured me. "Or die like those poor wretches on the *Whitby* last month."

That sounded ominous. "What happened?" I asked, unsure I wanted to hear the answer.

"Prison ship anchored next to us. The men managed to set fire to the ship. Seeing no hope, they chose death in the flames to the sufferings of disease and starvation. More than a hundred died. We could hear their screams…"

Kit stopped talking, lost in that horrible memory. Would I ever fall to that level of desperation? To defy the word of God and have a hand in my own destruction? I reflected on how far I had fallen. And then, on how much I had to live for.

"It don't matter," Kit suddenly blustered, "cause I don't intend being here that long."

Kit's youthful exuberance gave me some hope and raised my spirits for a while. Then I reexamined the fact that I sat in a pitch-black hell with my back resting against a dead man.

CHAPTER 49
Old Bill

November, 1777
Wallabout Bay, New York

"Traitors! Bring up your dead!"

The shouted orders from the open hatch jolted me awake. I had been dreaming of Jane, and the sudden return to reality brought tears to my eyes. Enough light entered the gun deck for me to remember where I was and see it for the first time.

Hundreds of men lay upon every available space. Most slept with their backs against a comrade, as Kit and I had. Others curled into tight balls, filthy straw pulled into pitiful nests. Here and there, men sat up, blinking at the light, rising to their feet. Others moved not at all.

Men with long, scraggly beards, hair twisted and filled with straw, dressed in filthy rags and pieces of canvas, shuffled past me.

The wretches were so encrusted with grime that they were indistinguishable from the dozen or so Negros among us. I could also see that most were extremely sick. You would not be surprised to know that dysentery was rampant on the ship. I shudder even as I write these words with the memory of the overflowing latrine tubs and the openings to the deck below where men relieved themselves. It does not need to be described.

Never once did I see a man rise from the orlop deck below us. If any soul lived there, he was no longer human.

Avoiding that thought, I turned to my new friend, who was rousing himself. Now that I could see, I was appalled that such a young boy would be held in these conditions. His sparse beard failed to hide the handsome face and intelligent blue eyes. He smiled at me and held out a hand.

"Nice to meet you, Fergus."

"And you," I said, taking the offered hand. "What do we do now?"

Kit looked beyond me at the poor soul whose place I had taken and leaned against all night long.

"First, we need to get old Bill on deck. If we're late, there'll be no food for us."

Together we shouldered the corpse of the recently departed Bill up the ladder to the main deck. Thankfully, someone helped pull the body up out of the deck hatch. We dragged him to the side of the ship, where four other bodies lay on the snow-covered deck.

Men huddled together, arms wrapped about their chests, shifting from foot to foot in a feeble attempt to stay warm. I saw that many were barefoot. None had coats or hats.

Within minutes, at least 400 men filled the deck. How many more remained below, trapped in their own nightmare, I do not know.

"What happens to them," I asked Kit, indicating the dead men.

"Burial detail will be assigned, then they will call out the mess number. During the next four hours, we will all eat."

However, I was to be immediately disappointed.

359

Because my group of prisoners came aboard so late the night before, we were not assigned to a mess. Similar to the method used in the Montreal prison, all prisoners were divided into groups of twelve men. A mess cook served for a week, retrieving the food from the steward who boiled the meat, peas, and occasional potato into a chewable stew.

When Kit's number was called, he hurried forward to the foc'sle where the galley stove was located.

He returned with a bucket full of steaming gruel and a stack of wooden bowls under his arm. His messmates gathered close to receive their allotment, like wolves at a kill. Hoping to be included, I joined them.

"You ain't part a this mess," one man growled. The others grumbled in agreement.

"He's taking Bill's spot," Kit said, trying his best to plead my case.

"If'n he gets assigned to our mess, he can eat!" the more intimidating of the group stated. Kit did not argue further.

I was then jostled and shoved out of the way. Even though the food smelled no better than it looked, it reminded me that it had been three days since my last meal. The soldiers who had brought me from Poughkeepsie to New York had been no more inclined to feed their prisoners than the men in charge of this ship.

Finding a corner of the deck out of the wind and snow, I huddled against the bulkhead and tried to think of anything other than my complaining stomach. Kit came and sat beside me.

"I can spare one spoonful," the wonderful lad said. "I need my strength, too, you understand."

I nodded dumbly, and he handed me his spoon. The taste was so repulsive that I almost spit the mouthful of broth onto the deck. Whatever kind of meat it was had gone off long ago. Only the act of boiling the greasy slime for hours kept it from poisoning us outright.

Kit told me that I needed to get a mess number from the steward once he finished cooking for the morning.

"We'll tell him you're taking old Bill McKinnon's place in Mess 21. Do you have any money?"

"No," I answered honestly. "The Indians took mine long ago."

"Too bad. Money always helps."

The cold and lack of food was starting to eat into the depths of my body. I sat shivering while Kit licked his bowl clean. Not one unpleasant drop remained.

"Let's see what we can do for you," Kit said as he gathered the spotless bowls from his messmates.

"Old Bill croaked?" the steward asked. "That's a pity."

"Last night," Kit replied. "This is Fergus. He's taking Bill's place."

The steward grinned at me and stuck out a greasy hand. "Abraham Neilson. It's a pleasure to meet you, sir."

As you would expect, the man responsible for feeding the prisoners suffered from no lack of food himself. He was paid for his labor with a tithe from each mess. Neilson's stomach bulged from beneath a stained and ripped nightshirt cut off at the waist. His beard and hair had been used to wipe his hands more than once.

Taken aback by such refined words from this fellow, I shook Abraham's hand without thinking about it.

"And you, sir," I responded with equal civility.

"Whence do you hail, if I may ask?" Neilson spoke with an educated Yankee accent.

"Pennsylvania, west of the Alleghenies," I said with

361

pride in my voice.

Nielson nodded his head in appreciation. "Indeed? A true pioneer! Well, we need to get you fed. You can join young Kit's mess. Number 21."

Much relieved, I anxiously looked for a bowl.

"So," Nielson said brightly, "I'll see you tomorrow, then." He turned back to his work, and I stood with my jaw hanging.

"Come on," Kit said, pulling at my sleeve. "There's no more food today."

Numb and disappointed beyond words, I followed Kit out onto the open deck. My stomach continued to protest loudly for an hour afterward.

The snow was falling harder, an inch or two covered the ship, and the wind was strong from the north. Dark streaks ran through the gray sky. Back home, someone would look at a sky like that and predict a blizzard.

One of the guards blew his whistle, starting me out of my reverie. Our four hours in the fresh air were done for the day. Climbing back down the ladder to the gun deck was like stepping from a winter cellar to a hot, humid summer day. It was remarkably warmer below deck, even though the smell hit me like a wet blanket.

As I approached the spot where poor old Bill had died, the place I now claimed as my own, I came to a sudden halt. A scarecrow of a man was lying in my nest, tucked up tight in a ball.

Kit stood beside me.

"Is this the right spot?" I asked.

"It is," he assured me. "This happens all the time." He kicked the man's foot. "Oi! This spot's claimed already. Move on!"

The man on the deck moved only his lips. "Shove off!"

he wheezed. "It's mine now!"

Hungry, scared, with a headache pounding deep behind my eyes, I was in no mood to be civil. I grabbed the man by an ankle and pulled him into the pathway between other reclining bodies. No one seemed to care what I did to him.

"Get out!" I shouted.

The man uncoiled and came menacingly to his feet. He was taller than me, but I outweighed him even in my emaciated condition. From nowhere, a knife was in his hand. His lips drew back in a snarl, and he lunged at me, arm straight and stiff.

Luckily, he was sick and slow. I grabbed his arm, pivoted on one foot, and used his forward momentum to throw the man to the deck. He landed hard, the knife skittering toward another man who made it disappear beneath his rags.

I took one step forward and kicked the scarecrow hard in the stomach. Crying out in pain, he collapsed and made no further attempt to move. The fight was out of him.

"Well done," Kit said. He gestured at the empty deck with an actorly sweep of his arm. "The floor is yours."

The scarecrow disappeared into the gloom of the gundeck without a word. I had no more problems with him or any other fellow prisoner. It sorely disturbed me to have to resort to such violence, especially against a fellow American. I did not want to hurt anyone.

I fluffed the rotten straw to make it somewhat acceptable and lay down with my back against the hull. Beyond the stout timbers, the wind howled. Suddenly, the ship groaned and listed heavily, straining against its anchor line, and the blizzard came on.

We were not to be above deck again for two days.

CHAPTER 50
The Mud Flats

December, 1777
Wallabout Bay, New York

"You, you, and you two," the sergeant barked, pointing out men as we stood in formation. I was among the unfortunates selected for the day's burial detail. This was my first experience dealing with the daily collection of the departed. I prayed it was my last.

A week or two had passed in my new home — how long, I could not say for certain. One day was much like another. New men arrived, and others died. I ate once a day, enough to keep me alive, not enough to get healthy.

This day, I stood with the others, freezing and shuffling our feet on the deck during turnout.

My cough got worse shortly after I arrived, and I ran a fever for two days. Men died daily from the same ailment, but I had recovered somewhat and was assigned this grim job. Besides, our guards cared nothing for the condition of our health.

Six men had died during the previous night. Our job was to get the bodies down the ladder to the floating platform and then into the rowboat.

Me and an older man with weeping sores on his arms

and face, picked up the first stiff corpse and wrestled it down the ladder. Once on the platform, we helped our mates as they lowered the other bodies from above.

Not only did we make up the burial detail, but we also had to do the rowing. The four of us took up the oars and pulled toward the shore. Two soldiers sat in the stern-sheets, looking as miserable as we felt. The snowstorm had passed, but it was bitterly cold.

The bodies took up most of the space in the boat. The old man next to me said, "This is the best part of our confinement, so it is. Nothing like a wonderful day on the beach!" He laughed with a wide, toothless grin. "Best part!"

Deciding that the poor man was touched, I turned my attention to our destination.

Wallabout Bay is on the western end of Long Island. Farms occupied most of the low, flat land, dotted here and there with bare apple orchards. Not too far to our south was the town of Brookland. Beyond the bay, across the river to the west, smoke rose from the crush of houses in the city of New York.

In August of '76, it was around Brookland that General Howe came close to capturing Washington's entire army. However, because of a well-played subterfuge, the wily general got all 9,000 of his men and most of the supplies safely to Manhattan island. From there, they managed to escape to New Jersey. Once again, Washington's luck rather than his skill saved the day.

Abraham Nielson said there are men still alive on our ship captured during the Battle of Long Island. Sixteen months in that hell. Hard to believe. I wondered what condition I would be in if I lived that long.

"Toss oars!" one of the soldiers shouted. We brought our oars in as the bow slid onto the mud next to a rough stone jetty.

Only two guards came with us, which surprised me now that I could see how desolate this section of the shore was. We could easily overpower them and make our escape — in broad daylight, in British-held territory.

The time would come.

I sighed in exhausted resignation and handed up the first body.

The other three men had done this before. Working silently, they dragged the first dead man over the rocks. The soldiers stood on the stones, watching us closely, muskets half-cocked and at the ready.

"Far enough!" shouted a soldier when the first body was halfway up the jetty. The tide was out, so a long stretch of black mud lay between the water and dry land. Then, two by two, we dragged each corpse to join the others, bumping across the stones with a sickening sound.

Two of the men sat on the rocks and took off their shoes. The toothless fellow was barefoot, and I had my worn-out moccasins.

"Take off your mocks," a gray-haired old man told me. I did as he directed.

Without ceremony, we rolled the poor fellows off the jetty and climbed down after them. Immediately, I sank into the stinking, black ooze. Despite the bone-chilling cold, the mud had not frozen. I assumed the river water was somehow warmer than the air. It felt damned frigid to me, though.

Pulling the bodies was a challenge. With each step, we sank to our knees while the mud sucked at our feet. My moccasins would have disappeared in the first step. I was quickly covered in slime and my legs ached.

"This'll do," the old man said. "Dig here."

Well, that was easier said than done. The short-handled shovels we carried with us could hardly clear the mud away before it slid back, filling the wet hole. Most of each shovelful was comprised of more water than muck.

Sticky shovelfuls flew in every direction until we had a pit roughly three feet deep and six feet long. All the while, we sank deeper and deeper, dangerously close to being buried ourselves in a common grave.

Then the six men slipped into the pit, one on top of the other. I tried hard not to look at their faces, but that memory haunts me still.

Covering them up required no effort at all. The morass swallowed the bodies before we even started shoveling.

Such was the ignoble end to the thousands of men who died on the British prison ships during the long, bitter war. (21)

As I extracted one leg and then the other and started slogging back to the jetty, I asked the old man how many bodies were buried in this mudflat.

He shrugged his bony shoulders. "I been burying men out here for more than six months," he said slowly. "Half a dozen a day, most days, from our ship alone. You figure it out."

I did not want to.

At the landing float, we threw buckets of icy river water on each other to wash off the filth caking our bodies. The smell was appalling, though no one cared at that point.

Twenty unfamiliar faces greeted us as we climbed, stained and soaking wet, to the main deck. The new prisoners eyed us with horror as they listened to Captain Hughes give his welcome speech. We looked like the specter of death from the depths of hell. A young boy, not much older than Kit, quietly wept when he saw us, fully understanding his fate.

Later that same day, as I lined up for my turn as mess cook for our group, Abraham Nielson said, "Mr. Moorhead! A grand day to you, sir!"

"And you, sir!" I responded, amused by the game of civility our steward insisted on playing. Over time, Abraham told me of his early career as a merchant captain from Boston. His ship had run into a British frigate during the blockade. Of his entire crew, Abraham was the only man still alive.

"Have you met our new arrivals?" he asked.

"I have not had the pleasure," I said. "But, based on their faces, the sight of me put the fear of God in them."

"I believe it. And it is proper that you did!" he chuckled. "No one should think themselves safe aboard this ship. They do have news to tell, though. Seems General Washington is wintering his army in your home state, a place called Valley Forge. Do you know it?"

"I don't."

Nielson smiled at his superior knowledge. " 'Tis not too far from Philadelphia." He shook his head while ladling watery stew into our communal pot. "It is a harsh winter to be camped in Pennsylvania, I can tell you that! I hear they have no food, and many are dying every day. Not much different than here."

I looked at his haggard face, red burn sores standing out on his arms, and vermin-infested beard, knowing that I looked every bit as pitiful. Could it be any worse than what we were experiencing?

The next day, my cough and fever returned. The mud-flats and river water bath had done me no good. For others, it was worse. The new arrivals brought smallpox with them. Within two days, one entire quarter of the gun deck fell sick. Sixty men died during the next week.

For once, I was content to be sick with a fever. It relieved me of the constant burial details. One day, too weak to go on deck, Kit brought me a little broth in the bottom of his bowl.

"It ain't much, Fergus," he said, propping my head on his arm, spooning broth into me with the other.

"I appreciate it. Truly I do," I said, my throat too sore to speak above a whisper.

"Just don't die on me. I don't want to have to find another mate."

I smiled weakly. "I'll do my best," I promised and coughed until my breath was gone.

My illness progressed from the cold I had fought for weeks to a consumption of the lungs that threatened my life. It would have been easy to fall into a slumber and let my spirit go. I was so tired, so beaten that the will to fight on was slipping away. If it had not been for the continual admonishments from Kit, I would not be alive today.

The next morning, he brought me a half bowl of oatmeal, the first we had received.

"What's the occasion," I asked, working hard to swallow the thin gruel.

Kit smiled broadly. "Why don't you know? It's Christmas Day!"

My head fell back against the bulkhead, emotions overpowering my need for food. Christmas! Nine months since

I left home. Nine long months, without the smile and warmth of my Jane or the comfort of my children. What were they doing today? Were they thinking of me? Unnoticed, tears came to my eyes.

"Here, now," Kit said softly. "Keep eating. You'll be up and around soon enough."

"To what end?" I asked, trying not to start my coughing again.

Kit got up on his knees and smiled broadly. "Well, I've got good news! I've been exploring further aft where there's a cannon still sitting in front of a gunport. No one sleeps there. So, over the past week, while you've been sleeping, I've made a friend on the outside!"

This got my attention. We never had any contact with people from the surrounding area. Even the guards, unhappy with their lot in life, refused to speak to us.

Seeing my interest, Kit continued, "Her name is Lizzy Burgin. She's an old bat that goes round the prison hulks, selling bread or scraps of meat to those she can reach from her dinghy. The guards pay her no heed cause she's been doing it so long."

"She can get us better food?" I asked, hopefully.

"Better than that!" Kit said, eyes bright even in the darkness of the hold. "Fergus, she's going to help us escape!"

CHAPTER 51
The Lone Cannon

January and February, 1778
Wallabout Bay, New York

Over the next month, my health improved to the point where I felt I might not die. Not immediately, anyway. Weak and bonier than ever, I had enough strength to visit Kit's secret gunport.

He had found the perfect location. A huge twenty-four-pounder still remained aft of the mainmast. For some reason, it had not been removed when the ship was decommissioned. Whether an oversight or intentionally abandoned, the cannon sat on its carriage, chocked and braced to prevent it from rolling around the deck. Its gunport was barred like all the rest, but the outside cover gapped slightly.

Forward of the gun, stairs led to the upper deck. The hatch at the top of the stairs was permanently locked, so no one ever used it. Aft of the gun was a bulkhead that separated the central gun deck from the area claimed by the captured officers.

We seldom saw any officers because they were not required to turn out as we did each morning, and they had their own cook. Not to seem resentful or anything, I never saw an officer's body dragged to the mudflats, either.

Crawling in beside the big gun, I realized how secluded we were. The space was unoccupied since the gun took up so much room. To even see out the gap in the cover, we had to lie on our sides, squeezed in beside the iron monster.

"So, Lizzy comes round every three or four days," Kit explained. "I found this space while searching for fresh air. No one claims it. I saw Lizzy pulling past and hailed her one night. She's quite nice, actually. Only old, like you."

I let that go and asked how he knew she was willing to help us escape.

"We talked through the gap there," Kit said. "She was mighty upset when I told her I was fourteen. She almost cried, thinking how terrible it was."

I peered at Kit in the shadows. "I thought you were seventeen."

Kit grinned. "I figured she'd be more sympathetic to a kid."

"You are a kid," I said.

We found Nielson on deck one morning during turnout. He was standing by himself, staring at the shore.

"Let me understand this," Abraham said, a greasy spoon leveled at my chest. "You want me to misplace my meat hatchet."

"I was thinking, maybe you left one out, careless like, and it somehow disappeared."

"I have two, and the Captain knows it. If one goes missing, they will shoot someone to get it back."

The sun was out, periodically hiding behind dull clouds, yet the temperature was mild. All 400 men pressed onto the main and quarter decks, literally cheek to jowl, enjoying the change in the weather.

"If you don't report it missing, who's to know?" Kit said. "They don't check, do they?"

"Well, no…"

Kit patted Abraham on the back. "Great! We'll do our best to return it."

When Kit went to collect our soup for the day, a battered carpenter's hatchet lay on the corner of the counter. Kit placed his communal bowl alongside the hatchet while Abraham poured in the day's ration. Neither man looked at the other. When Kit picked up the bowl, the hatchet was gone.

Thunder echoed across the bay, instantly jarring me awake. A winter storm was approaching. The ship creaked and rolled as the wind hit her broadside, nearly making enough noise to cover the moans and cries of its inhabitants.

"Kit!" I whispered as loudly as I dared. He sat up beside me. I could not see his face, but I knew he was awake and alert.

"We've got work to do," I said. "Hurry!"

Kit and I had often discussed the plan to cut our way out of the ship with Abraham's hatchet as soon as the opportunity presented itself. A thunderstorm was exactly such an event.

Moving carefully in the pitch black of the gun deck, we worked our way aft, trying desperately to avoid the mass of humanity lying on the decks. We found our way by memory, hands outstretched before our faces. Now and then, a curse came out of the darkness as we inadvertently stepped on someone's body part.

We wiggled our way in beside the nine-foot cannon, one on each side. Forged iron bars set in a wood frame secured the gunport. Beyond the bars was the gunport lid. There was a gap at the bottom edge through which Kit communicated with Lizzy. She came by every four days. According to Kit, tomorrow was the day we should expect her.

A flash of lightning over Long Island was quickly followed by a frightening clap of thunder.

"A winter thunderstorm!" Kit exclaimed. "The Lord is with us, Fergus!"

I said a silent prayer in case he was and turned my attention to the job at hand. Extracting our hatchet from the muzzle of the cannon, I studied the frame supporting the bars and chose a section that looked to be the least secure. The heavy clouds glowed just enough for me to see my target.

Kit's head was bobbing up and down in anticipation, intently watching my every move. Lightning flashed again, and I raised the hatchet. The thunder followed so quickly that I almost missed my chance. I swung viciously at the wood frame and noted the damage with satisfaction. A large chunk of the frame fell to the deck, and the corner opened an inch.

I waited an eternity for the next flash. The thunder followed in a second or two, and I swung at the loose corner with all my pitiful strength.

The corner of the frame parted completely. We were making real progress if only the storm would last. The next thunder rolled an interminable amount of time after the lightning. The thunderstorm was moving away. Our time was limited.

"Grab hold," I instructed.

Kit had better leverage from his position than I had. Together, we placed our hands on the broken corner of the frame and waited. The thunder was soft and distant when it reached our ears, and we gave it all we could. The frame rotated in the gun port with a crack and groan of twisting wood and fell to the deck with a horrendous crash.

"What the hell was that?" a startled voice exclaimed.

Terrified that our work would be discovered, we held our breath, not daring to move.

"Shut up!" another admonished.

"But…"

"Shut up," the voice in the dark growled.

We waited for many minutes until the snorts and gurgles of sleeping men returned. Luckily, as a result of the tight stairway and the bulkhead, no one was near us. I gathered up the wood chips and threw them out of the portal. Then, we carefully retrieved the frame, straining to lift the weight of the combined iron bars and wood. It was misshapen but fit roughly back into the gunport. I felt it would pass a glancing inspection.

I replaced the hatchet in the cannon bore, and we made our way back to our sleeping area, drenched in sweat and shaking from the exertion of the past hour. We spoke not at all; neither did we sleep.

The next day was a nightmare of tension. My heart pounded in my chest all day, and each unexpected sound made me jump. The turnout lasted a lifetime.

Whenever a guard approached the starboard side of the ship to spit or piss, I fretted that they would see evidence of our work.

After our meal, Kit and I went to see Abraham.

"Your hatchet is in the gun barrel below," I told him.

Nielson snorted. "Lot of good that'll do me. How am I to retrieve it, now?"

"I'm sorry, Abraham," Kit said. "I was just too scared to bring it back to you."

"What's done is done," he said, shaking his head. "Chances are, no one will ever notice. If they do, I'll simply blame the two of you."

"Fair enough," I said with a smile.

"When do you go?"

"Lizzy promised to come tonight," Kit said.

Abraham nodded his head, mouth pulled tight. "Well, gentlemen, it has been wonderful to know you. I wish you all the luck in the world."

We shook hands and left him cleaning his greasy pot.

"What if Lizzy doesn't show," I asked as we joined the multitude on deck.

Kit did not answer.

CHAPTER 52
Lizzy

February, 1778
Wallabout Bay, New York

"She isn't coming, is she?"

Kit's nose was pressed to the bars of the gunport. He had not moved for an hour.

It was well past midnight, the time Kit had arranged with Lizzy four days before. I tried not to despair, aware that waiting more days greatly increased the chance of someone discovering the damage to the gunport frame.

Kit turned from the port and settled his back against the cannon. He let out a long, disappointed sigh.

"We'll swim…" he said, his voice trailing off in uncertainty.

The weather had been warm for February, but I knew the water was numbingly cold. Taking stock of my physical condition, I knew my chances of making the shore were slim. The river would sap what pitiful reserve I retained. I was kidding myself — I had no reserve.

The alternative was equally grim. I was not getting stronger. Time was running out for me and every other man on this ship. Men died every day. The burial details never stopped making trips to the mudflats. It was only a matter of time before my body joined the rotting dead on that stinking shore.

"Let's do it," I said, clenching my already chattering teeth.

Together we pulled the frame out of the portal and quietly lowered it to the deck. This time, the scraping sound woke no one. The gunport lid pushed open with a slight squeak of the rusted hinges.

"I think we should swim down the coast a piece before venturing ashore. There's patrols all along the bay. I'm a strong swimmer, and the current should help," Kit said. He hesitated, looking at me. "Can you do it?"

I did not know. Once was, I could chase a baby through river rapids and save us both. Times had changed, and so had I. I took a deep breath.

"I'm right behind you," I said and wryly shook my head despite my nervousness.

"What?" Kit asked, seeing my face in the dim light.

"It occurred to me that this will be my fourth escape attempt."

"Don't worry," Kit whispered, "this time it's gonna work."

Without another word, he turned and pushed his legs out the portal, sliding on his belly until he hung suspended six feet above the water. He positioned his arms on the edge of the hull, gave me a quick smile, and then lowered his body into the frigid water.

We had agreed to meet at the ship's stern, which was facing the south shore. I did not waste any time, knowing that every minute in the water was draining Kit's energy, no matter how strong a swimmer he claimed to be.

Getting my longer frame out the gunport took more squirming than it had for Kit. I worked out over the edge, my legs dangling in the air, holding on with only my elbows. It was a short, silent drop to the water from there.

The water was so cold it took my breath away. I knew it would be bad, but I did not expect the numbness to attack my hands and feet so quickly.

Trying to be silent, I bobbed down the side of the ship. It took only moments to navigate the short distance to the stern, helped by the river current. I kicked toward the empty rudder posts and got a hand on the gudgeon.

Kit was not there.

I kicked hard to raise my body higher in the water, frantically searching for any sign of him. Moonlight illuminated an empty stretch of black water, and choppy waves agitated the surface. That was all I could see.

I did not dare call out. Right above my head was the officers' quarters, and above that, the guardroom. My mind reeled with the thought that Kit had abandoned me. Or worse.

The closest shore was three or four hundred yards away, in the direction of the burial mudflats. Still, I remained mindful of Kit's warning regarding the British shore patrols. I must work my way downstream, toward the open farmland south of the bay.

Perhaps Kit was already heading in that direction. I needed to follow.

With my last ounce of courage, I let go of the ship and started breast stroking. My moccasins had come off as soon as I entered the water, and my rotten trousers soon threatened to do the same. I could feel them loosening as I swam.

Part by part, my extremities lost all feeling. First my feet, then my hands, then my arms. My teeth chattered so loudly that I feared the guards would hear them. Soon my lips were numb, and, with a degree of shock, I realized I no longer shivered. I have no idea when I lost my britches.

The *Scorpion* was the westernmost of the four hulks anchored in Wallabout Bay, so I would not have to pass another ship on my way down the East River. If I lived that long.

Each stroke brought ice pain to my lungs while my kicking became erratic and labored. A rogue wave hit me square in the face, and I coughed, treading water, desperately trying to keep my head up. I could no longer feel anything in my legs. My flailing arms were not working as I wanted.

Frantic, I searched for the closest shore. Patrol or no, my slowing brain told me I must get out of the water. I glimpsed dim lights that might have been Brookland and turned in that direction.

At once, I knew I could not make it. Every second, the current carried me further away. I bobbed up and down, kicking as hard as I could, but my body was not obeying my commands. Swallowing another mouthful, I tried to turn on my back and only succeeded in submerging my entire body.

Black water enveloped me, my numb body failed to respond. Thrashing instead of swimming, my head came to the surface, gasping for one last breath of air.

And strong hands clasped my arm like a vice.

Scrapping against the gunnel, I was hauled bodily out of the water and dumped into the bottom of a battered, old dinghy.

"My Lord!" Lizzy Burgin laughed. "Are you a sight! Tiniest pecker I ever seen!"

Numb and in shock, I threw up in the bottom of the boat.

"Well, leastways, it's only water!" Lizzy chuckled.

"Where..." I tried to say. "Where is Kit?"

Lizzy took up her oars and turned her boat down current. "I seen him climbing up on the rocks near Brookland," she said. "I think he fared better than you."

Elizabeth Burgin was a strapping woman with dark hair pulled up under a cocked hat. Her square face, weathered beyond her thirty years by a life on the water, showed deep creases beside intelligent eyes. She was what people kindly call 'handsome.'

"Do you intend to follow him?" she asked, unabashedly handing me a dirty canvas tarp to cover my nakedness.

I thought about that. Kit intended to go east on Long Island and then head home to Providence. I, on the other hand, desired to go west.

Climbing onto the forward bench, I asked, "Is there any way to get me to New Jersey?"

Lizzy laughed out loud. "Jersey? You don't ask for much, do you? Which way you headed?"

"Pennsylvania," I said through chattering teeth. My shivers had returned, which I took as a good sign. At least my body was attempting to recover from the cold.

Rowing in silence for a while, Lizzy regarded me with her dark eyes. "Well, seeing as how I was late, and you all but drowned, I figure I can do that for you. Feel kinda responsible for you losing your britches!" And she laughed again.

She pulled hard on one oar and turned the bow west. I looked back toward Long Island and wished Kit a long life. He had been a memorable friend. (22)

The sun was high before we slipped north of Staten

381

Island. Lizzy found a secluded cove for a few hour's rest. Discussing my plans, she decided to put me ashore at sundown, so I would not draw too much attention to myself. She apologized for not having anything to eat and shared a small jug of rum. I dozed, exhausted and warm, wrapped in the old tarp, while she talked, not seeming to care if I listened or not.

I did learn, however, that two children and the man with whom she lived waited for her in New York. She was not well-off but insisted on doing what she could for the men on the prison ships and those confined ashore.

Over the years, Lizzy helped more than 200 men escape. When the most notorious of all the prison ships, the old *Jersey*, came to the bay, Lizzie had her hands full. That floating hell was responsible for more deaths than all of the other hulks combined. Whether they escaped or not, many men owe their lives to Elizabeth Burgin. (23)

Late in the afternoon, with a dull red sun low on the horizon, Lizzie grounded her dinghy on a muddy bank south of Elizabeth Town. She had brought me twelve miles from Wallabout Bay.

"This is a far as I can go, Fergus. It's a long hard pull back up to New York, and I mean to catch the tide." She looked me over and shook her head in sympathy. "You are a sight. I think I can count every bone in your body, even through your shirt."

I looked down at the tarp covering my waist. "Do you suppose you can spare this tarp?"

Her eyes crinkled, and a wide grin showed large, white teeth. "I'm of a mind to make you leave it behind, but I don't believe you'd make it far otherwise. Take it and find a barn to hold up. Find an old sack or something easier to wear."

Holding the tarp tight, I climbed into the freezing mud of the riverbank.

"I can't thank you enough," I said, my heart in my throat.

"It's what I do," she said, backing the dinghy away from the shore. "You take care of yourself, Fergus. I wish you all the luck in the world."

I stood in the mud and watched her row away.

Lizzy's return would be much more difficult, having to go upstream to her home in the city. Even with the tide, it would be a hard, long row. I suspected, however, that those broad shoulders were up to the task.

I shook my head in wonder. It was because of people like her that we would win this war.

Then I turned my face at the setting sun. I was cold, half-naked, barefoot, starving, and unsure of my way home.

But I was free once more. This time, I intended to stay that way.

CHAPTER 53
Naked and Lost

February, 1778
Somewhere in New Jersey

I awoke to the sound of singing.

Curled up tight and covered with straw, I thought for a second that I was still dreaming.

Daylight streamed through the gaps in the barn siding, dust motes floated leisurely in the slatted rays. Below me, the barn door was open, and a woman was scooping grain into the stall holding a single cow.

Moving as slowly as possible, I uncoiled my body and peered over the edge of the loft to obtain a better view. Naturally, the straw shifted, and a handful fell to the floor below.

The woman turned with a quick cry of surprise, staring up at the loft.

"Who's there?" she demanded.

I thought that staying quiet was my best bet until her next action changed my mind. She drew a small pistol from a deep pocket in her apron.

"Show yourself, or I'll shoot!" Her voice was measured and firm. I did not doubt her words.

"Please, ma'am," I said, showing my empty hands. "I'm

not gonna hurt anybody. I just needed a place to sleep."

The woman was young, rather stout, with a round face and apple-red cheeks. Her blue eyes sparkled in the sunbeams. She moved back to the barn door to get a better view of the loft.

"Show yourself," she said calmly.

I poked my head out of the straw and grinned down at her like a madman. For what she saw surely was crazed. Watery, feverish eyes shining out from a face covered with long, stringy hair and beard presented itself.

She took an involuntary step back and aimed the pistol at me. Her hand was steady.

"Come down from there."

That presented a problem. Other than my shirt, which only reached to my backside, I was completely naked. The tarp was under the straw somewhere.

Climbing down the loft ladder might be somewhat revealing.

"I can't," I said. "I've got no trousers."

"What!" she exclaimed and took another step back. This time the pistol wavered slightly.

I quickly launched into a full explanation, trying to convince the young woman not to shoot me or flee in terror, either of which might bring more people to the barn.

Thankfully, she lowered the pistol, but the stony look in her eyes told me she was not sympathetic to my plight.

When I finished, she said, " 'Tis a good story, although you've come to the wrong farm, mister. We are loyal to the King in these parts."

I assured her I intended to move on as fast as I could find some trousers. A flicker of a smile crossed her face.

"Fine. I'll help you with that, then I want you gone."

I promised. "Couldn't spare a bite of bread, could you?"

I ventured.

"Now you're pushing your luck," she said.

Many minutes passed before she returned. All the while, I could not stop thinking that she had gone for the authorities.

"These belonged to my brother," she said, throwing an old pair of wool britches up to the loft. "You people killed him." Then she tossed me an apple. "And this is all you'll get from us. Be on your way. My husband works late and will be getting up soon. Don't be here when he does, or it will go poorly for you."

She turned on her heels and left me alone with the cow. What a sweet girl.

I pulled on the britches, retrieved my tarp, and climbed down with the apple. Taking a bite, I cried out in pain and extracted a tooth from my mouth. It was a bad sign, one I immediately recognized.

Most of the men on the prison ships suffered from this new disease called scurvy because of the dreadful food. I knew that in the Royal Navy, they gave sailors lime juice to keep them healthy. For me, an apple was going to have to do.

Lizzy's tarp was a godsend. I used the edge of a scythe to rip off two square sections and then more, which I tore into long thin strips. Then I wrapped the squares around my feet and bound them with the strips. Next, I tore a hole in the remaining piece of tarp and made a serviceable cloak that fit over my head.

Taking the apple with me, I left the barn and started my journey west. Thankfully, the temperature was above freezing, and the light snow from the previous day was melting. I felt a hundred times better, even if my stomach growled and pleaded for the apple.

Soon as I could, I smashed the apple on a rock and sucked the pulp as I walked, contemplating my future. It was limited.

I could not possibly head for Indiana, which was more than 300 miles west. Even if I found someone with whom I could hitch a ride, I could never make it that far.

My family's place in Chamber's Town was the logical destination. At the time, I did not know the whereabouts of Jane and the children, or any of my family. If I could make it there, I could recover and then set out to find Jane.

Math came slowly to my starving brain. I figured I could walk fifteen miles a day, maybe add a day or two for weather or exhaustion, getting me to Chamber's Town in two weeks.

Ahead of me were three major river crossings and innumerable streams and creeks, most of which had no bridges. Crossing the Delaware, Schuylkill, and Susquehanna rivers would require all the luck I could find.

To do this, food, better clothes, and shoes were my top priorities. Did I mention food?

For the first ten miles from the barn, my path was the Kings Highway connecting New York and Philadelphia. It was a dangerous road to be on since the British held both cities. Traffic in either direction would be British Army or Loyalists, all of whom I must avoid. However, the road went in the direction I needed to go. I kept a sharp lookout.

The rumble of horses provided enough warning for me to scramble down an embankment and hide among the cattails standing beside a frozen creek. As I lowered my head below the reeds, a light cavalry troop cantered past, heading east. They were in a hurry to make New York before the weather closed in.

A mile on, I took a chance and crossed the old stone bridge at Brunswick. The town seemed oddly inactive. From the top of the bridge, I could see a handful of people scattered here and there but no evidence of village life. I moved on quickly before more soldiers appeared.

Then I followed a narrow road that wound more or less westward. I kept up a strong pace, staying warm and making three miles an hour for several hours straight.

With a bitter wind came a light rain and the temperature fell during the afternoon. By dusk, the rain turned to snow, making it difficult to see the road. I struggled on, slipping in the wetness. Fat, wet flakes melted on my head and ran down my back.

The silence was complete. The only sound was the soft hissing of the snow as it fell through the trees on each side of the road.

Half a dozen miles past Brunswick, I came to the most picturesque grist mill you could imagine. The snow was sticking to the trees, and the narrow stream cut a black band in the forest. The name Blackwell was above the unlocked front door.

The interior was still. No one had been there for days, so I felt it was a safe place to spend the night.

In one corner, I found a second burlap bag and added it to my wardrobe. Another treat waited for me. A tiny amount of cornflour hid in the crevices of the grain chute, neglected by the mice that ran from me in every direction. I scooped up a handful and chewed it methodically until I could swallow the thick paste. It sat like a lump of concrete in my empty stomach.

A dusty office sat in the back of the mill, and I decided to make it mine for the night.

I staggered to the open roll-top desk and whooped with delight. A broad brim straw hat lay among old, scattered papers. I apologized to the Lord and Mr. Blackwell and placed the hat firmly on my head.

I crawled into a corner of the office and pushed together a soft bed of rotting bags. As I fell asleep, I thought of Samuel and his attempt to build a mill. I wondered where he was now. I wondered if I would ever see him, or Jane, again. I wondered...

Sometime during the night, my cough and fever returned. It took more than one attempt to convince my aching body to move on.

I retied the canvas moccasins, added the burlap bag as a coat, and covered it all with the tarp cloak. Hat pulled down low, I left the mill and encountered a blindingly white world with a brilliant blue sky above. The snow was wet and heavy, hanging from the trees. The previous day's bitter wind was gone, so it did not feel as cold as it had.

Crossing the narrow wooden bridge, I turned south beside the stream. Outlined beneath the snow was a towpath that made my walking easy for six or seven miles until I came to a road heading west again.

My feet were frozen, and my nose ran continuously. I tried not to cough, but it kept creeping up on me until I could not hold it back any longer. It was during a particularly violent attack that a voice spoke to me from the deep woods.

"You need to care for that cough, son," a disembodied voice proclaimed.

I stopped dead and searched the surrounding snow-covered forest for the source. Then, from nowhere, a man was standing no more than twenty feet from me. His hunched shoulders and white beard partially hid a craggy, weathered old face.

Taking an involuntary step back, I tripped over a hidden stump. The old man laughed wetly and spat a wad of phlegm into the snow.

"Don't fret," he said, still laughing at my condition. "I'm not gonna hurt ya."

Finding my voice, I asked why he was hiding then.

"No tellin' who might be comin' along this road," he said, climbing down the bank to join me on the path. "You're a sight for sore eyes, if'n ya don' mind me sayin' so! Where ya comin' from?"

I was quickly convinced that the old fellow meant no harm. His coat and leggings, I noted with surprise, consisted of white rabbit skins. On his head was a rabbit-fur cap that might have come from the previous century. He blended into the snowy landscape so well that I had not seen him standing beside the road.

He held out an arm to indicate we should continue walking. I briefly told him about the prison ships and my escape.

Clucking his tongue in amazement, he said, "I'm only goin' a short distance more. Live off the road a piece. I made myself a little cabin before the last war started. Wanted no part a that foolishness. Don't want none of this one."

Somewhat irked by his attitude, I said, "Many a good man has died so we can be free."

Bob laughed until he had to spit again. "Do I not look free to you?" he asked.

I had no energy nor inclination to argue politics with this crazy old man, so I let it go. "How far is it to the

Delaware?" I asked.

"Well," he replied, scratching at his beard, ".'tis a long walk to Coryell's Ferry right down the Brunswick Pike. That's where ya need to cross. Don't go further south, or you'll run into Redcoats, sure as we stand here. They've been guarding places like McConkey's Ferry ever since General Washington got his army across there on Christmas Day in the year of our Lord, 1776."

He stopped suddenly on the path, and I halted beside him.

"Well, this is where I leave ya," he said. "My cabins 'bout a mile off the trail, there."

Though I saw no evidence of a trail, I did not doubt he could find one.

"I'd offer ya a bite of food, but haven't caught a rabbit for a while…"

"No. Thank you," I said, coughing hard. Understandably, Bob did not want anyone to know the location of his cabin. "I need to move on."

"Ya *need* to care for that cough, or ya won't make it home." He looked at me with deep-set, crinkled eyes and then rooted in one of his oversized coat pockets. "Take these," he said, holding out a handful of bright red teaberries. "Can't do better than to chew these nice and slow. Will help that cough."

I accepted the berries gratefully and popped two in my mouth. The mild flavor was immediately soothing to my throat.

"Thank you," I said.

"When ya get to the river, tell John Coryell that old Bob said to take care a ya. He'll know who ya mean once ya describes me! Ha!" Bob laughed again and turned off the path. He moved from tree to tree then disappeared completely.

From deep in the woods, a voice called out, "Good luck, son!"

I have met many unique characters in my day, but I must say old Bob ranks right up there. Meeting him, however, made all the difference in the world when, late in the day, I came to the ferry crossing on the mighty Delaware.

Pennsylvania was just across the river.

CHAPTER 54
Pennsylvania Dutch

March, 1778
Somewhere in Pennsylvania

I sat a while on the eastern riverbank before a farmer with four cows showed up and offered to pay the sixpence fee to the youngsters working for Coryell. No one objected to me joining the party. No one wanted to talk to me, either.

Partway across the river, I thought I might have made a mistake. The cows were not happy standing on the swaying barge. As the ferry operators poled against the current, the cows began to bellow and shift their weight, eyes showing white. The farmer tried to calm them, cooing softly and rubbing their ears, to no avail. I thought I might have to swim to avoid being crushed by the panicking animals.

We reached the western shore none too soon.

"He's up yonder," a young Negro boy responded when I asked where I could find Mr. Coryell. He pointed at a handsome stone house sitting high on the riverbank. The ferry business must be quite lucrative.

The girl that answered my knock took one look at me and ran back into the house. Coryell came out and stood on his front porch with his hands on his hips. I tried to explain why I was at his door.

"So you met Bob, did you?" he asked, still wondering whether to receive me. "Tell me about him."

Surprised at the question, I tried to remember anything unique the old man had said. Trouble was, I had done all the talking. Of Bob, I had learned nothing at all. Coryell stood waiting, head cocked to the side.

"I think he might be touched," I ventured. "He might be a magician, too. He appeared out of thin air and vanished the same way…"

Coryell put his head back and laughed heartily. "That he does! Bob has lived in those woods since I was a boy. I do not think he has set foot inside a real house his entire life. You will excuse my inquiries. We get our share of stragglers and deserters these days. I shall not abide it. Well, go on back to the stable and make yourself comfortable. I will send Sally out with hot food. You can stay the night, get some rest. Looks like you could also use shoes, if I might say so."

I looked down at the wet canvas tied to my feet. "Moccasins, if you have a pair, would be fine, sir," I said. "I don't think I could wear shoes, I've been so long without."

Coryell laughed again and showed me the direction to the barn. I cannot say why he was willing to take an endorsement from that old man, but so he did. And, he was true to his word. After a hot bowl of mush, I slept like the dead that night in the comparative warmth of the stables, surrounded by soft sighs of two draft horses.

John Coryell's boats were burned, commandeered, and stolen by one side or the other throughout the war. His loyalties, however, never wavered.

Later than intended, and braving the freezing wind, I started off with a fried egg and a glass of milk in my belly and new, dry moccasins on my feet. My cough, however, was deep and wet in my chest. The coughing fits were so bad from time to time that I was forced to stop and bend over, hands on my knees until it passed.

Still, I made decent progress. That night I slipped into another barn next to a log cabin somewhere in Pennsylvania. There were lights in the house, but I did not announce myself. The barn was empty, and frost hung in the air. By dawn, I was on my way, staggering and shuffling down the road like a sixty-year-old man.

You might wonder why I did not ask more people for help than I did. Although I knew plenty of folks were willing to help me, I also feared they might mistake me for a deserter, or worse, if I knocked on the wrong door. The last thing I wanted was to be arrested or conscripted into the army.

My only thought was to get to Chamber's Town as quickly as possible while avoiding as many people as I could. I felt I had been lucky so far. For the most part, the people I met following my escapes from Ticonderoga and New York had been friendly and helpful. However, I did not want to push that luck, so I kept my head down and walked west.

The highway ran from Trenton to York, so it was not surprising when riders trotted into view. I kept a careful watch for travelers in both directions and hurried off the road before anyone saw me. It required constant surveillance and tired me out.

At noon the next day, I came to the Schuylkill River at a place called Royer's Ford. The river was fast-moving and shallow, not much more than 200 feet wide. I studied it for a while, choosing my path with care. No one was near, so I took off my moccasins and wool trousers and waded in, holding the precious dry bundle high.

Within minutes, my legs went numb. Midstream, the water rose to my waist. I gasped but kept my footing and soon clambered up the far bank. Sitting on a log in a patch of sunlight, I pulled on my britches and briskly rubbed my legs until some feeling returned. It was an hour before I could go on, and I could not stop shaking.

Morgantown was still ten miles ahead when I found a collapsed house to spend the night. I kicked a pile of leaves against a stone wall and burrowed in. Overhead, the stars shined through the partially collapsed roof. The sky grew darker, and soon, exhaustion took its toll. I felt poorly and knew I was getting sicker and needed to rest. I also had to find something to eat or I would never be able to go on.

In the morning, I was so weak that I could barely rise from my nest. I placed a hand against my forehead like Jane does when our children do not feel well. It was damp and hot, yet I could not stop shivering in the morning air. Pulling the flour bag and tarp closer, I limped back onto the road, took two unsteady steps, and collapsed unconscious, face down in the snow.

"He does not look so good, mama. He is dying, I think."

Consciousness returned when large, rough hands rolled me over. The next words, spoken by a woman, were familiar but unintelligible. It was the strange form of German we often heard in my area of Pennsylvania.

The man lifting me from the road was Amish, those we now know as Pennsylvania Dutch. I am not sure why we call them Dutch — many of them did not come from the

Low Countries at all.

I stood weaving back and forth as the man put an arm around my waist.

"Come, now," he said. "You cannot lie in the road. Someone will be running you over, I am sure."

The man walked me to his wagon, where a woman held the reins of two swayback mares. She frowned and snapped at her husband. He responded with a steady, controlled voice that did not require a knowledge of their language to understand. His wife gave a 'humph,' crossed her arms on her ample bosom, and turned her head away from us.

"Jacob Stoltz is my name," the man said, pronouncing it with a Y. "And that mean old woman is Rachel, my wife of forty years, hard as that might be to believe!"

Holding on to the side of the wagon, I told him my name. I was so dizzy that it took both my hands and his arm to keep me upright.

"Mama believes we should leave you here, in the hands of God," Jacob said. "However, I am thinking God put you in our path, and we must not ignore Him." He was a sturdy man with large brown eyes, pushing sixty. A thick gray beard fell to his chest. His wife, by contrast, was plump and severe.

Jacob spoke to his wife, then guided me to the back of the wagon. "I can't spare much. Only a ride toward Lancaster, I can offer." He retrieved a stoneware jug and offered me a swig of cider. It burned my throat and started another coughing fit, but it felt wonderful in my stomach.

He helped me climb into the back of the wagon, where I collapsed among the dry corn ears, instantly asleep.

The sun was high overhead when I finally climbed out of a deep sleep, awakened by the inviting smell of frying bacon. My ragged clothes were soaked with sweat, but I felt somewhat better.

"Ach! Alive, are you?" Jacob called from the campfire. "Do you think you can eat?"

"Thirsty," I croaked. My throat was burning sore.

Jacob handed me a mug. "Warm water is what you need. It will not hurt so much, I'm thinking."

Sitting on a crate as close to the fire as I could get without bursting into flames, I managed to get a spoonful of beans to go down my tortured throat. I washed each mouthful back with warm water, wishing it was tea.

My head still buzzed, and I ached from head to foot. The shivering would not stop.

Mrs. Stoltz spoke to me in German, and her husband translated. "Mama asks, you have come how far?"

"I don't know," I whispered. "Kittanning to Montreal to New York. Almost a year."

Jacob whistled softly. "So, looking like you do, it is no wonder. A hard time, I'm thinking." He spoke to his wife, and her eyes widened. She looked at me and nodded her head.

Morgantown had come and gone while I slept, Jacob told me. We were now ten miles from their farm, located in a tiny hamlet outside of Lancaster called Bird-in-Hand. There, he said, Amish, Mennonites, and Quakers lived together in harmony. However, the Continental Army raided the farms periodically in retaliation for the locals' refusal to fight in the war.

The army stole two of Jacob's cows and all of the grain to feed the soldiers and their livestock. Their single remaining milk cow needed corn, so Jacob and his wife hauled a load of late-season pumpkins to trade at Pottstown. They had just pulled onto the York road when I collapsed in front of them.

After dinner, he carefully covered the fire, and we continued on our way. The sun was warm on my face, and despite the raw wind, I lay comfortably in the back of the wagon. Lulled by the rocking of the wagon, I fell asleep again and did not wake until Jacob shook my foot.

It was late afternoon, and the trees cast long shadows across the road. The sky was leaden and filled with snow.

"Lancaster is ahead," Jacob said. "We must go back a fair piece for the road home. I must have fallen asleep and driven right past it." He chuckled at his little joke.

Mrs. Stoltz spoke quietly to her husband.

"Ja, ja. I hear you!" He laid a gnarled hand on my shoulder. "She is right. We can go no further. Here, we must say goodbye. A warning, however. Go south of Lancaster. Many prisoners they kept in that town. Mostly Hessians, a few British. The townspeople are frightened of any stranger. It would be best, I am thinking."

I shook his hand and waited while he turned the horses in the center of the road. As they passed me, going back to their road home, Mrs. Stoltz raised one hand from her lap. That small wave meant much coming from her.

CHAPTER 55
The Continental Congress

March, 1778
York, Pennsylvania

As much as I had dreaded the idea, crossing the Susquehanna proved to be no problem at all. As Jacob Stoltz suggested, I skirted Lancaster, stumbling through winter fields and frozen streams, avoiding the roads entirely. Then I circled north again to the only river crossing within twenty miles.

Wright's Ferry was a major operation. They had an unusual method of getting across the river. A flatboat, mounted on wagon wheels, was pulled by four oxen. Horses, men, and supplies loaded on the flatboats, which then rolled into the icy river, drawn by the oxen. When the flatboat began to float and the wagon wheels left the river bottom, the oxen swam, pulling the barge behind them.

I would not have believed it possible had I not seen it for myself. The drover said, although rare, he occasionally had to cut a floundering ox loose before it drowned the entire team. The oxen were well trained.

I begged passage with a man taking horses to York to sell to the army. No one seemed alarmed at my looks or poor health. I was simply another victim of the war, something they were getting very used to.

The Susquehanna River was the last major obstacle on my way home. Before moving on, I took time to reflect how far this water had meandered since my last time upon it — in a canoe with Rebecca and Cornplanter, paddling for our lives.

Now, a mere fifty miles separated York and Chamber's Town. I was determined to do it in two days. First, however, I required food and a place to sleep. Walking the last hard miles into York, sleet began to fall, and soon, it was snowing again.

York was impressive and frightening. The once sleepy mill town was teeming with soldiers and congressional supernumeraries. The wide streets resounded with men marching or riding with immense importance. No one paid me the least amount of attention as I shambled down Market Street.

The Golden Plough Tavern was my destination, a place my father had taken Samuel and me many years before. I remembered it as crowded and hot. My father allowed me my first taste of beer.

From the street, I was disappointed to see that no light showed from the tavern windows. All of the activity was taking place next door at a finely built two-story stone house. Two soldiers stood at the front door, doing their best to stay undercover.

Every window in the house was ablaze, and shadowy figures moved about inside. While the snow was falling heavily by this time, muffling the sounds of the horses and carts on the street, it did little to dampen the voices emanating from the house. A boisterous party was underway.

Around the corner was the tavern's backyard. It shared the open space with the house hosting the party. Indeed, the two buildings practically leaned against each other.

Attached to the back of the house by a small passage-way was a separate cookhouse. As I entered the yard, the kitchen door opened, and a young girl in an apron came into the yard, carrying a pitcher. She clutched a shawl to her shoulders, and her loose hair blew about her head. She went to the pump and gave it a couple cranks, then blew on her bare hands. I heard a frustrated exclamation, where I stood in the shadows.

"It's frozen," I said.

The girl squealed and bolted for the door. I showed my-self in the light, and she took another step back. It seems I had the same effect on all the young women I met. She was ready to run or scream for help.

I held up one bony hand. "I mean no harm, miss," I said in as quiet and reassuring a tone as my sore throat allowed. "It's just that I'm so hungry. I've come far…"

I trailed off, sensing the uselessness of my plea. The girl was not much more than eighteen, frail and pretty in a farm-grown sort of way.

"The tavern's closed for the night," she said, pulling her shawl tighter. "There's a big banquet at General Gates' house, here, for all the hoity-toity congressmen."

"Please," I said, "may I come in, get warm?"

A woman's voice called from inside the kitchen. The girl looked at the door and then back at me, pursing her lips as she made up her mind.

"You can come in the kitchen and sit by the fire for a spell," she said and quickly retreated.

I followed her to the cookhouse of General Horatio Gates, the man who had defeated Burgoyne at Saratoga. I wondered if he would like to hear my story.

A plump middle-aged woman was ladling soup into an

array of bowls on the table. She looked up at me in surprise and missed one of the bowls.

"Lord be, Katie!" she barked. "What's this?"

"Please, ma'am," I said before Katie could speak. "I begged the girl to let me sit by your fire until I thaw out. I'll be no problem, I swear. I'm trying to make my way back home."

The woman held the ladle in front of her like a weapon. Based on the size of her, I believed she could do real damage with it.

"Where is home?" she asked, squinting at me with mistrust.

"I come from Chamber's Town. No more than fifty miles west. Not far, considering..."

She lowered the weapon. "I know folks in Chamber's Town." She pointed to a wooden bench beside the hearth. "You can sit there, but don't let them congressmen, or the General, see you. And eat nothing until we come back. I will see what I can spare."

She turned to the young girl. "Take the tray, Katie. I will bring the bread."

Katie gave me a quick smile and did as ordered. The cook gathered up a wicker basket covered with a red cloth. As she approached the door where I sat, she paused and reached into the basket.

"No one will notice a piece of bread missing," she said, handing me a crust. "Suck on it and eat nothing else, you hear me?. Your stomach won't stand for it. I have seen my share of starving men of late."

She followed Katie up the steps to the rear of the stone house, leaving me alone in the wonderfully warm kitchen. I sat quietly, somewhat shocked at my sudden turn of luck, and sucked on the bread crust. It was heavenly. I considered looking for a drink to wash it down, but decided to obey the cook and not abuse my welcome.

Suddenly the door to the back of the house opened, and the merry sounds of a well-lubricated party rolled out. Still hidden, I cracked the kitchen door an inch to listen. Two men stepped into the space between the house and the kitchen. They were arguing, splashing wine from crystal glasses as they emphasized each sentence.

From where I sat, I could see their breath in the frigid passageway. The cut of their clothes impressed me greatly. Each wore a jacket of elegant brocade with lace at the wrist and a silk cravat tied at the neck. Clearly, these were important delegates of the Continental Congress, dressed in their finest.

"I don't like it one damned bit," the younger of the two gentlemen said. "Conway is an ass and lucky not to have been hanged. We should not be discussing this." I could see this man in profile. He was in his mid-twenties, with a sharp chin and prominent nose. Although he towered over his companion, the older man did not seem the least intimidated.

"Alexander," protested the older man, "Washington is making no progress. I know George is your friend, but Gates has practically won the war! If he were in command, I do believe we would more quickly finish this affair and to our advantage. The fact that Conway has been discredited does not change the need to replace Washington."

"Why is Conway even here?" demanded the taller man. "Did Hancock invite him? I tell you, Samuel, this is a dangerous thing, meeting here tonight. Simply being in the same room with Conway makes us guilty by association. I shan't be a part of it!"

I listened with great interest as these men discussed the

Commanding General of the Army of the United States, a man whom I had never heard spoken of in exemplary terms. As my old friend Major Walsh once explained, Washington had failed at most of his military endeavors. He was not holding his own against General Clinton, and now he was holed up seventy-five miles away at Valley Forge while his army died or deserted. I held no sympathy for the man.

The gray-haired older man tried a different approach. In a calmer voice, he said, "What if Lafayette agrees to replacing him with Gates? Would that change your mind?"

The young man studied his wine before answering. "As much as it pains me, Samuel, we need Lafayette, and we need France. More than we need George…"

The old man let his breath out in a plume of vapor. "I agree, Lafayette is the key. If he — "

Just then, a junior officer came to the door. The two men looked up in alarm, looking guilty in their conspiracy.

"Mr. Adams, Mr. Hamilton, your pardon, gentlemen. Mr. Hancock asks if you will join him in the parlor. I believe he wishes to make a statement." (24)

Somewhat abashed, the two congressmen followed the young officer back inside.

I could not help myself. Even in my weak condition, I realized that a historic event was taking place here tonight. I had been listening to Alexander Hamilton and Samuel Adams discuss replacing George Washington as head of the Continental Army, an act that could completely change the face of the war.

Praying that my cough not return, I crept from the kitchen and climbed the steps. Directly inside the door, it was stiflingly warm. A long table set for twelve occupied most of the dining room while a blazing fire in the hearth and candelabras on the table gave the room a golden glow.

The cook and Katie looked at me in shock.

"Get out of here!" the older woman hissed. "What do you think you're doing?"

Honestly, I did not know. The men in the next room were the leaders of our new country — men whose names we would soon know by heart and teach in school. Perhaps it was my fever or the weakness that starvation had brought on, but I wanted to hear more.

Holding a finger to my lips, I picked a slice of cheddar from a plate, scooted to the parlor doorway, and sat on the floor, back against the wall. No one would see me unless they came into the dining room, and that was not likely to happen because every man in the other room was speaking at once.

The idea of replacing Washington with Gates was not a secret, and each man held a strong opinion. The voices were loud and angry, fueled by the wine splashed so liberally on the ornate carpet.

Samuel Adams called for a vote, others shouted him down. It was obvious that Adams and Hamilton stood on opposite sides of this argument.

Suddenly three sharp raps of a walking stick on the floor rang out. Risking a quick glance, I saw that the interruption came from a pale and sickly-looking man sitting in the corner of the room. The gathering quieted immediately.

"Gentlemen," the seated man said, his voice not more than a whisper. "Gentlemen, this is getting us nowhere. We must have order." He looked across the room to a remarkably young man in a brilliant blue uniform with gold epaulets. The young man found himself standing alone as others shied away from him, as if hearing that he had the plague.

"Monsieur le Marquis wishes to speak?" the man in the chair asked, raising his glass toward the young officer.

The French general stood straight, his intelligent eyes scanning the group of officers and delegates. He had a soft, round face with a receding hairline incongruous with his obvious youth. He bowed to the seated man.

"Thank you, Mr. Hancock. I was not sure how to gain the attention of such a...spirited room!" A small, self-conscious laugh came from the men whose attention the general now intently held.

"Gentlemen," the Marquis de Lafayette began in a firm, measured tone. "Although I fight for America, I am proud to say my voice is still heard in France. France sits on the sideline of a conflict with global import. With modesty, I say that whether she moves from that sideline depends on my report."

Lafayette looked around the room, meeting the eyes of each man. "My country knows the name of few Americans," he continued. "However, she *does* know your commanding general, a name I have not yet heard raised in toast tonight."

Some rumblings sounded from a corner of the room. The Marquis stood straight and held his glass high. "Gentlemen! To the health and success of General George Washington! May victory ever be his!"

Well, you could have heard a pin drop. No one moved. Then one or two delegates raised their glasses to their lips but did not sip; others carefully placed theirs on the table or mantel. No one spoke.

A moment passed in awkward silence. Then a rather paunchy man, looking every bit of fifty years, separated himself from the group of men on the far side of the room. General Gates raised his glass to the Marquis and said in a clear voice, "To General Washington!"

A deflated 'hear, hear' responded, and most of the men took a sip from their glass. With one gracious toast, the near disloyalty of the party was thoroughly extinguished. The debate was over. Washington would remain Commander in Chief.

Years later, I read an account of this banquet meeting. I was disappointed, but not surprised, that the history-changing speech by General Marie-Joseph Paul Yves Roch Gilbert du Motier, Marquis de Lafayette was not mentioned. Instead, so the story ran, a toast was made to the success of General Washington at the end of a lively evening with good friends. (25)

"Here! Who the fuck are you?"

I started so violently, my head banged against the dining room wall. Two Continental corporals stood in the rear doorway, each pushing to enter the house and lay their hands on me.

Even in my weak condition, I leapt to my feet and bolted like a jackrabbit through the crowded parlor. I bounced off Adams, ran past a handful of shocked dignitaries, and aimed for the front door. As I approached it, the door opened for me as if by magic. The two guards out front were investigating their comrades' shout and the ruckus I was creating.

Without slowing down, I pushed between the startled soldiers, out onto the snow-covered street and collided with a couple walking arm in arm.

The man assumed I was a thief. He grabbed at my arm in an attempt to restrain me. With a strength that belied my wretched condition, I pulled free, turned west, and ran, slipping and sliding past the courthouse.

Behind me, I heard the soldier's shouts of anger, but no one fired a shot, fearful perhaps at hitting any of the people on the street.

Breathing in painful gasps, I ran across the bridge, cut down a street to my left, and collapsed in the snow. I pulled up against a fence in front of a darkened house and coughed violently. My head spun, my chest heaved, and I slowly realized my ankle hurt like the devil.

Knowing that I had to keep moving did not give me any extra strength. Eventually, I got my feet under me and stood up. I held tightly to the fence until I could muster the energy to stagger on.

An insane chuckle rose in my throat. It grew within me until I laughed out loud at the absurdity of the last half hour. What else, I thought? I was sick and starving, moving forward by the force of will alone, and now I had sprained my ankle. And, I laughed again — I had also forgotten my stolen cheese!

I turned my face into the driving snowstorm, laughing like a man who had lost his mind, and continued west.

CHAPTER 56
Jane

March, 1778
The York Road, Pennsylvania

I have no coherent memories of the next two days, only fragments that may not be linear. It does not matter.

Continuing throughout the night, I hobbled on a very painful ankle until I found a dry sapling to act as a walking stick. I laughed again, thinking about the Biblical image I presented — a dying man, dressed in rags, hobbling down a deserted road at night, leaning on a staff.

The snow continued to fall, though I hardly noticed. A numbness penetrated my body. Only the sharp pain in my ankle kept me focused on the road ahead. I accepted the pain, fixated on it with the vague understanding that it meant I was still alive, still walking. Of the rest of my body, I felt nothing — not the cold that had seeped into every bone, not the hunger that had haunted me for so many days. Even my fever had receded behind my eyes.

As the sun came up, exhaustion overwhelmed me once again. I knew I could go no further without sleep. A broken-down wagon provided meager shelter from the sharp wind. It lay half overturned on the side of the road, the axle broken and a wheel missing. I crawled under the wagon bed and collapsed unconscious.

I do not know how long I slept in the frozen grass beneath the bed. When next I opened my eyes, the sun was out, and the storm had passed.

An unusual sound near my feet brought me wide awake. Sitting on her haunches, a bone-thin hound with a black head watched me with intent brown eyes. I sat up in surprise, and she stood and backed out from under the wagon. Standing in the snow, the dog cocked her head, big floppy ears pulled back in a questioning manner. I think I had appropriated her den.

"Are you lost?" I asked. At the sound of my hoarse voice, the dog turned and bolted across the road and into the tall grass. I felt an unreasonable loss and sadness at her departure.

With a deep sigh, I crawled into the sunlight and worked myself upright. The weather was improving, and I must move on. I took one step, and with a cry of pain, collapsed bodily in the wet snow. My ankle was twice the size of its opposite, tight, and red in the moccasin. It took all the will I could muster to push myself onto my hands and knees. Then, I crawled back under the wagon and fell exhausted in the patch of grass I had recently vacated.

Here I will stay, I thought. Here they will find me one day. I pulled my throbbing leg up to my chest and lapsed once again into a deep sleep.

There is no way to know how long I lay there. It might have been hours, or it could have been the next day. Night had descended, so I knew I had slept a long time, either way.

At my feet, head up, watching me intently, lay the hound. Not wanting to spook her, I remained silent. Then, when I shifted my position, she jumped up and backed out of the den.

The dog studied me as if trying to make up her mind, then ran up the bank to the road. She stood there, looking back at me. Then she returned to the wagon and whimpered.

"I'm hungry, too," I said, the words barely leaving my cracked lips. The dog turned her head to the side and barked once. Then she ran up to the road once again. The message was clear — get up and get moving!

I found my walking stick and used it to keep the weight off my bad ankle. Bit by bit, I crawled from under the wagon and stood, holding tightly to the weathered bed. The world swirled around me. I held the edge of the wagon until the feeling passed.

Then I joined my new companion, whom I named Dog. Her tail wagged a few times once I reached the road, telling me that I was doing good.

I grasped the stick, shifted my weight, and took a tentative step. The numbness of the previous day was replaced with a body ache that started in my head and ended in my foot. With Dog following behind me, I started down the road.

The sky was low overhead, the wind picked up from the north, and it began to sleet. I staggered on, step by painful step. More than once, I tripped in a pothole and fell to my knees. Each time, climbing back to my feet was more difficult and more taxing.

Inevitably, I trod on a rough stone in the road and turned my bad ankle again. The pain shot up my leg, and lights flashed before my eyes. I fell to the road with a strangled moan and pulled my leg to my chest, rocking back and forth in the mud.

"I can't, I can't," I sobbed, my tears mixing with the freezing rain. "Oh, Jane. How much more? How can I go on?" I asked the sky above me, expecting no answer.

However, an answer did come in the form of soft brown eyes and a warm tongue. Dog stood beside me, her head low beside mine, whining softly. Then she lay down, her back tight against my stomach, her head resting on my arm, her heat surrounding me.

A final prayer and a sad last sob of resignation escaped me as unconsciousness returned. Together we lay on the side of the road, man and dog, in the winter rain.

A wet nose against my cheek forced me to open my eyes and peer at the rising sun breaking beyond the trees. In wonder, I sat up, trying to understand what I saw.

I was home.

Chamber's Town lay in the distance, cooking smoke rising from a dozen houses in the wintry morning air. My father's house was only two miles away in the gently rolling pastureland south of town.

Dog scampered to her feet as soon as she saw I was awake. I reached my hand out in thanks, unable to speak. Slowly, like a dead man crawling from his grave, I worked my way more or less upright.

I took a tentative step, leaning heavily on my staff. Then another. Dog watched me carefully as if prepared to catch me should I fall.

I could not even see where I walked, so blurry was my vision. Step by exhausted step, I plodded on until

413

somehow, I realized I was standing on the path to my father's house.

Dog sensed the end of the journey and barked at the house, running ahead and then back to me. She got the attention of a young girl I did not know who came out onto the porch, wiping her hands on a rag.

The girl's eyes flew open in horror when she saw me standing on the path. "Begone!" she shouted. "We've got nothing for you!"

I stretched out a hand, lost my balance, and collapsed to my knees. Dog ran back and forth between me and the porch steps, barking frantically.

"What in the Lord's name is going on out there?" a voice called from within the house.

I raised my head, squinting into the morning sun, wondering if I imagined the vision of a woman with a fiery halo about her head.

Jane stood at the top of the porch steps, taking in the sight of the dying creature before her.

We looked into each other's eyes.

And she knew me.

CHAPTER 57
Epilogue

May 21st, 1781
Indiana, Pennsylvania

I stood overlooking a ruined cabin at the edge of the forest. Leaning against my shoulder and holding my hand was the love of my life. Her red hair, so beautifully streaked with gray, was loose and blew back from her face in the early morning breeze.

The night before, our caravan of six wagons and twelve families rolled into the meadow at the end of a long journey. We had come home to Indiana, the first of our family to reclaim what we had abandoned so many years before.

" 'Tis not much to look at," Jane stated. Her voice was soft against my shoulder. "It shall require some effort to rebuild."

"I've been thinking a great deal on that," I said, looking at the caved-in roof and the collapsed chimney. "Whether we should tear it all down and start over. I want to tear it down, Jane. It would be best to have no remembrance of our old life. It's been violated by marauders, and I want nothing to do with it. We'll start over, like the first time."

Jane smiled up at me. "Grand words, Mr. Moorhead," she chided me, "but yer wrong. We built a life here, we cleared that land there, just the two of us. We built a home and added to it as our family grew. Here, Fergus, this is where we lived, that's the cabin where we lived, and we won't be tearing it down. We will fix it right. We will pull out the rot and the cinders and rebuild because it is more than a cabin. That was our home. And it still is."

God, I loved this woman. "Well," I said after clearing my throat, "it's good that we have such a ready workforce."

She laughed and looked about for our children. We had eight now. Janie sat on a nearby stump, alternately sucking her thumb and conducting an intense conversation with her rag doll. Baby Samuel was in the basket at Jane's feet, and Dog sat beside it, intently watching us all. The rest of the horde was busy exploring or wading in the stream beneath the meadow. Fourteen-year-old William took his responsibility seriously; none of the young ones would wander off. (26)

In fact, there was no need to worry; this part of the country had been safe for some time. Although the war raged on, the fighting was now concentrated in the south, primarily North and South Carolina. New York and Pennsylvania had become quiet enough that a few of our community had decided to retake their land. Even the Indians were quiet, having had enough of the war, and retreated to their towns or moved further west.

Samuel and Mary Elizabeth were expecting soon, so they had decided to stay in Chambersburg, as we now called it, for the next six months. Other than that, our caravan resembled the first in many ways, except there were many more children. Forbes Road was now the fastest route to this part of Pennsylvania. It was rough going but shorter than the old Braddock road we had traveled years before. There was even talk of the government improving the road so more settlers could move west of the Alleghenies. Perhaps when the war ended.

I pulled Jane tight against my chest. We stood silently as the sun rose above the trees behind us, casting long golden streaks across the meadow.

"It is beautiful, isn't it?" I whispered, thinking back to that first morning when I stood in this spot and watched the deer, so unconcerned with our presence.

" 'Tis that," Jane said with a little sniff. Then she detached herself from my arms, gathered up the baby, and stood straight. "All right, then, if we're going to rebuild our home, we best get to it. The day's a-wasting!"

Watching Jane walk back to the wagons, I smiled to myself, marveling once again at the strength and courage of this woman. With a deep sigh, I followed her as the sound of men hard at work echoed throughout the valley.

The End

APPENDIX

1. Terminology
Indian

The term "Indian" was widely used during the 18th and 19th centuries and would have been the word of choice in a narration written in 1816. Since that time, especially in the late 20th century, several other terms have been used to describe the indigenous people of North America, including American Indians, Native Americans, and Indigenous Peoples. No consensus regarding a preference seems to exist.

In this story, Fergus intends no derogatory connotation when he refers to the native populations as Indian. He makes it clear that there were good and bad Indians. Overall, he had great respect and fondness for the majority of Native Americans with whom he had direct contact.

Squaw

The term 'squaw' is as controversial as 'Indian.' Squaw has been a familiar word in American literature and language since the 16th century and generally means an Indian woman or wife. It originally appeared in the Algonquin language and spread among the other languages in one form or another. Again, it would have been the term used by any writer in the early 19th century.

In general, whether or not it is offensive must be related

to the context in which it was used, just as the term 'woman' could be used as an insult today. Fergus meant no disrespect.

Patriot

Also called Rebels and Traitors during the Revolutionary War, Patriots wanted complete separation from Great Britain. The signers of the Declaration of Independence pledged "to each other our Lives, our Fortunes, and our Sacred Honor." It was not an idle promise, and their perseverance was instrumental in the formation of our country.

Loyalist

Loyalists were American colonists who stayed loyal to the British Crown and were often called Tories, Royalists, or King's Men. Many argued for 'Home Rule,' while others wanted to remain as colonists and subjects.

Many Loyalists moved to England, Canada, and the Bahamas after the war. Some of them lost the fortunes and land that they had built up over the years in the Americas. In some cases, the British government paid them for their loyalty, but it was usually not as much as they had lost.

Indian Town and Village

In reference to Native Americans, the terms Town and Village are essentially synonymous. For example, the Mohawk word for both town and village is *Kan-a-ta*, which happens to be a fairly common word among the Native Americans of the northeastern woodlands. While standing in the center of a village along the St. Lawrence River, Samuel Champlain asked the natives what they called the area, and they answered, "Canada." The name stuck.

2. Braddock's Road vs. Forbes Road

The decision to have Fergus and company take Braddock's Road instead of Forbes Road is open to debate. While Forbes Road was undoubtedly shorter, Braddock's saw more traffic at the time Fergus crossed the Allegheny Mountains. Braddock's Road is over extremely rough terrain but far less mountainous than Forbes Road. In the end, we don't know which road Fergus and his family struggled over. I chose Braddock's Road for this story.

Braddock's Road was constructed by General Edward Braddock's troops in 1755. Starting from Fort Cumberland, Maryland, Braddock's army cut a path through the wilderness, roughly following a Lenape Indian trail.

In 1758, General Forbes was determining how to move his 6,000 men across the mountains to attack Fort Duquesne. Forbes opened the more direct route through the very steep portions of the mountains and captured Fort Duquesne.

The western expansion following the Revolutionary War owes its success to both routes west of the Alleghenies.

3. Beeson's Town

Henry Beeson and his young wife, Mary Martin, moved to Fayette County in 1768. He built a grist mill on Red Stone Creek the following year. A settlement soon gathered around him. It was first known as Beeson's Mill and then as Beeson's Town. Today it is known as Uniontown, Pennsylvania.

4. Colonel James Smith

In the 1760s, James Smith led an unofficial posse called

the "Black Boys" (so-called because they blackened their faces) to protect settlers in central Pennsylvania and eastern Ohio from attacks by Native Americans. On March 6th, 1765, they stopped a pack train and burned illegal goods, including rum and gunpowder, that British official George Croghan sought to supply to Native Americans.

However, British authorities supported Croghan's illegal trading, which led to the Black Boys Rebellion, perhaps the first armed resistance to British rule in North America. The rebellion subsided when the Black Boys forced the British 42nd Highland Regiment under the command of Lieutenant Charles Grant to abandon Fort Loudoun in November.

See James Smith's account of running the gauntlet below.

5.   The Dunlap Broadside

The Declaration of Independence was first published as a large-sheet broadside printed by John Dunlap of Philadelphia immediately after its acceptance by Congress. One broadside was pasted into the Congressional journal, making it the "second official version." Dunlap's broadsides were distributed throughout the thirteen states. A version of this broadside would likely have been read to the colonists by riders moving from settlement to settlement.

6.   Wm. Lochry and John Moore letter to the President of the Council of Safety

"26th of December, 1776

Sir, by the removal of Col. Mackay from Kittanning, the frontiers of this County is laid open and exposed to the Mercy of a faithless, in certain Savage Enemy, and we are Informed by Andrew McFarland, Esq'r, who lives at

Kittanning, that, he is much afraid that the Mingoes will plunder the Country, and that he will not think himself Safe if there is not a Company of Men Stationed there, and if he Removes, a number more of the Inhabitants will follow; the Kittanning is a post of Importance, and we think a few men Stationed there would awe the Indians, and perhaps prevent much mischief, and as we are not certain there is any legal Representatives of the People of this State now sitting but the Council of Safety, we beg the favour of you to lay this letter before them, not doubting but they will take the matter into Consideration, and take such steps as the importance of it Requires."

7. Running the Gauntlet

As a young man, James Smith (4) was captured by Indians near Fort Duquesne in 1755. Near the end of a remarkable life, Smith wrote his memoirs in 1831 to great acclaim. His account is remarkably similar to the story attributed to Fergus, below.

"On approaching the fort, through large numbers of naked, painted savages who were formed into two long ranks, I was obliged to run the gauntlet. I was told that if I ran quick it would be so much the better, as they would quit when I got to the end of the ranks. I started in the race with all the vigor and resolution I was capable of exerting. When I had got near the end of the lines I was struck to the ground with a stick or the handle of a tomahawk.

"On recovering my senses I endeavored to renew the race, but as I rose someone threw sand in my eyes, which blinded me so that I could not see where to run. They continued beating me until I was insensible; but before I lost consciousness I remember wishing they would strike the final blow, for I thought they intended killing me, and that they were too long about it. I was sent to the hospital, and carefully tended by a French doctor, and recovered quicker than I expected.

"I asked a Delaware Indian who could speak some English, if I had done anything to offend them which caused them to beat me so unmercifully? 'No,' he replied, 'it was only an old custom the Indians had, and was like "how do you do?" After this,' said he, 'you will be well used."

"An Account of the Remarkable Occurrences in the Life and Travels of Colonel James Smith (Late a Citizen of Bourbon county, Kentucky) During his Captivity with the Indians, in the Years 1755, '56, '57, '58 & '59" Philadelphia: J. Grigg, 1831, pgs. 228 & 229

The same story is attributed to Fergus Moorhead, captured in 1777:

"After kindling a large fire the whole company, men, women and children, danced around it for a long time, and then formed into two lines, armed with hatchets, ramrods and switches. Having thus arranged matters, they called Moorhead to run the gauntlet, but as he had never before heard of such a ceremony, he did not understand them. His captor endeavored to explain it to him, saying he was to pass through the two lines and receive a blow from each individual as he passed, and exhorted him to run his best, as the faster he ran the sooner the performance would be over.

"Moorhead entered upon the chase with the feelings of a man who supposed he was running for his life, and was severely switched along the line, three-fourths of the way, when a tall chief, more devilish, if possible, than his companions, threw sand in his eyes, which added to his pain and completely blinded him. He tried, however, to proceed, but in his efforts to grope along, he was pushed about from one to another, and struck and switched, until two young warriors each took him by the hand, and ran with him into the wigwam, where he was quickly visited by his captor, who asked him if he felt sore.

"Moorhead replied that he felt much hurt and inquired what he had done to merit such usage. The Indian told him that he had done no harm, but this was the customary treatment of their prisoners; that he had now seen all their ceremonies, and that in the future he would receive better treatment."

"Indiana County Pennsylvania, Her People, Past and Present", Vol. I, by Joshua T. Steward, Chicago, J.H. Beers and Company, 1913, pg. 11:

8. Cornplanter

John Abeel III (born around 1740), generally known as Cornplanter, was a Seneca war chief and diplomat of the Wolf clan. As a chief warrior, Cornplanter fought in the French and Indian War and the American Revolutionary War.

During the American Revolution, Cornplanter argued for the Iroquois nations to remain neutral. He believed the Iroquois should stay out of the white man's war.

In 1796, Cornplanter and his people were granted 1,500 acres in Pennsylvania along the western bank of the Allegheny River, just south of the New York border, allotting it to him and his heirs "forever."

During the War of 1812, Cornplanter supported the American cause and offered to bring 200 warriors to assist the U.S. His offer was refused.

Cornplanter died on his Allegheny reservation on February 18, 1836.

The speeches by Cornplanter and others at the Great Council Fire related in this novel are taken from Reference 12.

9. Iroquois

Known as "People of the Longhouse," the Iroquois was a powerful northeast Native American confederacy comprised of the Mohawk, Onondaga, Oneida, Cayuga, and Seneca. In 1722, they accepted the Iroquoian-speaking Tuscarora people into the confederacy, and it became known as the Six Nations.

10. Letter from Samuel Moorhead to Colonel Morgan

"21th of March, 1777,

Sunday morning my brother and Andrew Simpson left here to go home. Myself left it (for Twelve Mile Run) on Tuesday and found on the road, Simpson killed and scalped; my brother either killed or taken; a war mallet left on the road, and a tomahawk, with a letter, of which I have sent you a copy, enclosed."

11. Salamanca, New York

The land along the southern turn of the Allegheny granted to Cornplanter (8) was inundated by the 1960 construction of the Kinzua Dam. Approximately 600 Seneca were forced from the 10,000 acres they had occupied under the 1794 Treaty of Canandaigua. They were relocated to Salamanca, near the northern shore of the Allegheny Reservoir, created by the flooding of land behind the dam.

The Indian village of Salamanca that Fergus visited on his way north is now the home of the Seneca Nation and site of a prosperous casino and resort.

12. Mary Jemison

Mary Jemison, born in 1743, was a Scots-Irish frontierswoman who became known as the "White Woman of the Genesee." She had been taken as a youth and adopted into an Ohio Seneca family, assimilating to their culture, marrying two Native American men in succession, and having children with them.

History tells us that Mary did see her husband and son again. As the war wound down in 1779, Washington sent a vindictive force, led by General Sullivan, into Iroquois land. His army destroyed every Indian town they came to as punishment for the Iroquois' disloyalty. Mary escaped the carnage and eventually reunited with her family.

In 1824 Mary published a memoir of her life and died in 1833, at the age of 90.

13. Joseph Brant

Joseph Brant (1742 - 1807) is one of the best-known Native Americans of the late 18th century. Born in the Mohawk tribe, he soon became a friend of several influential English military officers who helped guide his career. Most notably among them was Sir William Johnson, who was in a relationship with Brant's sister Molly. Additionally, Sir William was the father of Sir John, who fought with Brant at Fort Stanwix.

Although he was not a chief's son, Brant earned his title of Mohawk war chief after his successful career in the French and Indian War. During the Revolutionary War, Joseph Brant (now a sachem of the Mohawk) became affiliated with England. His war efforts brought great fame. He went to England and met King George III. He also obtained substantial infamy in the United States. After the war, he retired to Canada, where he received a vast amount of land from the British.

14. Blacksnake

Tekayetu was born sometime around 1748. Known in English as both Governor Blacksnake and Chainbreaker, he was a Seneca war chief and leader, nephew to Chief Cornplanter. Later, he supported his maternal uncle Handsome Lake, who was a prominent religious leader.

Blacksnake allied with the United States in the War of 1812 and later encouraged accommodation to European-American settlers, allowing missionaries and teachers on the Seneca reservation.

He died in 1859 at a very advanced age.

15. Lt Colonel Barrimore St. Leger

Barry St. Leger (born around 1733) was a British Army officer who enjoyed varying levels of success during his career. Following his involvement in General Burgoyne's 1777 Saratoga Campaign, St. Leger remained on the frontier for the duration of the war. Later, he briefly as commander of British forces in Quebec. Due to ill-health, St. Leger returned to England in 1785 and died in 1789.

16. The Flag of the United States

There is considerable controversy surrounding the design of the flag raised during the siege of Fort Stanwix. Congress had determined that the official flag was to have thirteen stars in a circle on a blue field and thirteen stripes. Several reports state that the flag at Fort Stanwix was made of red, white, and blue stripes. Considering the remoteness of this outpost, it is not unlikely that the Americans in the fort did their best to create a symbol of resistance.

Regardless, it is considered the first time that the American flag of any design was raised in battle.

17. The Battle of Oriskany

The battle of Oriskany (August 6th, 1777) was devastating to both sides, yet both claimed victory. Losses to the Tryon militia may have been as high as 500 killed, wounded, or captured out of the 800 engaged. Casualties on the Iroquois and Loyalist sides were much lighter. Around 60 Native Americans were killed or wounded, and only a handful of loyalists were killed or wounded. Yet, the losses they suffered greatly demoralized the Iroquois, particularly the Seneca.

As the siege wore on, the British would once again call on the Native Americans to be the main fighting force, and their enthusiasm for supporting the siege cooled considerably. In the end, all these factors contributed to the Native American's desertion of the British Army besieging Fort Stanwix. This, in turn, forced St. Leger to abandon the siege and retreat back to Canada, adding to the failure of the Saratoga Campaign.

18. Release of Kittanning Militia

General Edward Hand, Commander to Captain Samuel Moorhead, 14th of Sept., 1777

"Being convinced that, in your present situation, you are not able to defend yourself, much less render the continent any service, you will withdraw from Kittanning, bringing everything away portable, leaving the houses and barracks standing."

19. The Murder of Jane McCrea

Jane McCrea's (1752-1777) family lived near Saratoga

when the Revolution began. Different loyalties divided her family. Her brothers supported the American efforts and joined the Albany militia. Jane's fiancé, David Jones, joined the Loyalist army in Quebec.

Hearing that Jane was staying at a home near the British fort, General Burgoyne sent a group of Wyandot scouts to accompany them to the British encampment on July 27, 1777.

While the events that came next are a source of some disagreement, it is generally accepted that the Native Americans became involved in a dispute and, as a result, killed Jane. They then scalped her and took the trophy with them back to General Burgoyne.

News of her murder caused an outcry throughout the colonies. Some historians believe that the killing of Jane McCrea solidified the opposition to the British in the colonies. The incident was used effectively to help recruit soldiers to the American cause throughout the colonies. Years later, John Vanderlyn's propagandist painting added further to anti-Native American sentiment.

20. The Siege of Fort William Henry

The story of the 1757 siege is famously recounted in James Fenimore Cooper's 1826 novel *The Last of the Mohicans*. The depiction of the attack on the unarmed British army and their families is accurate. The exact role of General Montcalm and other French leaders in encouraging the actions of their Native American allies, and the total number of casualties incurred, is a subject of historical debate. The memory of the killings influenced the actions of British military leaders for the remainder of the French and Indian War.

21. Prison Ships in New York Harbor

One of the most horrific events in the Revolutionary War occurred in the waters of New York Harbor, near the current location of the Brooklyn Navy Yard. From 1776 to 1783, the British forces occupying New York City used abandoned or decommissioned warships to hold captured soldiers, sailors, and private citizens.

Some 6,000 to 11,000 prisoners died aboard the prison ships over the course of the war, most from disease or malnutrition. Some historians assert that more men died on the prison ships than in all of the battles of the war combined. Many of these were inmates of the notorious HMS *Jersey*, which earned the nickname "Hell" for its inhumane conditions and the obscenely high death rate of its prisoners.

22. Christopher Hawkins

Kit Hawkins (1764–1837) was born in Providence, Rhode Island. His journal, published in 1864, tells the story of how, at only 13 years of age, he joined a privateer to fight the British. During his early life, Kit was captured and escaped more than once. Eventually, he was held on the infamous prison ship called Old *Jersey* (21). In the journal, he describes escaping from the *Jersey* by stealing an ax from the ship's cook and breaking his way through a barred porthole during a thunderstorm.

In this story, Kit's history has been moved up in time so that his adventure coincides with that of Fergus.

23. Elizabeth Burgin

Elizabeth Burgin was born before 1760 and died after 1790. Not much else is known except that she was a true American Patriot, helping more than 200 prisoners of war escape the British prisons and prison ships.

She was a mother of three and probably a war widow. In 1779, she was approached by George Higday, a member of the Culper Spy Ring, to officially help prisoners of war escape. She was eventually recognized for her service:

George Washington to the Continental Congress,

"Regarding Elizabeth Burgin, recently an inhabitant of New York. From the testimony of our own (escaped) officers…it would appear that she has been indefatigable for the relief of the prisoners, and for the facilitation of their escape. For this conduct, she incurred the suspicion of the British and was forced to make her escape under disturbing circumstances."

24. Continental Congress in York

In September 1777, the Second Continental Congress, under threat of the advancing British, moved the central government from Philadelphia to Lancaster and then to York, Pennsylvania.

During the nine months York was the Capital of the United States – until June 27th, 1778, Congress adopted the Articles of Confederation, proclaimed the first National Day of Thanksgiving, and signed the French Treaty of Alliance.

Some of the Continental Congress members in York at that time include John Hancock, Henry Laurens, John Adams, Samuel Adams, and Alexander Hamilton.

General Horatio Gates, who had recently defeated Burgoyne at Saratoga, Baron von Steuben, and Marquis de Lafayette also spent time in York during the winter of 1777-1778. Meanwhile, Washington and his army were 75 miles away, freezing and dying at Valley Forge.

When Gates defeated Burgoyne, he sent word of the

victory directly to the Continental Congress in York, by-passing his superior officer, Washington. Soon, there were secret efforts to replace Washington with Gates. Not long after Gates' victory, France announced its support of the new government.

25. Conspiracy to replace Washington

The Conway Cabal was a group of senior Continental Army officers who, in late 1777 and early 1778, attempted to replace George Washington as Commander-in-Chief of the Army. It was named for Brigadier General Thomas Conway, whose letters criticizing Washington were for-warded to the Second Continental Congress.

When these suggestions became public, supporters of Washington mobilized to assist him politically. Conway was forced to resign from the army, and General Horatio Gates, a leading candidate to replace Washington, issued a public apology for his role in the affair.

The banquet described in this story actually took place earlier, in January 1778, but its date is not important. Whether the toast by Lafayette actually happened is open for debate. Some historians call it the 'Toast that Saved America.' It could be argued that, had it gone differently, this one dinner party might have resulted in Horatio Gates becoming the first President of the United States. Regard-less, Washington retained his position as Commanding General, and Gates was reassigned. The actual words spo-ken by Lafayette are not known.

26. Fergus and Jane Moorhead

As the Indian Wars, following the Revolutionary War, became more violent, the Moorheads and other families constructed a two-story stone fort. The stone building, or one very similar, existed west of Indiana Borough until the 1980s.

Fergus and Jane Moorhead left "a numerous and respectable progeny." They had nine children who lived: William, Joseph, Euphemia, Thomas (who may have died of smallpox), Samuel, Margaret, James, Fergus, and Jane. Three others died in childbirth. The exact dates and order of the children's births are not known.

Fergus Moorhead died in 1822 at the age of 80. Jane White Moorhead died two years later, at the age of 79.

HISTORICAL NOTE

As mentioned in the Preface, the story of Fergus Moorhead has been central to the early history of Indiana County. It has been told by Arms and White, Stewart, and innumerable newspaper articles, yet it remains mostly undocumented. Little is known of his early life in Chambersburg, his profession, or even the birthdates of his children.

His trek to Indiana County is basically a retelling of the standard pioneer tale of hardship and heartbreak in the older literature. The difficulties faced by Fergus and his family are undoubtedly real because many other families endured and documented the same challenges.

There is documentation that Samuel Moorhead was stationed at Kittanning during the early days of the war and that Fergus was captured on his way home following a stint at the fort. The literature, however, is exceptionally vague when describing his time as a captive of Native Americans.

Arms and others reported that Fergus was taken to Canada and traded to the British, where he remained a prisoner for eleven months before being exchanged back to the Americans. They further state he traveled to New York, eventually making his way back to his family in Chambersburg.

There are many problems with this scenario when one compares the timeline of his capture on March 16th, 1777, to actual events. The Seneca, the most likely tribe to take Fergus north, were not operating as far south as Kittanning at that time. Additionally, the Delaware, his most likely captors, would not have carried Fergus very far north. My solution is to have the Delaware capture Fergus at Blanket Hill, and, through a series of events, the Seneca march him north to the Mohawk Valley.

As a prisoner of the Seneca, the timing works perfectly for Fergus to attend the Great Council Fire of Oswego. All Iroquois Nation members, and specifically the Seneca, were headed there a few months after his capture. Hence, my creation of his involvement in the siege of Fort Stanwix and the Battle of Oriskany. It follows that Fergus would have come in contact with well-known Native Americans such as Cornplanter and Joseph Brant.

After St. Leger's failure at Fort Stanwix, most of the Iroquois either returned home or followed Brant east to join Burgoyne. This led to my conclusion that Fergus was taken to Canada by the British and not by Native Americans.

Other problems exist with the timeline in stating that Fergus was taken to Canada, held for eleven months, and then exchanged back to the Americans. Following Burgoyne's surrender, the Americans marched their British prisoners away from British-held territory, eventually going to Pennsylvania. The Northern British Army abandoned Fort Ticonderoga and withdrew back to Canada. No one was attempting to exchange prisoners at this time, and Washington, himself, expressed his unwillingness to do so.

Even if there had been exchanges, freed American prisoners would not have gone to New York because, at that time, the British still held the city. The idea of Fergus and Rolf traveling to Fort Ticonderoga and their escape made for a more likely account.

The horrors described aboard the British prison ships in New York harbor are real. The only evidence that Fergus may have been aboard those death ships is in the claim that he went to New York after his exchange in Canada. I moved Christopher Hawkins' story up in time so he could meet Fergus. All of the authors state that Fergus made his way back to Chambersburg, bearded, starving, sick, and close to death, recognized only by his wife, Jane.

So, regardless if it is real history or historical fiction, I have made every attempt to "print the legend."

REFERENCES

1. Richard L. Kirkpatrick, "Fergus Moorhead (1742-1822), Pioneer: Documentary History" (December 2018), with 383-page document compilation on file with the Cumberland, Franklin and Indiana County Historical Associations PA
2. A Journal of the Captivity of Jean Lowry (Conococheague Institute, 2008)
3. Jean Lowery, A Journal of The Captivity of Jean Lowry and Her Children, Giving an Account of Her Being Taken by The Indians, The 1st of April 1756. Printed by William Bradford, Philadelphia, 1760.
4. J Jordan, History of Westmoreland County, Pennsylvania (Google Books, 1906)
5. History of Cumberland and Adams Counties, Pennsylvania (Google Books: Warner Beers, 1886)
6. C T Arms & E White, History of Indiana County, Pennsylvania: 1715-1880. J.A. Caldwell, Newark, OH, 1880
7. J T Stewart, Indiana County, Pennsylvania, Her People, Past and Present. J.H. Beers & Co. Chicago 1913. *Note: Stewart's 1913 account of Fergus Moorhead was taken almost verbatim from the earliest volume of county history, Arms & White (sometimes referred to as "Caldwell"), published in 1880. The same basic story of Fergus and Jane Moorhead has appeared numerous times in Indiana newspapers for 150 years.*

8.   A.T. Moorhead, History of the Moorhead Family
      from Later Part of the 16th Century to 1901. Indiana,
      PA A.T. Moorhead, Publisher, 1901

9.   Clarence D. Stephenson, Indiana County 175th Anni-
      versary History. The A.G. Halldin Publishing Co. In-
      diana, PA, 1979

10.   George P. Donehoo, A History of Indian Villages
      and Place Names in Pennsylvania. Telegraph Press,
      Harrisburg, PA, 1928

11.   Frederick Drimmer, ed. Capture by Indians,
      Firsthand Accounts: 1750-1870. Coward-McCann,
      Inc. New York, 1961

12.   Thomas S. Abler, ed. Chainbreaker, The Revolution-
      ary War Memoirs of Governor Blacksnake as told to
      Benjamin Williams. University of Nebraska Press,
      Lincoln, NB, 1989

13.   Thomas S. Abler, ed. Cornplanter: Chief Warrior of
      the Allegany Senecas. Syracuse University Press, Sy-
      racuse, NY, 2007

14.   Mary Jemison, Captured by Indians, 1758. EyeWit-
      ness to History, www.eyewitnesstohistory.com, 1999

15.   Richard M. Ketchum, Saratoga: Turning Point of
      America's Revolutionary War. Henry Holt and Co.
      New York, 1997

16.   Christopher Hawkins, The Life and Adventures of
      Christopher Hawkins. The Holland Club, New York,
      1858

17.   Robert P. Watson, The Ghost Ships of Brooklyn. Da
      Capo Press, 2017

18.   Chester Hale Sipe, Indian Chiefs of Pennsylvania.
      Ziegler Print Co. Butler, PA, 1927

19.   Samuel P. Hildreth, Pioneer History: Being and Ac-
      count of the First Examinations of the Ohio Valley

and the Early Settlement of the Northwest Territory.
A.S. Barnes & Co. New York, 1848

20. Brady L. Crytzer, War in the Peaceable Kingdom:
The Kittanning Raid of 1756. Westholme Publishing,
Yardley, PA, 2016

21. John Mack Faragher, Daniel Boone, The Life and
Legend of an American Pioneer. Henry Holt and Co.
Inc, New York, 1992

ACKNOWLEDGEMENTS

A novel of this scale requires a considerable amount of help, including editing, historical insight, and general encouragement when it all seems insurmountable.

I owe special thanks and a great debt of gratitude to the following people:

Charles Spence, Historical and Genealogical Society of Indiana County, PA, for his early guidance and help with the history of Fergus' home.

Richard L. Kirkpatrick, Esq. for his exhaustive work on the life of Fergus and his family.

Brian C. O'Connor, Ticonderoga Historical Society, for his continued support and historical perspective on the events around Fort Ticonderoga.

John Buxton for the use of the beautiful painting gracing the cover of this book.

Cheryl Moorhead Stone, for her archival research.

And Judy Hoffman, Patricia Black, Cynthia Olcott, and Jerry Kiely for their invaluable edits and suggestions.

THE AUTHOR

Craig Pennington's maternal lineage is Moorhead, and he proudly traces his family directly to the first settlers in Indiana County. Additionally, his family tree includes Fergus' comrade James Thompson, and Daniel Boone as a distant cousin.

Craig met his wife, Claudia, in Key West while working for a salvage company searching for Spanish shipwrecks. They continued their nautical adventure in Montserrat and Dominica. Following their marriage, Craig managed offshore construction projects for the Navy, while Claudia became the director of major maritime museums in Washington DC, Newport News VA, and Key West. Craig always had an extra job as 'museum husband.' Today they enjoy retirement, book collecting, writing, and horses in Bradenton, Florida.

His first novel, "Dead Reckoning," is a nautical thriller set in the Caribbean and has received excellent reviews. Watch for his next novel "The Heart of the Run" coming in September 2021. It is an epic tale of five generations of the Moorhead family in Scotland and Ireland. Both books are available on Amazon in paperback and Kindle.

Printed in Great Britain
by Amazon